About the Author

Ilsa Evans has published fifteen books across a range of genres, from light fiction and short stories to memoir, murder mystery and YA fantasy. Two of her books have been shortlisted for the prestigious Davitt (Sisters in Crime) Awards, while her novel about domestic violence, *Broken*, was an Australian best-seller and selected as *Women's Weekly* Book of the Month. Ilsa also works in academia, writes social commentary, and has been published in several newspapers and online journals. In 2011, she received the Eliminating Violence Against Women (EVA) Award for online journalism.

ALSO BY ILSA EVANS

The Unusual Abduction of Avery Conifer

family baggage

Ilsa Evans

FICTION

First Published 2023
First Australian Paperback Edition 2023
ISBN 9781867270744

Family Baggage
© 2023 by Ilsa Evans
Australian Copyright 2023
New Zealand Copyright 2023

Published by
HQ Fiction
An imprint of Harlequin Enterprises (Australia) Pty Limited (ABN 47 001 180 918), a subsidiary of HarperCollins Publishers Australia Pty Limited (ABN 36 009 913 517)
Level 19, 201 Elizabeth St
SYDNEY NSW 2000
AUSTRALIA

Printed and bound in Australia by McPherson's Printing Group

MIX
Paper | Supporting
responsible forestry
FSC® C001695
www.fsc.org

This book is dedicated to the four Diamant sisters,
who led the way for me and mine.
Mimi, Hilde, Charlotte and Ilse.
My love and thanks to you all. Apologies that
we dropped the baton.
Miss you, Mum.

Prologue

Enid Tapscott was dying. She knew this with a certainty that felt congealed within, thick and visceral. Like marrow itself. The odd thing was that she felt removed from it all, as if the inevitability of her dying had robbed the concept of power. Instead she was utterly relaxed, her blood warm, limbs heavy, mind deliciously foggy. Enid thought that she hadn't felt this tranquil for years. Certainly not since the seventies anyway, when for a brief period of time she had floated through life on a cloud of weed.

Even if awareness of her own imminent demise hadn't been curled within, it was easily discerned from the attitudes of those around. Fatalism wafted into a miasma that hung from the ceiling like mist. The hushed voices of the nurses, the shiny-eyed solicitude of her children, and especially the sudden appearance of her mother. This last had been a dead giveaway, in every sense of the term, as her mother had been cremated nearly half a century ago. Yet there she was, superimposed on the IV drip stand, gazing beatifically down on her daughter. Clearly death had done wonders for her personality.

Under normal circumstances, as in when she wasn't busy dying, their defeatism would have irritated Enid. But then, she supposed, if she wasn't dying, then it wouldn't be an issue. She blinked slowly, trying to unravel this philosophical enigma. Soon it too drifted away. Her mother sighed. It was the soundtrack of Enid's childhood. She wondered if at some point her life would flash before her eyes. Maybe it already had and she'd missed it. Typical. It would have been a short feature anyway. Childhood, marriage, motherhood, death. Hopefully reincarnation was actually a thing, and she got another shot.

Her mother sighed again. It occurred to Enid that she was being judged not on her lack of achievements but on the detritus left behind. She wanted to explain that she'd had no warning. Otherwise she would have spring-cleaned the house and scrubbed the casserole dish from last night's stew. She would have done that load of washing. She would have also pre-purchased one of those funeral plans, chosen the songs (anything but 'Amazing Grace'), prerecorded a stoic goodbye message and written her own eulogy. She would have put together a will. And she most definitely would have burnt that old diary, destroyed the letter hidden in her wardrobe, culled her memorabilia box, and discarded the vibrator nestled amongst her sensible white underwear. Actually, she probably would have thrown out the underwear also. Soon people would be literally rifling through her smalls.

But Enid had been given no warning. She'd been as fit as a fiddle until six o'clock last night. She knew the exact time because the ABC News had just begun and she'd been standing at the kitchen bench with her cup of tea, wondering, as she did most evenings, where the past eighty-three years had gone. After that her memory was less clear. The cold of the kitchen tiles through the long night, the rubbery feel of her face, then disembodied voices and the smell of the ambulance. All leading up to this state of rather delightful laissez-faire consciousness. She could have done without her mother's presence though. After all these years, it was probably time she told her that. She opened her eyes but instead found the view blocked by a fleshy face, millimetres away, every pore magnified. Enid recoiled, making a noise somewhere between a gasp and a gurgle.

The face immediately pulled back, blurring and then elongating into a body before separating into two more. Like a triple exposure. Enid blinked, trying to focus. Realisation blossomed. These were her daughters. The ties that tether. The Sorter, the Settler and the Sook. Not that she would ever use those words out loud. She tried to smile, but the corners thickened within her cheeks. Now she could also see her grandchildren, standing over by the wall, and ... her eyes darted around the room. There he was, curled in an armchair in the corner, head down. Her son. Enid's gaze softened. She willed him to look up but understood why he could not. How hard this must be for him.

Enid dragged her attention back to his sisters. She felt a rush of urgent energy and, for the first time, fought against the inevitable march of death. She needed more time. She needed to tell them to watch out for their brother. She needed to extract promises. He was so vulnerable. She ran a tongue around her mouth, moistening it in preparation. But the words congealed even as the faces merged back into one, and then slowly faded. Soon all that remained was a soundless smog of colour and light. Her mother's sigh was a feather-soft breeze, beckoning her towards the darkness. And she realised ruefully that she had simply waited too long. It was over. The story of her life.

Chapter One

Monday morning

Today I went to Ethel Ferguson's Tupperware party. I have no idea why. She didn't even serve booze. The only interesting bit was when they were talking about favourite pastimes (because Connie Duff was trying to spruik Hobbytex), and Ethel's fat sister-in-law said hers was diaries. Writing them kept her from murdering her family. So I thought it worth a try. Anything is worth a try.

George found the diary almost immediately. She hadn't been looking for it; hadn't, in fact, even suspected its existence, but when she rifled through the desk drawer, there it was. The size of a slim paperback with a padded cover that, judging by the binding, had once been crimson but had since faded to the colour of dried blood. She'd picked it up only because it seemed out of place amongst the jumble of receipts and cheque stubs. It smelt old, like archives and dust. George slipped her glasses on, flicking the book open to the first page. Then she sat down hard on the desk chair, blinking with surprise.

There was no doubt that it was her mother's, and that it was a diary of some sort. She knew that writing as well as her own. Tightly contained cursive with the odd curlicue that bled into words above and below, making them sometimes difficult to decipher. The acerbic observations were also typical Enid, but the diary itself was most definitely not. The introspective nature of it, even apart from the edge of desperation.

From the hallway came the sound of a key in the front door. George tensed guiltily and then remembered, with a fresh shaft of pain, that her mother was dead. Enid Tapscott was not about to walk through the door and catch her daughter going through her personal items. There would be no withering look that, no matter her age, made George feel like a child again. Her eyes welled. They had been doing that a lot over the past week.

She could hear her sisters bustling along the passage now. George thrust the diary back into the drawer, reburying it. This was as instinctive as her earlier guilt. It was fuelled by a fierce desire to keep it to herself, at least temporarily; to be the first to devour the words. It was like being offered a final get-together. Just her and her mother. She pushed the drawer closed and then ran her hands down her pants, as if ridding them of the diary's dusty scent.

Both her sisters were in the kitchen. Kat was putting away milk while Annie unwrapped a bakery box. George plonked herself at the table, pushing aside some papers to make room for her elbows. She propped her chin on cupped hands and watched them, drawing comfort from their presence. They had always been close. They even looked similar. Fair complexions with hazel eyes, neat features and mousy hair that each, to varying degrees, kept short and livened up with highlights. Kat had lately opted for a rather dramatic pixie cut with dark streaks, while Annie always went for attention-grabbing colour. This month was plum. George herself preferred low-maintenance, with just enough colour to hide the odd strand of grey. Their looks were all Enid. Even their brother resembled her a little, certainly far more than he did his father. It made George a little sad sometimes, that this lovely, devoted man had left such a faint stamp behind.

Some variety lay in their sizes though, and in reverse proportion to their age. As the eldest, Kat was also the slightest, while Annie was a couple of inches taller and wider. George sat in the middle, which seemed to be her wont in life. The mediator between the two. But the main difference had always been in their personalities, marking them even in their fifties.

'Already made a start then?' asked Kat. 'Please tell me you found a will or something equally helpful?' She got three mugs down from the cupboard. She was wearing a lovely sleeveless lemon top and skinny jeans. George hadn't worn jeans for a decade. Skinny or otherwise. Her sister turned, displaying the tattoo that encircled an upper bicep. It featured leafy roses, very pretty until a closer examination revealed a thread of barbed wire intertwining the foliage. Kat had gotten it in her early twenties, much to their mother's disgust. George didn't have any tattoos either.

'Well?' asked Kat now, looking at her enquiringly. 'Is that a hard question or something?'

George blinked. She thought of the diary. 'Oh no,' she said, rather airily. She waved a hand for good measure but then thought it might look a little like she was channelling the queen. She propped it back beneath her chin.

Kat lifted an eyebrow. 'Are you all right?'

'Yeah, sure.' George followed this up with a shrug, because she wasn't all right. She hadn't been all right for a week. She was the opposite of all right. She was asunder.

'Look what I brought!' exclaimed Annie. She tilted the bakery box to reveal a selection of pastries. 'Something to help us get through. I thought … you know. She'd have liked this.'

George smiled at her sister even as she felt her eyes glisten again. Their mother always had pastries when they were visiting. Neenish tarts were her favourite. The sight of them here, now, actually churned her stomach. She'd eaten little since it happened, which was odd because usually food was her crutch. But it was like the enormity of what had happened filled her belly. There was no room for anything else. Kat abandoned her coffee-making and came over to the table. She dropped her bag on the table and pulled out a chair, flopping down with a groan.

'Bloody hell,' she said in her husky voice. George had always envied her older sister's voice. She could have worked in radio, or on telephone sex-lines. The only time George sounded like that was when she had a bad cold, and then the surfeit of mucus generally negated the sexiness of the voice.

'How weird does this feel?' continued Kat. 'Being here like this?'

'I keep expecting her to walk in,' said Annie slowly. She looked towards the lounge room. 'And tell me off for taking over. Make me go sit down.'

'Yep,' said George. She took off her glasses and rubbed her eyes.

Kat nodded. After a few seconds of silence she dropped her head and began rummaging through her bag. She took out an iPad and her mobile phone, laying them neatly on the table. Then she looked up again. 'So … how have you both been?'

George shrugged. There were no words. She guessed that Annie felt the same way as she didn't reply either, instead busying herself with arranging the pastries on a plate.

Kat persevered. 'Recovered from the funeral yet?'

'Oh. My. God.' George grimaced. This was easier to discuss. In fact, the funeral had been so bad that it was almost funny.

Annie stopped what she was doing. 'Worst funeral ever.' She shook her head and then let out a snort of laughter. '*Fawlty Towers* awful. It was only missing John Cleese.'

The sisters fell silent again, remembering. On one level, of course, a funeral *should* be relatively awful. George imagined few people turned to each other after burying a loved one and said, 'What fun! Can't wait to do *that* again!' But their mother's funeral had taken this to new heights. Or depths. For her, the day had even begun badly. Fierce altercations with both offspring over outfits, one wanting to wear ripped jeans and the other shades of red (the former arguing that her grandmother would prefer her to be comfortable and the latter that *his* grandmother had been a fan of colour. Both were wrong). By the time that was over, nobody was on speaking terms and George herself had only minutes to get ready.

Not that it mattered. Gale-force northerly winds whipped her hair into a beehive. They'd arrived at the funeral home only to discover that the slideshow USB had been left at home. Her son Leo made the dash back while she went to mingle with the family and friends now gathering, buffeted by wind. Platitude after platitude, each accompanied by a hand on George's arm, anchoring her in place. She'd taken on so many layers of grief that even her ankles felt thick.

Then came the commencement music, where the carefully selected orchestral piece had been replaced by what sounded like the soundtrack from *Jaws*. The mourners all straightened as one, gazing around with surprise. They'd looked like startled meerkats. When finally they began filing inside, their footfalls keeping time with the build of the beat, George had thought it couldn't possibly get worse. She was wrong.

The celebrant, chosen during the fog of raw bereavement, delivered a service so monotone that he made Enid's life seem more depressing than her actual death. Great-Aunt Astrid had fallen asleep, her moist snores punctuating the speech. The celebrant was followed by Aunt Margaret, who tried to liven things up so much that she'd sounded like a stand-up comedian. Just as she declared that Enid had *always* liked to make an entrance, Leo had done just that. He'd also changed his grey suit jacket for one of a cranberry hue that matched the hatband on his fedora. As he stood there, looking like a flamboyant version of Indiana Jones, the wind caught the door and slammed it shut with such force that even the coffin shuddered. Great-Aunt Astrid promptly fainted, smacking her head against the back of the chair. Everything had been put on hold until an ambulance attended, eventually giving her a cautious all clear.

Things hadn't improved from there. The slideshow froze on a close-up of her mother, the whites of her eyes glowing like a dystopian movie-still. The celebrant mislaid his notes for the closing. Somebody's child got a bloody nose. When finally the coffin rolled back through the curtain, the moving strains of 'Amazing Grace' were abruptly replaced by 'Everything is Awesome' from *The Lego Movie* as their brother's mobile went off. They left the building straight into a crowd of windblown strangers assembling for the next funeral, only to discover that Great-Aunt Astrid had been mislaid, eventually being discovered inside enjoying her second funeral for the day. All of which meant they were subsequently so late to the wake that most people had already left. All that remained was the catered food, still in the fridge, and so many flowers that the floral scent lodged like a potpourri lump in her throat. It was still there.

'Remember that *Jaws* music?' asked Kat now. She rapped her knuckles against the table, sounding out the beat. 'Da dum, da dum, da dum.'

Annie rolled her eyes. 'What about the celebrant?' She lowered her voice to mimic him. 'We are gathered here together to blah, blah, blah. Snore.'

'No, *that* was Aunt Astrid's contribution,' said George. 'And how about the slideshow? When it stuck on that bit with Mum looking possessed?'

'Bloody hell,' said Kat. She was playing with her iPad now. 'And you do realise that we're now blessed with a DVD of the whole shitshow? Which is just weird. Even if it was a lovely funeral, does anyone *ever* want to relive these things?' She glanced up. 'I don't re-watch movies I enjoy, let alone funerals.'

Annie brought over the laden plate. 'I don't know. I did have a favourite part.' She straightened the pastries, not making eye contact. 'You know when Kat started doing the eulogy and got stuck? Then we both got up at the same time and went to stand with her. So that she could finish. I'd re-watch that bit.'

George nodded. She smiled. It *had* been a lovely moment. The three of them, united in grief and solidarity. She suspected that they would need to draw on that, going forward.

'Well, we'd better get started,' said Kat, as if thinking the same thing.

They'd given themselves the weekend to recover; a sort of timeout, a bubble of normality that was anything but. Today, though, was the start of the sorting that followed a death. It was a convoluted process, George knew, just from being on the periphery of her father-in-law's death a few years before. And here it was complicated by their brother, who had yet to make an appearance despite having the least distance to travel.

The kettle began to boil, but Kat remained where she was. Annie took over, putting together mugs of coffee that she brought over to the table. She lowered herself into a chair with a sigh and wrapped her hands around her mug. George thought that her younger sister seemed tired, and her makeup was heavier than usual. A small glob of mascara nestled in the corner of an eye. George felt a surge of affection.

'Okay,' said Kat decisively. 'Here we go. I've put together an agenda.' She slid the iPad towards the centre of the table. Sure enough there was an agenda there, complete with dot-pointed action items. George blinked.

'You're unbelievable,' said Annie, leaning forward.

'Unbelievably good,' replied Kat smugly. Then she raised one eyebrow. 'Although do let me know if either of you would like to take over? I know I can be a little … bossy.'

George exchanged a glance with her younger sister. Bossy was an understatement, but then Kat was undoubtedly also the most capable. Annie would probably over-complicate things and then take offence when it went awry, while she herself … well, with a to-do list as long as her arm and her own life something of a mess, she was hardly the best choice to organise the clean-up of someone else's.

'No?' asked Kat now. 'Okay then.' She tapped one finger on the iPad to bring it back to life. 'So, first item. Let's recap. The lawyer has all the paperwork in hand but the whole process will take a while. The funeral's paid. We've got an appointment at the cemetery on Thursday afternoon to select the plot. Spot. Whatever they call it.' She cleared her throat and continued more quickly. 'But in the meantime we need to sort her bills.' She nodded towards the paperwork that George had pushed aside. 'We can check her desk for any other outstanding things.'

'I'll do that,' said George quickly.

Kat nodded. 'O-kay. And of course we need to discuss the elephant in the room.'

This was one of the things that had kept George awake for much of the night. Right on cue, the footfalls of the elephant himself could be heard beneath them. They echoed along the floorboards and then a door creaked, followed by the sound of Harry coming up the stairs. This house, their childhood home, wasn't large. Just a compact L-shaped lounge and dining, with the island bench serving as the divider between dining and kitchen. A hallway ran down the centre of the house, with living areas to one side and bedrooms to the other. At the end of the hallway were stairs leading down into what had originally been a garage and workroom. During their childhood, this workroom had been repurposed as an extra bedroom and then, twenty years ago, after her husband's death, their mother had embarked on a major renovation. Upstairs, this had just meant turning the second bedroom into a study, but downstairs was unrecognisable. An entire apartment for their brother, complete with bedroom, living area, and ensuite. All self-contained yet still dependent. Just like him.

Annie let go of her mug and drummed her fingers on the table. Nobody said anything. Moments later Harry entered the lounge room. He was wearing a pair of tracksuit pants and a t-shirt that featured Iron Man. It stretched across his midriff, giving Iron Man a lopsided girth that would have severely hampered his ability to fly. Middle age, or perhaps Harry's epilepsy medication, had erased the last traces of the slim, fine-boned boy. He stood awkwardly, casting them a rapid glance.

'Come on, mate,' said George kindly. 'Come here and sit down.'

He pointed towards the area by the island bench. 'That's where she was.'

All three sisters swivelled to follow his finger. They already knew, of course, and had each since been to the house for various reasons and spent time staring at the tiles, but there was still something magnetic about the area. Kat was the first to recover.

'But she didn't *die* there, Harry. She just had a fall. We've *all* done that at some time.'

Harry gazed at her. Their father used to say that Harry was a slow thinker but a deep one, and that was far better than the opposite. George could almost see him digesting this new angle. She tried to nudge him along.

'Even Mum has! Remember that time she slipped in the bathroom and broke her collarbone? Or when she fell off the chair putting up the new light?'

Annie joined in. 'That's right! C'mon, Harry. There wouldn't be a square inch in this house where *someone* hasn't fallen! It's what makes it a home.'

'Odd definition of home,' said Kat to her. Her lip quirked. 'Not sure OHS would agree.'

George was still gazing at Harry. He seemed almost convinced. She patted the chair beside her. 'Sit down. Join us. We're talking about what's next. You're part of this.'

Harry hesitated, and then shuffled over to the table. He sat.

'Did you enjoy yourself staying with Aunt Margaret?'

'No.'

George grinned at her sisters. They were very fond of Aunt Margaret, their father's sister, but there was no doubt she was the chatty type. Harry most definitely was not.

'Who rang you?' asked Annie suddenly. 'At the funeral?'

Harry looked at her, puzzled. 'No-one.'

'But your phone went off! With that Lego song!'

'That was my alarm.'

'Your *alarm*? What on earth did you need an alarm for?'

Harry looked at her as if she herself was a bit slow. 'For the funeral.'

'What? But you were already—'

'Leave it,' said Kat. She shook her head. 'We love you, Harry. You're a hoot.'

He nodded, as if this was indisputable. They fell quiet for a while. George found her attention returning to the tiles. Even though it was January, they must have been so cold overnight. She started as Annie pushed her chair back, scraping it across the floor.

'Coffee?' she asked Harry.

He nodded. She put the kettle on and then began, incongruously, to scrub a casserole dish that sat by the sink. George looked over at Kat, but her older sister was now examining her mobile. After a few minutes the kettle whistled, a muffled shrill that cut uncomfortably across the silence. George closed her eyes momentarily. She didn't think she'd taken a deep breath since it happened. She had a sudden urge for camaraderie.

'It's not even been a full week,' she said. She chewed at her bottom lip. 'I keep thinking what I was doing this time last Monday. Before … you know.'

Kat lifted her gaze from the mobile. 'Not wanting to be pedantic, but this time last Monday she was already in trouble. We just didn't realise yet.'

George stared down at her coffee. In trouble was a nicer way of saying dying. Dying, dying, dead. Her mother was dead. The sentence was an oxymoron; the words jarred.

'I know what you mean,' said Annie suddenly. 'And what's more, I think we'll always do that. Soon it'll be this time last month, then it'll be this time last January. Eventually we'll just say this time in 2020. But it'll always be there.' She paused to pour boiling water into Harry's blue mug. 'Like a wall. Before and after.'

George's throat felt thick. She gazed at Annie, willing her to make eye contact. But her sister kept her attention on Harry's mug. Steam wafted across her face. From beside her, George sensed Kat watching too.

'The Berlin Wall was erected in 1961,' said Harry, filling the silence. 'Some people say that it came down in 1989, but that's not right. Demolition officially began in 1990 and was completed in 1991.'

'Thanks for that,' said Kat brusquely. '*Totally* relevant.'

Harry flushed. George reached over to pat his hand. 'No need to be mean, Kat.'

Kat didn't reply. She stared down at the iPad for a few moments and then reached for the plate of pastries, sliding them across the table towards Harry in lieu of an apology. Annie brought his mug over to the table and took a seat.

'Okay then, let's get started,' she said. She sighed. 'No point putting it off.'

Kat nodded. She tapped on the iPad again. 'Back to the agenda then. And I have an idea I'd like to run past you.'

'Arson?' asked George. A small part of her wasn't joking. At around two that morning she had fantasised about the house being hit by a bolt of lightning. Preferably, of course, while it was empty. But that would negate the need for any decisions. It would all be done for them.

'Best not put that in the minutes,' said Annie. She leaned across to grab a muffin.

'Female arsonists aren't common,' said Harry around a mouthful of danish. 'And they usually do it for attention.' He frowned for a moment. 'Except with Terry Barton. In 2002 she burnt a love letter and set fire to 138,000 acres in the United States of America.'

'Impressive,' said Kat, lifting an eyebrow. She shook herself and looked back at Annie. 'I'm not taking minutes, smart-arse. Now do you want to hear my idea or not?'

'*I do*,' said George. She also wanted to ask Harry if he knew what was in Terry Barton's love letter but didn't want to receive a lecture on the US postal service. The amount of trivia he kept in his head was astounding. One of her mother's pet peeves had been that after the movie *Rain Man* came out, people began comparing him to the main character. But this essentialised people like Harry, as if one similar characteristic made them all the same. For starters, unlike that character, Harry could be relatively affectionate, never had meltdowns, and could not fathom maths. Even numbers only made sense in relation to objects. To him, the 138,000 acres just mentioned might as well be the size of their backyard.

'So then, it's like this,' continued Kat. 'You know how I've been sharing with Kathy Sheffield ever since I got back?' She waited for her sisters to nod. They all knew that she had sold her apartment early the previous year while undertaking a secondment in London. On her return, seven months ago, she had moved in with a friend. Kat took a sip of coffee and continued. 'Well, she met some bloke on Tinder and he's all but moved in, so it's a little crowded. I've been looking to buy, but to be honest, I don't mind putting that off until I'm sure I'm staying at the Melbourne office.'

'You're thinking of heading off again?' asked George. The words caught in her throat.

'No, not really,' said Kat. She shrugged. 'Anyway, here's my idea. I move in here for a year. So we can take our time with …' she paused, her gaze sliding across to Harry and then away. 'Things. And we can make a few repairs, spruce the place up. Get it, you know, ready.'

George gazed at her. She loved the idea, instantly, even if a tiny part of her felt dislodged by the fact that it was Kat providing a solution for Harry. Usually that was her role. Regardless though, it was procrastination with purpose. Her favourite combination.

She got up to get a glass of water as she played with the notion, examining the edges.

'But that'll give you a longer commute,' said Annie now. She was frowning. 'Besides, aren't we better off just biting the bullet? Putting it on the market?'

George glanced at her quickly as she sat down again. In the last decade or so, Annie had developed a soft v across the bridge of her nose, which capitalised when she frowned. It was doing that now. It occurred to her that Annie might have money issues. She had long suspected that she was still partly supporting her adult son, so it was certainly possible.

'Nah,' said Kat. 'We'll get a better price if we fix it up a bit.' She waved a hand towards the kitchen, which featured mosaic tile and mission-brown trim. 'If we invested say, ten grand, we'd get ten times back at point of sale.'

'Ten grand!' exclaimed Annie.

Kat gave her a shrewd look. 'Yes, but it can come out of Mum's savings. You do realise they were fairly reasonable? As soon as probate comes through, we'll be splitting that four ways.'

'Oh.' Annie sat back as she digested this. 'Oh, okay. Of course.'

'I think it's a great idea,' put in George. She felt lighter already. 'I really do.'

'Harry?' Kat smiled at their brother. 'You get a say too. How do you feel about me moving here for a year?'

Harry was brushing icing sugar from his fingers. 'William Wordsworth lived with his sister Dorothy,' he said, without looking up. 'They were very happy.'

'Well, there you go,' said Kat. 'Perhaps we shall write poetry together.' She turned back to her sisters. 'But there's two conditions. One is that I'm not a replacement … carer. If you know what I mean.'

George knew exactly what she meant. And she could help anyway. She nodded.

'No poetry,' said Harry. 'I don't like poetry.'

'Like with his finances and everything,' said Kat, still addressing her sisters. 'We have to share the … responsibilities.' She slid her gaze across to Harry for a moment and then brought it back. 'And the other condition is that we need to clean this place out first.'

'What?' Annie's v deepened once more. 'Clean it out? All of it?'

'No poetry,' said Harry, more firmly this time.

George patted his hand lightly. 'There'll be no poetry, Harry. We promise.'

'All of it,' said Kat emphatically, as if there had been no interruption. 'I don't want to live in a shrine. Nor do I want anyone asking in a year's time what happened to this or that. What I'm asking is that we spend this week clearing *everything* that's upstairs. There's lots people will want, but after we divide it up, we donate the rest. I've got my own things in storage.'

George considered this. One week wasn't a lot of time. It might be a small house, but it was crammed with belongings. And memories. Every drawer full, every surface crowded, every wall laden. But if that was the price, then she was more than willing to pay it. She opened her mouth, but Annie spoke first.

'Apart from anything else, not all of us can take a week off just like *that*.' She clicked her fingers for emphasis. 'We have jobs. *Regular* jobs.'

George rolled her eyes. She knew that this last had been directed at her because it was a dig that Annie made quite regularly, mostly good-natured but with, she suspected, an undercurrent of envy. In fact George's job required the same input as a more traditional one, like Annie's nursing. She taught professional writing part-time at the local TAFE, and also produced a column for a national newspaper weekend supplement. But Annie often conflated flexibility with leisure. Besides, she acted like George just cribbed information from Wikipedia. She was very wrong. Mostly.

'Plus I've got Tom staying,' continued Annie. 'And he's only here for this week.'

George had more sympathy with this. Annie's son had flown down from the Gold Coast as soon as he'd heard that his grandmother was ill, and was leaving again this coming weekend. 'You don't have to be here every day though,' she said now. 'And maybe Tom'd like to be involved anyway? He could pick a few mementoes to take back with him?'

'I've already spoken to the removalists I used last time,' said Kat. 'They can bring my things over next Monday. Sorry, Annie, but if I'm going to do this, I'd rather get it done.'

'You were pretty confident we'd say yes then?' said Annie, raising her eyebrows.

Kat shrugged. 'I haven't locked it in, but, well, you have to admit it makes sense. We could do a SWOT analysis if you like? I've already done my own but happy to do one together.'

'No need,' said George quickly. 'I've just swotted in my head. The strengths and opportunities *clearly* outweigh the weaknesses. The biggest one being of course *you*'—she turned a rueful expression on Annie—'not being there.'

Annie snorted. 'Don't lay it on *too* thick.'

'But we'll do our best to push through despite the pain,' continued George, laying a hand against her heart. 'My two can help. We'll cull and divide and sort out what we think you'd like. Then you can just come around next weekend and check out the fruits of our labour.'

Annie's eyes widened as she processed this. She shook her head slowly. 'No. I suppose I could swap a few shifts. I've taken the next few days off anyway. We should all be here. Tom too.' She flicked a glance at George. 'And yes, I know what you did just then.'

'And *that*, ladies and gentlemen, is how it's done,' said George smugly. She hadn't raised two children for nothing.

Annie grinned, then turned back to Kat. The grin vanished. 'Although, hang on … *how* will we divide things up? We need to make sure it's fair.'

'Actually I had a thought about that too,' said Kat. 'Given there's four of us, and four grandchildren also, we need to have a plan. A friend did this thing with her family. Stickers.'

'Stickers?' asked George. She had a sudden recollection of her mother doing something similar when she'd cleared out downstairs prior to the renovation. 'Like what Mum did?'

'That's right. Except we each do it. With everything.'

'Can't we just talk about who wants what?' asked Annie. She was frowning again.

Kat shook her head. 'I don't think that'll work. Not by itself. There'll be arguments, and people feeling like they've been talked out of stuff. There's definitely some things that more than one person will want. I just want us to come out the other end still talking to each other.'

'So what happens if we all put stickers on the same thing?' said Annie stubbornly. 'We'll *still* have to discuss it. And there *still* might be arguments.'

'Not if we also include priorities,' said George slowly, thinking it through. 'Like every person gets to put say, an asterisk on one of their stickers for the thing they absolutely want. Their favourite thing. One for each person.'

'Two,' said Kat so quickly that George knew she had been thinking along the same lines. 'Two each. That way, even if they miss out on one, they have to get the other.'

'I don't know,' said Annie. Her v seemed indented. 'It seems a bit overly complicated.'

Kat shrugged. 'It's just a suggestion. I'm happy to put it to a vote.'

'I like it,' said George quickly. The last thing she wanted was conversations with others about memorabilia. About what meant something, and why. She gazed into the lounge room and then shook her head. Even the thought made her feel nauseous. 'I vote yes.'

'Huh.' Annie sat back. 'Well, then it seems I lose anyway.'

'In 2016, two sisters had their brother murdered over an inheritance,' said Harry. He turned his blue mug slightly to the right, and then straightened it. 'They used one of their sons to do it. He's now serving eighteen years behind bars. United States of America again.'

'Well, nobody's murdering anyone here,' said Kat firmly.

'Besides,' added George. 'If we're talking about my son, then there's no problem. He rarely does anything I ask.'

Kat had already turned back to Annie. 'I don't want you to feel like you're being talked into anything. If you come up with another idea, feel free to pitch it.'

Annie shrugged. She reached across for another muffin and then plucked out a blueberry, staring at it. 'Seven days, hey? That's a lot to get done in seven days.'

'Absolutely doable,' replied Kat firmly. 'All we have to do is plan it out and remain solution-focussed. Eyes on the prize. We've got this.'

George nodded slowly. She felt the familiar burn behind her eyes, but even so, felt better now that plans were being put into place and she had a framework within which to move forward. Although Annie was right. It would be a tall order within seven days. Doable, especially with Kat in charge, but at a stretch. It was also a little biblical. Except in this case it was seven days to dismantle a world. To sort through the belongings of a life-time, finalise paperwork, divide possessions, draw a line between then and now. This last would be the most challenging because drawing lines was not her forte. They usually blurred, the leakage meaning that everything stayed with her. Baggage accumulated across a lifetime. Maybe at some stage, one day, she would have to sort through those also. But not just yet.

Chapter Two

Monday afternoon

I'm not sure what the proper way is of doing this. Do I call you Dear Diary? Is it like confession? Forgive me, Father, for I have sinned, it has been oh, about a thousand days since my last confession. And there's no real point me going now either, not when I'd sin again in a heartbeat.

There were no dates on the diary entries, just a short paragraph per page. George flicked forward, skimming the surface in a search for keywords. She wasn't even sure what keywords these might be. Murder? Mayhem? A genealogy proving they were actually royalty? But nothing stood out. There were only a couple of dozen entries anyway, taking up around a third of the book. Following this were just blank pages. On impulse she lifted it by the spine and gave a gentle shake. A small rectangle of thin paper fluttered out, landing on her lap. George stared at it for a moment, stunned by the unexpected success of this venture. She leaned forward. It was a ticket for *The Rocky Horror Show* at the Regent Palace Theatre, dated 25th October 1975.

George's eyebrows shot up. She could not imagine a scenario where her mother would have attended *Rocky Horror*, other than by force. She did some quick maths. In October 1975, Enid would have been thirty-eight years old. She herself had been ten. She could distinctly remember the hype that accompanied the stage show, and even an occasion when their teenage cousin Lesley had taught them a rather vigorous version of the Time Warp. She could also recall the expression on her mother's face when her three daughters lined up to demonstrate their new skill.

George stared at the ticket. Her mother had been no fan of either science fiction or fantasy, let alone shows featuring gender-fluid aliens that couldn't keep their clothes on. But did this date the diary then? And what about the sinning, which she would do again in a heartbeat? As far as George knew, apart from her admittedly sharp tongue, her mother had led a fairly blameless existence. It didn't make sense.

'How's it going?' asked Kat from the doorway.

'Good!' exclaimed George without turning around. She pulled a pile of bank statements from the desk to her lap. 'Just getting these together for shredding. All good here.'

'Excellent! We're right on schedule.'

George waited until she heard her sister leave before sliding the diary into a bottom drawer. Reading it in tense, guilty snippets wasn't doing it justice. She needed to save it for total immersion. She resolved to be the last to leave so that she could grab it on the way out. With this decision made, George closed the drawer. It was like putting chocolate in the pantry. She stood and carried the pile of statements through to the lounge room. Harry was sitting on the couch, the shredder beside him. Tentacled strips of paper protruded from an overfull garbage bag nearby, giving testament to his previous endeavours. Judging by the faint music however, he was now playing a game on his mobile phone.

George dumped the bank statements beside him and then squeezed his shoulder lightly before going through to the kitchen. Annie was half in the pantry, her backside the only thing on view. It strained against her yoga pants. A jumble of packets and bags of assorted ingredients lay across the island bench. George collected her glass of water from the table as she went past, opening the sliding door to the veranda. It was one of those beautiful summer days where the sun splashed across cottonwool clouds like egg yolk. A light breeze rustled the agapanthus that edged the steps to the backyard. Next door, snow-white sheets billowed from the washing line like surrender flags.

The only furniture on the veranda was a hanging egg-chair and a wrought iron, semicircular plant stand pressed hard against the railings, holding a rather unhappy fiddle leaf fig. George took a sip of water and then poured the rest into the plant. She noticed that the railing behind looked in poor shape, so slid the plant stand away and then bobbed down to examine it further. The middle railing in particular was quite rotten. She glanced up and sure enough the guttering above was also in poor repair. She made a mental note to tell Kat. Funds would have to be put aside for repairs also.

George straightened, both knees voicing their displeasure. She left the plant stand aside as a reminder and leaned against the more solid part of the railing, gazing down into the backyard. This was the quarter-acre she had grown up in. Always that little overgrown, with nooks and crannies that were the venue of a million games, of hide and seek and tree-climbing. Of fairy dells and roads for Matchbox cars. Hopscotch and elastics on the concrete pathway, and secret treasures buried beneath the shrubbery. Dusk falling softly across days that felt like endless summer, with her mother standing right where George was now, calling them in for dinner. Their games had changed over the years, but Enid had been the one constant. Always calling, always answered. Eventually.

The memories caught in her throat. They felt like sandpaper. She thought it might be easier if it was winter. If the weather matched the mood. Rain should be lashing the rippled perspex over the veranda, and turning the grass to mud. Although then the heater would be on inside, lending the house a cosy warmth that held its own set of reminiscences. She felt a surge of angry bitterness, but there was nobody to be angry at. Except perhaps her mother, for not taking better care of herself. George closed her eyes and took a deep breath of the sunshine, then went back inside. She needed to keep busy.

In the study once more, she took stock of what remained to be done. Apart from the bank statements, all she seemed to have done is move things from one place to another. The wardrobe was still full, as was the bookshelf, and much of the filing cabinet. It was a little overwhelming, like being sent to clean your room as a child. George took a deep breath. She was fifty-five years old. She could do this.

For the next hour she worked steadily at the filing cabinet. It seemed that her mother had kept every statement, every invoice, every quote received for work she hadn't even followed through with. George put aside only the most recent, along with Harry's records. She flicked through the remainder, pausing when she came to a manila envelope labelled *Department* in her mother's writing. The entire word was underlined with a curlicue that swirled down from the t. The envelope contained a single sheet of paper. George read it several times before registering that it was the photocopy of an application for her brother to be put on the waiting list for communal housing. It was dated February 2001.

This was another surprise. Not as momentous as the diary, but unexpected nevertheless. George had no idea that her mother had ever explored options for Harry. She turned the single sheet over but there was no way of knowing if the application had even been submitted. If it had, that would mean that Harry had been on the waiting list for nearly twenty years. Surely that wasn't possible. This application had been filled out shortly after her father had died. George's chest tightened at the thought. Had it been a kneejerk reaction? What was her reasoning? And why had she never discussed it?

Kat came back into the room, her mobile phone pressed to one ear. Tinny on-hold music could be heard. Wordlessly, George passed her the photocopy and waited for her older sister's reaction. She was rewarded seconds later by one of Kat's eyebrows disappearing beneath her jagged fringe.

'That's all there was,' explained George in a low voice. She held up the envelope. 'It was in here. So you didn't know either?'

Kat shook her head. The on-hold music was replaced by a faint voice. Kat nodded at George and then left the room, taking the application with her. George could hear her voice, clipped and impersonal, fading down the passage. Leaning back in her chair, she stared at the nearby gilt-framed painting of apples as she thought about the ramifications of the application. She was washed by a fierce desire to have her mother back. Even if just for a moment, even if just to ask some questions. There should be a warning before someone's death, a grey zone for exchanges of affection, and a proper handover. She *needed* to see her. George wiped roughly at her eyes behind her glasses and then swivelled around, sliding the desk drawer open. Before she could extract the diary, Kat returned.

'Sorry, that was the electricity company.' She held up the application as she lowered her voice. 'This is ... a little surprising.

I'll give them a call. Outside though, coz I don't want Harry to know. Not yet. Can you keep an eye on him? Make sure he stays in here?'

George nodded. She pushed the drawer closed with one foot and then gathered up a pile of discarded papers. On her way through the lounge room, she dropped them atop the bank statements from earlier. Harry glanced up briefly from his game. In the kitchen, Annie's backside still jutted from the pantry. The island bench was even more crowded.

'Do you know you wiggle as you do that?' asked George, pulling out a chair at the table.

'Thanks.' Annie straightened, holding a cloth in one hand. 'Very useful information. Although it's probably more a wobble than a wiggle nowadays.' She gestured towards the bench. 'Would you believe that she had three full packets of macaroni? And two of semolina! What do you even use semolina *for*?'

'Porridge, I think.'

'Okay, fair enough. But what about kelp noodles then? And forbidden rice?'

'Only for the emperor,' said Harry from the lounge room. 'Once upon a time. But high in antioxidants. Can boost eye and heart health, and protect against cancer and other things.'

'Really?' Annie picked up the packet. 'Maybe she should have opened it then.'

There was an edge of bitterness in Annie's voice that George thought matched her own. It gave her a sense of solidarity. Growing up, she and Kat had probably been the closest, but then as young adults, Kat had shot off in a different direction and she and Annie had come together. They'd had similar interests, overlapping circles of friends, even married around the same time and shared their first pregnancies. But it was the aftermath of Annie's marriage breakdown a few years later that had really solidified their adult friendship. There had been little choice. Because quite abruptly Annie's husband, Brad, had turned from a rather boring, slightly pompous git into the ex-husband from hell.

Their divorce had heralded, for Annie, thirteen years of emotional and financial manipulation. Thirteen years of court appearances for minor changes to the parenting orders. Thirteen years of regular no-shows for access and then unannounced drop-ins because by god, didn't Brad have a right to see his son? Not to mention the constant threats of litigation if ever she herself tried to alter the routine. Things only eased when Tom turned eighteen. And then, last year, Brad had retired to the Gold Coast and Tom promptly followed. George could only imagine her sister's pain. And now this. Their mother. She closed her eyes and tilted her head back, feeling the muscles strain.

'Don't let Kat catch you napping,' said Annie with a snort. 'She'll put you on report.'

George straightened but didn't take the bait. She massaged her neck.

'I'm going to leave some plastic bags here,' continued Annie. She pointed towards the pile on the bench. 'Grab whatever you want. Then I'll donate the rest to the local food bank.'

'Good idea,' said George. She already knew she wouldn't be taking anything.

'You know something?' asked Annie. She gazed down at the array of packages. 'Mum wanted me to go with her to Costco last week. I said I was too busy.' She picked up a container of two-minute noodles and balanced it precariously atop the macaroni, watching it teeter. 'Too busy,' she repeated wonderingly.

George nodded slowly. She didn't trust herself to speak. There were countless times that she had also been too busy. But then maybe, for her own sanity, she needed to focus on the occasions when she *hadn't* been. Through the sliding door she could see Kat on the veranda, on her mobile. Every so often she would animatedly wave the hand holding the application. A few of the puffy clouds had now joined forces, elongating across the sky and turning the glow of the sun into an omelette. Below were ranks of serrated blotches, marching towards the horizon. Once, when George had been about eight or nine, lying on her back in the grass, she had been joined by her father. He was not an overly playful man so when he suddenly lowered himself to the ground, it had felt more awkward than companionable. Minutes moved as slowly as the serrated clouds above. *Soldiers*, her father had then said, pointing. *See? They're on parade. Like damn sheep. Never be a sheep, Georgie girl. Promise.* And she had.

'Penny for them?' asked Annie now.

George turned to her sister. 'I was just thinking of all the games we used to play out there. Remember? Hide and seek? Mum used to stand on the veranda and call us in?'

Annie was quiet for a moment. 'Sure I do. I also remember you two hiding from me. All the time. And me getting sent to bring you both in. I used to scream with frustration.'

The edge of bitterness was back, but this time it afforded George no pleasure. Overlaying her earlier memories were another set, of she and Kat smothering their giggles as they buried further into whatever hiding place, spurred on by the growing anxiety in their little sister's voice. But Annie was wrong, it wasn't *all* the time.

'Oh, forget it,' said Annie, her voice back to normal. 'You're right. There's plenty of amazing memories out there too. I'm just being miserable.'

'No, you're right. We did that sometimes. I'm sorry.'

Annie shrugged. 'You were just being bratty. To be honest, I blame Mum more. She should have done her own dirty work.'

George wanted to agree, if only for Annie's sake, but any companionable maternal criticism felt inappropriate now. Yet another thing gone. In the lounge room, the shredder started up again. The noise was a steady whine that rose gratingly as Harry fed paper into the machine. She took her glasses off and rubbed at the bridge of her nose. Suddenly she felt Annie's arms encircle her from behind. George stiffened with surprise, and then relaxed into the embrace. She felt a sudden rush of love for her sister. They weren't an overly tactile family, but sometimes words weren't enough. Only a hug would suffice.

Annie gave one last squeeze before breaking away. She returned to the bench and busied herself moving packets around. 'You know how everyone finds their own niche in a family?' she asked after a few moments.

George blinked. 'Huh?'

'It's a sociological theory, I think,' explained Annie. She leaned forward on the bench, the pile of macaroni nestling against one elbow. 'Children slip into their own roles. I was thinking about this just before. See I suspect that for me, the roles were already taken by you two. Even when we were playing games like Barbies or whatever, I just got the ones neither of you wanted. And if I pushed back, then you wouldn't let me play at all.'

There was a pause, which George wasn't sure how to fill. She also wasn't sure if Annie was getting to a point or just returning to her earlier complaint. She'd preferred the hug.

'So,' continued Annie. 'I think I just took the good girl role. Even if it meant you two would call me a suck-up. But you know what the worst thing was?' Annie frowned, the v in her forehead deepening. She went on without waiting for an answer. 'A lot of the time I did it for Mum, but I think that's what she liked *least*. Sometimes I'd be helping her or whatever.' She waved towards the piles of food. 'And then I'd see her glance at me with, I don't know, almost disdain.'

'Really?' asked George. She suspected her sister had revelled in the good girl role. Certainly if she or Kat had gotten into trouble, usually Annie would be standing nearby with a smirk. Maybe they *had* bullied her a bit though. She felt annoyed that her memories were being muddied.

'Really,' said Annie. She closed her eyes for a moment and then pushed away from the bench. 'Anyway, no matter. Coffee?'

'Sure.' George picked up a piece of paper from the pile on the table and gazed at it. Without her glasses it was just blurred lines. She put it down. 'What about me then? If you were the good girl, what was I?'

'Oh, let's see. Kat was the naughty one. No, not naughty. More stubborn. Bossy.'

'Yes, but what was *I*?'

Annie flicked the gas on under the kettle and then paused, thinking. 'Hmm. Bit of column A, bit of column B? I don't think you *had* a definitive role.'

George stared, a little affronted. She made her sound inconsequential. 'What about mediator then? All the times I sorted out issues between you both!'

Annie raised her eyebrows and then shrugged. 'Maybe, I suppose. Sometimes. But more often you just took her side. Like before! When you two ganged up over those stupid stickers. C'mon, George, you don't really want that, do you? Can't we just discuss things like adults? You know, negotiate? Compromise? You're always saying how good you are at that.'

'No,' said George curtly. Any doubts she might have had were vanquished by this conversation. And she had no recollection of ever saying that she was particularly skilled at compromise, just that life demanded it, at times. Annie was now making her sound inconsequential *and* a wet blanket. 'Plus for your information, I'm not *ganging up*. I happen to think it's a good idea.' She hesitated, then went for it. 'Besides, not *everyone* is good at compromising.'

Annie's eyes had narrowed. 'What do you mean by that?' She waited, but George didn't answer. 'Unless …' Annie gave a slow smirk. 'You shouldn't be so hard on Rhyll, you know.'

George blinked. She hadn't been referring to her daughter. And what's more, she knew that Annie knew that. She opened her mouth to retort, but at that moment the sound of the shredder rose and then jammed grindingly before abruptly falling silent. Harry could be heard muttering from the lounge room. But the brief interruption had given George time to pull back. This was not the time.

'I wasn't talking about anybody in particular,' she said more equably, skirting around the truth. 'Just that everyone has different, ah, skills in that department. Kat could talk anyone around and Harry'll just quote historical facts. As for Rhyll, yes she'd probably do a bit of sulking.' George paused for a moment after throwing her own child under the bus, and then forged on. 'And Tom, well …' She shrugged, letting the words hang.

Annie's lips had thinned. Harry shambled into the kitchen and glanced at both of them briefly before going out to the veranda. The kettle began to whistle and finally Annie turned away. George grimaced at her sister's back. She didn't understand her opposition, unless it was just for the sake of it. Of all of them, Annie should have been most keen to avoid negotiations. George was very fond of her nephew, but there was no denying that collaboration was not Tom's strong suit. He was also fairly attached to getting his own way.

The screen door opened and Kat came through. She frowned at George. 'Thanks for that.'

'What?'

'I asked you to keep an eye on you-know-who.' Kat gestured towards the veranda where Harry was now sitting in the egg-chair, gazing intently at his phone.

'Whoops,' said George. She grimaced. 'He must have snuck past.'

'Yeah, sure.' Kat looked from one of them to the other. Her frown deepened. 'You two aren't arguing, are you?'

'No,' said George as Annie shook her head.

Kat didn't look convinced. 'Because we've got no time for that sort of crap.'

'I *said* we weren't,' said George. It sounded like a whine, even to her. She busied herself straightening the pile of bills. She could feel Kat's eyes on her, but after a moment her sister turned away, passing the DHS application to Annie at the bench.

'I've just been on the phone with them,' explained Kat. 'The crux is that yes, she made an application years ago, but they don't prioritise those who have secure accommodation with a parent.' She glanced towards the veranda. 'Now of course things are different.'

Annie finished reading. 'Wow. She never said. I didn't know …'

'Yeah, neither did we.' Kat shrugged as she took the application back. 'Look, she may have just been putting things in place for the future. Anyway, someone's ringing me back later this week. The woman said it's still a decent wait time, but he'll be moved up categories now, that's for sure.'

'Maybe he'd like it,' said Annie slowly. 'Maybe we should ask him. After all, he likes the day centre.'

'Barely,' said George shortly.

'Well, let's not ask right now.' Kat folded the letter over. 'Wait till we hear back. Get our ducks in a row.'

'Did she give any hint of how long?' asked George. She kept her mind on the logistics and not the thought of Harry in some type of supported housing. The latter made her stomach curl.

'She didn't say. But she was very informative about other things. Like we'll need to think about applying for financial guardianship. Otherwise the State Trustees will look after his income; however they take a cut. She also said …' Kat cast another glance outside. 'That we need to recognise he's entitled to a greater share of the assets than us.'

'What?' Annie stared at her.

'Because he was more dependent, and has greater needs into the future. She said we should discuss things with a lawyer, and that we'll probably have to engage a separate, independent lawyer for Harry.'

George nodded slowly. It made sense. She had no problem with Harry getting a larger cut if it meant he would be financially secure. It was the supported accommodation idea she was having problems with. But the alternative, which had him moving in with one of them, was equally unpalatable. She loved her brother, but her life was already a little complicated. She glanced over at Annie. Her sister was staring at the coffee mugs. George was more convinced than ever that Annie was having financial difficulties. She resolved to speak to her at some stage. Harry came back inside.

'The Spanish flu killed between seventeen and fifty million people,' he said.

'O-kay,' said Kat. 'Thanks. Interesting.'

He nodded. 'It actually started elsewhere, not Spain, but wasn't reported because of World War I. King Alfonso XIII was gravely ill. There's another one now.'

'Another Alfonso?' asked George, trying to follow. 'Or another Spanish flu?'

'No, another disease. Some people eat bats.'

'Well, that's fine then,' said Annie curtly. 'None of us have any intention of eating bats.'

'So you think,' said Harry darkly. He went through into the lounge room.

The sisters looked at each other. They were well used to Harry's odd injections into the conversation. One of his favourite hobbies was cross-referencing the news with Wikipedia, which he treated as a type of bible. His other hobby was Lego. An old table tennis table in his apartment held streetscapes of shops and post offices, museums and theatres. Dozens of little Lego mini-figs peopled the landscape in ever-changing poses. It occurred to George now that those would never fit into supported accommodation. She blinked.

'Anyway, I think we should start winding up for today,' said Kat. 'Start afresh tomorrow.'

Annie nodded. She brought George's coffee over. 'I'll just finish the pantry.' She waved at the bench. 'And please take some of this stuff. Otherwise I'm donating it.'

Kat cast her eyes over the pile of packets. 'Yeah. Also, I thought I might stay here for a few nights. I don't really want to leave Harry alone at the moment.'

'Are you sure?' asked George. 'I sort of expected I'd take him home with me. Just for now.'

'Nah. Let him settle back into his routine. Besides, it'll save me driving back and forth.'

George nodded. A flash of relief made her feel guilty. She also suspected that the roommate's romance had worn even thinner than Kat had let on. Her sister wasn't usually quite this altruistic.

George closed her eyes tiredly, then picked up her coffee and rose. 'I'll check the study. Finish up there.'

She left the room, passing Harry, who was now pulling crinkled worms of paper from the cogs of the shredder. In the study, she slipped the diary from the desk drawer and stood for a moment with it in her hands before opening the wardrobe doors. Both the hanging space and shelving were crowded with boxes and books and baskets. A plastic bag lay partly open, spilling skeins of wool. George didn't think she had ever seen her mother knit. It was going to take a full day just to sort through the things in here, not to mention the rest of the house. For a moment she felt overwhelmed by the task ahead, let alone the emotion that would be contained within each box, each basket. The stories that would emerge, with threads that dangled, the questions that would never be answered. Her stomach tightened and, quite suddenly, bile surged up to coat her throat. She pushed the door closed with one hand just as she was hit by a paroxysm of coughing. She bobbed, trying to be as quiet as possible as tears streamed from her eyes. The coughing abated, but the pain did not. It enveloped her from the inside out, holding her in a grip that was almost as agonising as her loss.

It was not the first time this had happened during the past week. Once when she had been in the shower, pressing her down onto the tiles as if she had been liquid herself. On another occasion she had been weeding, pausing abruptly to curl over into the garden bed, emitting a keening that felt almost organic. The last time she had been in the supermarket, stupidly staring at her mother's favourite brand of butter, with just enough time to abandon her groceries and run to the centre bathroom. Where she sat on a toilet, arms wrapped around herself, eyes clenched against the pain. Eventually, as always, it eased enough for her to function.

It was no different now. After a few minutes, her limbs loosened and she rose with one hand against the wardrobe for support. Already the intensity of the attack was fading, leaving just a dull bruise behind. She could hear the low murmur of her sisters talking in the other room and the sound brought a warmth that helped enormously. She pushed aside the minor disagreement with Annie as she took a deep breath and hugged the diary against her chest. Misery really did like company. They were in this together.

Chapter Three

Monday evening

I should have had more guts. That's the bottom line. The glossier version of course, is that I did the right thing, put the kids first, went with the numbers and all that. Three against one. Blah, blah, blah. Except we know the truth. They're all goddamn excuses. I could have been eating apples in Mount Isa. But when the chips were down, I was all talk. I didn't have the guts.

Before leaving, George had taken the time to read one more diary entry. She had given up on the idea of taking it home, as there was a chance her sisters would have noticed. They probably wouldn't have said anything, not knowing what it was, but one or both might have recalled the occasion when she revealed its existence later this week. That wasn't the only reason though. Throughout the afternoon, George had come to the realisation that to devour the diary in a single meal would be to relegate her mother's voice into the past. One bite at a time kept it alive. The self-denial itself felt rewarding; almost deliciously masochistic. Pain was pleasure.

Unfortunately there was also self-denial in not being able to discuss each entry. What did her mother mean by not having enough guts? Three against one? And why on earth would she be eating apples in Mount Isa? Even apart from the fact that part of Australia was renowned more for mining than produce, it seemed a little unremarkable in terms of life goals. As far as George knew, the furthest north that Enid had been was a family holiday to Coffs Harbour. There was a photo somewhere of her holding Harry's hand alongside the Big Banana. Wrong fruit. Apples themselves did not seem to have achieved any particular notability within their lives either, except perhaps in the form of apple pie which had been her father's favourite. Then again, maybe the reference was biblical and was more about temptation. The combination of these last two trains of thought conjured up the classic image from the movie *America Pie*. George blanched.

A burst of laughter interrupted her thoughts. She glanced across into the living room where her family, and Leo's friend Evie, were seated around the table feasting on leftovers from the funeral. Platters of spinach and feta triangles, vol-au-vents and mini quiches covered the surface, along with stubbies of beer and, in Evie's case, a bottle of something strawberry-red. Her husband Simon caught her eye and gave a rueful, apologetic grin. She smiled back automatically, giving tacit approval to their merriment. She *wanted* them to be happy, but she also felt a bilious resentment that they could.

'Come join us,' called Simon in his hearty, get-with-the-project voice. 'Have something to eat. It'll do you good.'

Everybody was looking at her now. Simon. Leo and Rhyll, clones of their father with their dark hair, olive complexions and hooded nut-brown eyes. Evie, solid and spiky with her shock of pink hair, multi-pierced ears and faint air of condescension. Even their old dog glanced up from his bed in the corner. George summoned up another smile and shook her head. 'I'm fine. I'm not hungry.'

They turned away, one by one. Simon was last, his eyes narrowing as he assessed her statement. Then he too was gone. George tucked her legs beneath her bottom on the couch, curling into a comma. On the television, Monica was wearing a turkey and Chandler had just declared his love. George flicked the channel. Now there was an update on the fires that were currently raging across the eastern states. They had been burning since before Christmas, devouring huge expanses of land. Lives lost, houses destroyed, wildlife decimated. George closed her eyes. It was all too much. The scale of destruction made her own tragedy seem inconsequential, and her grief self-indulgent. She resented that too.

She fumbled at the remote and turned off the television before she opened her eyes. With that gone, the voices from the dining room seemed even louder, even more jovial. She thought that there should be some sort of timed progression on grief; a set of instructions that delineated the process. Perhaps the Victorians had it right with their strict mourning period and graduation of colours. She needed a template like that. Guidance. Something that told her when the gut-punches would ease, when her appetite would return, whether she was allowed to be pissed that her family were having fun.

When her father had died, after spending the day at the hospital, she and her sisters had gone back to the family house, where they sat for hours, stripped raw with grief. She hadn't left until nine that night, utterly drained, returning home to have Simon lead her straight to the bathroom. There she found a steaming bubble bath, soft music, scented candles, a glass of wine. He had helped her out of her clothes and then sat on the floor while she lay in the bath and just cried. Afterwards he'd dried her off, tucked her into bed and spooned himself around her. He had *encompassed* her grief.

George glanced back towards the table. Now the only thing he was encompassing was a vol-au-vent. He was also talking through mouthfuls. It seemed to be an anecdote of somebody's lunch being stolen at work and the convoluted detective work that ensued in order to catch the culprit. *That* should enthral the younger generation. George uncurled herself stiffly. One of her knees cracked. She got to her feet and went past the table into the kitchen. Once there, she wasn't quite sure what to do, so she started collecting the catalogues and assorted brochures scattered across the bench, intending to put them in the bin, but then changed her mind. Maybe there was something important there. Instead she pushed them to one end, where they joined the discarded mail, and put the kettle on. Puddles, their elderly labrador, had followed her. She bent to pat him, feeling an additional wrench as she gazed at his cataract-filmed eyes. He'd better not die anytime soon. She didn't think she could take it. If she'd been alone, she would have sunk onto the floor and gathered him into her lap. Wallowed in his devotion.

Instead, George got one of his soft chews from the bag that had spilled in the pantry and fed it straight into his mouth. He licked her hand with gratitude and emitted a soft fart. The kettle boiled, so she made herself a cup of tea and then sipped it at the bench. Now Leo was telling a story about a client who insisted his at-home smart technology had been corrupted by paranormal activity. It was a much more entertaining tale than his father's. George waited for him to wind down.

'We're going to start dividing up her things tomorrow,' she said.

All heads turned towards her, their smiles so deliberately being replaced by expressions of concern that it was almost comical. Leo's hair looked like it had been caught in a snow drift. For months he had been growing out a platinum dye-job applied for a Halloween costume party, where he had gone as Spike from *Buffy the Vampire Slayer*. George liked it now; it gave him luminosity. Her eyes slid to Rhyll, sitting opposite. She could do with some luminosity herself. The only thing sparkling was the tiny diamond in her nostril. As usual, she was slouching over in her chair, looking two shades away from miserable. George felt a familiar urge to poke a finger into the small of Rhyll's back, like her mother used to do to her, with a remonstration to stop hunching. Sit up straight. She could only imagine the reaction that she would receive.

'Are we allowed to just say what we want?' asked Leo now. 'Coz if so, can I have that hanging chair on the veranda?'

His father looked at him, bemused. 'Where the hell would you put it?'

'In my room. I'll hang it from the rafters.'

'You don't *have* any rafters! You'd need to drill it into a joist in the ceiling. And ... no!'

Leo shrugged. 'Then I'll keep it till I get my own place. With rafters.'

'You do realise that rafters are—'

'It doesn't matter!' interrupted George, irritated by this segue into architecture. They all fell silent as they looked at her cautiously. She took a deep breath and then focussed on both her children. 'I wanted to know if you could come by tomorrow.'

'Sure,' said Leo immediately. 'I was going to ask if you wanted a hand. I'll chuck a sickie.'

'Actually, *I* wouldn't mind the hanging chair,' said Rhyll. She was looking at her brother.

'What?' asked Leo. 'Why?'

'It's got memories.'

'Of what exactly?' queried her father. 'You fell off the thing at Christmas!'

'That's coz she was high,' said Leo. He grinned as he took a sip of beer, not taking his eyes off his sister.

'I wasn't fucking high!'

'Language,' said Simon, but so mildly that it seemed like a comment rather than an admonishment. 'And if you're so desperate for a chair, please god *one* of you ask for the Eames! That thing's a work of art, *and* it doesn't require rafters.'

'Forget about the bloody rafters!' snapped George. 'Who cares about the bloody rafters!'

Simon's eyes widened. He made a timeout gesture. 'Hey, calm down, love.'

George jerked her gaze to his. Her irritation teetered on the edge of anger.

'Oh dear,' said Evie, speaking for the first time. 'Don't you know you should like, *never* tell a woman to calm down?'

'Huh?' Simon turned to face her. He looked puzzled. 'Why on earth not?'

'Because it invalidates whatever she's annoyed at.' Evie reached out to snare a mini quiche. 'It's like saying she's overreacting.'

'God, Dad, even *I* know that,' said Leo with a grin.

'Lol,' said Evie. She examined the quiche. 'Hey, George, is this chicken or tuna?'

'Um, chicken I think,' said George. She was feeling a rush of warmth towards the girl. Perhaps she could give Simon a few more pointers.

'Bugger. I've gone pescatarian, see. It's like, my first step towards veganism. Save the planet and all that.' Evie replaced the offending item on the platter. She used a cobalt-blue fingernail to prod at the edge of another and then took the one next to it.

George felt her warmth dissipating. 'I see.'

'So what happens then, Mum?' asked Leo. 'If we both want the same thing?'

'What? Oh …' She dragged her gaze from Evie. 'Well, we'll have a system. Stickers. Like when your grandmother did that big cull years ago. Except this time you both also get two priority picks. To let us know the things you *really* want.'

'I bet that was Kat's idea,' said Simon with a grin. 'Hey, do you want me to send someone around to quote on a spruce-up? If you're putting the place on the market?'

'We're not,' said George shortly. She didn't know why she felt offended by this. She softened her voice. 'Kat's moving in for a year. It'll give us time for decisions.'

'Oh, *great* idea. Market's a bit down at the moment. And good for Harry too. I half-expected you'd bring him home with you.'

George nodded. She'd thought the same thing. 'So anyway, first up is a clear-out this week, and dividing all the stuff. So that's why I need you two tomorrow.'

'Hanging chair,' said Rhyll firmly. She cast her mother a low, hooded glance.

Leo shrugged. 'Same.'

'Christ almighty,' said their father.

George took a sip of tea, but it had gone cold. She stepped over Puddles, who had curled up on the floor by her feet, and poured it down the sink. Outside, darkness was settling and the solar lights created splashes of illumination amongst the garden beds. A possum made a dash along the deck railing and disappeared into a nearby tree. George sighed tiredly. She suddenly wanted to be in bed, alone.

'So hey, Mum,' called Leo. 'What happens if we both put one of these priority stickers on the same thing?'

'We'll work it out,' said George. She rinsed her teacup and put it in the drainer.

'Yeah, sure,' said Rhyll darkly. She stared at her stubbie. 'May as well give it to him now.'

'Don't be ridiculous!' exclaimed George, now thoroughly irritated. She looked from one family member to the other, willing them to recognise her own pain. Even though she knew this wasn't entirely fair. They had all loved her mother; they were all suffering. Just yesterday she had come across Leo and Rhyll bent over the old photo albums, both shiny-eyed and almost brusquely embarrassed. She took a deep breath and kept her voice even. 'It'll all be done fair and square. I promise.'

'Besides, I *did* say it first,' said Leo mildly.

His sister's head snapped up. 'Piss off!'

'Seriously, guys?' said their father. He did another of his time-out gestures. 'You're really going to start arguing over your grandmother's stuff before she's even cold?' He whipped around to George. 'Sorry, that was a bit insensitive.'

'Anyway, I'm not sure you can use that expression when someone's been cremated,' said Leo. He rocked his chair back, teetering it precariously on two legs. Opposite him, Rhyll slid down in her own seat and used her foot to hook one of her brother's grounded chair legs. Leo let out a hoot of laughter and shot forward, securing himself before beginning a foot fight with Rhyll under the table.

'D'you know, that saying's probably *more* apt,' said Evie, ignoring the fracas beside her. 'Like a cremation is *literally* hot. Literally.'

'Guys!' exclaimed Simon. He made yet another of his time-out gestures, but stopped abruptly as the table rocked. He used his hands to steady it instead, but not quickly enough to stop his own stubbie toppling over. Foamy liquid gushed across the mini quiche platter. With the dumb luck of youth, both the combatants' drinks remained upright.

'Christ! Enough!' yelled Simon. 'You just spilled the drinks!'

Leo reached over and righted his father's stubbie. 'Not wanting to be pedantic, Pops, but only *one* drink got spilled. Singular, see? Not plural.'

'And given it was yours,' added Rhyll, 'it seems you should take responsibility also.'

Leo nodded. 'That seems fair.'

'Imagine working there,' mused Evie. She had lifted her own drink during the disturbance and now nestled it against her chin. Her words echoed into the rim. 'What a shit job.'

It took George a moment to realise the girl was still talking about the crematorium. She closed her eyes, then opened them to look at Simon. 'I'm going to bed. Can you make sure you put everything away? And take Puddles out?'

'Sure,' said Simon distractedly as he mopped at the spillage with a serviette. 'Hey, are you okay?'

'Fine. Just fine. Goodnight, all.'

There was a chorus of goodnights as she left the room. She half-expected Simon to follow, even if just for a moment, but was also relieved when he didn't. In the bedroom, she stripped off her clothes and threw them in the hamper, then went through to the ensuite. Stepping beneath the shower, she tipped her head back and let the water cascade down her body. It was almost orgasmic. She stood there, mind numb, until it almost felt like she was at one with the water. Light, buoyant, free-flowing, transcendent.

'Everything okay in here?'

George jerked back to earth. Simon was standing in the doorway, peering at her.

'Only because you've been here for ages,' he continued, half-yelling to be heard over the shower. 'Everything good?'

'Have you been watching me?' asked George, a little stunned. She didn't know whether to be offended or flattered.

'Hah! Course not. It's just you can hear the pipes rattling out there. They're really loud.'

'Oh. I see. Well, *sorry* for disturbing you.'

'That's not what I meant. I thought you might have drowned or something.'

George turned off the shower. The abrupt cessation of the water left her feeling exposed. She reached out to snag a towel.

'Do you need anything?' asked Simon. 'Cup of tea? Coffee? Glass of wine?'

'No thanks. I'm fine.'

'Hmm. Okay. Well then, I'll leave you to it.'

George waited for him to leave and then stepped from the cubicle and dropped her towel. Her skin glistened. Once upon a time, a little episode like that would have had a very different ending. Or at least an appreciative comment. Instead it seemed that Simon had performed one of his annoying timeouts on their relationship. George flushed guiltily, because she certainly had.

Turning to the full-length mirror, she took hold of the bum-bag of flesh that hung below her belly. It wasn't *too* bad, but there was no doubt it was there. She moved her hands to her breasts, lifting them up. They cooperated obligingly but, as soon as she let them go, dropped back into relaxed mode. Perhaps her fifty-five years showed more precisely in her face. She leaned forward to examine it. Pouchier by the year.

'Middle-aged,' she said in a low voice. 'Middle-aged, muddled and motherless.'

George dried herself off quickly and then ran a comb through her hair. Back in the bedroom, she pulled on an oversized t-shirt and sat down on the side of the bed. Part of her wanted to return to the dining room, surround herself with family and just let their noise wash over her. Like with the shower. But she also knew that theory was often more appealing than practice. The conversation would not so much wash as prod, much like Evie's fingernail into the mini quiche. And no doubt it would only take about twenty minutes before Rhyll found *something* objectionable about her mother; whether it was words, or deeds, or even the expression on her face. She would then sulk for a bit before flouncing off. And when Rhyll flounced off, she always managed to leave much of her mood behind, like smoke from a faulty exhaust. A perfect analogy, because Rhyll could indeed be exhausting.

George had several friends with daughters also in their mid-twenties, and in every case their relationships had metamorphosed into friendship. Photos on Facebook showed them with their arms wrapped around each other, or enjoying shopping expeditions and brunch and pedicures. Rhyll would no more agree to a mother–daughter pedicure than she would have her toenails removed with needle-nosed pliers. Those Facebook daughters also all had jobs and boyfriends and vibrant social lives. They posted effusive messages on Mother's Day. *Best mother ever! Can't thank you enough for everything! Love you to bits!* Last Mother's Day, Rhyll had handed her a pot plant that looked suspiciously like it had come from someone's garden. They weren't even friends on Facebook.

George suspected that a therapist would trace their difficulties back to the birth itself. Twenty-six hours of labour followed by an arrival so explosive that George had to have surgery to repair the damage. And Rhyll had begun her rejection almost instantly. Breastfeeding had been like force-feeding a suffragette. Reflux meant that even formula was projectile vomited. No baby books had prepared her and Simon for the trembling bone-weariness that bracketed their hours as days crept into weeks, and weeks into months. It had been a full three before they even had sex again, and perhaps the therapist might point the finger there also. Because what that singular occurrence had lacked in enthusiasm, it had made up for in effectiveness. She had fallen pregnant again.

Even all these years later, George could still clearly recall their blank-faced shock as they'd stared at the pregnancy test, with Rhyll's colicky wails serving as a soundtrack to their hell. They had even briefly considered a termination, given that infanticide was frowned on. Two months later Simon had a vasectomy and six months after that, on New Year's Eve, Leo had been born. For them, 1995 had literally been bookended by babies. But the saving grace had been the production of a vastly different type of child. Happy, contented, grasping at life with both chubby hands, as sociable as his birthdate. When she took the two babies out in their bulky double-pram, passers-by would pause to return his sunny smile and then blink when their gaze slid across to his scowling sister. They were like chalk and cheese then, and had remained so ever since.

Not for the first time, George compared the relationship with her daughter against that she had enjoyed with her own mother. Would Rhyll feel as gutted when she herself died? Or would she emerge from her bedroom just long enough to revel in the funeral leftovers? George felt a sudden swell of self-pity. It caught in her throat. But it was bigger than just Rhyll, with lumpy, lacy edges that snagged her breath. Dying, dying, *dead*. She stared at the wall for a few moments and then reached out for her mobile, which was charging on the nightstand. She put her glasses on. There was a new message there, from Guy.

Hope it all hasn't been too ghastly. Don't forget, if you need to get away, there's a spa here, and wine, and my magical hands ;)

Trust an author to use the word *ghastly*, George thought. Nobody else did. It was one of those words that was sliding into disuse. Like jentacular, or kerfuffle, or crapulous. But it was also more than fitting. Everything *was* ghastly at the moment. She pulled up the group chat that Kat had launched the week before and typed quickly. *This is so hard.*

Only a few seconds later came a reply from her older sister. *You should try being here, in her room. It's weird. Really weird.*

George nodded to herself. *It's all ghastly,* she texted. And then: *How's Harry?*

Seems fine. The only bit of normal was the death glare he gave when I went down to his room!

After a moment a message popped in from Annie. ♥ *To you both.*

Same, typed George. The script appeared just as the identical word was sent from Kat. She entered a laughing emoji and then a care one. They said their goodnights and George waited a few moments but nothing else arrived. She scrolled through the wealth of communication that had got them through the difficulties of the last week, willing it to do the same now. It helped, a little. She tossed her glasses aside and put the phone down, then flopped backwards, gazing at the ceiling for a while before coiling into the bed, pulling the sheet over her. The tears came before her head even reached the pillow. Not noisy and gulping, as they had been those first few days, but just a silent and uncontrollable leakage. They *seeped* from her, pooling beneath her nose and soaking the pillow.

She got up, throwing the sheet aside and returning to the ensuite, where she scrabbled through the drawer of jumbled hotel shampoos and cosmetic samples. She was sure that at one stage there had been a No More Tears sachet there. Locating it with a grunt of satisfaction, she tore the foil open and then tipped her head back to drip the contents into each eye. They stung. She dabbed at them with a towel but the burning continued. So did the slow leakage of tears. She squinted at the mirror but her reflection was now just a damp shadow. Taking the sachet with her, George went back into the bedroom and put her glasses on to read it properly. She blinked at the blurry text until it fell into focus. *Tears Ahoy*, it proclaimed proudly. *For dry eyes*.

She let out a sound that was half sob, half gulp of laughter. It seemed that when the universe had you in its sights, there was no escape. She flipped the sachet over and read the instructions. Strictly one drop in each eye. There was also a picture of a jaunty sailor, holding his cap aloft, although any association between seafarers and troublesome tear ducts was left unexplained. George threw the empty sachet onto the bedside table and then flopped back onto the bed. This time, when the tears came, they were accompanied by a burning sensation that was reminiscent of hangovers. She pulled the sheet over her once more and gave in to the misery.

The loss of her father had been gut-wrenching but this, this was something else altogether. Describing it as ghastly didn't even come close. She felt physically damaged. Hollowed out by the enormity. It was reminiscent of a movie she once watched where an explosive device had been detonated in a paddock. All that remained was a smoking crater, with earth crumbling at the edges, while tall grasses around the rim lay flattened from residual impact. That was how she felt. A grenade had been lobbed into her life and although right now she was in the worst of it, the epi-centre, she already knew that the after-effects would reverberate for the rest of her days. There would never be a time where she would be free. Her mother was dead. It was a life sentence.

Chapter Four

Tuesday morning

It's been almost two years since the last letter. A lot can happen in nearly two years. Whole lives can change. And begin. Of course on the other hand, things can stay exactly the same. Morning, noon and night. Same, same, bloody same.

Well, Elvis Presley just died. The way that Anna is carrying on, you'd think they'd been bosom buddies. Apparently he died on the loo. Trifle embarrassing, but I suppose there's worse ways to go. I'm betting this doesn't happen for many women anyway. For starters, it'd require us being left alone long enough to get the job done.

George slapped the diary closed before self-control deserted her altogether. Earlier that morning she had figured that allowing herself only three excerpts per visit would make the document last the entire week. And these should be spaced out across the day as a type of reward system. Deferred gratification. That hadn't even lasted five minutes after arrival. At this rate, if she didn't get a grip, she'd be finished by tomorrow. She pulled her mobile from her bag instead. There was another message from Guy. She swiped it aside and searched for Elvis Presley. He died on the 16th of August 1977. Not quite on the loo, but certainly in the vicinity. But this now dated the diary precisely, and also meant that the *Rocky Horror* ticket, from October 1975, must have been a keepsake. After all, October 1975 was almost two years before August 1977. Almost …

George stilled for a moment and then flicked open the diary to the initial entry read that morning. *It's been almost two years since the last letter.* Her eyes widened. There had to be a connection. She re-read the entire entry, trying to decipher the meaning. A logical scenario had Enid going to *Rocky Horror* with somebody special who soon afterwards ceased writing letters. But why had they been writing letters anyway, if they were close enough to attend a musical together? And could all this also involve the choice her mother had regretted, where she hadn't had the guts to eat fruit in Mount Isa? What about the sin that she would repeat in a heartbeat? Could her mother possibly have been having an *affair*? With a flush of guilt, George dismissed the thought as quickly as it formed.

'What the *hell* are you doing here?' asked Kat from the doorway. She was wearing a hip-length sleeveless t-shirt, knickers and a frown. Much of her streaked hair was vertical, as though even it was surprised. She looked like one of the good luck troll dolls they had used to collect as children, except minus the cheerful expression. And with a bicep tattoo.

'I thought I'd get an early start,' said George, covering the diary with her hand.

'It's not even six bloody thirty!'

'Hence the word early,' replied George. She shrugged. 'I couldn't sleep.'

'So you thought you'd share the pain?' Kat waited, as if she genuinely wanted a response to this question.

George shrugged again, even though the answer was easy. Yes.

'And what on earth's wrong with your eyes?'

'You're determined to make me repeat myself, aren't you?' asked George, more cheerfully than she felt. 'I already said that too. I didn't sleep well.'

'Christ!' Kat stared at her and then shot a glance at the grey light that glowed along the edge of the blind. She shook her head as she turned back. 'Who would have thought that *you*, of all people, would rise at the crack of dawn to do some cleaning?'

'Hey!'

Rather than answer, Kat just lifted an eyebrow questioningly.

George grimaced. 'Okay, fair call. But in this case, the proof's in the pudding.' She waved her spare hand conjuror-style, taking in her body as Exhibit A. 'And you should be grateful, not make disparaging insinuations about my domestic skills.'

'You have no domestic skills,' said Kat. 'Well, the bare minimum anyway. But I'll take what I can get. Anyway, it's too early for banter. Now that you've woken me up, you may as well make coffee.'

'Sure.' George tipped her head to one side. 'Do you know that your hair defies gravity? What sort of product do you use? Builder's bog?'

Kat ran a hand through her hair. It made no difference. 'Can we also save the sharing of beauty tips until after I've had a shower? Coffee. As soon as possible.'

George waited until her sister left before returning the diary to its hiding place. As she crossed the hall, the grandfather clock gave a low chime to signal the half-hour. With a jolt, George realised that she could prioritise it with a sticker. It could be hers. The thought brought her to a temporary halt. The same with the pewter knight bookends that her parents had received as a wedding present, and the walnut secretaire, the Spode dinner set, her father's Eames chair, the lovely frames her mother collected. The set of Encyclopaedia Britannica. Everything. All the items that had belonged to her parents, been *part* of her parents, were about to slide their way down the family tree. Rather than owners, her mother and father had become footnotes. Their time was done.

Grief washed over her, anew. To distract herself, she tried to imagine any of these items in her own house, but they didn't fit. For the first time she also wondered what her sisters would choose, and whether their shared history would mean similar choices. Similar points of nostalgia. Or would they simply go for the big-ticket items, like the Eames chair or the dinner set? What about this clock? Did anybody seriously want to be reminded every half-hour of time passing? Kate came out of the main bedroom carrying a large toiletry bag and gave her a questioning look.

'Whatcha doing?'

'Nothing,' said George, which was mostly true. She got moving again before she could be asked to elaborate.

In the kitchen, she put on the kettle and selected a croissant from the bag she'd picked up from an all-night supermarket. She estimated that she'd had around five hours of sleep, in snatches full of surprisingly tranquil dreams that made those first few waking moments even worse. It had been like groundhog night. She took her glasses off and rubbed at her eyes. It felt like sandpaper had been shredded and inserted beneath each lid. It was hard to know how much was due to lack of sleep, and how much to the liberal application of Tears Ahoy. One thing was certain, it wasn't a product that was going on her shopping list.

She took a bite of the croissant. It tasted like cardboard. On the fridge was a magnet shaped like an apple, holding a shopping list. *Milk, bread, bicarb of soda, jelly crystals for Harry.* George pulled it off, magnet and all, and threw them in the bin. Harry would have to do without his jelly crystals. She took another bite of the croissant, grimaced, and then went over to open the sliding door so that she could toss it outside for the birds. The sun had broken free of the horizon, leaving a pearly-saffron glow that promised a warm day to come. A magpie began warbling. The kettle whistled and George went back to make their coffee. The steady thrum of the hair dryer started up from the bathroom. She wondered if Simon had realised she was gone yet. Or whether he was just taking advantage of the extra space by spread-eagling himself across the bed.

She took the mugs and croissants over to the table and sat down with a groan. Her mother's scuffs still sat by the sliding door. It was as if any moment she would come in with her trolley full of shopping, kick off her shoes and slide her feet into the scuffs with a sigh of relief. 'You need something nice to go with that cuppa,' she would say, before digging through her trolley for some treats. It didn't matter how many times that George told her that she'd sworn off pastries, there would still be mini muffins and cupcakes and Neenish tarts. 'Diet?' her mother would say with her slight English accent. 'Don't be a damn fool. Life's too short for that sort of nonsense.'

'Six bloody thirty!' said Kat again as she came into the room. Her hair was once more a side-swept cap of streaky layers. She stood in front of the open sliding door for a moment, then flopped into a chair and took a gulp of her coffee. 'Shit! That's hot!'

'Not really a morning person then?' asked George. 'Anyway, it's just about seven now.'

'Oh, well *that* makes all the difference! Especially after barely sleeping all night!'

George looked at her with interest. 'You too?'

'Yeah.' Kat leaned back in her chair. 'I just kept waking up. Couldn't settle.'

'Ah. Yes.'

They sat in silence, drinking their coffee. The open door allowed ingress to a light breeze and an early morning crispness that felt quite soothing. The lone magpie was joined by others, the warbling now undulating in chorus. George thought about all the cups of coffee she'd had at this table, all the hot chocolate and tea. Orange juice and cordial. Milkshakes and lemonade spiders.

'Do you know Harry has Lite n' Easy meals in his freezer?' asked Kat. 'I suggested we get some takeaway together, but apparently that's not on. Every day except Friday and Sundays are all Lite n' Easy. No exceptions.'

'Yeah, I know. The other two days he ate with Mum. How was he though?'

'Oh, fine. Hardly saw him. I suppose the big thing is just keeping his routine.'

George nodded. She tried to imagine how he would cope if he got offered supported accommodation, but it was difficult to visualise. His Lego alone required a massive amount of space. The rising sun was now dappling across the veranda. She thought of the conversation she'd had yesterday with Annie. 'Hey, do you remember those games we used to play out there?' She gestured towards the backyard. 'Hide and seek and all that?'

'Of course I do!' Kat grinned at her. 'Such fun! My god, remember how Mum used to get so annoyed, calling us in? And we'd pretend it was just part of the game?'

'Yes!'

'And when we used to swing on the old Hills hoist? Bent each of the arms!'

'Yes!'

'Oh! What about that time we used those old bricks to make a cubby up by the fence? Just piled them on top of each other. And Dad flipped his lid because it was so unstable?'

'My god! Yes!'

'Oh, good times,' said Kat. Her grin faded. She sighed. 'Okay then, better get organised.' She pulled over the bag of croissants and tipped them onto the table, smoothing the paper bag before grabbing a pen. 'We need to get her wardrobe done today. Aunt Margaret's coming later and she's going to take the clothes. Apparently she volunteers at some charity shop. Unless anyone wants any, of course. The garden shed's another job. There's old tools of Dad's there too.' Kat was writing quickly. 'And also the wardrobe in the study.'

'I'll do that!'

'Love the enthusiasm. Let's keep that going all week.' Kat dug the end of her pen into a croissant to drag it across. She took a bite. 'Mmm. Hey, did you tell your two about the whole sticker thing?'

'Yes. They're coming around later to lend a hand too.'

'Excellent!' She peeled a strip of pastry from the croissant. 'How's it going with Rhyll?'

George shrugged. 'As good as can be expected. Same as.'

'Don't be too hard on her,' said Kat. She waved the strip of pastry at George. 'She was pretty close with Mum. This can't be easy.'

George kept her face expressionless. It wasn't easy for anyone. She appreciated Kat's concern for her niece, but then her sister didn't have to coexist with a twenty-five-year-old university dropout who still lived at home, spent most of her time in her room, and seemingly had no direction in life.

Kat peered into her mug and then held it out. 'More?'

George had just risen when she heard the front door. She glanced at the clock. It was still only seven-thirty. The door closed quietly and then a floorboard creaked. Kat caught her eye and grinned. Moments later Annie crept into view and immediately froze, gaping at them. She was wearing a cream shift covered in huge red dots that clashed with her hair. She was also holding another bakery box.

'Morning!' said Kat brightly. 'What kept you?'

Annie's gaze raked across the croissants and coffee mugs before settling on George. Her expression darkened. 'Is this a private meeting or can anyone join?'

'I couldn't sleep,' said George with a shrug. 'Coffee?'

Annie nodded slowly but didn't move. And now George could see movement above and behind her sister. 'Tom!' she exclaimed as her nephew emerged. 'You're up early!'

'I was lured under false pretences,' said Tom cheerfully. 'Promised a big breakfast only to discover she means that crap.' He pointed a disparaging finger at the bakery box. 'Enough carbs there to sink a bloody ship.'

Kat raised an eyebrow as she regarded his neat frame. 'Hmm, not sure you have anything to worry about. Besides, since when did carbs sink ships? What, do they form icebergs?'

'Carb-bergs,' said Tom, still grinning. 'That's what *really* brought down the *Titanic*. The iceberg was framed.'

George had a sudden image of the jaunty sailor from Tears Ahoy aboard the *Titanic*, sinking slowly. He wasn't looking as smug now.

'Well, glad you're here anyway,' said Kat. 'We need all the help we can get.' She waved at the nearby chairs. 'Pull up a pew.'

Instead Tom flopped down into the armchair and swivelled it to face the table. He hooked one long leg over the armrest and swung it idly as he regarded his aunts.

'Tom's here for the whole day,' said his mother brightly. She put her box down on the bench. '*So* generous of him, especially when he's on holidays.'

'Not sure funerals count as a holiday,' said Tom dryly. 'But each to their own. Plus I'm doing this for Granma.' His gaze shifted to a point between his two aunts, almost as if he expected to see his grandmother standing there.

'Oh, Tom,' said his mother.

'Yeah, well. Hey, George, where's Rhyll and the Dick?'

George knew that he meant Leo. Years before, as a young teen, Tom had declared that as Harry was Harry, and he was Tom, all they needed was a Dick to make the trifecta. He had promptly renamed his only male cousin and despite George's lack of enthusiasm, continued to do so. '*Leo* will be here later. Along with Rhyll. At a more decent hour.'

'Lazy buggers,' said Tom. 'So, Mum, how about some coffee for the only grandchild dumb enough to turn up at the crack of dawn?'

'Just about to make some,' said George, putting a hand up towards her sister. She continued into the kitchen and put the kettle on. She felt slightly resentful at Tom's appearance; not that she wasn't fond of her nephew, more that his presence was not conducive to sisterly chats. Annie was different when her son was around. More watchful, more prickly, more oddly eager.

And Tom himself, alongside his undeniable charisma, had a confidence that could be a little annoying. Ironic really, because of all four grandchildren, he had been the one with the most dysfunctional childhood. His father had treated him as a chess piece while his mother grabbed at him like she was drowning. Rather than fold under the pressure though, Tom had emerged with a sense of importance that translated, mostly, to a vaguely amused air of condescension towards lesser mortals. In that, he was a little like his father.

George was also currently holding a mild grudge on account of his move to the Gold Coast, even though she knew it wasn't entirely fair. Brad *was* his father after all. But he was also the man who had put Annie through hell. She slid her nephew a quick glance now. He had pulled out his phone and was frowning as he scrolled through messages. The saving grace was how much he loved his mother. It was undeniable. He spoke to her daily, and visited regularly. He'd just been down for Christmas, and booked a flight the instant he'd heard about his grandmother. It was likely that Annie had paid for both those trips, but still.

The kettle boiled, so she busied herself making the coffees and then passing them out. A few magpies had swooped down to the veranda to squabble over the discarded croissant. Annie was now sitting at the table, having said barely a word since arriving. George knew exactly what her younger sister was perturbed about, and she smirked inwardly as she considered that Annie would no doubt not be finding her so *inconsequential* now. This, along with her gritty tiredness, combined into an irresistible urge to poke the bear.

'That was a great chat,' she said to Kat cheerfully as she pulled out a chair. 'Good fun.'

Kat shot her a look of surprise. 'Well, just goes to show you need to socialise more.'

George let out a trill of laughter, as if highly amused. She knew, without needing to glance in her direction, that Annie would be dissecting each word even as she pretended this conversation meant nothing. 'Well, *I* enjoyed it. A very pleasant breakfast. We should do it more often.'

'I hardly call that breakfast!'

George shrugged. She sipped her coffee and waited. It didn't take long.

'Hmm,' said Annie. 'So what were you both talking about then?'

'Just this,' replied Kat quickly, tapping the handwritten agenda with a fingernail.

'And memories,' added George. '*Shared* memories.' She tacked on an exaggerated sigh.

'Oh for god's sake,' said Kat. She turned to Annie. 'Can't you see she's trying to press your buttons?' She flashed an irritated look at George. 'As for you, bloody hell, it's one thing to talk about the past, but let's not revert to childhood while we're at it.'

George shrugged again. She snuck a glance at Annie and smirked.

'It's like being in a bloody time machine,' grumbled Kat.

'Jules Verne invented a time machine,' said Harry from the lounge room.

George twisted with surprise. 'I didn't even hear you come in! Were you tiptoeing?'

'No. His middle name was Gabriel. His nephew was called Gaston. Like in *Beauty and the Beast*. He shot him twice.'

'Huh?' Tom had lifted his head. 'Jules Verne shot his nephew?'

'No. His nephew shot Jules Verne. Twice.'

'Brutal,' said Tom. He flashed a grin towards his two aunts. 'See how lucky you guys are?'

Kat ignored him. 'D'you know,' she said to her brother, 'I'm sensing a theme here. Your anecdotes often seem to involve homicidal family members.' She looked over at her sisters, one eyebrow raised. 'I don't think it's nephews we need to be worried about.'

George laughed. Annie had risen. She slid the door half-closed and then went into the kitchen to rinse out her mug. Tom had returned to staring at his phone while Harry lowered himself onto the couch nearby. Tendrils of shredded paper studded the nubbly fabric. George wiped her glasses with a corner of her t-shirt and then slipped them on. She closed her eyes briefly. Her eyelids felt heavy, almost swollen. She wished fervently for the day to be over, so that she could crawl into bed.

'Look.' Kat held up her phone to show a small gif of a fox enthusiastically working a hula hoop. 'From Aunt Margaret. Anyone got a clue as to why she'd send me this?'

'Maybe she's trying to tell you you're foxy?' suggested George.

Tom made a snorting noise but didn't look up. His mother grimaced apologetically.

Kat was examining her phone again. 'Hang on. There's a message coming through. Here we go. *Be there at noon will bring lunch stop.*'

'Good,' said Tom. 'I'm starving. Tell her to come now.'

'Does she realise it's not pay per word?' asked Annie. 'And that you don't have to *say* stop, you just stop. It's not like a telegram.'

Harry cleared his throat. 'Samuel Morse invented the telegram. He was a painter first, before an inventor. He hated Catholics and liked slavery. He said it was allowed by his god.'

'Charming,' said Kat. 'And did he attempt to murder any relatives?'

'You know what?' asked Annie before Harry could respond. She leaned against the island bench and gazed at George. 'You should hire Harry as your assistant. Think of all the anecdotes you could share! And how much time you'd save on research!'

'Okay,' said Harry agreeably.

George sent a glare towards her sister. 'For the *hundredth* time, I …' She petered off as she saw a corner of Annie's mouth twitch. Realisation dawned. 'Ah, I see. Touché.'

'Don't drag Harry into your bickering,' said Kat tersely. For a moment she sounded so much like their mother that George's eyes widened. In her peripheral vision, she saw Annie doing much the same thing. Maybe that's what would happen now, Kat would slip seamlessly into the role of mother. George found the thought oddly comforting.

'I actually *am* starving,' said Tom. 'Literally.'

'I doubt that,' said Kat, still sounding like Enid. She reached over to slide the door open once more. 'Besides, there's croissants here. And your mum brought morning tea. There's food aplenty.'

'Nah. I think I'll go with a Macca's breakfast. Mum, you can shout seeing you dragged me here. And I bet Harry'd like some too. Whaddya say, Harry?'

'Okay,' said Harry. He folded his hands on his lap expectantly.

Annie smiled. 'Sure! You order. Use my Uber Eats account. Save you driving anywhere.'

George exchanged a fleeting glance with Kat. It spoke volumes. Apart from anything else, how was a McDonald's breakfast better in terms of carbohydrates? She looked guiltily at Annie, to make sure she hadn't seen that exchange. Tom was her sister's Achilles heel. He was also Kat's, but in an entirely different way. Her phone pinged and she pulled it from her handbag. It was a text from Simon. *You must have got up early! Have a good day. Yell out if you need help.* George felt a surge of irritation. She shouldn't have to yell out. He should have taken a few days off work to come with her.

Annie had poured herself a glass of water and now removed a bottle of tablets from her bag, shaking two out onto her palm. She swallowed them along with a gulp of the water. George tilted her head slightly to read the label. *Marvellous Menopause*, it said. Along with a picture of a daisy with a stylised face that managed to look both cheerful and vacant.

'They're very good,' said Annie, a little defensively. 'Minimises those damn hot flushes.'

'Really?' George's own hot flushes had dissipated a few years ago but even so, she wasn't sure she would trust anything that called that period of her life 'marvellous'.

'I keep telling her not to bother,' said Tom, swinging a leg. 'That herbal crap just amounts to expensive urine. You're better off simply developing strategies to deal with it. There's nothing that can't be managed.' He tapped his head. 'Mind control.'

'Are you kidding?' asked Kat. She was staring at him. 'Are you seriously mansplaining menopause to us? Really?'

Tom's leg stilled and although his grin remained in place, it too looked a little fixed. George tensed; the last thing she wanted was for Kat and Tom to enter into one of their spiky debates.

'I'm sure that's not what he meant,' said Annie hurriedly. 'Tom's done a lot of research on supplements and the like. That's all.'

Kat lifted an eyebrow and then shrugged. After a few moments where nobody added anything to the conversation, she pushed her empty mug away and rose. 'Okay, can't sit here all day. I'm going to duck into town and pick up a few things from my place. I'll stop at a newsagent on the way back, get the stickers.'

'We're still going with that then?' asked Annie with a distinct lack of enthusiasm.

Kat looked at her with surprise. 'I thought it was decided? Look, honestly I don't give a shit. You can discuss it while I'm gone. Let me know.' She grabbed a croissant and then headed out, pausing in the doorway. 'I should be back before Aunt Margaret gets here.

Maybe you guys could concentrate on clearing out Mum's wardrobe? You can pack all the clothes ready for her to load in the car. Check the pockets first.'

'I'm sure we'll manage,' said Annie. She waited until Kat left before closing the sliding door all the way. She sat back down and looked at George. 'Does she think we're incapable of doing anything without her?'

'She's probably right,' replied George equably. 'At the moment anyway.'

'Huh.' Annie continued to gaze at her for a few moments, and then transferred her attention to her son. 'Breakfast all ordered then?'

'Yup.'

'Oh. Good, good. Lovely.'

Tom was fixed on his mobile. His leg was swinging once more. George felt a sudden burst of sympathy for his mother.

'Hot flushes, hey?' she said brightly to her sister. 'They're a real bugger.'

'They are.' Annie frowned as she focussed on George. 'Your eyes are like an albino rabbit. Are you okay?'

'Yeah. Just having trouble sleeping, that's all.'

Annie lowered her voice. 'Mum? Or problems in paradise?'

'Shh!' George flicked a glance at her nephew but his head was still down. Annie was the only one who knew about Guy. After it had happened, the first time, George had needed to tell somebody, and clearly Simon had been out of the question. It had also been quite gratifying telling her sister, who seemed to think George's life was much more exciting than it actually was. It was lovely, at the age of fifty-five, to be suddenly seen as an adventuress of sorts. 'No,' she said now. 'I'm just ... I don't know. Can't get to sleep, can't stay asleep. And then I'm so bloody tired that it makes everything ten times harder.'

Annie had been staring at George fixedly through this short speech. She nodded slowly. 'Same.' She gave a sigh that was almost guttural. 'The worst thing is that every time I wake up, I forget ... for just a moment. Then it hits all over again.' She placed a hand across the centre of her chest. 'Right here.'

George nodded slowly. Words were too difficult. She felt her eyes well. It was like tears were never far away, no matter her mood. Always poised, biding their time. She wondered if this was her future. When she herself was eighty-three, thoughts of her mother would still have the same effect. Annie reached out a hand and laid it atop of George's. Her eyes were shiny too. They looked at each other for a few long seconds. That was all it needed.

'We all miss her,' said Tom from the armchair. 'I can't believe she's gone.'

George nodded again. She didn't really want to discuss this with her nephew, and not just because of the threatening tears. It seemed too personal, as if emotion rendered her vulnerable. Annie responded to him instead while George took a sip of her coffee. She grimaced. It was tepid, and she'd already had three this morning. Coffee had the same effect on her bladder as thoughts of her mother had on her eyes. She rose, taking the mug over to the sink. Tom had now moved on to complaining to Annie about being called a mansplainer. The irony being that his complaint included a mansplain of what, in his opinion, mansplaining actually was.

George stared out into the backyard. The sun now glimmered across the shrubbery as it continued to rise, marking yet another day without her mother. Another day between now and then. What life needed, she thought suddenly, was a remote control. Then she could hit rewind. She would burst in here, scoop Enid up and rush her straight to hospital. George wallowed in this fantasy for a little while before the logistics became too complicated. The next best thing would be fast forward. She would shoot past this entire week. It would be Sunday already, and instead of gearing up for yet another day of sorting memories, they would be saying goodbye to them. Then she could just go home. But the problem was that she didn't really want to be there either.

Chapter Five

Tuesday afternoon

Those three girls are going to be the death of me. The older they get, the more they bicker. Even when they're getting on, the least thing will set them off. Someone used up all the hot water, or moved something, or looked at the other one funny. Or spoke when a favourite song was on the radio and they missed whatever lyric that they knew by heart anyway. One day my head is going to explode. And then they'll bicker over who has to clean up the mess.

Today I did tuckshop duty. God almighty. I don't understand other women. Are they really as happy as they seem? Is it all an act? Am I the only one who didn't get the script?

'So I said Lesley, Lesley, Lesley. There's absolutely *no* point you coming all this way just for the funeral. Not when I've just been over there for Christmas and you've already got flights booked for midyear.' Aunt Margaret paused for breath. 'It's all a wee bit far for a few days. So I said, you just stay in London. God darn it, I'm sure the girls will understand. You can pay your respects later. Georgette, are you listening? What on earth are you reading?'

'Just some papers of Mum's,' replied George. She closed the diary and reflected on the latest entries. She had decided to ration herself to two at a time. Having started that way this morning, it seemed only right to continue. A precedent had been set. Plus this meant she would finish it quicker and be able to share with her sisters. It was almost altruistic.

'Ah yes, your mum was a great one for keeping everything. And now you poor girls have to go through it all! My neighbour Gladys is a bit like that. Clutter everywhere! I saw her last Wednesday and she ... hold your runaway horses, was it Thursday? I'd remember if it was Friday, of course, so it has to have been either Wednesday or Thursday. Or maybe Tuesday.'

George tuned out. Had her mother always been so unhappy, or was the diary written during a particularly difficult year? She and Kat would have been young teens during 1977 and she knew, from her own children, how difficult that could be. Still was, in many respects. The thing was that she didn't *remember* her mother as being unhappy. She had never seen her staring mournfully out the window, or take herself to bed, or neglect her appearance. Nor had she been much of a drinker. But then she didn't remember her mother as having been particularly happy either. She had just been ... herself.

'So we hadn't spoken for a while because Gladys likes that Trump fellow and I have no time for that nonsense. The man's obviously retarded. And god darn it, yes, I know that's not a word we're supposed to use nowadays. Am I allowed to say he must've got dropped on his head a few too many times as a child? Georgette? Don't you agree?'

George nodded, although she doubted there was a yardstick for babies being dropped on their heads. Even once was probably too much. Aunt Margaret had fallen silent, so she turned to give her a look of attentiveness lest the older woman think that she wasn't listening. Which of course, she really wasn't. Aunt Margaret was a large, buxom woman whose chin had almost entirely disappeared in old age, leaving behind a set of fleshy vertical pleats that wobbled whenever she became animated. A long-time advocate of the perm, she had clung stubbornly to this hairstyle despite her white hair becoming so thin that each tight curl was encircled by glimpses of pink scalp. She also had a habit of punctuating her speech with malaphors such as 'god darn it', which always sounded to George like her aunt was demanding the Almighty pick up the slack in the mending department.

'Did you want any of Mum's books?' she asked her aunt, waving towards the bookshelf. The contents were mostly by authors who were rather dated nowadays, and she doubted that any of her sisters would be interested.

'Oh, yes. I rather think I might.' Aunt Margaret peered towards the shelves. 'I wouldn't mind the Georgette Heyer set, but only if you don't, dear. After all, you're named after her.'

'Not a chance. You're welcome to them.' George cast a disparaging glance towards the row of Regency romances. Her name had been a bane of her existence for years. Always called Georgie as a child, she had been quickly christened Georgie Porgie the moment she entered the schoolyard. Then, at university and doing an arts degree, she'd shortened it to George and had to contend with all those who thought that she was channelling George Eliot or George Sand. But it could have been worse. Right alongside the Georgette Heyer collection in her mother's bookshelves were those by Cornelia Otis Skinner.

Interesting though, now that she thought of it, was that her mother had been drawn to Regency romances at all. She wouldn't have pegged Enid as the bodice-ripping type. Maybe it had been the history that attracted her, rather than the romance? Or perhaps, like with the diary, this was yet another side of a woman she had never known. The thought was a little confronting. She went to rub her eyes but stopped herself just in time. They were only just starting to feel better. Her aunt was now listing her favoured authors, so George waited patiently for her to draw breath and then leaped.

'Aunt Margaret, did Mum particularly like apples?'

'Apples? Well, I suppose as much as the next person. Granny Smiths are *my* favourites. Or Golden Delicious. But then your mother did make a mean apple pie. Dab hand at pastry, she was. We went strawberry picking once. A big crowd of us. Of course that was when she met my brother, your father. Oh!' Aunt Margaret pointed towards the still life hanging near the desk. 'Do you mean because of that picture?'

George opened her mouth to reply but was interrupted by a shout from the other room.

'FUCK ME!'

George's mouth fell even further open. She and her aunt stared at each other with surprise and then George jumped up. She thrust the diary into the wardrobe and hurried out into the passage.

'Ew! Ew! *Ew!*'

She now recognised the voice as coming from Rhyll. George rounded the corner into her mother's bedroom and nearly ran into Annie's back. She peered over her shoulder. Rhyll was standing in the middle of the room, wiping her hands repeatedly down her jeans as she stared at an open bedside drawer. She turned, her face screwed in disgust.

'I am *never* going to be able to unsee that! I'm going to need *therapy!*'

George felt like saying that might not be a bad thing but restrained herself. 'What is it?'

'A freaking vibrator!'

'A *what*?' Annie shook her head and then snorted. 'No. You must be mistaken.'

George ducked around and went over to the drawer. Unbelievably, it was indeed a vibrator. Nestled amongst neatly folded white underwear; salmon-pink in colour, with an impressive array of ridges. She gaped at it, momentarily incapable of speech. This cast Regency romances into the shade.

'Oh. My. God,' said Annie. George could feel her sister's breath on her neck.

'What's all the fuss?' asked Aunt Margaret from the doorway.

Annie whipped round. 'What? Oh, nothing! Nothing! Rhyll just saw a mouse!'

'Ew,' said Rhyll again. 'I *touched* it!'

'Oh, you young ones,' said Aunt Margaret with a laugh. 'Scared of a wee mouse. I don't know. When *I* was young, they were everywhere! Couldn't move without tripping over them. Everyone had them!'

'Fun times,' said George. She was still staring at the vibrator. 'Aunt Margaret, would you mind putting the kettle on? We'll be out in a moment.'

'Peanut butter,' said Aunt Margaret as she was leaving. 'People say cheese is good, but peanut butter is the bee's knees. Easier to apply as well. It smears better.'

'That's it,' said Rhyll, backing away further. 'I'm done. I wanna go home.'

'Oh for god's sake,' snapped George. She felt suddenly protective of her mother. 'It's just a vibrator. People *do* still have a sex drive after fifty, you know.' She caught sight of Rhyll's darkening face and slid her irritation smoothly into humour. 'Besides, didn't you hear Aunt Margaret? Back in her day, *everybody* had one.'

'Fucking gross,' said Rhyll. She sat down on the bed and then looked around wildly, as if that too might be scattered with sex toys.

Annie had returned to staring at the vibrator. 'I think I'm in shock. I mean, where did she even *get* that?'

'Maybe she went to Sex City,' said Rhyll with a grimace. 'Probably got a senior discount.'

Annie blanched. 'God almighty. I never thought, never even suspected ...'

'Well, it's hardly something she would have shared,' said George curtly. 'Thank god.' She leaned forward and folded a pair of the white underpants around the vibrator so that she could pick it up. It fitted with disturbing neatness into her hand.

'Tegan is here!' trilled Aunt Margaret from the lounge room.

'Great,' muttered Rhyll. 'Saint Tegan has arrived. This day just keeps getting better.'

George ignored her. She gazed at the bundle in her hand and then thrust it towards her sister, giving her no choice but to take it. 'Take care of this? I'll keep the others out.'

'Take care? Like how?' Annie was holding it at arm's length. The underwear had partly fallen away and the moulded pink tip peeked out cheerfully.

George was already heading towards the door. 'Given I'm guessing nobody's going to want to put their sticker on it, how about you wrap it up, put it in a bin liner and chuck it?'

She left them to it. In the lounge room, Aunt Margaret was regaling Tegan with the story of why her daughter Lesley hadn't come for the funeral. Tegan had the enviable knack of making people feel that they had her undivided attention even when, as she once admitted to George, she was usually revisiting the plot of whatever movie she'd watched recently. One of her traits was

that while she listened, she would tilt her head to one side and
then idly stroke her side ponytail. To George, it always looked like
her niece was grooming a small pet. There was something a little
disturbingly Austin Powers about the habit, even though Tegan
herself was about as far from Austin Powers as one could get. Tall,
blonde, with a willowy figure, straight teeth and a lovely personality. They were all very fond of her.

She greeted her niece and then continued into the kitchen. The
light breeze had turned a good deal gustier, and branches could
be heard scraping across the perspex above the veranda. She could
see Leo and Tom playing totem tennis with an old pole they must
have found in the shed. Leo was wearing a rather startling paisley
waistcoat in shades of orange. Every so often the wind caught the
ball in an undulating puppet dance. Harry stood by watching.
She would have preferred if they were doing something actually
useful, but at the same time, it was nice to see them enjoying
each other's company. A side benefit was that it kept them out of
the house. Things already felt too crowded in here and now that
Tegan had arrived, it was unlikely to improve.

In an odd quirk of fate, all four of her mother's grandchildren
had been born within the same year. It was a circumstance that
Enid always enjoyed telling new acquaintances. *That's* what you
call efficiency, she would say with a smile. Efficiency was not the
word George herself would have used to describe her own bookended babies, but then her mother had the luxury of handing
them back. A silver lining about the proximity though, was that
it was not difficult to remember the ages of her niece or nephew
and, in fact, all four children were the exact same age for almost
the entire month of January each year.

First to be born had been Rhyll at the end of January, followed
a fortnight later by Tom. That had been the end of the planned

babies. A few months down the track, ironically around the time Leo was conceived, her parents had answered a knock at the door and their world had been turned upside down. On the doorstep was a very angry middle-aged couple and a very plump girl of around twenty. It had quickly become clear that she wasn't so much plump as pregnant, and that she also had an intellectual disability. But the story they initially threw at George's shocked parents, which painted Harry as a sexual deviant, quickly unravelled. Mainly because Harry himself had scuttled over to the other side of the room and begged them not to let the girl near him.

It eventually emerged that Vanessa, as she was named, had developed a crush that was fervently unreciprocated. Nevertheless the two of them had sexual relations once, at their special learning centre after a Christmas party the year before. How they'd managed that was something that Vanessa's father now transferred his fury to. According to Harry, he'd thought she would stop talking if he went 'all the way'. He had no wish to repeat the experience. But once was all it took.

The two sets of parents eventually shared a bottle of riesling as they discussed, more calmly, what to do. Some things had been off the table, like the inherent flaws within Harry's methodology for ending conversations, or why it took so long for Vanessa's parents to realise she was pregnant. But it was too late for a termination, and adoption was soon dismissed. Instead they arrived at a shared care arrangement that meant that suddenly, in their late fifties, George's parents had abruptly taken on partial responsibility for another child. In this respect though, they got lucky. Despite her unconventional start, Tegan was never any trouble. She eventually graduated as a social worker and now worked with the homeless. She was, in short, everything that Rhyll was not. Hence the one-sided antipathy.

George helped herself to a sandwich from the platter that Aunt Margaret had brought. She ate some at the sink, still watching the boys. Tom thwacked the ball so hard it whipped around the totem tennis pole several times before Leo could hit it back. Her mother had a vibrator in her drawer. A vibrator. Salmon-pink, with ridges. George threw the rest of the sandwich away and instead massaged her temples with her fingertips. Obviously she knew that Enid had had sex, at least four times, but the notion that an … *urge* had continued, and to such a degree that it necessitated an *aid*, was beyond disturbing. As was the thought of her browsing the aisles at a sex shop. The Regency romances had clearly not been enough.

'Headache?' asked Tegan, coming into the dining room.

'Yes. It started just over a week ago. Amped up in the last twenty minutes.'

Tegan looked at her sympathetically. 'I know. It's so hard. When my mother died, it was such a shock. But I was lucky; I still had my grandparents.'

'Oh, Tegan. And you were so young!'

'Yeah, but like I said, I still had Nannie and Pops then. And also Granma. Let's be honest, they were the real parental figures.' Tegan paused as her gaze flicked across to an array of framed photos on the wall. She sucked at her top lip and then visibly shook herself. 'Hey, I'm here to help anyway. I need to keep busy. What can I do?'

George grasped at her offer. For a moment she had feared that Tegan would get teary, which would have set her off in turn. She needed to keep it together today. 'Let's see. Actually, could you take the boxes of clothing out to Aunt Margaret's car?'

'I'm back!' announced Kat, coming round the corner. She dumped a shopping bag on the table. 'Sorry! Took longer than I thought. Traffic.'

'What? Did you go via Sydney?' asked George.

'Not quite. Tegan! Lovely to see you!' They hugged briefly and then Kat turned back to George. 'Did I miss anything?'

Only the discovery of your mother's vibrator, thought George. But she shook her head. 'No, but in the *hours* that you've been gone, we've finished her wardrobe. Annie and Rhyll are just doing the drawers.'

'Rhyll's here?' asked Tegan with delight. 'Oh, I'll go say hello.'

Kat watched her leave, then spoke in a low voice. 'Do you think she realises that Rhyll avoids her like the plague? Or she's blissfully ignorant?'

'Bit of each,' said George. 'Listen—'

'Kathryn!' cried Aunt Margaret, appearing behind her niece. 'I'm glad you're here! I wanted to explain why Lesley wasn't able to make it for the funeral.'

Kat leaned forward to kiss her aunt's cheek. 'You already have. At the funeral itself. And it's all good. We'll catch up when she's out here in June.'

'About time you're back,' said Annie, crowding into the room also. 'What, did you go via Sydney? You missed all the fun. We had a ...' She paused to register the array of interested faces. 'A situation. I'll tell you about it later.'

'Just a mouse,' said George quickly as Kat opened her mouth.

'What!' Kat grimaced, stepping back and examining the floor rapidly. 'A mouse! Here?'

'Pfft,' said Aunt Margaret merrily. 'I'd hardly call it a situation, Anna. Goodness.' She turned to Kat. 'And you can relax, anyway. I'm sure your sister has it in hand.'

From behind her mother, Rhyll snorted. George clapped a hand to her own mouth to hide her grin. She met Annie's eye and winked. The screen door slid open and a flurry of wind accompanied the boys inside. It lifted the pile of papers on the table and sent them flying across the room. Somebody cursed and somebody else slammed the door shut. As Tom and Leo bent to collect them up, Tegan bounced over to give her father a hug. He stiffened but took it gracefully. The room was now very crowded. Greetings and sandwiches were shared as several distinct conversations began at once. Harry backed away to stand against the wall, his eyes sliding from one family member to the other. Aunt Margaret was explaining, yet again, why her daughter was still in London.

Kat leaned over the bench towards George. 'Where's this mouse? I *hate* bloody mice!'

'It's okay,' George whispered. 'There's no mouse.'

'What?'

'Shh. I'll tell you later.'

'*What?* No! Tell me now! Is there or isn't there a bloody mouse?'

George leaned even closer. 'It was a vibrator.'

'What the hell? The mouse was a vibrator?'

'This sounds interesting!' said Leo, reaching past for a sandwich. 'Was it a mouse-shaped vibrator or a vibrator for a mouse? Can't see either taking off. I'm guessing they'd be very niche markets.'

George looked around wildly. Several people had paused to stare in their direction. 'You misheard me,' she hissed at Leo. 'And get your mind out of the gutter.'

'Can't,' he replied cheerfully. 'It has free parking there. So what *did* you say then?'

'None of your business!'

'Come here!' Annie grabbed Kat by the arm and pulled her over to the sliding door. They went out onto the veranda and Annie shut the door firmly behind her. She immediately began talking, her hands waving in emphasis.

'You definitely said vibrator,' continued Leo around a mouthful of sandwich. 'I am particularly attuned to certain words. Vibrator is one of them.'

'Shut *up*,' snapped George. 'I'll explain later.'

'And I'll hold you to it.'

George waved him away. Through the window she could see that Annie was still talking rapidly. She was also holding her hands out about 30 centimetres from each other. George raised her eyebrows. That seemed a slight exaggeration.

'I'm even more interested now,' said Leo.

'Shut up,' said his mother again. It seemed that Annie had come to the end of the explanation. Kat's back was to her, but it was obvious from the shaking of her shoulders that she was laughing. George rolled her eyes. A part of her wanted to laugh also, but it felt incredibly disloyal to their mother. Even humiliating. She was struck by the sudden notion that there really was such a thing as spirits and that Enid, or her essence, was even now wafting across the ceiling, furious at this invasion of her privacy. The back of her neck prickled. Then again, if there were spirits, perhaps they were beyond such mundanities. Perhaps instead they just wanted connection. George put her hand on the counter, slightly curled, and stared at it. Perhaps all it needed was focus.

'Is that a mousetrap?' asked Tom, looming over her as he swept up the sandwich platter. 'Not sure it'll be very effective. Hey, Dick, did you leave *any* decent sandwiches?'

That was another habit of Tom's: dropping comments and then leaving as if a response wasn't necessary. George flexed her fingers as she turned away. She put the kettle on and lined up a row of mugs, castigating herself for her stupidity. Spirits indeed. Next thing she'd be getting out a ouija board to conjure up the dead. This thought gave her pause, but then she shook her head. Even more stupid. She slipped her glasses off and polished them with her t-shirt. It was best, she decided as she contemplated the mugs, that she practise compartmentalisation. It had served her well in the past. She slipped the pink vibrator into a drawer of her own and then reached for the coffee canister. The number of conversations behind her appeared to have multiplied.

'Can I have your attention please!' called Kat. She had come back inside and was holding her hand up like a traffic controller. As everybody turned towards her, she reached forward and upended the shopping bag that she had left on the table. Rolls of brightly coloured tape tumbled out. A lime-green one cycled towards the edge and was deftly caught by Tom. He picked up another and began juggling them.

'Hmm,' said Leo. He stroked his chin. 'Very colourful. Rainbow themed bondage?'

'No, idiot,' said Kat. 'And you're a fine one to comment on colours, given that waistcoat you're wearing.' She moved her gaze back to the group. 'I couldn't find eight different types of stickers so I bought these instead. You can cut bits off. Everyone gets to choose a colour.'

'Actually ...' said Tom, still juggling two of the rolls, 'Mum and I were talking and I've got a better idea. Not that yours wasn't good, of course.' He caught the roll in the air and grinned at his aunt. 'But hear me out. What about if we each write down what we want and then just pass the lists over, all at once? Doesn't that seem a bit simpler? Not quite so OTT?'

Kat's expression had stilled during the course of this suggestion. 'Thanks, Tom. Appreciated. But why don't we just move ahead with the original plan. OTT and all.'

'Ah, but I thought you said you didn't give a shit?' said Tom. He tossed the roll back up again and then snatched it, overhand, from midair. His grin wound back to a small, quizzical smile. 'You said discuss it while you were gone. So we did.'

George raised her eyebrows at this last. There had been no discussion that she was aware of. She glanced over at her younger sister, who was gazing at her son with an odd mix of pride and trepidation. George felt a surge of irritation. Tom had been at the house since early this morning and had done very little except wander around chatting, and then playing totem tennis. And now he was trying to derail the plan for division. Not that his idea didn't have merit; in fact George would have been quite happy to go with that also. But given it was Tom who suggested it, with Kat on the other side of the net, she wouldn't.

The tableau around the table had turned into something of a still life, all attention focussed on Kat and Tom. They weren't a family who argued much, but they could certainly recognise a stand-off when they saw one. With these two, also, everybody was well aware of how their similarities grated. Tom tossed the roll of tape up once more, without taking his eyes off his aunt. His smile had now become more of a smirk. George's irritation swelled. She cleared her throat.

'Not a bad idea, Tom,' she said sweetly. All heads swivelled in her direction. Tom looked a little surprised. 'But it's pretty similar to Kat's anyway. So let's just stick with that.'

Tom raised an eyebrow. 'How about putting it to the vote?'

'No,' said Kat tightly. '*That's* over-complicating things. And then you have a new issue if there's a draw or whatever. No, your mother, George and I are executors. So the thing is that *we* decide together.'

Annie snorted. 'Sure we do.'

If it hadn't been for her current irritation at her nephew, George probably would have opted for the vote idea. She would have liked everybody to be part of this, to have felt they *owned* the decision. But not now, and not like this.

Rhyll stepped forward suddenly and leaned over the jumble of tapes. She extracted a yellow roll. 'If I had a vote, I'd vote for the stickers anyway. The other way ...' She glanced sidelong at Tom. 'It's not like, transparent enough. You know?'

George looked at her with surprise. She would have expected Rhyll to back her cousin up, given they were quite close. She glanced across at him. His expression now had an odd, flat look to it. George sensed that he was devoting a lot of effort to keep that half-smile in place. Despite her irritation, she felt a little sorry for him. Finally he shrugged.

'Who needs democracy anyway?' he asked, of nobody in particular. He dropped one of his rolls back on the table and then tossed the other up once more. But this time Leo leaped forward and snatched it out of the air.

'Mine!' he yelled, taking off into the lounge room. Tom looked stunned for a moment, but then sprung into pursuit. George suspected he was taking advantage of this opportunity to make a somewhat dignified exit. He bounced off the couch and then the two of them could be heard running through to the hallway. This was followed by a dull thud as somebody actually hit the wall. George flinched. So did Annie.

'Well,' said Kat. She took a deep breath. 'Let's do it then. Everyone else choose.'

'I already have,' said Rhyll. She picked at the yellow roll with a chewed fingernail.

Tegan came forward. 'Then I'll have this.' She took a sky-blue roll. 'But, um ... can I ask why?'

Kat looked at her, surprised. Then her face cleared and she continued enthusiastically, as if glad of the change in focus. 'Of course! Nobody's told you. Okay, I'll explain. It'll be good to recap anyway. So, I'm moving in here for a year while we get the house ready for market. But we're clearing all your grandmother's things out this week beforehand. And given there's a lot of stuff, we thought everyone could put stickers on whatever they wanted.'

'Oh, great idea!' exclaimed Tegan. She beamed at her father. 'Won't that be marvellous, Dad! Do you want some help? Picking what you'd like?'

'No,' said Harry.

Annie coughed. '*I* thought we could just discuss things. But I was outvoted.'

'Yes, you were,' continued Kat smoothly. 'And what's more, Tegan, each person gets two priority picks. Just put an asterisk on those stickers if you like. That's for the things you'd really like the most. No guarantees of course. Then come Saturday, Annie, George and I will do the final dividing. Also, all hands on deck this coming weekend please. As soon as the division is done, we'll need everything moved.'

'One question,' interjected Rhyll. She flashed a narrow glance towards her mother. 'What if two people want the same thing?'

'Exactly,' said Annie with a smug nod.

Kat took a deep, exasperated breath. 'Oh for god's sake, nobody's saying that there can't be any discussion. This isn't some weird type of silent auction. We're just trying to take some of the bloody pressure off.' She kept her eyes on her youngest sister for a moment and then turned to Rhyll. 'If you find that somebody else has put their sticker on whatever it is that you want, then sure, try and talk it out. If that doesn't work, just leave it. We'll make sure that everyone gets at least one of their two priority picks. Okay?'

Rhyll shrugged, clearly unconvinced. Leo came back in, his white-tipped hair tousled, and grabbed an orange roll of tape.

He held it against his paisley waistcoat and grinned at Kat, then twirled it around his finger a few times and disappeared once more.

'Oh that's lovely of you girls,' said Aunt Margaret. 'So thoughtful. But I'd really just like one thing to remember your mother by. And those books George promised me. And maybe something for Lesley also. She would have been here you know, but—'

'Great idea!' exclaimed Kat. 'What about a brooch? Mum loved her brooches. Would you both like a brooch? Tegan, maybe you could show Aunt Margaret the brooches!'

Tegan grinned. 'Sure thing.'

Harry shuffled across to the table as his daughter left and touched each of the rolls with the tip of his finger before taking the bright-red one. The wind picked up outside; a tree branch scraping gratingly across the roof of the veranda. It was like nails on a chalkboard. George gave in and rubbed her eyes. That didn't help. Instead she put her glasses on and scanned the three rolls that were left. Purple, lilac and salmon-pink. She grimaced but before she could even react, her sisters had both reached over and grabbed a roll each. And just like that, she was left with the one colour that was the exact match for her mother's vibrator. She stared at it. Clearly, compartmentalisation was not going to work here.

Chapter Six

Tuesday evening

*I've decided that I just have to get through this year. My mother used to
say that you could get used to anything. Mind you, she was usually looking at me when she said it (cow), but that doesn't change the truth of it.
I need to count my blessings instead of the opposite, and just persevere. If
I think about the rest of my life, I get so dizzy I have to sit down. But
only till the end of the year? I can do that.*

*Just read what I wrote about my mother the other day. Maybe that's
why I struggle with the girls? Is it because I never had much of a mother
myself? Not a good role model, as they say these days. Sometimes I hear
her in me. It makes me ill. But then she never had a mother at all. So is
this something we each pass down? Will my girls be bad mothers too?*

George mulled over the last two entries as she washed dishes at
her sink at home. There wasn't a lot to do as both Leo and Rhyll
had gone back to Tegan's apartment for pizza after they'd finished
for the day. This had been something of a surprise as Rhyll and
Tegan didn't normally socialise much, but probably owed more to

Tom having also been there. George thought that he was probably Rhyll's favourite. *His* favourite was probably, marginally, Leo,
who was likely also to be Tegan's favourite. Not all that surprising. As for Leo, she doubted he *had* a favourite. It wasn't something that would even occur to him.

Regardless, the unexpected cousin-fest had meant it was just
her and Simon for dinner, along with his go-to gnocchi. He'd
begun meal prep before George even realised, otherwise she
would have skipped dinner altogether. Especially as they had a
firm cook-doesn't-clean rule, which meant that she'd paid for
her three bites of gnocchi with having to clean the kitchen. Or
at least the dishes. Thankfully Simon was not one of those men
whose ratio of implement to recipe was so disproportionate that
the cleaner-upper had to devote the entire evening to the task.

Wind squalled through the garden outside, rising to a crescendo
that flattened the shrubbery before dying off abruptly to rebuild
momentum once more. It was extremely irritating, even though
George recognised that it was something of a fitting backdrop to
her mood. She felt bruised by the events of the day. The sorting
of her mother's wardrobe, the full house in the afternoon, people
rifling through her mother's possessions, the vibrator. All on top
of a lack of sleep that now formed an almost rhythmic throb at
her temples. *You. Need. More. Sleep. You. Need. More. Sleep.* Along
with the residual burn from the Tears Ahoy mishap. But worst by
far was the ache of knowing that her mother had been unhappy.
That she'd thought herself a bad mother.

Enid had not been perfect. She'd been sharp-tongued and, at
times, short-tempered. She'd had no patience for fools. She had
doled out approval as if it was in limited supply. She had not been
particularly tactile, nor had she been one for spontaneous bursts
of affection. But she had been a wonderful mother. She had loved

fiercely, and been loved fiercely in return. The depth of which could be measured by the chasm left behind. George fervently hoped that her mother had been conscious enough at the end to see that her entire family had gathered around her bedside. Bad mothers didn't get that.

They had never met their grandmother. George knew that the woman had herself been raised mostly in children's homes, and that she in turn had dropped her own daughter off with various relatives throughout her childhood. She also knew that her grandmother had abruptly become a born-again Christian in Enid's early teens, taken the girl back, and hitherto made her life miserable. It had given her mother a lifelong aversion to organised religion, and also driven her immigration to Australia at the young age of nineteen. George remembered the day that the letter had arrived, informing Enid of her mother's death, many years ago. It had heralded an unprecedented set of events. Her mother retreating to her room, with the house wrapped in a shadowy grief that required them to walk on eggshells. Then just as suddenly as the letter had arrived, her mother emerged, back to her brisk self, apron in place, and things had returned to normal.

George resolved to check the details of her grandmother's death. Could it have given impetus to the diary writing? Could her grandmother have emigrated also, perhaps to Mount Isa? Could she have had a fetish for apples? Maybe Enid's rejection of her own mother had been the sin she was talking about. George put away the last of the cutlery and then left the kitchen, pausing to pat Puddles on her way into the lounge. Simon had now fallen asleep on the couch in front of the television, his head tilted back, his mouth open. She could see his tonsils. From this angle his emerging bald spot looked like a helicopter landing pad.

Scenes of devastation were playing out on the television with aerial vision of the fires. Kilometre after kilometre of charred landscape, studded with the skeletal remains of buildings. George watched as the coverage cut to an interview with a survivor, her face blank with shock. She spoke in halting sentences while incessantly plucking at her shirt, as if it too was on fire. Behind her the sky was gunmetal grey. It was tragedy on a grand scale.

George turned away. It was simply too much. She sent a fervent wish that they too weren't getting this blustery wind closer to the fires, and then went through into her study.

Once there, she sat at the computer, staring at the screen for a few minutes before giving it life. She slipped on her glasses. There were no classes at the moment as it was the summer break, but a column still needed to be submitted. *Peripherals*, as her regular column was called, offered a pithy snapshot of a female figure from the past. Particularly those who had their stories so romanticised that their relationships took precedence over their achievements. She opened the folder and went straight to the file with her spares. These were the extra pieces put together when she was most productive, for those times when she wasn't. Like now.

George loved her work. She loved writing, the linkage of words into sentences, into paragraphs, into story. She always had done. Every report card had praised her creative writing skills. At the age of thirteen, she had created a weekly newsletter called *The Tapscott Times*, which included a serialised tale of a rabbit family whose relationships would have given *The Bold and the Beautiful* a run for their money. She'd had her first published story while still at university, and after graduating landed a plum job in the publishing industry. Once the children arrived she turned to freelance writing and teaching, and then the column eventuated about a decade ago. The one thing she hadn't done, which was also her biggest regret, was write a book. She even knew what it would be about. A fictionalised biography of a distant ancestor, Mary Monks, who had grown up in Nottinghamshire and been arrested for the interestingly named 'offences against the currency' before transportation. George had everything sorted, except time to write.

For now, she scrolled through the contents of her spares file until she found a piece that was complete. All her columns started with the popular version of her subject. In this case it was Louisa Lawson who was remembered, if at all, as simply the mother of the poet Henry Lawson. Yet the woman had raised a passel of off-spring singlehandedly, founded a newspaper, run a printing press, patented her own inventions, written poetry, and in her spare time lobbied fiercely for the vote and championed women's rights. Her decline only set in after an unfortunate altercation with a tram.

George read the column through and made a few altera-tions. An interesting story *plus* a message about road safety. Win-win. She put the column aside for a final edit and then worked methodically through her emails, deleting most and answering a few others. There was even one from her cousin Lesley apolo-gising, yet again, for not having come over for the funeral. She replied quickly. *You're forgiven. But only if you let me swap lives with you. I'll shift into that garden flat near Hyde Park and you can have my character abode (aka in need of renovation) in the foothills of the Dande-nong Ranges. I'll even throw in an incontinent dog. Deal?*

She leaned back and took her glasses off, gingerly rubbing her eyes. Wind buffeted against the windows. Despite the difficul-ties of the day, it had been very productive. All the unnecessary paperwork was now shredded, the pantry cleared, the toolshed somewhat emptied and her mother's clothing gone. She was par-ticularly glad that the latter was over with. Taking each piece off its hanger and folding it into the boxes had brought forth her mother's smell. A miasma of soapy lavender. It infused every shirt, every cardigan, every scarf. There were even little bags of netted lavender hanging between the clothing. A potpourri of emotion.

George massaged the back of her neck. She felt a little like she herself had had an altercation with a tram. For a second, an image of Louisa Lawson flashed into her mind. She had steely eyes and a determined chin. She would have strode through life with her focus firmly on the next milestone. No mountain too high, no valley too far. Or shallow, or something. But the odd thing was that pre-diary, she would have thought her mother and Louisa were cut from the same cloth. Now, post-diary, they seemed poles apart. Directionless. That was the Enid of 1977. In fact, more like the Georgette of now. This revelation brought George upright. *I need to count my blessings.* How many times had she told herself that? She leaned forward and clicked on the minimised column. A smudgy photo of Louisa appeared alongside the words.

'What would you do, Lou?' she asked the photo. Louisa gazed back enigmatically. Although there *was* a slight sneer on her lips. George raised an eyebrow. 'I'm not asking for judgement, missy,' she said out loud. 'Just advice.'

Her phone pinged. George blinked, and then gave a short laugh. Even if Louisa did manage to communicate from beyond the grave, it was doubtful that she'd choose an Apple iPhone. She slipped her glasses back on to read the incoming text. It was from Guy.

Just checking to see if we will be having our usual Friday Frolic? I'm thinking we concentrate on the letter f. Fruity wine, feta, figs, and of course a you-know-what ;)

George took a deep breath. This was getting out of hand. She thought about sending back a frowny face, which at least went with his theme, but in the end simply deleted the message. Just as she did, another message came in. This time from Leo.

A vibrator? LMAO!!!

George took another deep breath and then closed her eyes briefly. She texted back. *How did you know?*

Rhyll just told us. Go Granma go!

She stared at the mobile. It was difficult to know exactly how to respond to a son who had just discovered his grandmother kept a vibrator. Normal etiquette didn't cover this. The phone pinged again.

Told you she liked colour!

George's eyes widened and then, almost despite herself, she felt a grin form. It really was funny. Very, *very* funny. Her eighty-three-year-old mother, who had pursed her lips at profanities, had kept a vibrator in her bedside drawer. Within easy reach. The grin turned into a chuckle and before she knew it, George began laughing. She could see the vibrator, its salmon-pink so *fleshy*, the ridges so *precise*, nestled neatly amongst the crisp white granny underwear. Her *mother's* underwear. Her laughter thickened. This had been so far from the ballpark of what she expected this week that it hadn't even been in the same suburb. Or country.

'Everything okay?' asked Simon from the doorway.

Her laughter stilled, but a smile remained as George turned to face him. She nodded. 'All good. Just … thinking about things.'

'You were laughing though. You sounded a bit …'

'A bit what?'

Simon ran a hand through his hair. 'Well, a bit manic.'

'Ah,' said George. She tried to reconcile this. Admittedly, her laughter probably had danced along the edge of hysteria, but for a moment, it had felt pleasurable. A partial solution would be to include Simon, to explain *why* she'd been laughing, but she simply

couldn't summon up the energy. Her shoulders dropped at the
thought. Plus it was one thing for her to laugh at her mother, and
even for Leo to LMAO but a whole other matter to have Simon
snigger at Enid's expense.

'Okay then,' said Simon a little awkwardly. 'I'll leave you to it.'

George felt a wash of guilt. 'I'll be out soon. Maybe we could
watch something together?'

'Oh! Um, sure.' He shrugged. 'I suppose. If you want to. Or
hey!' He gave a sudden grin. 'Maybe we can think of something
else, given we've got the house to ourselves?'

George lifted an eyebrow. She waited a few beats. 'Really?'

'Up to you of course,' he went on hurriedly, no doubt remembering that her mother had just died and sex might not be upper-
most on her mind. 'Just an idea.'

'As much as I would *love* to celebrate life in the face of death,'
said George sardonically, 'I am afraid I'm just a little tired. You
know, after clearing out my late mother's possessions.' She paused
to allow this full effect, and then matched his earlier grin. 'But
given you'd like to do something together, I have a better idea.
Monopoly?'

'What?' He visibly blanched. 'Oh. Well, if you *really* want to.
Let's chat about it later?'

'*So* looking forward to it.'

He shut the door behind him and George made a timeout gesture that finished with her giving him the finger. The odds of
Simon getting any action tonight were about as high as that of
the salmon-pink vibrator. She grimaced at the analogy and then
took off her glasses again and polished them with a corner of her
top. She knew she was being unfair, that she was keeping him at
arm's length while simultaneously feeling resentful that he wasn't
moving closer. Especially given what she'd been up to for the

past year. But the effort to do something about it felt simply too cumbersome.

They had come close to separating a few years ago. Leo had finished high school and been accepted into the same university as Rhyll. Graphic design for her and information technology for him. Shortly afterwards they had both moved into a student share house in Burwood. For years Simon and George had joked about the anticipated bliss of an empty nest but the reality had been very different. It came with the weight of empty space, and extra time, and the echo of their own voices when they spoke. And when they did, they had less and less to say. One of the things that remained unsaid was the growing awareness that the marriage had run its course. The question had not been if but when. Then Rhyll had abruptly dropped out of university and moved back home. She had been followed a year later by Leo, who had finished his course but was economising in order to launch his own business. Their own issues had taken second place, metamorphosing instead into an adversarial residue that shadowed every conversation, every gesture. It was like sediment in a creek, every so often being stirred to cloud the surface.

And then about a year ago, she had done the unthinkable. Guy Weston, the successful author of hefty biographical tomes, had been the keynote speaker at an industry event. Afterwards they had enjoyed a few glasses of wine and a fascinating discussion about the arts. Nary a mention of real estate or building contractors or troublesome offspring. Guy had seemed so worldly, with an anecdote about everything and a wealth of knowledge that made her feel like a suburban housewife. He was living the life that she'd thought she would, once. Before she knew it, they had been flirting. George hadn't flirted in thirty years. The attention had been intoxicating. That, and the wine. The combination had propelled her back to his apartment, and then somehow, without seemingly any effort on her part, evolved into regular meetings. Usually on Fridays.

At first she had convinced herself that this arrangement was exactly what was needed to keep the pulse going in her own marriage. She was taking one for the team, so to speak. But then, over time, guilt began to outweigh the advantages. Plus the fascinating discussions became more tedious, his anecdotes more gossipy, and the wealth of knowledge more opinion than fact. He also had unusually hairy knuckles and a kink in his penis that he was bizarrely proud of. But he was also the most interesting thing that had happened to her in years, and without him she would go back to being just George. She didn't know if she could face that either.

She took a deep breath, then pushed it all aside so that she could give the column a final read. After a tweak, she sent it through to her editor. Buoyed by the resultant sense of accomplishment, she tapped her fingers lightly against the keys and then searched for information about supported accommodation. Much of it seemed like an exercise in slick marketing. She clicked on images and was confronted by a plethora of communal bliss. People enjoying meals together, or sitting on couches, or engaged in arts and crafts. Nowhere was anyone enjoying a solitary meal of Lite n' Easy while surrounded by Lego.

She opened the group chat on her phone and sent a message to her sisters. *How would he cope in one of those group homes?*

Annie replied fairly quickly. *What's the alternative?*

George's fingers hovered over the keypad, but there wasn't really an answer. Kat chimed in while she was thinking.

TBH, he'll hate it @ the start. Doesn't like change anyway. But we have to give it time. 4 all we know, he'll love it. Eventually.

The door opened again. George swivelled her chair around to face Simon.

'I'm just making some tea. Want one?'

'Yes, thanks. That'd be lovely.'

'Good.' His eyes flicked to the phone in her hand and then back. 'Um, there's a documentary on mighty machines. I thought I might watch it in bed.'

'Oh. Well, that *does* sound like fun. But weren't we going to play Monopoly?'

He lifted an eyebrow. 'You really want to play Monopoly?'

'Absolutely. I've been looking forward to it.'

'Oh. Okay.'

George returned his searching look with a bright smile. She kept it in place until he closed the door. She wondered what he would say if she suddenly announced that she was having an affair. And rather than play Monopoly, they needed to talk, seriously, about the future. That plodding along without making the leap was doing neither of them any favours. Given projected lifespans, she had another 26.6 years left and he had 20.4. She knew this because she'd looked it up last week. If they both stuck to the script, that gave her exactly 6.2 years without him if they didn't act any sooner. Every day was one day less. But what would separation mean? Would there be enough equity in the house to enable both of them to buy their own properties? How would they divide superannuation? And most compelling of all, who would get Rhyll?

She looked back at her phone. The conversation had finished without her. Her sisters appeared to have come to the conclusion that given time, there was even a chance that he might flourish amongst peers. That he would become some sort of social butterfly. George grimaced. Harry tolerated his day centre, but only because he was a creature of habit and the activities came in small doses. But then perhaps their mother agreed; maybe that was why she'd put his name down in the first place.

The door opened again and Simon leaned in. 'Puddles made a puddle. I've cleaned it.'

'Great.' George looked at him expectantly. She knew that he was waiting for some thanks, so withholding it felt like a power of sorts. The ensuing silence gave her a chance to examine him. He wasn't a bad looking man. Tall, relatively fit for his age, with just a slight paunch. Nary a hair on his knuckles and a nice, straight penis. Once on the open market, he would be snapped up quickly. Her eyes widened at the thought.

'What about a David Attenborough documentary?' asked Simon finally. 'You like that sort of thing.'

George was still stuck on the idea of him moving on so fast. Guy was certainly not a long-term prospect for her. She knew that much of her attraction for him came from the fact that she was essentially unavailable, while his attraction for her had been the clandestine nature of the whole thing. And even that had long gone. No, she would be living alone in her tiny unit, motherless, while Simon was being fought over by a bevy of divorcees and widows. He would probably lose that paunch within months, buy a convertible and start dating women half his age. She felt a surge of anger. It was so unfair.

'George? David Attenborough? Come on, I know you fancy him.'

She glared at him. 'Oh, naturally. Because a ninety-year-old is the best *I* can hope for?'

'What?' Simon gaped at her. 'Oh, um … what?'

'Monopoly,' said George firmly.

'Really?'

'Yes, really.'

'I didn't think you even *liked* Monopoly.'

'The question isn't whether I like Monopoly,' said George conversationally. 'But which type you'd prefer? We have several varieties. There's even the original if you'd rather stick with the tried and true?'

'Good lord. Well, I suppose I'd better go check them out. Maybe there's a more exciting version than the original.'

'I'm sure there is,' said George. There was no doubt about that, at least. She waited for him to shut the door and then leaned back. A squall of wind rattled the windowpanes. Fortunately for him, there was every chance that his exciting new girlfriends would be more obliging about sex. Even if their mother had just died, rather than feel resentful, they would probably see the act as life-affirming. Maybe they'd even chuckle about how sex could become stale within long-term relationships and swear that it would never happen to them.

She'd have to buy a vibrator, just like her mother. Ridiculously, even this thought brought tears to her eyes. She removed her glasses to wipe at them roughly. She wondered what Louisa Lawson would have done. No doubt, with a marriage like George's, she would have pulled up stakes far earlier. In between baking bread and lodging patents for new inventions, she'd have packed her carpet bag and started a new life. Where she took on the media moguls, fought against patriarchy and climate change, and launched a career in politics. In her spare time she would have volunteered as a firefighter. Instead here George was, watching it on television. Living with a man who she both loved and didn't, about to play a game of Monopoly, which she most definitely didn't. Trading seven minutes of something she actually did enjoy for several hours of mind-numbing boredom. Simply because it felt like a win, of sorts.

Chapter Seven

Wednesday morning

Now that I've decided to take one step at a time, I feel much better. Just this lot of clothes to iron, this floor to wash, this one meal to cook. I even made crumbed sausages last night, with macaroni pudding for dessert. The girls' favourites. I did draw the line at playing the Game of Life with them though. Huh! Living it is enough!

I often wonder what would have happened if Bel hadn't got accidentally pregnant. We'd saved for so long and were just on the verge of booking our tickets. London. One more time. And then I put it off until I found another travelling companion and instead I met Ronald. So if not for Bel's inability to keep her knickers up, I might have been living a different life altogether.

I was watching Ronald tonight. I've decided that he's a Norm. A potato.

George closed the diary before she could be tempted to read yet another entry. She leaned back in the study chair, resting the book on her lap. There was no doubt that her mother had been going through some type of midlife crisis in 1977. Something happened to precipitate a dissatisfaction with her life that she had fought to slough off – not, it seems, very successfully. As children, they'd had no idea. But as an adult, the notion that her mother experienced this slump now made George feel even closer. Sad, but closer. Some of the words even resonated within her own life. Not the reference to Bel's knickers of course, and certainly not the part about her father being like a potato. That was a little confusing. It did seem that Enid had had a rather odd obsession with produce.

Another correlation was that her mother had been planning to go back to London before she'd met her future husband. The 'one more time' suggested it was just for a visit. This was almost exactly what had happened to George. Except of course, that she'd been born in Australia and had never been to England at all. But she too had once dreamt of heading to London, even collecting brochures and pamphlets and maps of the different boroughs. She had planned to live in a garret, whatever that was, and become a fully-fledged writer. Her cousin Lesley was already living there then. George had been conscious of time slipping away, that already it was past the heyday of the Earl's Court expats, yet nevertheless she did more dreaming than actual saving. And then came Simon, and the wedding, and mortgage, and babies. One day around sixteen years ago, having run out of newspaper for their new puppy, she had found those old brochures and used them with barely a second thought. Life had literally pissed on her dreams.

George sighed as she replaced the diary. Sliding doors. Missed opportunities. Maybe in another dimension there was a slimmer, leaner George, with a cutting sense of fashion. Who had written several bestsellers while floating through continental literary circles. And who met people like Guy at industry events and instantly noticed their hairy knuckles because she wasn't swept away by facades. But then that meant she would never have met Simon either, and neither Leo nor Rhyll would exist. Impossible to imagine. This current dimension might be a trifle complicated, but she wasn't sure the trade-off was worth it.

Apart from all that though, how had she not known this about her mother? Surely when George herself had spoken wistfully of London, it would have been just a tad relevant for Enid to mention that she'd once had similar plans? She could have omitted the downward trajectory of Bel's knickers, but at least shared the dream. George shook her head, bemused. Thus far the diary had brought more questions than answers. She took off her glasses and slipped them into a pocket, then stretched. It had been another restless night. As a result she'd slept in, only rising during that chunk of morning she thought of as the grey zone – which was after Simon and Leo had left for work, and before Rhyll rose. Puddles, not having been taken outside, had lived up to his name yet again. Nevertheless she arrived at the house at the same time as Annie, beating her into the driveway by the merest whisker. It had given George a sense of triumph out of all proportion to the deed.

The agenda for today was to finish the toolshed, empty the bathroom cabinets, sort through a suitcase of loose photos, and also the jewellery box, and then lay out the Christmas decorations ready for stickers. It sounded a lot, but as Kat had pointed out, things would probably be easier without the mass of helpful hands from yesterday. George pulled over the desk chair and clambered up with a groan. She wedged a knee into the wardrobe architrave to stop the chair rotating as she levered down first the box of Christmas decorations and then the tree. A few rolls of wrapping paper bounced out and she flinched as they tumbled past to the floor. She got down and stared at the haphazard pile. It was only a few weeks ago that she had helped her mother pack all this away.

George carried the decorations out to the lounge room. Annie was sitting on the couch, the jewellery box on her lap, laying the contents neatly on a piece of black felt atop the coffee table. She was wearing a maxi dress in a batik pattern and, barefooted, looked a little like an ageing hippy setting out a market stall. Except that every piece was personal. Annie held up a gold fili-gree brooch with a spray of red ruby droplets.

'Remember this?'

George nodded. They had gone in together to give that to their mother on her eightieth birthday. It had been very expensive, but it had been difficult to tell whether she had liked it as much as they had. 'You should put one of your priority stickers on it.'

'Yeah, sure.' Annie finished the sentence with a snort. She laid the brooch gently alongside another, this one with a pair of oversized pearls that resembled cataract-eyeballs. She looked up at George. 'What have you got there?'

'Christmas stuff. Where did Kat want it?'

'Does that really matter?' asked Annie. She kept her eyes on George for a few moments and then dropped them to the jewel-lery again. 'Make up your own mind.'

George frowned, both at Annie's tone and the implication that she couldn't think for herself. She gazed at her younger sister for a few moments. 'Are you okay?'

Annie shrugged. 'Fine.' She ran a finger over the pearls. 'Just ... sad, I suppose.'

'Yeah.' George let the silence settle. It was swollen with loss. 'I still can't quite believe it, you know. I mean, we've had the funeral and everything, but I still keep half-expecting someone to announce that there's been a mistake. It's too huge to be true.'

'Same,' said Annie, still staring at the pearls. 'I rang her last night. How stupid's that?'

'Not stupid at all!'

'But I just got Leo's voice of course, on her voicemail. Which was probably just as well. If she'd recorded her own message, I think that would have been the end of me.'

'Ring me instead,' said George quietly. 'When it gets bad, like that, ring me.'

Annie nodded. 'Thanks.'

'I mean it,' said George. She chewed her lip. 'Listen, there's something else I wanted to ask you ... are you having money problems?'

'What?' Annie looked up, clearly surprised. Her v was a soft indentation. Her eyes bright with unshed tears. 'No. Not really. Why did you ask?'

'Just your reaction the other day when Kat suggested putting off the sale of the house.' George rested the corner of the box against the armrest. 'I thought things might be a little tight. And I'm guessing you subsidised a lot of Tom's move up north so, well ...'

Annie nodded. 'I did. But don't you dare give me a lecture on that subject.' Her face broke into a sudden grin. 'You're as bad as me in that department.'

'True,' said George ruefully. 'But then we've got two wages coming in.'

'That's not Tom's fault,' replied Annie immediately. 'And he shouldn't be penalised.' She paused for a moment. 'If anything, the opposite. He didn't ask for his parents to split up.'

'Yes, but—'

'Don't say it.' Annie held up a hand. 'No really, George. I know you mean well, but you have no idea. You've had your perfect family. Your steady husband, your pigeon pair children.

You don't know what it's like to feel guilty that you couldn't give your child that.'

'Oh, Annie.' George couldn't think of anything to say beyond that. Her family was by no means perfect, far from it, but she didn't think pointing that out was going to help here. She pushed the box a little further onto the armrest to free up one hand. This she rested on her sister's shoulder, giving it a squeeze. Annie reached up and took it for a moment, returning the pressure, and then broke free.

'Now, we'd better get back to work. Otherwise the sergeant major will come back and put us on a charge.'

'Okay, but if you are having problems then promise you'll let me know. And I meant it before, about ringing me. Anytime. Okay?'

Annie nodded. 'Thanks.'

George gave her sister's shoulder a final squeeze, then hefted the box up and took it back into the study. These brief exchanges, about shared sorrow, brought a warmth that was as unexpected as it was welcome. From there, her thoughts slipped to her husband, and the stilted half-game of Monopoly they had played the previous evening. Maybe if she shared her grief with him also, then the evenings would be easier. She paused in the centre of the room, considering this. Maybe it was up to her to make the first move. Maybe this was it.

After a few moments, she compartmentalised the idea, determining to explore it a little later. Apart from anything else, the box was getting a little heavy. She looked around for a good place to unpack it. The desktop looked fit for purpose. The next hour was spent sorting through the decorations and throwing away anything broken. Those pieces with particular meaning, like the fur-trimmed angel that sat atop their tree for as long as she could remember, were laid carefully on the desk. Other bits and pieces, useful but not nostalgic, were left in the box on the floor. There were also unopened packets of gift tags, more wrapping paper, even a new box of crackers. Her mother had clearly hit the Boxing Day sales in preparation for the following year. The thought formed a knot in George's belly.

But how much worse would it have been had her mother died a month ago. Then the whole house would have been still decorated, the tree dominating the lounge room, Christmas cards crowding the mantelpiece. There would have been that peculiarly Christmassy smell, of pine cones and mulled wine. Even if you had neither, it seemed to be obligatory. Both fridge and pantry would have been full of delicacies. Turkey and ham and Christmas pudding. This room would have held the Christmas presents, wrapped and tagged, waiting to be placed under the tree. George tried to imagine how it would have felt, handing those out. Gifts from the grave.

Her phone pinged so she pulled it out from her bag. There was a message from a TAFE friend, sending her best wishes, another from Rhyll, asking what they were up to that day, and another from Guy querying again whether Friday was on. This one was a little terser. George frowned. The last thing she needed was another person putting pressure on her. Besides, the least he could do was give her some space given the circumstances. This was becoming as complicated as everything else. Maybe it was her. She was like Midas, except everything she touched turned problematic. Gold would be more useful.

'Bad news?' asked Kat, leaning in from the doorway.

George shook her head. 'No, just some guy.' She was rather pleased with the witticism.

'Oh?' Kat raised an eyebrow. 'Anyone of interest?'

George shook her head again, this time with conviction. She dropped the phone back into her bag.

'Anyway, I came to see if you wanted a break. Morning tea.'

'Sounds good.' George rose, one of her knees cracking. A bauble rolled off the desk and she caught it deftly. 'Hey, Kat, what did you get from Mum for Christmas?'

'Um, I can't remember. Oh! A new Fitbit. Why? Making comparisons?'

'Certainly not!' said George, affronted. If it had been an issue, she'd have remembered.

'O-kay. Well, I'll go put the kettle on.'

A Fitbit would be replaced within a year or two, just like the e-reader that George herself had asked for. She should have gone for something memorable. Earrings maybe, or a filigree brooch. She kicked at a roll of wrapping paper and it spun across the room. By the time she emerged, Harry had also made an appearance. He was sitting at the dining table with his blue mug before him, examining his mobile. George massaged her neck as she took the chair beside him. In the kitchen, Kat had lined up three more mugs and was ladling coffee into them. A plate of chocolate-chip cookies sat on the table, along with a bowl holding the coloured tape and a piece of paper that detailed which colour belonged to which person. George's own name had *SALMON-PINK (LOL!)* written beside it.

'Very funny,' she said to Kat.

'That was me,' said Annie, giving her an odd look as she came in.

'How do you both take your coffee?' asked Kat. She had paused with the spoon in the air.

George raised her eyebrows. 'How do you *not* know how we take our coffee?'

'Because she never makes them,' said Annie. She went over to the bench and peered into the mugs with a grimace. 'For good reason. Good god, Kat, I'm having a hard enough time sleeping as it is. If I drink this, I'll be awake until February. Here.' She took the spoon from her sister. 'Let me do it.'

'Voltaire drank about fifty cups of coffee every day,' said Harry. He took a sip of his own coffee and his eyes widened. He put it down.

'Give me that.' Annie came over and took his mug, casting a disparaging look towards her eldest sister. 'Voltaire could have saved time and just had one of these.'

Kat shrugged. 'In my defence, I rarely make the stuff. You do know you can buy it? At places called, hang on … cafes?'

George tuned out as her sisters began bantering about the cost versus the merits of takeaway coffee. She leaned back and gazed outside. The gusty wind of yesterday had vanished, leaving behind a stillness made eerie by the cod-grey sky. Smoke from the distant fires had blown in overnight, now hanging like a pall as if the entire city was in mourning. Something else caught her eye, closer to the sliding door. It looked like the hanging chair had been wrapped in metres of thin cord. George put on her glasses. It wasn't cord but two different colours of tape. Yellow and orange. She glanced down at the list. Rhyll and Leo.

'It's awful, isn't it?' said Annie, having followed her initial gaze. 'Those poor people. And all the animals.'

'Yep,' said Kat. 'This smoke's from Gippsland. Apparently it'll be here for days.'

They remained in silence, each staring outside. The horizon was like the setting for a dystopian movie. Somewhere, not that far as the crow flies, other people were having their lives destroyed. The fortunate ones were emerging shell-shocked from the ruins, faces smeared with ash and pain, while others never would.

'The worst fire ever in the whole world was in Peshtigo,' said Harry as the kettle began to whistle. '1871. Northeast Wisconsin in the United States of America. 1,200,000 acres burnt. Number of deaths estimated between 1,500 and 2,500.'

'Oh my god,' said Annie from the kitchen. 'Really?'

Harry look at her, surprised. 'Yes.'

'Was that one started by a love letter too?' asked Kat.

Harry frowned. He bent to his mobile, perhaps to find out. George was trying to get her head around the scale of lives lost. Entire communities. The haze outside now felt like a shroud. She slid her gaze across to Harry, who was scrolling through his phone. How on earth would he cope in supported accommodation? Would anyone there be the least interested in his trivia? Or would the very idiosyncrasies that made him so wonderfully unique within his family, make him just peculiar within theirs?

'Why're your sandals on the railing?' asked Kat now, looking over at Annie.

George glanced back outside. Sure enough, her younger sister's sandals were balanced atop the railing near the wrought iron plant stand. This latter was still in the askew position she had moved it to a few days before.

'I had to hose them off,' said Annie. She sighed. 'Stepped in dog poo. Story of my life.'

George exchanged a quick grin with Kat. Annie could be so melodramatic.

'Where's the dog?' asked Harry with interest. He was very fond of dogs but that was one of the few things their mother had denied him.

'No idea,' said Annie. 'But if you follow the trail of faeces up the nature strip, maybe you'll find it. Take a note of where it lives so I can give the owner a piece of my mind.'

'Okay,' said Harry.

'No,' said George, frowning at her sister. 'She didn't mean it, Harry. *Don't* follow the trail.'

'Okay,' said Harry again. He looked back down at his phone.

Annie brought the mugs over to the table. She sat down heavily and then pulled across the sheet of paper with the coloured tape division. She gave another sigh, this one even more audible. George felt a flash of impatience. Both of her sisters were given to habitually sighing, but with Kat, it was more like an escape valve. As if her sister was expelling energy, and simultaneously allowing others to catch up with her. Annie's were different. With her the expulsion of breath carried the weight of the world. In the dying stages of their marriage, her ex-husband would mimic her. This recollection dissolved George's irritation. She sent her sister a sympathetic smile, but she was still staring at the paper.

'I have an idea,' said Kat abruptly. 'How about you both stay Friday night? It's Harry's night to eat en famille, so it'd be lovely for us all to be there. We could get heaps done and then just relax with some takeaway. Have a glass of wine. Plus it might be your last chance while it looks like … this. You know, before everything starts getting cleared the next day.'

Annie looked up. 'Nice idea. And thanks, but I can't. Tom's only here till Sunday.'

'*I* can,' said George. The thought had instant appeal. 'Woo hoo! Slumber party!' She nudged her brother. 'Won't that be fun?'

'The slumber party massacre happened in 1982,' said Harry without looking up. 'All these girls were killed with a power drill after eating pizza. It was not good. Only two survived.'

'I think that might have been a movie,' said Kat with a grin. 'But if it makes you feel better, we won't have pizza.'

'Or use power drills,' added George. 'This will be a strictly pizza and power drill free occasion. And we'll make sure the chainsaws are out of action too.'

Annie had been watching them, her v deepening. 'Maybe I *can* come. I'll see.'

'Great,' said Kat airily.

George sipped her coffee. In her opinion, never actually voiced, Annie would be better advised *not* to wrap her entire life around that of her son. She was willing to bet that Tom spent very few evenings at home anyway. More likely he was catching up with friends while his mother waited by the phone, just in case.

'Great to see a few people putting their stickers on stuff yesterday,' said Kat. She glanced out at the hanging chair and grinned. 'Some being more enthusiastic than others!'

Annie had followed her gaze. She shook her head slowly. 'That's what I'm worried about. Wouldn't it be better if they'd just talked about it with some maturity? Now *we're* going to have to decide who gets it. And someone's going to miss out.'

'With some maturity?' repeated George. It sounded very much like Annie was having a dig at her children. Admittedly, neither were particularly mature, but still. She frowned at her sister. 'What do you mean by that?'

'Like just discussing it. Sitting down and working out who wants it more.'

'C'mon, Annie,' interjected Kat. 'That was never going to work. And I'm at a loss as to why you're so fixated on this! Unless, is it because Tom doesn't like it? Or is it just because *I* suggested it? Seriously, think about it. You'd just have people trying to one-up the other with why something meant so much to them. I don't know about you, but I have *no* desire to go through that. And even afterwards, someone's still going to miss out.'

George nodded. She heartily agreed. She was also still stuck on the particular allusion to Leo and Rhyll. At least they'd made a start; all Tom had done was put forward alternative ideas that had even *less* discussion attached.

'And so instead we'll have people manipulating your overly complicated system,' retorted Annie hotly. 'Yesterday, I heard Tegan say to Leo that if she put her number two sticker on that chair also, then she'd be sure to get her number one! That's manipulation!'

'So what?' Kat shot back. 'Apart from the fact she was probably just joking, even if she *did* do that, then she only gets one of her priority picks. More fool her! Besides, if you think people are so bloody underhand, then how on earth did you expect them to discuss things reasonably anyway?'

'Because I'm not underestimating them!'

Kat jabbed a finger in her direction. 'You're the one who just accused people of being manipulative!'

Annie sat back, folding her arms. Her v had deepened. 'You're twisting my words.'

'No. You're just not making any sense!'

'I'm making perfect sense. You're not listening! As usual!'

'Hey, you two,' said George uncomfortably. Things appeared to be escalating. She needed their camaraderie, not this. 'Don't you think that—?'

'And besides,' interrupted Annie, her eyes still on Kat. 'It's got nothing to do with who suggested it. The bottom line is, *I* just think it's what Mum would have liked.'

'Oh!' Kat got up hurriedly, one knee knocking the table. Coffee spilled from the mugs. She stared at her youngest sister, red blotches staining her cheeks. 'What the fuck? Where do *you* get off telling us what Mum would have liked?'

'And what does *that* mean? What, you get to say what Mum would have liked because you're the eldest? Is that it?'

'Bloody hell!' snapped Kat. 'Don't even start with that! All you're doing is pulling the Mum card because you didn't get your own way!'

Annie glowered at her. 'Bullshit. Absolute bullshit. I *never* get my own way!'

'Well maybe if you stood up to your son a bit more, you would!'

Annie's mouth dropped open. After a moment it closed again, and her eyes narrowed.

'Mum liked tapioca pudding,' said Harry, glancing up from his phone. 'With cream. And so do I. You spilled my coffee.'

George was staring from one sister to the other. It was like she had been left behind at the point that her two children had been accused of immaturity, and then the train had shot from the station without her. Her stomach churned. She disliked conflict at the best of times, and this week was certainly not that.

'Well, I tell you what,' said Kat now, her voice terse. She grabbed her bag from the back of a chair. 'You know what *I* think Mum would have liked? She would have liked *you* to organise *yourselves*.' She waved a hand towards the pile of papers that had been there all week. 'You can ring the lawyers, and the gas company, and the water, and Veterans' Affairs to cancel the pension from Dad. There you go, it's all yours! Discuss *that*!'

George gaped as Kat flounced from the room. She felt physically ill. She also wasn't sure why she'd just been thrown under the bus as well. The front door slammed and the lounge room window juddered in its frame.

'Well, that went great,' said Annie. Her voice shook, just slightly.

George turned on her. 'What on earth was the point?'

'Of course *you're* going to take her side,' said Annie. She rose abruptly, taking her mug over to the sink. 'Even after what she said about Tom! Well don't panic, I'm sure she'll be back soon. Then you two can get all cosy again.'

'Do I *look* like I'm panicking? I just want *everyone* to get on; is that too much to ask? It's hard enough anyway, without all this shit!'

'The word shit comes from Latin,' said Harry. 'It means to split apart. Separate.'

'Well, then congrats, Annie,' continued George, her gaze still on her sister. 'You're doing a great job of shitting us up.'

Annie shrugged but didn't reply. She turned away and began filling the sink. George used the silence to replay the conversation and try to ascertain at what point it had gone awry. She was still annoyed at the comment about Leo and Rhyll, but this had been overlaid by the nauseous weight that had settled in the pit of her belly. She glanced over at Harry, but he seemed to be engrossed in his phone once more. One of the best, and worst, things about Harry was his complete obliviousness to tension.

Annie came over to the table and wiped it down with a sponge. She took the mugs back into the kitchen and began doing the dishes. After a few seconds, George realised that her sister's shoulders were shaking. Her eyes widened. Annie was crying. Without thinking, George got up quickly and crossed into the kitchen. Once there, she wrapped her arms around her sister from the back. Annie stiffened and then pulled away.

'You two *always* gang up on me,' she muttered without turning. '*Always.*'

George felt affronted, especially after her gesture of affection. 'How am I even remotely responsible for this? I hardly said anything! Even after *you* had a go at *my* kids! Sorry, Annie, but you brought this on yourself.'

'I'm going home.' Annie wiped her hands on the tea towel and then turned. Her eyes shone and mascara had smudged beneath, highlighting the puffiness.

George felt sympathy butt against her frustration. 'Oh, Annie. *Nobody's* ganging up on you. Really, they're not. We're in this together.'

'Al Capone joined the James Street Boys gang,' said Harry. 'He was Public Enemy Number One in 1929.' He looked up, sending them a narrow glance. 'He also did a massacre.'

Annie had kept her eyes on George. 'So it's all in my imagination, is it? You two have *never* ganged up on me?'

'I didn't say that,' protested George. 'I just said—'

'Whatever,' interrupted Annie. She rubbed roughly at her eyes. 'I'm going home.'

There didn't seem to be much to add. George could have retorted that there were probably as many times that Annie and Kat had ganged up on *her*, but there seemed little point. She knew that she was arguing not against the events of the past few days, but a perspective of the past. Instead she watched as her younger sister went out onto the veranda and started banging her sandals against the railing. Droplets of water flew off. With a flash of insight, it occurred to her that Annie might even be creating this conflict subconsciously, that she needed a target to bypass her grief. Certainly the vigour with which she was beating her sandals suggested the need for some type of outlet. After a few minutes, George followed. It was worth one more try.

'Look, you might have a point about when we were younger,' she said, sliding the screen door shut behind her. 'But not now. Now we just want to get through this. Together.'

'Yeah, sure.' Annie had fastened the left sandal. She stood on one leg, trying to sort the right. The straps seemed to be caught beneath the sole of her foot.

'Come on. Don't leave like this.'

Annie didn't reply. She curled over, still on one foot, and balanced awkwardly as she tried to ascertain the problem. The maxi dress was not helping.

'I'm sure Kat didn't mean what she said about Tom. They just clash a bit because they're both, well, alpha types. But we all love Tom. And she'll be back soon. We can sort this all out. We need you. *I* need you.'

Annie began to hop backwards, trying to wrest the sandal strap free. The hem of her dress now appeared to be caught in the buckle. She flashed a furious glance at George, as if this too was her fault. Somewhat unfortunately their eyes met just as George gave an involuntary giggle at the sight. Annie's expression darkened.

'I'm sorry!' said George. She took a step towards her sister, arms out. 'Let me help!'

'Fuck off!' shrieked Annie, jerking herself away just as George's fingers brushed her arm. She took another hop backwards as she tried to wrench the dress free. It tore, the sudden release propelling her backwards even more, but this time with force. Still bent over, she hit the railing hard with her butt and there was a splintering sound as the rotten railing gave way. For a second they stared at each other, their faces mirroring each other's shock. And then Annie was gone.

George stood, frozen, staring at the severed section of railing. It gaped like a missing tooth. Her brain was having problems processing what had just happened. She blinked, and then rushed forward to lean against the solid part of the remaining railing. Her heart literally felt like it had filled her throat. Annie lay spread-eagled on the ground about a metre below, on her back. The maxi dress was gathered around her hips, her legs pale and fleshy, her plum-coloured hair fanned around a pale face. She gazed up at George, her eyes round.

'Oh my god!' said George. 'Are you all right?'

Annie sat up slowly. She moved her head from side to side and then wiggled her feet experimentally. She ran her fingers over her left wrist and flinched before pulling it to her chest and holding it still. She started to rise.

'Wait!' said George. 'I'll help!' She hurried down the steps and crossed the lawn to her sister who was now on her knees. She took her arm, trying to assist. 'Should you be moving? Should I ring an ambulance?'

'Who. Moved. The. Planter?' asked Annie.

'Um, what?'

'The planter,' repeated Annie. Her voice was thready with shock. She rose to her feet. 'Mum put it against that damaged bit of railing. Who the hell moved it?'

George grimaced. 'Look, that *might* have been me. I was going to tell Kat to get it fixed.'

'I see.' Annie pulled away, straightening slightly as she hobbled towards the steps, holding her wrist against her chest. The left sandal flopped, still undone. George followed her up to the veranda, asking the sort of questions one should ask in such circumstances. Was Annie sure there wasn't spinal damage? Had she hit her head? Was her vision clear?

Annie slid the door open and began gathering her things from the table with her good arm. She hooked her bag over her right shoulder and then in a sudden, furious movement, swept the bowl containing the coloured tapes from the table. The bowl was saved from destruction by landing sideways on the nearest chair, while the rolls hit the floor, scattering in all directions.

'Annie!' exclaimed George. Then she shook her head. Pick your battles. 'You need to see a doctor. Seriously. We need to make sure you're okay.'

'I'm going home,' said Annie flatly. 'I'm fine. No thanks to you.'

George shook her head. 'I have to make sure.' She grabbed her own bag, extracting her car keys. 'You can't drive. I'll take you.'

'Not a chance in hell.' Annie turned to face her. Her expression was set. 'I am going nowhere with you. Understand? I will see my own doctor, myself. Now. Leave. Me. Alone.'

George watched helplessly as her sister strode from the room. A few moments later the door slammed. The window juddered again. She slid her bag from her shoulder and let it drop back onto the table, then picked up her mobile. She typed a quick message to her nephew. *Your mother just had a bit of a fall but won't let me take her to the doctor. Please make sure she goes.* Sighing unhappily, she put the phone back down. She turned to Harry, who was still sitting in the exact same position at the table.

'And then there were two.'

He hunched his shoulders, staring at his phone. George rolled her eyes and turned away. She went into the kitchen and got two Panadol from her mother's medicine cabinet, washing them down with water. It did seem that Annie had had a remarkably lucky escape. The veranda was not particularly high, but any fall could be dangerous. She was willing to bet that her sister would have quite a few bruises by tomorrow. But this latest episode wasn't going to help things.

Outside the sky was like lead. It seemed only fitting. She put on the kettle and got Harry's mug from the drainer. It probably *had* seemed to Annie that her two sisters paired up as children, but that was mainly because there were only two years between them, and four years between her and Annie. That made a lot of difference once. As adults though, Kat probably could have made the exact same argument. And it was certainly untrue for Annie to claim that she never got her own way. She most certainly did.

Although not in the overt way favoured by Kat, but more a passive aggressive undermining. Like just before.

The kettle whistled. She made Harry a fresh mug of coffee and took it over to the table. Then she picked up the rolls of tape from the floor and piled them back into the bowl. Nearby was the sheet of paper where she had started the to-do list. She scanned it, searching for a reference to the railing repair, which she was sure she'd included a few days ago. It wasn't there. She sighed, and then added it in block letters. Better late than never.

'Look,' she said to Harry, waving the sheet of paper. 'At least I'm *doing* something. Besides, what difference would it have made? It's not like she did a risk assessment before sticking her butt through the damn thing. Am I right?'

'No,' said Harry.

George put it back down and sighed again. She felt a surge of resentment that they had both left. It would serve them right if she left also, except that there was nowhere she wanted to be more than here. She stared out at the veranda, with the egg-chair gaily covered with metres of tape and nearby, the gaping, accusatory hole in the railing. She couldn't believe that Annie had just fallen through that. She felt sick. Behind her, Harry abruptly rose. She turned to watch as he rearranged the cookies so that he could balance his mug on the plate. He lifted it carefully and shambled from the room. Shortly afterwards she heard his heavy footsteps on the stairs. When they ceased, it was like the silence itself was cumbersome. She took a deep breath, letting it out slowly as she gazed around.

'And then,' she said to nobody except herself. 'Then there was one.'

Chapter Eight

Wednesday afternoon

This afternoon I just watched my Harry having his afternoon nap. I never had time to do that with the girls. Or maybe it never occurred to me? But he's so beautiful. Different from his sisters. Less independent maybe, more mine. He needs me. Or maybe the real difference is simply that I loved his father so much. Maybe that's it.

George was instantly aware that something about this entry jarred. And not just the surfeit of maybes. At first she assumed it was the favouritism, something she and her sisters had always just accepted as the way things were. After all, Harry was the baby of the family, and the only boy, and it had been clear, early, that he had a disability. Even though it was still a little confronting to see the favouritism laid out in black and white, there was something ... more. She frowned as she re-read the short paragraph. It took a few moments for the real issue to land. When it did, she rocked backwards and put a hand on the wall to steady herself. Her eyes flew over the entry yet again in disbelief, but there was no mistaking the meaning. The real difference was *his* father. As opposed to *their* father.

The wording wedged in her throat like something swallowed the wrong way, and then dropped abruptly to the pit of her stomach. With diary still in hand, she walked over to the other side of the room and then back. She stared towards the array of Christmas decorations spread across the desk, but they were just blurs of red and gold and silver that splodged across her vision.

It was like the pieces of a jigsaw puzzle had just fallen into place. The sin, the letter, the *Rocky Horror* ticket. Even the decision Enid had to make, which was three against one. The three had been her daughters, and the one had been her son. This child who had arrived six years after the last. After all the baby paraphernalia had been given away. George's eyes widened further as each piece became the whole. Her mother had indeed had an affair, and Harry was the result. Her mother. Had. An affair.

Suddenly the diary was too great a weight. She dropped it onto the desk, where it nestled against a green-and-red-striped Christmas stocking. Harry was the result of an affair. He was their half-brother. Her mother had met with another man, gone to musicals and god knows what else. Probably seedy motels with half-lit vacancy signs and stained candlewick bedspreads. Or perhaps an inner-city apartment with a spa, where she indulged in fruity wine, feta and figs. George's mind spun away from this last. It was one correlation too far.

Had her father been aware? She searched back over his behaviour, his placid affection towards their mother. She felt a wash of almost painful pity for him, regardless. It had certainly never affected his parenting. If anything he had treated Harry even gentler. Overcompensation perhaps? An awareness that he had come within a whisker of losing his wife?

Now she *had* to share the diary – sooner rather than later. This was too huge to contain. At the same time, the thought of watching as her sisters read it through, when she herself still had about half to go, was unthinkable. She stared at it. The only solution was to finish it now. She had no choice. She hooked the desk chair with her foot and pulled it over, then dropped down heavily. After polishing her glasses, she picked up the diary, opening it gingerly and shaking her head as she re-read the last entry again.

'What's that?'

George started. She slapped the diary closed and stared across at her daughter. 'Rhyll! You gave me a heart attack!'

'Hmm. Maybe not?'

'You know what I mean. What on earth are you doing here?'

Rhyll's eyes flicked across the decoration-strewn desk and then to the Christmas tree leaning against one wall. 'I've come to help.'

'Really?'

'Yes really.' Her gaze settled on her mother. 'You don't have to act like it's such a shock. I messaged before. She was my granma too, you know.'

'Of course!' said George quickly. 'It's just I didn't expect you here. Right now.'

'Must be your lucky day then. Where are the others?'

'Oh, um. Just running errands.'

Rhyll looked at her from under her fringe and then shrugged. 'Whatever. So whaddya want me to do?'

'Let's see,' said George, injecting enthusiasm into her voice. 'I know! Your Aunt Annie was laying out Granma's jewellery on the coffee table. You could finish that for her?'

'Sure.'

George watched her leave. She looked down at the diary and chewed her lip as she came to a decision, then rose to follow Rhyll into the lounge room. Her daughter had already settled herself on the couch and was gazing at the jewellery. George went past into the dining room where she slipped the diary into her handbag and zipped it firmly closed. She looked over at Rhyll and briefly toyed with the idea of sharing this bombshell. *Hey, you know your recently deceased grandmother? The one with the pink vibrator? Well she also had an affair. With an apple afficionado in Mount Isa. And your Uncle Harry is the result.*

'What are you staring at?'

'Huh?' George blinked. 'Oh! Um, just you. I was thinking how nice it was for you to help.'

'Yeah. Besides, Dad was home early, watching the tennis. I hate tennis.'

'Ah, okay. How did you get here anyway? Did you catch the bus?'

'Not likely,' said Rhyll, a reply that made little sense given public transport was her usual mode of travel. She plucked a seed pearl bracelet from the jewellery box and draped it over her wrist. 'Nah, Leo gave me a lift.'

George frowned. 'And he didn't want to come in?'

'No.' Rhyll glanced at her mother through her fringe. 'Sorry. You'll have to wait to get your Leo fix. He and Evie were off to meet Tom.'

George took a deep breath and counted to three. 'Firstly, can we please not start with this rubbish about Leo fixes? Let's just have a pleasant afternoon, shall we?'

'And?'

'And what?'

Rhyll laid the bracelet on the black felt and then took an exaggeratingly deep breath. 'You said firstly. That implies there's a secondly to come.'

George narrowed her gaze. She didn't particularly care for being mimicked. But neither did she have the energy for yet another confrontation. 'You said they were meeting up with Tom. Why didn't you join them?'

'Nah,' replied Rhyll with a grimace. She straightened the bracelet and then picked up the pearl brooch. 'Hey, I don't remember Granma wearing half of these. Especially this one. They look like Puddle's eyes.'

George flinched. 'Yes. But back to Tom. Why did you pull a face just then? I thought you were all getting on? You went back to Tegan's for pizza!'

Rhyll shrugged. 'We were. We did.'

'And?'

'And like, he's just being a bit of a flog at the moment. That's all.'

'What's a flog?'

Rhyll rolled her eyes. She replaced the brooch and ran a finger over the pearls.

George watched her, waiting. She guessed that the term was derogatory so when no answer was forthcoming, continued with that assumption. 'So in what way is he being a flog then?'

'Come on, Mum.' Rhyll gave a snort of laughter. 'Surely even you picked up on the fact he's pissed off about all this?' She waved a hand, taking in the room. 'And like, he's great fun to be around when things are going well. But when they're not, then he *really* isn't. Besides, I think he's particularly pissed at me for not coming aboard his idea. You know, the piece of paper instead of the stickers.'

'Oh.' George recalled her daughter coming forward during the stand-off the day before, and helping to tip the balance by stating her preference. 'I meant to thank you for that too.'

'Sure.' Rhyll flashed another glance at her mother. 'Anyway, how come I'm the one doing all the work while you're just standing around?'

'I *am*,' retorted George, 'I was just taking a few minutes' break. If it's okay with you.'

'You don't need my permission,' said Rhyll dismissively. 'You do you.'

George lowered her brow, but it was wasted as Rhyll's attention was now wholly on the jewellery. She had picked up a ring inset with tiny diamond chips that matched the one in her nose. After a few moments, George turned away, going into the kitchen. There she put the kettle on but almost immediately flicked it off again. She'd had more than enough coffee. Outside, the sky still hung dark and leaden. It was like the world had been given a ceiling. Beneath it all, the veranda served as a stark reminder of what had happened earlier.

Since then, George had googled various delayed reactions to a fall, the most concerning of which was a subarachnoid haemorrhage. Despite its rather confusing name, this had nothing to do with spiders but instead referred to a ruptured membrane. One third of sufferers had a good recovery, one third were permanently disabled, and one third died. This did not seem like very good odds, but George's concerns had been somewhat allayed by a laconic reply from her nephew to the request that he take his mother to the doctor. *Lol. Okay. Sure.* It wasn't much, and she wasn't sure what was so humorous, but George now felt she had officially passed over the responsibility. Plus, of course, Annie herself was a nurse. Surely she would know a subarachnoid haemorrhage if she saw one, or felt one.

Annie's fall had now also been superseded somewhat by the news about Harry. George rolled it around in her mind, examining the edges. There were plenty. She shook her head, opening the pantry door instead to stare at the shelves. There were only a few staples left: some coffee, sugar, teabags, a few packets of biscuits. A few days ago Annie had commented about how there had been so many doubles in here, along with weird ingredients. But they both knew why. It was a rare visit to this house that any of them didn't leave without something pressed upon them. *Have you ever tried proper Canadian maple syrup? Here, have some of this sourdough! Look, mandarins were on special so I bought more than I need. Why are you still standing there? Grab a plastic bag!*

Her mother had once commented on the immense pride she took in a full pantry. Having grown up on World War II rationing, the ability to buy whatever she wanted, whenever she wanted, was something that never ceased to afford pleasure. George ran a finger along the edge of a bare shelf. She wished Annie had left the pantry to last. In stripping this, they had taken their mother back to where she had started. Enid would have hated that.

But then how well had she known the woman anyway? After all, who would have guessed that in amongst stocking her pantry, she'd also purchased a vibrator? And before that, she'd managed to have an *affair*. Right under their father's nose. Who knows what else she did with that proper Canadian maple syrup? As for Harry, was this then the reason she had always treated him differently? Nothing to do with his sex, or his birth order, or even disability, but because of this affair itself? That she did not seem to have regretted nearly as much as the decisions made afterwards.

From the lounge room came the faint sound of a musical beat. George supposed that Rhyll had plugged herself to her mobile with earphones. There wouldn't be anything else from her for a while. She needed to keep herself busy also. Both physically and mentally. Keep her mind well away from Harry and affairs and maple syrup. She checked her phone to see if Annie had finally replied, or if Kat had checked in, but there was nothing. On a brighter note, there was also nothing from Guy. Perhaps he had finally taken the hint.

She looked around, her gaze settling on what had always been known as the Tupperware cupboard. She had copied this moniker in her own house, where this had also been the one cupboard where toddlers had been allowed free rein. During those years, the contents had spent as much time on the floor as inside. Those were better memories. She began the task of clearing out her mother's. Along with the Tupperware, there were a multitude of takeaway containers, glass jars, and a staggering amount of spare lids.

'Are you and Dad going to get a divorce?'

George froze, her hand around an ancient jam-preserving jar. 'Pardon?'

'I said are you and Dad going to get a divorce?'

George rose slowly. She put the jar on the bench and dusted down her pants before walking around the corner. Rhyll was still on the couch, her attention seemingly on the additional jewellery now laid out neatly across the felt. One earbud was in place but the other dangled across her shoulder. The music had stopped. George stared at her daughter, willing her to look up. '*What* did you ask me?'

'If you and Dad were going to get a divorce.' Rhyll moved a pair of earrings a little to the right. 'It's like, a yes or no question. Simple really.'

George ignored the second part of this statement. It was far from simple. She played for time. 'Why would you ask that?'

'A better question would be why won't you answer,' said Rhyll. She finally turned to look at her mother. 'Which probably says everything, really.'

'It says *nothing*!' protested George. 'Of course we're not getting a divorce. I don't know why you'd even *think* that!'

Rhyll lifted an eyebrow. It disappeared into her fringe. For a moment she looked very much like her Aunt Kat. 'Oh, *I* don't know,' she said. 'Maybe because you never spend any time together? Or because you avoid each other whenever you can?'

'I'll have you know we played Monopoly last night!' said George hotly. 'Together!'

'Sure you did,' said Rhyll with a smirk.

'We did! Why would I even say that if we didn't?'

Rhyll shrugged. 'Why would you do half the things you do?'

George felt a surge of exasperation. She swallowed it before it could break free. The conversation seemed to have taken an unexpected turn.

'Forget I asked,' said Rhyll. She returned her attention to the jewellery.

George stood in the doorway, uncertain how to respond. She really didn't want to have this discussion, but nor did she want to leave it like this. She was washed with a sense of unfairness. Her mother had managed to have an affair right in front of them, which had even produced an additional child. Yet nobody had been the wiser. While she, George, couldn't even negotiate through a flat, slightly adulterous spot in her own marriage without getting the third degree.

'I said forget it. You can go back to whatever you're doing.'

George continued to gaze at her. Such a prickly child. She might look like her father, but in personality, George had long suspected, her daughter was far more like Annie. She also recognised that in her own way, Rhyll was reaching out. She cleared her throat. 'So if we ever *did*, um, separate and I'm not saying we would, but if we *did* ... would you be upset?'

Rhyll shrugged again. 'Not really.'

'Oh.'

'Like, if you're not happy together, then do something about it.' Rhyll looked over again. Her face was serious. 'I mean, life's short. And you're both well over halfway through.'

'Ah, yes. That we are.'

Rhyll kept her gaze on her mother for a few more moments, as if expecting her to add something, then looked back down at the jewellery. She picked out a fragment of tarnished necklace, with an oversized, clearly fake diamond. There must have been a sentimental reason for keeping such a piece. But it was too late to ask.

'Who would you go with?' asked George abruptly.

'What?' Rhyll glanced across. She sneered. 'Why? Are you going to like, battle over custody?' She snorted. 'That'd be the day. Besides, I'm not a kid. I can make my own way.'

This last statement was so obviously false that it wasn't worth a response. Rhyll currently enjoyed free board and lodging and still couldn't even afford to run a car. Let alone anything else. George turned away, catching sight of the gaily wrapped chair on the veranda.

'I see what you and your brother did with the chair,' she said, looking back at her daughter. 'We're not going to have any problems there, are we?'

'Nah,' said Rhyll, still focussed on the jewellery. 'We're just shit-stirring each other. Might as well have some fun. Otherwise this is all ...' she hesitated, laying the tarnished fragment gently on the felt. 'All too frigging sad.'

'Then you don't really want it?'

Rhyll shrugged. 'We'll see. So are you going to tell me the real reason that the aunts aren't here?'

George blinked at yet another change in conversation. But then, maybe it really wasn't. 'They had an argument. Pressing each other's buttons. Shit-stirring. But it went too far.'

'Ah. Interesting.'

'Yes, your Aunt Annie has a bee in her bonnet about—'

'The sticker system,' said Rhyll, finishing for her. She looked up. 'I know. Tom said.'

'Hmm. And did he happen to tell you *why* she's not happy about it?'

'Just that you two always bully her. Especially Aunt Kat. And now she's stuck with this rush job when she'd have rather taken the time to talk about things.'

George grimaced before she could stop herself. She could think of nothing worse. It wasn't that she didn't want to share memories, but only as addendums. She opened her mouth to reply but was stopped by the sound of keys in the front door. Shortly afterwards her older sister appeared in the doorway. She took in the scene, nodding approvingly at the sight of Rhyll on the couch.

'You've come to help? Great! The more the merrier! Oh, and actually I was going to ring you. I wanted to ask you if you were doing anything tonight?'

Rhyll looked surprised. 'Me? No, nothing. Why?'

'I was wondering if you'd stay here. I've decided I really need a break.' Kat sent a fleeting glance towards George before continuing. 'I thought I'd catch up with some friends in town. And we don't really want to leave Harry alone just yet.'

'Oh. Yeah. Sure.'

'Are you all right?' asked George of her sister with concern.

'Sure. It's just harder than I expected.' Kat shrugged. 'All this. Staying here. You know.'

George frowned. 'You're not having second thoughts, are you?'

'No,' replied Kat. She shook her head for emphasis. 'Not at all. I'll be fine when I get rid of all this.' She looked around the room. 'And get my things in. My own bed.' She grimaced, and then turned to Rhyll, continuing briskly, 'Anyway, sorry about the short notice. I'll be heading off soon anyway. I've got an appointment for my eyebrows later, so I may as well just stay in town afterwards.'

'Sure,' said Rhyll.

'Your eyebrows?' repeated George, confused. Kat had made it sound like they were pets, being taken for their annual check-up.

'Yeah, I'm getting them tattooed. Feathered style. Booked it months ago. This woman, she comes down from Sydney twice a year, best in the game. A true artist.'

'Cool,' said Rhyll. 'Just don't go all Frida Kahlo.'

'Ha! I won't.'

George was peering at her sister's eyebrows. There were two of them, and they were even. What more did anyone want?

'Much appreciated,' said Kat to Rhyll now. 'For staying tonight.' She flicked her gaze to George. 'So where's Annie?'

'She left just after you. Um, she had a bit of an accident. Hasn't been back. And Harry disappeared as soon as you both shot through. So it's just been me. I mean us. By the way, I'm glad you're having a break tonight.' George paused to give her sister a meaningful look, one that expressed her awareness of how hard it had been. 'You deserve it.'

Kat shrugged again. She slid her bag from her shoulder and dumped it on an armchair, then massaged her neck, flinching as it gave an audible gristly crack. 'What sort of accident?'

'Just, um, a bit of a fall. Oh, and I also got the bathroom cabinets done. Plus I've made a start on the Tupperware cupboard. Rhyll's finishing off the jewellery. In fact I think we should both get an award.' George put her head to the side. 'Are you sure you're okay?'

Kat shrugged. 'She just really gets to me sometimes, you know? So passive aggressive. I'd rather she just come out and say what she really means.'

'Hmm. I rather think she did.'

'You know what I mean.' Kat leaned against the armchair. 'Like where does she get off saying we're not acting like adults? Or how Mum would've wanted things? When it's really just how *she* wants things?'

'Um ...' George glanced over at Rhyll, who was listening to this exchange with interest. 'Maybe we should take this somewhere else.'

Rhyll snorted. 'Yeah, sure. That'd be right. Treat me like a five-year-old.'

'And she always accuses me of wanting my own way,' continued Kat. 'But she does it too! It's just *she* does it by undermining things. It's like fucking water torture. Drip, drip, drip.'

'Let's have coffee,' said George, making another attempt to move the conversation elsewhere. She did agree with Kat, but she also recalled Annie's accusation that they always ganged up. It felt like they were doing that now. Even worse with Rhyll being part of it.

'Okay. God, I've had more coffee this week than I've had in the past year.'

George led the way into the kitchen. Undeterred, Kat was still talking as she followed.

'And also, I *don't* actually get my own way that often! If anything, I give in just as much. Because you know what? I don't *care* if I get my own way, as long as the way is organised!'

'There were way too many ways in that sentence,' said George. She put the kettle on.

'What the hell?' exclaimed Kat. She was staring at the veranda with its severed railing.

'That was the accident,' said George. 'I told you before. It was rotten. The guttering's been leaking there. Annie fell through it.'

'You didn't say she fell through the bloody railing!' Kat went closer to the sliding door, staring. Then she turned to George. 'Is she all right?'

'I *wanted* to take her to the doctor,' said George defensively. 'But she was too angry. With both of us. Mostly you. Anyway, she left in a huff. Won't answer my texts now. But I let Tom know what happened. Asked him to make sure she went to the doctor.'

'Shit,' said Kat. She glanced back towards the veranda and shook her head. 'Well, that's not going to help mend fences.' She grimaced. 'No pun intended.'

'No. Probably not.'

Kat sighed. She sat down at the table and pulled over a sheet of paper, stared at it, and then slid it back. 'I don't know why she's so ticked off anyway. We put it all to the vote, didn't we? You agreed!'

'True.' George made a quieten-down gesture with her hand, flicking her eyes towards the lounge room. She continued in a lower voice. 'But see, that's the thing. She feels like we always pair up against her.'

'Oh, what crap.'

'Is it?' George frowned. She had a sudden image of their younger sister, in the kitchen, her shoulders shaking as she cried. 'You know, we *do* seem to be on the same page quite often. Maybe we don't give her enough space to catch up.'

Kat rolled her eyes. 'Well maybe it shouldn't take her so bloody long then. She fluffs around like there's no tomorrow! For god's sake, if it was up to her, we'd be still sitting here *discussing* things!'

'Look, I get what you're saying.' George paused as she got down two mugs. 'But everyone does things at a different pace. Maybe we did rush her a bit.'

Kat raised an eyebrow. 'You mean, *I* rushed her a bit.'

'I suppose I do.' George nodded. She spooned coffee into the mugs. 'And it's great when you get the bit between your teeth but it can seem, sometimes, a little … well—'

'Bossy?'

George flicked a glance at her sister. She softened it with a smile. 'Yeah. And let's face it, in that regard, Tom's a bit the same. So Annie gets it from both sides.'

Kat grimaced, but George wasn't sure whether it was in response to the comparison with Tom, or their sister's plight. The kettle whistled so she switched off the gas and then filled the mugs. Cookie crumbs were scattered across the bench from earlier. Annie had brought those. She turned back to Kat. 'It can't be easy being the youngest of us three. Maybe she brings a lot of this baggage from when we were kids. We *did* pick on her at times.'

'I suppose. But it wasn't easy being the oldest either!'

George gave a sudden laugh. 'Ha! You were *born* to be the oldest! Literally as well as figuratively! Imagine if *you*'d been the youngest? Oh my god! You'd have been giving us directions in utero!'

'I hardly think …' Kat paused as a grin spread across her face. 'Okay, point taken.'

'And then you've got the fact she's probably had the hardest road of us all as an adult.' The smile slipped off George's face. She kept her voice low. 'That bloody Brad.'

Kat nodded slowly. She took her mug of coffee from George and wrapped her hands around it. 'Maybe I'll give her a call tonight. Talk things over.'

George liked the sound of that. She slid her phone closer to see if Annie had answered any of the earlier messages. Still nothing. From the lounge room came Harry's voice, saying hello to Rhyll. He shambled into the dining room, putting his blue mug down on the bench before taking the chair beside Kat. He took his phone from his pocket and also a small model of a sarcophagus, lining up both neatly on the table before him.

'The word sarcophagus comes from the Greek word for flesh,' he said, as if picking up an earlier conversation. 'Sark. All together sarcophagus means flesh-eating. George pushed Annie off the veranda.'

'I most certainly did *not*!' said George hotly. She turned to Kat. 'I was reaching out for her, when she began sort of teetering. I did *not* push her.'

'Interesting,' said Rhyll from the lounge room.

Harry straightened his sarcophagus. 'And the Egyptians used to remove their brains through the nose with a metal rod.'

'What? As a hobby?' asked Rhyll. 'Seems a little counterproductive.'

'Unlikely to be a hobby,' said Kat. 'I'd say it'd be the sort of thing you'd only do once.'

Harry gave them both a puzzled look and then picked up his sarcophagus, turning it over in his hands. He appeared to be now lost in thought.

'I'm having second thoughts about moving in with you,' commented Kat with a grimace. 'You seem way too focussed on the macabre.'

George was still focussed on her sister. 'I did *not* push her!' she said insistently.

'Calm down,' said Kat. 'I believe you. Not your style.'

'Hmm,' said Rhyll from the lounge room. 'Methinks the lady doth protest too much.'

George rolled her eyes but didn't respond. She busied herself preparing Harry's coffee and then, while she waited for the kettle to boil again, glanced over at him crossly, still bothered by his accusation. Her irritation faded as she recalled the diary entry. They had always assumed that he took after their mother, like the rest of them, but what if the reason he looked nothing like their father was more straightforward? For all they knew, he might be the spitting image of his own. Somewhere there was a sandy-haired man with a penchant for apples and an eidetic memory for all things Wikipedia. If Rhyll hadn't been there, she thought, she would have shared the news with Kat right now, whether she had finished the diary or not. Instead she remained silent as she finished making the coffee, bringing the mug over to the table.

'Hey,' said Rhyll, coming into the room. 'Don't *I* get one?'

'Sure,' said George, refilling the kettle.

'Thanks a lot,' said Rhyll. 'Always nice to feel included.' She turned away, holding her phone out to her aunt. 'Look at this.'

Kat leaned over. She frowned. 'What the hell? Are you kidding me?'

George hurried across. Rhyll's mobile was open at Facebook, paused on a recent post from Tom. She polished her glasses so that she could read the small print. *Sometimes adversity brings out the worst in people. And relatives are just those who share your blood.* Her eyes widened.

'No prizes for guessing who he means there,' commented Kat. 'Charming.'

'Maybe he thinks you pushed his mother too,' said Rhyll, her gaze flicking to the veranda.

George moved back into the kitchen. She felt a surge of annoyance at her daughter, and Harry, and also at her nephew, for being a jerk. Just as she had started to smooth things over between Kat and Annie, he had to throw a spanner into the works. She picked up her own phone and opened Facebook, then scrolled through until she found the post. A few of Tom's friends had already queried what he meant, or asked if he was okay. A blonde called Tammy Wyncroft said *can't wait to c u again. I'll make everything better.* This was followed by a winky face.

'Bloody hell,' said Kat crossly. 'This is all because he didn't get his own way with his stupid idea. Little shit.'

Given Tom was easily the tallest in their family, this probably wasn't the most apt description. George continued scrolling through Facebook until she found her younger sister's latest post. It had been last week, on the day of the funeral. Seventy-six friends had sent their best wishes. The kettle came to the boil, whistling shrilly.

'And do you know what? I reckon a lot of that was because I accused him of mansplaining earlier that day,' continued Kat. 'I *knew* he was ticked off then. Well, he wants adversity? I'll give him bloody adversity.'

George put her phone down. 'For god's sake, don't reply,' she said as she made Rhyll's coffee. 'Maybe it's not about you. I mean us. Or maybe it's just loyalty to his mother. She's probably all bruised, from the fall. In which case, it's sort of nice, isn't it? Him protecting her?'

'I have no problem with loyalty,' said Kat tersely. 'But I can't stand this habit of plastering personal stuff all over social media. And what's with these stupid coded messages?'

'Nothing coded about that,' said Rhyll cheerfully.

'Samuel Morse was born in 1791,' said Harry. He rearranged his sarcophagus slightly. 'He was a painter before becoming an inventor and his first wife died of a heart attack just after having a baby. She was twenty-five years old.'

'Twenty-five!' exclaimed Rhyll. 'That's young. Maybe she got pushed off a veranda?'

George didn't bother replying. She passed Rhyll her coffee and turned back to Kat. 'They all do that now. Social media is like a conversation. These oblique messages are a thing.'

'God, Mum!' Rhyll snorted. 'Could you *sound* more ancient?'

George shrugged. At the moment she felt ancient. Grainy with lack of sleep, nauseous from the conflict, still jittery from Annie's accident, and heavy with the knowledge about Harry. It was a lump behind her ribcage, overlapping the hollowness of loss but, unfortunately, doing little to fill it. Regardless, Tom's stupid Facebook post was the least of her problems.

She drank her coffee slowly. All three of her companions appeared to be engrossed in their phones. As if on cue, her own pinged with an incoming message. She picked it up, curling her hand automatically when she realised it was from Guy.

Dropped flowers around. Your husband's a nice bloke, isn't he? Likes the tennis.

George blinked. She could hear Kat offering to take Rhyll home to collect her overnight things, but their conversation wafted in the margins of her shock. Guy had gone to her house. He had met Simon. She re-read the message, hoping desperately that she had misinterpreted. She hadn't. Another message pinged in.

Nice place you have. Very suburban.

George shook her head in disbelief. She was having problems absorbing what had just happened. Along with everything else, it was like information overload. She typed slowly. Her fingers felt fat.

You went to my house? Are you serious?

She pressed send and then stared at the phone, willing a reply. Within a few seconds the three little dots appeared, blinking, and shortly afterwards came a message.

How could I not? You didn't answer my texts. You left me little choice. I was worried.

George's lips thinned. Her incomprehension dissipated in the wake of sudden anger. It was not often that she did get actually angry, but this only served to deepen the intensity. In an instant, any residual affection, or lust, was swept away. She was mortified that she had ever taken him into her life. He was a pompous git, so egotistical that he thought the world revolved around him. He hadn't just overstepped the mark, he had crushed it between his hairy knuckles. They were definitely finished.

She typed quickly, angrily. *You're an arse. It's over.*

'Are you all right?' asked Kat.

George glanced up. Both her sister and Rhyll were gazing at her, the first with concern and the second with curiosity. George swallowed, and then took a deep breath to regulate her emotions.

'I'm fine.' She mustered a smile. 'Just some stuff happening at work.'

'O-kay.'

Kat didn't sound wholly convinced but George didn't have time for that now. She looked back down at her phone, but Guy hadn't responded. She took another deep breath as she thought things through. There was no doubt that he had gone around there out of spite, but there was also no doubt that he wouldn't have divulged their relationship. Nevertheless her guilt had never felt so weighty. Simon had met him. Her two worlds had collided.

But if she was to be honest, there was also a sense of relief. Her hand had been forced and she'd ended it. No more Guy, no more cringey text messages, no more having to cater for him alongside everything else. All she wanted now was to finish here as quickly as possible. Then she could go home, act nonchalant about the unexpected visit from a work colleague, and perhaps make Simon his favourite meal to dissipate some of the heaviness of her remorse. She would listen to him talk about work, or golf, or tennis, and act wholly engaged. Maybe she would even initiate sex. One thing was for sure, she would never do anything like this again. Not while the marriage was still intact. The brief moments of pleasure weren't worth it.

And once she had offset her culpability in this respect, then she would remove herself long enough to read the rest of the diary. Deferred gratification; a reward for being the perfect wife. She glanced over at her handbag. Maybe the very next entry would give lie to everything that had come before. Maybe it was all fantasy, or fiction, or the idea for a book. Even if the worst was true, as she already suspected it was, then at least she would know all. And she could bring the diary back tomorrow and hand it over. The whole thing. This would most likely even bridge the breach between all three of them. Maybe she could share the Guy debacle with Kat as well, and then let all three of her sisters commiserate with her about what a dick he turned out to be. Because there was one thing that Tom had omitted with his crap about adversity. It was so much easier when it was shared.

Chapter Nine

Wednesday evening

George stared at her pale belly, rising ever so slightly out of the water like an atoll. When she had first lowered herself into the bath, almost an hour ago, her belly, and everything else, had been covered with bubbles. Those were long gone, along with the warmth. She had shaved everything that needed shaving, anointed various parts of her flesh with scented body oil, and deep-conditioned her hair. Now she just needed to actually get out of the bath, get dressed, and await Simon's return from wherever he'd gone. It was just a little difficult to actually press the go button.

She finally hoisted herself up just as her oiled skin was turning prune-like. After drying off, she took some time selecting her outfit. It had to be flattering, but not obviously so. She settled on sleek leggings with a silky, bronze-coloured tunic top that she thought complemented her skin tone. Then she brushed out her hair, applied some makeup and sprayed herself with the perfume that Simon had given her for Christmas. She stood back to examine the effect and nodded. This was as good as it got.

In the kitchen, she bobbed down in front of the oven to check the spinach and feta lasagne that she had picked up on the way home. It was one of Simon's favourites. Music could be heard from the deck, where Leo was lounging at the outdoor setting along with Evie and a few other friends. They were having pre-dinner drinks before heading out for the night. One of the girls had a loud, braying laugh that periodically punctuated the music. This was another reason that George had stayed in the bath so long.

She turned up the air-conditioner and then put together a tossed salad before slicing up a baguette. The flowers from Guy sat on the dining room table. She would have thrown them out but she thought that would have looked suspicious. So now she would have to live with them for at least a few days, and then they could join all the others in the wheelie bin. Out on the deck, she saw Leo rise and shortly afterwards he came in through the French doors. He was wearing his paisley waistcoat again, this time with black pants. He leaned against the island bench and regarded her pensively. George kept working but after a few moments, when he still hadn't said anything, began to feel uncomfortable.

'Um, why are you staring at me?'

'I was just thinking. I don't *have* to go out. I can stay here if you'd rather.'

George was filled with a sense of warmth. She smiled at him. 'No, that's fine. I'm fine.'

'It's nothing special, tonight,' he continued. 'Just I told everyone to keep me busy this week. So I didn't … you know.'

'I know,' said George. She needed him to stop before her smile began to tremble, but she also needed him to continue.

'So I could easily cancel. We could watch something if you like. Netflix?'

She shook her head. 'Thanks, I really appreciate the offer, but it's fine. Your dad will be home soon. We'll have a nice quiet dinner. You go enjoy yourself.'

Leo pushed himself away from the bench and then, standing back, scanned her outfit. He grinned. 'Ah! And look at you, all dolled up. Message received. Romantic dinner, hey?'

'Don't be ridiculous.'

'Well, then I hope he's in a better mood than before.' Leo went past her to the fridge, removing a few stubbies of beer. He closed the fridge and then pressed one of the beers against his forehead. 'Shit, it's hot. Friend of yours, was he? The guy who pissed him off?'

'You were here?' asked George with surprise. She flicked to the latter half of his statement with rising panic. 'What do you mean, pissed off? What did he say?'

Leo shrugged. 'Nothing much.'

'So why was your father pissed off?'

'Probably looking forward to watching the tennis. Then he had to make polite chitchat. I think he holds you responsible. Because honestly, the bloke seemed a bit of a dick.'

'He is,' said George with feeling. She prodded at the lettuce with a salad server.

'How do you know him anyway?'

'Just through work. So you were here the whole time then? With them?'

Leo rolled the stubbie across his forehead. 'Most of it. Why'd you ask?'

'No reason.' George felt a wave of relief. If the conversation had turned to, say, adultery or pistols at dawn, then Leo would have known. She pointed towards the decking with her salad server. 'Aren't your friends waiting for their drinks?'

Right on cue, the girl on the deck burst into a cacophony of laughter. George flinched. From the decking, Evie waved at her cheerfully. She waved back, still feeling Leo's gaze. He was now leaning against the fridge and didn't seem in a hurry to leave. She prodded at the lettuce again and a mushroom skittered from the bowl. She bent to pick it up.

'Hmm. Is that spinach and feta lasagne I smell?'

'It sure is,' said George brightly as she straightened. She examined the mushroom and then tossed it back in the bowl. Two-second rule.

'So, here you are all gussied and perfumed, with Dad's favourite meal in the oven. Eager for me to get out of here. Exactly how badly did you stuff up?'

George stiffened. She took a deep breath before turning to face him. 'I'm not sure why you would assume I've stuffed up. Can't I cook your father a nice meal?'

'Probably not,' said Leo smartly. 'Given you usually buy them ready-made.'

'Very clever. Your friends must be dying of thirst by now.'

'They'll survive. Listen, has it got anything to do with Tom?'

George blinked. 'What?'

'Well, given he's pissed off with you too, and Aunt Kat, and then some guy turns up and pisses off Dad, who also seemed to be pissed at you, I thought, well, surely with so many people pissed off at my mother, there might be a connection.' Leo grinned. 'Deductive reasoning. I'm not just all looks, you know.'

'It has nothing to do with your cousin,' insisted George. She was on firm ground there at least. 'But how did you know Tom was annoyed with us?'

'Oh, he was carrying on about it this afternoon,' said Leo airily. 'Apparently the two of you are an affront to the democratic process. And the latest thing is that you had something to do with his mother now having a sprained wrist. Oh, and also you bully her. He went on about it so much that I ended up telling him to shut it.' Leo pushed off from the fridge and went over to the French doors. He turned as he got there and grinned at her. 'So now he's pissed off with me too. He was coming out with us tonight but pulled the pin.'

'Oh dear.'

'His loss,' said Leo, the grin still in place. 'Well, we'll be out of your hair soon and then you can enjoy your romantic dinner. Although, want some advice?'

'What?'

'You need candles. Maybe some wine. Soft music. Set the mood, you know.'

'Yes. Thanks. I'll keep that in mind.'

Leo opened the French doors awkwardly, his arms full of stubbies, and went through to the deck. He was greeted with cries of approval. Somebody must have made a joke because the loud girl began braying her donkey-laugh once more. George went into the laundry to check on Puddles. To her surprise, the dog wasn't there. Her heart stilled. She knew that cats often hid themselves away when it was their time, but did dogs? How would a twenty-five kilo, arthritic, near-blind labrador hide anyway? Her house wasn't the neatest, but it wasn't capable of absorbing that.

After a few moments spent staring at the spot where the dog should have been, George registered that the bed was missing too. Along with Sebastian the bear. It was even more unlikely that Puddles had taken his possessions for a final saunter into the unknown. She went over to the laundry window and pressed her face close to the flyscreen, peering towards the deck. And there was the dog, safely ensconced in his bed by Leo's feet.

Sebastian was tucked into his flank. George relaxed, smiling at the sight.

At that moment, Evie glanced across and met her gaze. The girl's eyes widened and George jerked back instinctively, then swore under her breath. She could have just waved again, instead now she looked like stalker-mum. Hiding in the laundry with her face pressed against the window. She sighed crossly and went into the kitchen to check her mobile for any messages. She slipped on her glasses. There were just two, in the group chat, from Kat.

Hi Annie, George tells me that you had a nasty fall. Hope everything is okay. And I'm sorry things went down so badly this morning. Let's talk tomorrow. Okay?

Hi again. Just reminding you both that we've got the appointment at the cemetery tomorrow afternoon. Although if that doesn't suit, happy to change it. Just let me know. I'm flexible.

George knew that this last message wasn't directed at her, but also at their youngest sister. Hence the extreme tractability. She could see that Annie had read it, but there was no reply. She typed one quickly herself, stressing her own flexibility. Then she sent a message to her husband.

Spinach & feta lasagne in the oven. Wine in the fridge. Rhyll's staying with Harry tonight and Leo's about to go out. Let's eat on the decking?

She considered this for a moment. Suitably nonchalant, but a little more friendly than she had been lately. She pressed send. The music outside stopped abruptly, leaving just the hum of the air-conditioner in its wake. The French doors opened and Leo and Evie came through, followed more slowly by Puddles. Leo was carrying the dog's bed and bear. He went past to return them to the laundry.

'You look good!' said Evie to George, with an evident surprise that rather negated the compliment itself.

'Thanks. Um, before, at the window, I was just checking on the dog.'

'Huh?'

'At the window,' explained George. 'In the laundry.'

Evie was chewing gum. She opened her mouth, stretching the gum from top teeth to bottom, as she gave this some thought. 'Huh?'

'Never mind,' said George, wishing fervently she hadn't mentioned it in the first place. Evie shrugged, then stuck a finger in her mouth and pierced the gum with a blue fingernail. She took it over to the bin.

Puddles had now made it into the kitchen. He dropped to the floor and curled himself near her feet, emitting a moist fart as he did so. Leo came back, brushing down his pants.

'Well, we're off! Enjoy your dinner date, Mum.'

'Oh, you have a *date*!' exclaimed Evie, as if this explained everything. 'How cute!'

'Yes. Precisely the word I would have used,' said George. She glanced towards the doors. 'Where are your friends?'

Leo went past, dropping a kiss on the top of her head. 'They went out the side gate. Okie dokie, see you tomorrow.'

As soon as they left, George stepped over the dog and went down to her bedroom to stare in the mirror. Perhaps the bronze top was too much, too obvious. She stripped it off and, after some deliberation, replaced it with a cowl-necked cotton number. But this wasn't enough. She pulled that off also and then gazed at the contents of her wardrobe. There really wasn't anything exactly right for the situation. She doubted there was anything at the stores either. It was a definite gap in the market.

After a few minutes, she returned to her original choice. Too much was probably just right, given the circumstances. She checked the time. It was just past six, which meant that surely Simon would be home at any moment. She hurried back into the kitchen and turned down the oven, then went out to the decking and wiped down the table. Now the question was how to arrange herself for when Simon first came in. Should she be in the kitchen, bustling busily, or in her study, seemingly focussed on work, or in the lounge room, watching television? After some consideration, she opted for the latter. The news was on, with more footage showing the devastation left behind from the fires. The good news was that they were now mostly under control. The bad news was that about 18 million hectares had been burnt, over 5,000 buildings destroyed, and thirty-four lives lost.

When George next glanced at the clock, it was six-forty. Simon was late. She got up to turn the oven down even further. She tossed the salad and then cracked open the wine, pouring herself a glass. When she returned to the couch, the weather was on. It was going to be hot again tomorrow, and the next day.

George checked her phone, but there were no new messages. She scrolled through to the one that she had sent Simon earlier. He hadn't even read it. She sighed as she put the phone down, then got some crackers from the pantry and ate them along with two Panadol while she finished her wine. She poured another glass and then fed Puddles, crushing his arthritis medication into the soft dog food. It was seven-thirty. She turned the oven off but didn't open it. The lasagne should stay hot for another twenty minutes or so. She went back into the lounge room to stand by the window overlooking the driveway. She stood with glass in hand, staring fixedly, as if by sheer will she could conjure Simon's car. At the same time, she readied herself to move quickly, not wanting a repeat of the laundry incident.

But quick reflexes weren't required. The only sign of life was a young couple who cut across from the small park over the road, walking their dog, and then disappeared around the curve of the crescent. It was now 7:50 pm. At 8:08 and then again at 8:15, a car did come down their road, but both times the occupant cruised past on the way to their own homes, where doubtless their monogamous spouses waited. At 8:30 pm, headlights began to appear on the main road in the distance. George took off her glasses and polished them with the hem of the tunic top, leaving scrunch marks across the bronze silk. The suspicion that Simon wasn't coming home for dinner at all crystallised. This happened occasionally, when he had been caught up at work, or had forgotten to inform her of a dinner meeting with a client, but certainly wasn't common. It was just horrid bad luck that it seemed to be happening now.

The lasagne, the baguette, the clothing and cloying perfume suddenly seemed ridiculous, even desperate. She finished her wine and then hurried into her bedroom, stripping the tunic top off again and pulling on the oversized t-shirt that she slept in. Back in the kitchen, she removed the lasagne from the oven. The edges had curled, and at some point it had bellied in the middle. George felt like doing the same thing. She covered it before sliding it into the fridge, along with the salad. She poured yet another glass of wine and ate some bread before storing the remainder away also. She wiped the counters down, furious at herself. Had she really thought it would be that simple? Was anything, at the moment, that simple?

The wine was starting to have a definite effect, most particularly around an enhanced ability to feel sorry for herself. George threw the dishcloth into the sink and then turned the air-conditioner down to its lowest setting. It was now 9:00 pm. Simon definitely

wasn't coming home for dinner. She reached for her mobile and
dialled his number, but it went straight to voicemail. For the first
time, a niggle of concern arose. Perhaps he wasn't out for dinner
with a client at all. Perhaps he had had an accident, and was even
now in emergency. On life-support. Being worked on so franti-
cally that nobody had time to ring his next of kin. She typed
quickly.

*Where are you? I'm worried! Answer me or I'll start ringing all the
hospitals!*

This time, after a few moments, the three little dots appeared.
And shortly afterwards, a message.

I'm fine. Staying at Callum's for a couple of days.

George frowned. Relief gave way to bemusement. While it
wasn't unusual for Simon to visit his brother Callum in Daylesford
every so often, he never stayed longer than one night because he
didn't get on with his brother's wife. Few people did, including
Callum. And he always gave George plenty of notice. But then ...
perhaps he had. George's frown deepened. There had been a lot
going on lately. It was possible that Simon had mentioned this visit
and she had simply failed to listen; a scenario far more likely than
him deciding on an impromptu visit without telling her. Plus, the
Australian Open was on, and both brothers were tennis aficiona-
dos. They did usually get tickets, particularly during the first week
of play.

All of which meant if she now queried the trip, he might very
well retaliate with the fact that he had told her. And she clearly
hadn't listened. Although, given what she was going through at
the moment, she did think he might have put her first. Changed
his plans to be here instead. Which gave her back the high ground,
apart from the fact she'd had an affair. She finished her wine, considering all angles, and then just sent a simple reply.

Say hi to them from me. Enjoy.

As George hit send, it occurred to her that there was a silver lining here. She now had the remainder of the evening to herself. And she also had the diary. Her spirits leaped with the realisation. Instead of spending time with her husband, she would spend it with her mother. She poured herself another glass, even though she was now well past her usual consumption, but the occasion seemed to call for it. Then she pulled over her handbag and rummaged within for the diary. It wasn't there.

George frowned. She opened the bag fully and peered inside. There was her purse, and sunglasses, a small packet of tissues, some chewing-gum, keys, four biros, an ancient lipstick, and a few crumpled receipts. But no diary. George tipped the contents out onto the bench. Coins spilled from her purse and the lipstick rolled in amongst the pile of catalogues at the end. But still no diary.

She thought back over the events of the day, questioning her recollection of storing the diary in her bag. The wine fuzzed along her thought processes. She was certain she had, but … perhaps she had *meant* to, but hadn't actually done it. Perhaps it was still in its hiding place. Disappointment clutched within. If it hadn't been for the fact she'd been drinking, she thought she would have gone right back to the house, now, and fetched it.

She leaned over the bench and lowered her head to her hands, staring down at the grey and black terrazzo pattern until it blurred into something resembling a chalkboard. She recalled doing the same at her mother's funeral when gazing across the rows of mourners, all dressed in greys and blacks. If it had really been a chalkboard though, she could have scraped her fingernails across and mirrored the sound within. After a few minutes, George lifted her head and wiped roughly at her eyes. Then she checked on the dog, turned the air-conditioner off and went to bed.

Chapter Ten

Thursday morning

George could hear Aunt Margaret's voice as soon as she opened the front door that morning. It wafted out from the kitchen area in a monologue that gave no clue who she was talking to. George grimaced as she closed the door quietly, and went straight down to the study to search for the diary. She tried the desk drawers first, then the wardrobe, and finally moved all the Christmas decorations aside in case it had slipped beneath. It wasn't there.

She stood in the centre of the room, her bag still over one shoulder, and frowned. Was it possible that the diary had somehow fallen from her handbag at some stage? Perhaps it was even now sitting in full view on the dining room table. Right in front of Aunt Margaret and whoever she was talking to. George paled. She hurried back out and into the lounge room, pausing to scan the couch, armchairs and coffee table. She could see the bulk of her aunt sitting at the table in the next room. She was explaining to somebody why Novak Djokovic was unlikely to win the Australian Open that year. Apparently his concentration wasn't up to the job. It was obvious that he was distracted.

'Probably because of that stuff going on back home,' said Aunt Margaret now. 'It's in all the papers. Terrible things. You know, with the war.'

George came into the room. Her daughter glanced up from the other side of the table and gave her a nod. Kat was in the kitchen, standing atop the island bench with her back to George. The kitchen clock was in her hands but she was frowning at their aunt.

'Um, I think you mean Syria,' she said. 'Djokovic comes from *Serbia* though. Not Syria.'

Aunt Margaret waved a hand dismissively. 'They're all the same.'

This was a statement of such sweeping racial ignorance that it clearly rendered Kat speechless. She stared at her aunt for a moment and then turned, as if registering George's presence. 'Thank god!' she exclaimed.

George started to smirk but was distracted by her sister's eyebrows. They were now batwings, several shades darker than her hair, edged by pink, puckery skin. Even more disturbingly, they glistened.

'The colour will fade over the next few days,' said Kat, a little defensively. She clambered down from the bench and put the clock aside, brushing her hands down her pants.

'Sure. If you say so,' said George. 'But um, why are they shiny?'

'That's just the gel. I need to put it on for a while. Keep them moist.'

'*I* think they're lovely,' said Aunt Margaret unexpectedly. She smiled at George. 'Nice to see you, dear. What do you think about me getting my eyebrows done too? Like Kathryn's?'

George transferred her attention to her aunt's pale, patchy eyebrows. She blinked, but then just nodded. There were more important things at stake. She came closer to the table, skimming her gaze across it. The bowl of coloured tapes, a pile of paper-work, a plate of mini muffins, coffee mugs. No diary.

'Looking for something?' asked Rhyll, following her gaze.

George shook her head. 'No. Just thinking of everything yet to be done.'

'There's not as much as it looks,' said Kat. She wiped dust from the clock and then brought it over to the table, laying it on top of the papers. 'We're right on track. And Rhyll got quite a bit done last night as well.' She turned to Aunt Margaret to explain. 'She stayed with Harry while I had a night off. Not that he can't look after himself, but we thought it's, well, a little soon.'

'Quite right,' said Aunt Margaret. 'Do you know, your mother would be so pleased with you all coming together like this. Step-ping up to the breach.'

George felt a flush of pride, moderated slightly by awareness that they weren't *all* quite coming together. She caught Kat's eye and grimaced. Rhyll called out a greeting to Harry and then he shuffled past, seating himself at the table opposite his aunt. George put down her handbag and went into the kitchen to put the kettle on. Through the window she could see that somebody, probably Kat, had transferred a large potted rubber tree from the front yard to cover the severed part of the railing. Was it possible that the diary had slipped out of her bag at home? Perhaps it had got caught up with the pile of discarded catalogues at the end of her kitchen bench and she just hadn't noticed. She *had* had a few drinks by then. It was the only explanation. Which meant the diary had to wait, yet again. She sighed with exasperation.

'So as I was saying,' said Aunt Margaret, 'Djokovic's out of the running this year. Mark my words. It'll be that wee Spanish fella. Nadal? Although with all his money, you'd think he could buy shorts that fit.'

Harry looked up. 'In 2006, Rafael Nadal and Roger Federer played the longest ever Wimbledon final until then. It lasted four hours and forty-eight minutes.'

'I rest my case,' said Aunt Margaret smugly.

Kat frowned. 'But how ... never mind.'

'Although it wasn't the longest match ever,' continued Harry. 'That went for eleven hours and five minutes. American John Isner won.'

'Good lord,' said George. 'Eleven hours? I get puffed just putting on runners.'

'When d'you ever put on runners?' asked Rhyll. She caught sight of her mother's face and shrugged. 'What? Am I not allowed to join the conversation?'

'As if that would stop you,' replied George. She got down a mug for Harry and then looked back at her daughter. Rhyll's eyes seemed a little puffy, as if she too hadn't slept well. 'Did Dad tell you he was spending a few days at Uncle Callum's?'

'Yeah. They're going to the tennis.'

George felt a wave of relief. So it *had* been planned. Albeit a little selfish, which pleased her. It provided balance for her own selfishness.

'And I'm staying here again tonight. Aunt Kat said it was okay.'

'Oh? Why?'

Rhyll shrugged. 'Maybe coz she likes me?'

'That's not what I meant and you know it,' retorted George. 'I meant ... oh, never mind.' She turned away from her daughter and finished making Harry's coffee. Doubtless Leo also had plans for the evening so she would be home alone, again. She took the mug over to the table before turning to the others. 'Coffee? Tea?'

'Cup of tea would be lovely, thanks,' said Aunt Margaret, resting her hands in her lap.

'This isn't my mug,' said Harry. He was gazing at it with a puzzled frown. 'It's not blue.'

'Your mug's not here.'

'It's in my room.'

'Well then—'

'I'll get it,' said Rhyll. '*I'll* look after you, Uncle Harry.'

George took a measured breath. She passed Harry's coffee to her sister, who was leaning against the bench with a grin. George put the kettle back on and dropped a teabag into another mug. Her sister pushed forward and came over to stand right by George. Her eyebrows were even shinier close up. She spoke in a whisper.

'Tom crossed out his priorities. On his stickers.'

'What?'

'Ssh!' Kat cast a glance towards the table. 'Tom. He crossed out his one and two. Rhyll told me. He and Annie dropped in last night while I was out.'

'But why would he do that?'

Kat shrugged. 'Don't know. But now his don't have priorities. There's just stickers.'

George puzzled this over. 'That's weird. Maybe he just changed his mind? Wanted to give it more thought?'

'Huh. *I* think he's telling himself that he's ticked off on behalf of his mother,' said Kat. 'He's trying to make a point. Like, he won't be part of all this. But I still think it's really because he's annoyed at me for not putting his idea to a vote.'

'But … then we just don't know what he really wants. What does that accomplish?'

'What are you girls whispering about over there?' asked Aunt Margaret.

'Nothing,' said George quickly. She poured boiling water into the mug and brought it over to the table along with the carton of milk. Opening her handbag, she removed her mobile and her glasses, slipping the former into a pocket and the latter on top of her head.

'Once upon a time they used to say whistringe,' said Harry. He was staring at his phone. 'Middle English. Now obsolete. It was for gossip.'

'Well, we're not whistringing,' said Kat firmly. She moved back to the bench. 'Just discussing what needs to get done today.'

Tegan came in through the sliding door. She was holding a pad and pen. 'Inventory of shed contents now complete.' She passed the pad to Kat and then spotted George behind her. 'Hello there! What'd you think of Aunt Kat's new eyebrows? Cool, hey?'

'Mega cool,' said George. 'You need sunglasses just for the glare.'

Rhyll came back with Harry's blue mug. She put it down on the bench and then flopped into her chair. 'Cool castle you're building down there, Uncle Harry.'

Harry glanced at her, clearly pleased. 'It's not Windsor Castle,' he said. 'I wanted Windsor Castle because Henry VIII is buried there. But the Lego Group don't do Windsor Castle.'

'Oh, shame.'

'He exploded in his coffin on the way there. Body gases. And fluids.'

'Brilliant!'

'I'm not sure that's the word I would use,' said Aunt Margaret. She stirred her tea. 'Although it's more common than you'd think. Your grandfather's brother did that. Big man. Teeth like a racehorse.'

George blinked. She wasn't sure what the teeth had to do with it. Except perhaps for shrapnel. She remade Harry's coffee and brought it over to the table, then brushed her hands together.

Today she was going to be organised and efficient. 'Right. I'm going to do my stickers then.'

'They called him Harry,' said Harry, turning his mug slightly. 'Like me. Even though his name was Henry. Like my friend Henry. But I don't think he liked peppermints.' He frowned for a moment, and then bent his head to his mobile, perhaps to check.

'Here you go.' Tegan had leaned over to check the list. She rustled through the bowl of tapes and then held out the salmon-pink roll towards George. 'This one's yours.'

Rhyll let out a yelp of laughter. 'Hey, that's the exact same colour as—'

'Yes,' said George. She grabbed it from her niece. 'I know.'

She made her departure quickly, leaving both Tegan and Aunt Margaret questioning Rhyll on what else was exactly that colour. Standing in the passage, George fiddled with the roll of tape as she examined the pictures on the walls. The only furniture was the bookcase with the set of Encyclopaedia Britannica and the grandfather clock. The latter bore two stickers, including a lime-green one that she assumed was Tom's as it had the number one crossed out. George shrugged. More fool him. She wished she'd brought the sheet of paper with her, detailing who belonged to which other colour. Just out of curiosity.

George's gaze settled on a small tapestry that she had always admired. It wasn't anything remarkable, just an embroidered country scene that had always reminded her of the rural town of Majic. They had visited there often as children. She wondered if that was why it had been purchased, and by whom. And for who? What was its story? George felt again that familiar heave of dull despair. There was nobody left to ask. Angrily, she tore a piece of tape off with her teeth and stuck it on the embossed silver frame. Her mother had always run a cloth over this frame, when she was cleaning. Then it had been the turn of the bookcase, after which she would lay the cloth down and wind the grandfather clock. Always an order to things.

And now, unless anybody else put a sticker on it, the little tapestry would be hers. And the encyclopaedias would go to whoever was lilac, and the grandfather clock to either lime-green or purple. Her mother's time as custodian was done. It made no difference to her now that the silver frame was polished, or the dinner set complete, or the grandfather clock regularly serviced. It rendered it all rather inconsequential.

Her anger dissipated. There was nobody, really, to be angry at. Tegan came into the hallway, holding her own roll of tape. It was blue. Her niece smiled at her and then examined the grandfather clock, her head tilted to one side as she stroked her hair pensively. George left her to it. She went into the study and stood staring at an array of items that had been laid out on the floor.

George slipped her glasses on and then bobbed down, steadying herself against the desk. There were a couple of old watches, a rather jaunty, very un-Enid like fedora, her father's old shaving kit, a stamp album, and some old school primers. Smiling with nostalgia, she leaned over and picked up *John and Betty*. The protagonists' shadows graced the orange cover. George flicked through it, recalling all the hours she'd spent trying to sound out John's and Betty's rather limited range of activities. On the title page was her own name, written in jagged letters. She wondered whether Marjorie Howden had ever written anything else or, having produced this opus, she had rested on her laurels. George sighed. Perhaps this was the only type of book that she herself was capable of writing.

This is George.

George is bereft. Her mother is dead.

She will never see her again.

But George still needs her mother. She also needs her sisters, including the one who fell off the veranda. She also needs to tell them that their brother has a different father.

None of this is easy.

Also, George has not been behaving well. She fornicated with a man who was, when all is said and done, a bit of a tool. He was also not her husband.

George is unhappy. She knows that she has brought most of this upon herself. Except for the mother dying bit. But certainly the rest.

Don't be like George.

She grimaced. It would probably be a fairly niche market. Tossing the book back onto the chair, she suddenly registered that there was a purple sticker on the front. George frowned as she tried to recall who was purple. Annie. Her lips thinned. Her sister had put a sticker on the book despite it not even being hers to start with. It was like she was determined to make things worse. George tore another piece of her own tape and pasted it straight across the front cover, beneath the title.

'How's it going?' asked Kat from the doorway.

'She put a sticker on my *John and Betty* book,' said George grimly.

'Huh?' Kat followed the pointing finger. 'Oh, I see. And this matters because you planned to what? Re-read it?'

'It's got my name in it!'

Kat shrugged. 'In all fairness, she may well have used it after you. Now that I think of it, I probably used it *before* you. No doubt you're just the only one who wrote your name.'

'Still—'

'Look, everyone's got a right to put a sticker wherever they want,' said Kat dismissively. 'Let's not go looking for things to be aggrieved over. There's enough crap going on anyway. That's what I wanted to ask you. Do you have Tom on Facebook?'

'What?' George frowned as she adjusted to the change in subject. 'Of course I do. Why?'

'Check it.' Kat waved a hand impatiently as George continued to stare at her. 'Go on. Just check and see if you've still got him there.'

'Um, sure.' George took her phone from her pocket and opened Facebook. She scrolled through to her list of friends and then searched for her nephew's name. It didn't come up. Her frown deepened as she tried again.

'Not there, is it?' asked Kat with some satisfaction. 'Me either. He's defriended us.'

George looked up at her sister. 'You're kidding.'

'Nup. I just went to see if he'd posted anything else there, and voila! He's gone.'

'Wow.'

'What's wow?' asked Rhyll. She came into the room, twirling her roll of yellow tape around one finger.

'Your cousin has defriended us both on Facebook,' Kat said, her batwing brows almost meeting. It was like she was announcing a fatality. 'Check yours, Rhyll; maybe you've been damned by association?'

'Doubt it,' said Rhyll with a shrug. Nevertheless, she fished her mobile from her jeans pocket and examined it. A minute late she raised her head. 'Nah, still there.'

'How did you know which cousin?' asked George curiously.

Rhyll swept a withering gaze across, letting it settle for a second before speaking. 'Because, dear mother, I'm not an idiot. But like, thanks for your vote of confidence.' With that Rhyll turned on her heel, leaving her mother gaping after her.

'What the hell did she mean by that?'

'Well, she's got a point,' said Kat. 'Tegan would hardly be here playing happy families if she'd just wiped us, would she?'

'I suppose not.' George considered this. 'But still, bit of an overreaction?'

Kat shrugged, then squatted down to examine the items on the deflated mattress. 'Then again, maybe it's more a culmination than a single incident.' She picked up the shaving kit and unzipped it, then lifted it towards her nose, taking a deep breath. 'Ah. Old Spice with a hint of Brylcreem. That takes me back.' She glanced up. 'Anyway, back to Tom. Can you believe that? He's defriended us!'

'Maybe overreaction runs in the family,' said George. 'It just skipped our generation.'

'But I don't get it. What does he hope to achieve?'

George was still holding her phone, with Facebook open. She hadn't posted any updates for days, but friends were still adding to old posts, sending their sympathies, and shooting these back up to the top of her feed. 'Maybe he wanted a break,' she said slowly, gazing down at it.

Kat snorted, giving her opinion on that theory. She zipped up the shaving kit and smoothed out the mattress so that it sat in a little indentation of its own. George slipped her phone back into her pocket. She frowned.

'Hang on. Back up. What did you mean before by culmination? About Rhyll?'

Kat took her time before answering. 'Well … and I don't want you to take this the wrong way, but sometimes you treat her as a bit, well, younger than she is. No offence.'

'Oh, none taken,' said George with a sweep of her spare hand. 'But thank god you tacked that on the end. Otherwise I may well *have* taken offence.'

'God, not you too,' said Kat. She sat back on her haunches. 'It's bad enough having one sister ultra-sensitive. All I meant is that the two of you don't seem to have settled into your, I don't know … your *adult* relationship.' She shrugged as she returned her attention to the items on the floor. 'I'm not a mother though, so I suppose I don't understand how hard that transition is.'

George stared at the back of her sister's head. She suddenly recalled begging her parents to go guarantor for a car loan just after she got her licence at the age of eighteen. At the time she had no savings, a part-time job at the local milk bar, and was about to start university. She had blamed their refusal on her mother, wailing, 'You need to start treating me like an adult!' To which her mother had replied, 'I'll start treating you like an adult when you start behaving like one.' Thirty-seven years later, George nodded in agreement. Her mother had a point.

'Hey, remember this?' Kat held up the fedora. She was grinning.

'Yeah, sure. So you think Rhyll and I don't have an adult relationship then?'

Kat shrugged. She put the fedora down and picked up the stamp album, flicking through the pages. 'Maybe you're still in the process of redefining it. Finding common ground.'

'Common ground?' repeated George. 'You mean I need to spend most of my time in my room as well, staring at my computer?'

Kat dropped the stamp album and turned around. She was grinning. 'Um, isn't that what you already do? Didn't you just describe your job?'

'You know what I mean,' said George grumpily. A headache was beginning to pulse. She took off her glasses and polished them on her t-shirt.

'You two have got so much in common,' said Kat. Her grin had gone. 'And don't look at me like that, I mean it. You're both great writers, for starters. I *love* Rhyll's blog. It's fantastic.'

'Rhyll's blog?'

'Yeah. You know. *Beyond the Peripherals*. Hey, hang on.' Kat was looking at her curiously. 'You *have* read her blog?'

'Of course I have,' snapped George. She searched for a change in topic. 'You shouldn't have told her that before, about Tom defriending us.'

'Why on earth not?'

'Because I don't need my daughter knowing about issues we're having with our sister, that's why!' exclaimed George. Her hitherto mild irritation flared as her sister raised an eyebrow. 'She'll just use it as ammunition! And it's none of her business!'

'But … never mind.' Kat got to her feet and dusted her knees off. 'She was crying last night, you know.'

'What?'

'Rhyll. She was crying.' Kat flashed a glance towards the door and lowered her voice. 'I ended up coming back at around one and she was still up, sitting in the dark and watching some of Mum's home movies in the lounge. She was crying.'

'Oh.'

'Yes. Well, I'll leave you to it then.'

George watched her go, the surfeit of information throbbing at her temples. Rhyll had been crying. Watching home movies. Sitting in the dark by herself. The image was a knot in George's chest, bringing tears to her own eyes. She wanted to rush out to wherever her daughter was, wrap her arms around her and just *enfold* her pain. But she also knew that any such gesture would be firmly rejected, especially with others around.

Instead, after a few moments, she dragged out her mobile and googled her daughter's name. Nothing came up. She tried to recall the name of the blog that Kat had just mentioned, but the name hovered at the edge of her consciousness. There was too much going on up there. She stared at the still life of apples as she thought, tapping one finger against the phone.

After a few minutes, she tried Rhyll Tapscott. This time there were several results, the top being *Beyond the Peripherals*, hosted by WordPress. How could she have forgotten that, when it was so obviously a play on her own column? She pressed it and instantly the screen filled with a rather nicely laid-out blog. The title was in graffiti-style font, surrounded by icons of the past embedded into postage stamps. They fluttered down the sides of the page. The archived entries to the side indicated that the blog had been operational for around two years. It had 17,345 followers. George blinked as she read this again.

'Hey, Aunt George,' said Tegan, bouncing into the room. She held up her roll of tape. 'This is *so* hard.'

'What? Yes. Yes, I suppose it is.'

'I don't want to put one on anything anyone else has, but then I don't want to regret things later either. You know?'

'Yes,' said George, still distracted. 17,345 followers! She slid her phone into a pocket and focussed on her niece. 'You need to ignore the others though. Put them wherever you want. Don't be a people pleaser.'

'Oh. Okay.'

'Good luck with that though,' said George with feeling. She left the room, passing Harry in the hallway. He too was now staring at the grandfather clock. One arm was extended, like a sort of salute. It was studded with neatly cut pieces of bright red tape. In the dining room, Aunt Margaret was still sitting at the table.

She had a magazine spread out before her and appeared to have settled in for the day. Rhyll was nowhere in sight. Kat looked up from behind the kitchen bench as George entered the room and gestured for her to come over.

'I've been thinking,' she whispered as soon as George approached. 'About Tegan.'

'And?' prompted George. She peered through the kitchen window to see if Rhyll was outside. *Beyond the Peripherals* indeed. Couldn't she have been a little more original?

'Yes.' Kat leaned in a little closer. 'I've been thinking that when the house gets sold, maybe we should offer Tegan some of her father's share upfront? Especially if he gets a bigger portion.'

'Huh?' George frowned, trying to concentrate. Her sister's breath was very warm. 'Why though?'

'Well, because things are different for her than the rest of them. They still have parents to lean on. And I know for a fact that Annie is going to give Tom some of hers straight up. She said so. But if Tegan got even a small lump sum, she could put a deposit down on a flat. Get into the market. I rather think Mum would approve.'

George nodded slowly. Her sister was right. Their mother would most definitely want Tegan looked after. If anything, she had been more of a daughter than a grandchild.

'So we'll put it to Annie as a united front then?' continued Kat, stepping back. 'That Tegan should get a portion?'

'Yeah, I suppose so. That makes ...' George petered off as her sister's eyes slid over her shoulder. She turned around. Aunt Margaret was staring at them, her fingers frozen in the act of turning a page.

'Everything okay, Aunt Margaret?' asked Kat brightly. 'Would you like another cup of tea?'

Their aunt shook her head, the pleats beneath her chin wobbling. 'I … that is, no. I'm sorry, couldn't help overhearing. Oh dear. Are you *sure* that's the right move?'

'Um,' said Kat. She shrugged. 'Yes, we think so. It'll set her up for the future.'

'But …' Aunt Margaret looked down at her magazine and then closed it. She smoothed the cover. 'Such a big decision. Although I'm so glad you're being supportive on this. Your mother *would* be pleased, about that at least.'

'Agreed,' said Kat. She flicked a quick glance at George, lifting one shiny eyebrow.

Aunt Margaret used the table to help her stand. She stayed like that for a few minutes, still staring at the magazine and then finally lifted her gaze. 'As long as there's no regrets, that's all. You can't go backwards.'

Kat frowned. 'Yes. We know.'

Their aunt nodded. She pushed away from the table and hobbled slowly from the room. Shortly afterwards she could be heard talking to Harry in the hallway. Kat looked at George.

'Do you think senility has started in?'

'Shh!' said George. Behind her sister, she could see a bright red sticker plastered to the edge of the microwave, and the pantry door. She turned slowly. There was also one on the edge of every cupboard, and the kettle, and the unopened packet of biscuits on the bench. If she blurred her eyes, they were like splatters of blood. The kitchen was a crime scene.

Kat laughed, following her gaze. 'He's having a lovely time. At least it keeps him busy.'

George nodded. She didn't really have room for Harry at the moment, or Tegan, or Aunt Margaret. She could feel her mobile pressing against her thigh. It felt heavier than usual, perhaps because of those 17,345 followers. What it didn't have was any communication from her husband.

'I'm going out onto the veranda,' she said. 'Need some quiet time.'

'I sympathise,' said Kat with feeling.

George went past, pushing open the sliding door and being hit by the warmth of the afternoon. It was so still outside that the heat felt all-embracing, like a doona. Blowflies buzzed somnolently in the thick air. She could see the jagged edges of the railing through the rubber tree. George tore a few of the bands of tape across the egg-chair and settled herself down, fishing her mobile from her pocket. She thought for a few minutes, her headache now a dull throb, and then typed a message to Simon.

Hope you're enjoying yourself at the tennis. Don't forget I'm staying with Kat on Friday night so I'll see you Saturday.

She gazed at the phone, willing a reply. None came. She frowned, but then told herself that it was just her guilty conscience reading more into things than were actually there. If Guy had said anything that was actually incriminating, then Leo would have known. And Rhyll had confirmed that the visit to Callum's had been planned. Through the sliding door, she could see that her daughter had come back into the dining room. Instinctively George began to rise, but Rhyll continued into the kitchen where she leaned against the bench and began talking with her aunt, their voices just a murmur through the glass.

She lowered herself back into the chair. 17,345 followers. Glad of something to distract her, she repositioned her glasses and picked up her phone, opening the saved page and then the archives. It made sense to start at the beginning.

George's jaw slackened with surprise as she read. It almost instantly became clear that the title was similar for good reason. It had begun as a parody of her own. Rhyll had used George's own column, week by week, as a springboard, and then poked fun at it before going quite literally beyond the peripherals. Where George had highlighted a major historical figure, Rhyll had turned to a related, but more marginal woman. The week George wrote about Marie Antoinette, it had been Rosalie Lamorlière, her maidservant. She had done the same for the others, concentrating on the women once-removed, who truly did populate the margins of history. And then, perhaps as her own popularity had grown, Rhyll had then abandoned the parody and concentrated on her own selections. In the past year, George's own column hadn't even scored a mention.

She lowered the phone to her lap and looked back inside. Both Kat and Rhyll had vanished. Leaning back, she closed her eyes, her stomach tight with conflicting emotions. Surprise, hurt, and an almost grudging, but steadily growing pride. Because Rhyll was good. A little bit too sweary for George's taste, but undeniably good. She utilised a clever mix of information and dry humour, together with the occasional dollop of self-deprecation. Her latest addition had been Cleopatra's little sister. *The child was doomed from the start*, she wrote. *Born into a family who either married or murdered each other, she was also saddled with the unfortunate name of Arsinoe. Which sounds more like a cure for haemorrhoids than a ruler of Egypt. It's unlikely that a name like that was ever going to feature on a Hollywood blockbuster.*

There had been over a thousand likes for that entry, and eighty-seven comments, including one from a Casey who had said *Omg, so funny! Mrs Hurley would be so proud! Tell me more when we meet up later!* The only Casey that George knew was one who had been friends with Rhyll in high school, and Mrs Hurley had been their history teacher back then, so it must be the same Casey commenting here. She hadn't known that they had even kept in contact, let alone met socially.

George rubbed at her temples. *Beyond the Peripherals* had been operational for two years. How had she not known this? She *taught* writing and editing, and yet she had never been aware that her daughter had been capable of this. Sure, Rhyll had been quite creative as a child, and her writing had been above average, but this was so sleek, so professional. So popular. Hadn't Rhyll been proud? Hadn't she wanted to share the success? What happened to that little girl who had insisted every stick-figure drawing be stuck to the fridge?

On top of this came another thought, slithering into centre-stage. Maybe she was the only one who hadn't known. Kat certainly had, and probably so did Annie and Tom and Tegan. Leo definitely would. And most likely so had her mother. Had they all just assumed that she didn't want to talk about it? That she herself wasn't as proud as punch? Or maybe that she felt *threatened* in some way? Her head throbbed, but this time with confusion and hurt as she tried to disentangle the different possibilities. Beyond the peripherals indeed.

Chapter Eleven

Thursday afternoon

Ferntree Gully Cemetery was separated into two distinct parts; the first, hugging the main road, was the original section, with faded headstones bearing the names of those long dead. No doubt by now so were their children, and their grandchildren and even, in some cases, their great-grandchildren. The Dandenong Ranges rose majestically in the distance. A few trees afforded some shade, but most plots were left to bake beneath the afternoon sun. Towards the upper end was the office, neatly separating the older part from the new. It was a pale, weatherboard-clad building that looked more like a portable classroom. This was where Kat and George met the cemetery manager, Robert, a middle-aged man with a buzz cut and ruddy complexion. This latter might have been due to the temperature though, which was now nudging the high thirties.

'So then,' he said now, pausing to wipe his brow with a handkerchief. 'As I explained on the phone, there are no spare spaces on your father's wall, but there are some available nearby. Just not on that one. I'll take you up there now.'

'Can we wait a few minutes?' asked Kat. 'Our other sister is joining us.'

Robert looked at her steadily, as if wishing to impress the importance of his time. Then he nodded, taking a step back into the shade of the office roof where he mopped his forehead once more.

'You can leave us here,' added George helpfully. 'We'll give you a call when she comes?'

'Nah. All good.'

George exchanged glances with her sister, but it was difficult to read Kat's expression, given she was wearing a pair of oversized sunglasses. The upper curve of her batwing brows almost blended into the ebony frames. She bent her head to examine her phone, yet again, in case Annie had messaged. George shaded her eyes to scan the carpark by the main road and then the one at the side. She wondered if Annie was trying to make a statement by being late, although it was difficult to know exactly what sort of statement this might be. She herself just wanted to get this over with.

'I just got the weirdest text from Aunt Margaret,' said Kat, still gazing at her mobile. 'Something about Tegan and feminism and aren't we glad we're not living in the US.'

'Interesting,' replied George, even though it really wasn't. For somebody who appeared to think texts were pay-per-word, their aunt was also capable of sending streams of consciousness that were maze-like in their complexity.

Kat slipped the phone into a pocket. 'I'll deal with that later.' She turned towards the carparks. 'She's here,' she said, pointing towards Annie's red Mazda, which was pulling into one of the empty spaces to the side.

They watched as Annie exited the passenger side of the car. George realised that Tom must be driving his mother, possibly because of the accident the previous day. He was just a vague shape through the tinted windscreen, and the driver door stayed firmly closed. She waved but it was difficult to see if he returned the gesture. By now Annie was making the trek along the concrete driveway. She was wearing a floppy summer hat, sunglasses almost as large as Kat's, and a snow-white bandage that covered her left wrist and most of her hand. Her expression was grim.

As her sister approached, George was surprised by a curdle of acrimony. Despite her placating words to Kat about giving Annie the benefit of the doubt, she herself was quite resentful that their younger sister was making things so much more difficult. It was horrible enough, all of this, without having to deal with Annie's prickliness. It seemed to have swollen in the past few days, taking up the space that should have been filled by the three of them. Together.

'Ouch,' said Kat cheerily as Annie came to a halt. 'Looks like you really did hurt yourself.'

'Yes,' said Annie. She turned her head towards George briefly. 'Yes, I did.'

'What's the damage?' asked Kat.

'Bad sprain.'

'Oh, okay. Tough break.'

'Fortunately not,' said George tightly, feeling like she should add something. 'Luckily.'

'Yeah, that's me. Lucky.'

Robert came forward before either Kat or George could respond. He held out his hand.

'You must be the missing sister,' he said, shaking her good hand briskly. 'I'm Robert, the manager here. And now how about I take you three up to the wall, show you what's available there.'

He set off without waiting for an answer, leading the way around the office and into the new section. George snuck a glance at Annie as they walked and to her surprise their gaze met. It might have been a meaningful moment but unfortunately, her eyes on her sister, George caught her right foot against the corner of a gravestone and her leg folded, sending her stumbling atop the last resting place of Maria Lombardi, dearly beloved. With her right knee and both hands on the gravestone, she stared at Maria's picture, mounted in the centre of the headstone in a glassy oval frame. The old lady didn't look impressed.

'For god's sake, George!' snapped Kat. Some distance ahead, she had turned to see what was keeping them.

Annie reached out her good hand and helped George to her feet. It was obvious that she was trying desperately not to laugh. 'Are you all right?'

'Yes.' George dusted herself down. She examined her knee where it had hit the marble and although there didn't appear to be any outward damage, she thought she might have a bruise the next day. It stung.

'Paying your last respects, hey?'

Despite herself, George grinned. Her resentment curled itself into a ball, dampened by the humour. It made the ignominy of flinging herself on a stranger's grave almost worth it. 'I tried to call you,' she said, her grin fading. 'Find out how you were.'

Annie shrugged. 'I just didn't feel up to talking. Needed some time to myself.'

'I'm sorry, you know. That it happened.'

'Yeah. I know.'

George examined her sister. 'Tom defriended us,' she blurted. 'On Facebook.'

'He told me.' Annie chewed at her lip. 'Look, don't read too much into it. He's hurting. Plus worried about me. And it was probably more aimed at Kat anyway, but you got caught in the slipstream. Besides, it's just Facebook. And it's only temporary.'

'Temporary would be blocking us. Defriending is a bit more, well, harsh.'

'My god, you sound like a teenager.' Annie paused as Kat called impatiently from up ahead. 'Best we get a move on anyway,' she said. 'Don't want to keep Her Majesty waiting.'

George gave her a flat look as her irritation bounced back. She hadn't taken the whole Facebook thing as personally as Kat had seemed to, but Annie's explanation still felt short. They were *all* hurting. She followed her sister into the new section, leaving Maria Lombardi behind. George was quite familiar with this space as it was where they interred their father twenty years before. She had visited with her mother, or one of her sisters, on many occasions since. Marking his birthday, father's day, the anniversary of his death. These visits had however lessened as the years went by. The last time she had come was for his birthday almost twelve months ago.

The graves were far newer here, lined neatly in rows like schoolchildren awaiting a lesson. In the centre was an ornate fountain, surrounded by a circular hedge, the sound of cascading water almost meditative in the silence. They skirted past, heading towards where Kat and Robert stood by the rank of interment walls against the far fence. There were about six of them, each with a marble-grey facade, jutting about a metre from the fence. Their father was in the second one along, his plaque centrestage and third from the top. *Ronald Vincent Tapscott. 23rd March 1933 – 1st September 2000. Beloved father of Kathryn, Georgette, Anna and Harry. Father-in-law of Simon. Grandfather of Rhyll, Thomas, Tegan and Leo. Always loved, sadly missed.*

George stared at the inscription. Brad had missed inclusion
only by months. But had their mother even hesitated when she
added Harry? Had she thought about his real father? She jumped
as a cockatoo shrieked from behind her, transferring her gaze to
watch as it circled in, landing on the edge of the fountain. If she
believed in signs at all, she might have thought it had been sent by
her mother to admonish her for not minding her own business.
A few other cockatoos joined the first, shrieking at each other as
they took turns drinking. This put any such thoughts to rest. Enid
simply hadn't been that sociable.

'So as you can see,' said Robert, gesturing towards their
father's wall, 'unfortunately these are all taken. However, there's
some spots over here.' He turned to the facing wall and pointed.
'There, and there. Or of course, there's a few further up that I
could show you.'

'Hmm.' Kat shaded her eyes as she examined the two walls.
'Would it be possible for us to have some time alone? So that we
could decide?'

'Sure,' said Robert with an enthusiasm that suggested he was
just glad of the chance to get out of the sun. 'I'll just be in the
office. Take as much time as you need.'

Kat waited for him to leave before turning to her sisters.
'Thoughts?'

'I wanted them to be together,' said Annie. She was hugging
her bandaged hand against her chest as she gazed at their father's
plaque. He was surrounded by several members of the Wethering-
ton family, for whom 2004 appeared to have been a very bad year.

'I did ask whether they could be interred together,' said Kat.
'It's possible, but complicated. They'd have to remove Dad's ashes
and put them in the same urn as Mum's. Then there'd be, um,
leftovers. Quite a lot.'

George grimaced. Even apart from the ew factor, there were some complications with this plan that so far only she was aware of. The knowledge felt heavy. Would her mother have wanted to be conjoined with their father for eternity? Had he, in fact, been the love of her life? She gazed at her father's plaque, the embossed lettering growing gradually darker. It had been nearly twenty years and she still couldn't wrap her head about him being here, like this. It was impossible to imagine her mother joining him.

'We could always scatter them,' said Annie slowly. 'The, um, leftovers that is.'

Kat screwed up her face. 'I'm not sure Mum was the scattering type.'

'Agreed,' said George. The idea of scattering some of Enid's ashes anywhere was not appealing. As difficult as it was to imagine, she needed a place that she could at least visit and know that her mother was complete, in a sense. Her mind skittered to the crematorium at nearby Springvale, where Enid would be waiting her turn. The thought was like a sledgehammer to her gut. She closed it down instantly.

'Pity she wasn't the type who left clear instructions then,' said Annie acerbically. 'An agenda perhaps.'

Kat gave her a slow smile. 'Yes, that would have been *very* helpful.'

They stood in silence for a while, each examining their father's plaque and then turning to scan the facing wall, and the positions of the vacant spaces. Each plaque had a tiny brass vase moulded to one side. Some contained fresh flowers, or fading clusters of artificial blooms. Others, like those of the Wetheringtons, were either empty or held arrangements long dead. Their father's had a spray of artificial lavender. George had a sudden, sharp memory of that same spray sitting on her mother's kitchen bench around

Christmastime. At the time, she hadn't even thought to ask what it was for.

She turned away as tears sprung to her eyes. Alongside the image of the flowers, on the bench, was another of her mother being here alone, carefully arranging the lavender in her husband's vase. Possibly even on Christmas Day, before they all came over for lunch. The idea of it clutched at her chest and burned the sockets of her eyes. She scrabbled in her handbag for her sunglasses. Her sisters had the right idea there.

'Are you okay?' asked Annie.

'Yep. Sure,' said George, a little embarrassed by the huskiness of her voice. She unzipped the side pocket inside her bag and fumbled within. Her fingers curled around the sunglasses, brushing against something else. Something hard, and book-shaped. She froze with surprise, and then pulled open the bag further so that she could peer within. And there it was, the faded crimson cover unmistakable. George stared. She was certain that she hadn't put the diary in the zip pocket. But then, how else to explain its presence?

'You sure you're okay?' asked Annie again.

George nodded. 'I'm just trying to find my sunglasses. That's all.'

'They're in your hand,' said Kat.

'So they are.' George slipped them on and jammed the bag closed before turning back to her sisters. 'It's such a mess in there,' she said brightly. 'Everything but the kitchen sink!'

Kat lifted one of her batwing brows. 'Okay, well if you're sorted, how about we make a decision.' She looked from George to Annie and then back. 'Any ideas?'

'I'd still like them to be together,' said Annie. 'Maybe we could also do a pilgrimage, scatter the rest somewhere they both loved. How about where they met the first time?'

'Problematic,' replied Kat. 'Given they met while fruit picking, and that whole orchard has been an estate for the past forty years. Even if we found the right spot, I doubt the occupants of whatever house would appreciate us scattering ashes over their driveway.'

Annie's v formed above the bridge of her sunglasses. 'Bloody hell. It was just a thought.'

'Sorry,' said Kat after a moment. 'I didn't mean to be dismissive. It was a good idea.'

George left them to it. She walked around their wall and then between two of the adjacent ones, away from her sisters. There were more spare spaces here, but that wasn't why she'd come. She needed a moment to gather her thoughts. She *really* couldn't remember putting the diary into the zipped section of her bag, and although that would explain why it hadn't tumbled out when she'd upended it last night, surely she would have felt it there? Was it even remotely possible that somebody had taken the diary yesterday, and then returned it again to the zip pocket of her bag?

Her sisters' voices floated across the top of the wall. They seemed to now be discussing the possibility of moving their father's spot also, so that both parents could be interred side by side. George opened her bag and unzipped the pocket. The diary was still there, nestled securely against the silk lining. If anybody had taken it, there was no way they would have remained silent about its contents. Which meant that she *had* put it there, and then simply forgotten. Just like she had forgotten about Simon telling her that he was spending a few days at his brother's. It was a scary thought, because it rendered her tenuous grip on everything even less secure than she had imagined.

George rubbed at her eyes behind her sunglasses. She had to concentrate on the silver linings, not the clouds. The main thing was that she had the diary. And she could tick other things off too.

She and Annie were on speaking terms again, Guy was no longer
an issue, Simon was enjoying the tennis and would return, no
doubt, in a good mood, which also gave her the upper hand as he
had chosen his own pleasure over her grief. Plus Rhyll was spending another night at Kat's. The thought of her daughter reminded
her of the blog. 17,345 followers. Perhaps instead of spinach and
feta lasagne, she would cook up a feast that was everybody's favourite when they all came together on Saturday night. Perhaps they
could eat out on the deck like they used to. And perhaps she could
tell Rhyll just how proud she was.

All of which meant that tonight it would be just her and the
diary. She would be spending the evening with her mother. Not
with her ashes or her house or the division of her possessions, but
with her voice. It *was* Enid, in a way that these marble walls and
clichéd plaques never could be. She closed her bag securely and
hugged it to her chest, feeling a moment of unexpected happiness.
It was a secret shared, and one that then she could share in turn.
Something to look forward to.

Chapter Twelve

Thursday evening

Today I worked out that the way my three girls keep their Derwents sums up their personalities. There's Kat, who has every pencil intact, all sharpened and colour coded, and George, whose tin is a total mess. Most of the pencils are lost and she just settles for the ones that are left (meaning her drawings have some _very_ odd colour combinations!). Then there's Annie, who has a few favourites she's worn to a nub and complains about constantly. She also keeps accusing the others of taking hers (she's probably right). The Sorter, the Settler and the Sook. But I think I've come up with an analogy for life. Derwent pencils. They should get me to write their new marketing slogan.

It was so windy this morning that other people's washing blew into our yard. Old man Roger's droopy drawers were stuck in the roses and I had to fish them out with a stick. I also found Annie draping Gladys next door's petticoat over the bushes in the corner. She'd moved most of her toys out there and set up a tea party. She said it was her princess tent because of the lace. I haven't laughed that much for a long time. Gladys wasn't quite as amused.

Last night the movie Old Yeller *was on Disneyland. What a tear-jerker! By the end all the girls were crying, but then five minutes later Kat and Georgie were chasing Annie around the house shouting 'No, Travis! No!' Their father ended up giving them both a whack on the backside and sent them down to bed. That's not going to help Anna though. The girl needs to develop some backbone. But then I was washing the dishes and I kept thinking of how loyal that dog had been and the price it paid. And everything seemed so unfair. What's the bloody point of it all?*

Maybe what this family needs is a dog. Like Old Yeller, or Lassie. Or Rin Tin but without the attitude. Unconditional love. I think I'd like a dog. Something that's just happy you're there but doesn't ask for all that much in return. I'd like that.

Things that really get my goat:
Wall-to-wall carpet
Odd socks
Textas
Clag
VFL
Humphrey B. Bear
Damp spoons being put in the sugar bowl
Children who can't amuse themselves
Boredom
That ridiculous song 'Afternoon Delight'. Really? And have to make the bed again? No.
Men
Romance books with happy ever after
Connie Duff
Hobbytex

Margaret when she won't shut up
~~Life itself~~

I found Kat's diary this afternoon while cleaning her room. Spent the
next hour curled up on her bed reading. Was I ever so daft? Mind you,
she's even a bossy-britches when she writes. Also it seems that she's in
love with a boy called Martin Pratt. She's even written a poem about
him. Apparently his hair is like cornsilk and his eyes as blue as emeralds.
Then she filled the rest of that page with all different ways of writing Kat
Pratt. I want to tell her that there is <u>no way</u> to make that sound better
than the punchline of a nursery rhyme. And that emeralds aren't blue,
you twit. They're green.

Burnt the meatloaf to a crisp this evening. Forgot all about it. Smoke
came pouring out when I opened the oven. What sort of imbecile burns
meatloaf? I nearly cried. So Ronald came over and put an arm around
me and said you go lie down, I'll feed the kids. That just made me feel
like crying even more. I hate it when he's nice.

The damn trains are on strike again. That's the third time this month.
I mean I do see why they're striking, but I also had an appointment at
the children's hospital for my Harry today. Now I have to wait another
month for them to fit me in. I'm worried about him. He doesn't seem the
same as the girls were at his age. Ronald says it's because he's a boy, but
then Ronald also has a habit of not seeing what's right under his nose.
As I well know.

Picked Annie up from Julie Frost's birthday party this afternoon. She'd
spilled orange cordial all over her party dress. It's ruined. And the Frosts
do have a dog. It's small and white and fluffy and has an underbite.
It also barks A LOT. Sixteen screaming eight-year-olds and the most

irritating thing was the dog. Knowing my luck, that's exactly the sort of dog I'd end up with. Ergo, we are no longer getting a dog.

<u>*More things that really get my goat*</u>
Dogs
Transport strikes
Tapioca pudding
Motor mowers
Ronald
Lego bricks
The theme song from Countdown
Barbie feet. And also the size of their chests.
The postman
Men who leer (like the above)

Enough is enough. Today I found myself watching everyone to find something to be annoyed about so that I could write it down. Either I'm not doing this right or this diary thing is daft. I've just read through this whole thing and all I sound like is a misery-guts. Plus I feel worse now than when I started. Ethel Ferguson's sister-in-law is an idiot. I just need to grow <u>my own</u> bloody backbone. Otherwise I might as well take a leaf from Old Yeller *and put myself out of my own misery! For starters, I have to start concentrating on what's good about my life, not what's missing. Count my blessings. After all, I was pretty happy before. All it takes is a bit of willpower and I can be pretty happy again.*

<u>*Things I like about my life.*</u>
Not having my mother in it
My children
Ronald (~~usually~~)
Margaret

My house
The grandfather clock
Food
Christmas
Sitting on the veranda on a summer evening
Bacardi and coke
The future

Chapter Thirteen

Friday morning

Somewhat to her surprise, George slept more deeply than she had since her mother's death. She woke feeling refreshed, and so befuddled by this unexpected achievement that it took several moments for the events of the previous day to slide back into focus. There had been no further revelations in the diary. More insight into Enid's unhappiness certainly, but also reminders of her strength. The familiarity came with a wash of relief. It was like the misalignment of seeing someone out of context – your school-teacher at the shops, or the mayor at the local nudist beach, only then to have them slot back into place the next time you met. Even if the fit was never quite as seamless.

But there were more correlations also. For starters, George considered their lists of pet peeves quite similar – although she wouldn't have included textas, dogs or her father. And she quite liked wall-to-wall carpeting, particularly in bedrooms. Connie Duff probably wouldn't score a mention either, whoever she was. These deletions would be replaced by things like grief, revelations from beyond the grave, Tears Ahoy, the use of your instead of you're, Monopoly, and Guy Weston. But the biggest difference between the two lists was not having her mother in her life had been on top of the things Enid liked about her life, but for George it was the opposite. Grief roiled within like frothy surf. It was still somewhere there, even when the tide was out.

After finally finishing the diary, she had been filled with the urge to take a highlighter (or texta) and go through the entire thing again, circling the important parts and adding notes. Like confirmation from Google that the transport strike mentioned had occurred in early September 1977, thus providing a date for that particular entry. And Christmas being included as a favourite in the last entry suggested that it had been approaching when Enid called it quits. George herself finished the diary with all the regret of a sudden parting. She leafed through the remaining pages carefully, but that was all she wrote.

She left that morning a little later than usual, revelling in the difference a full night's sleep made. The sun hung low but heavily in a mostly cloudless sky, promising another warm day to come. The smoke from the fires had dissipated, earlier than expected, leaving just the faint scent of smouldering ashes. George drove with peak-hour traffic towards her mother's house, arriving there just after nine o'clock to find that Kat's car wasn't parked in the driveway. This was a stroke of luck. Even so, it was with her heart pounding that she hurriedly entered the house and went straight down the passage and into the study, thrusting the diary back into the wardrobe as if it had become nuclear-reactive in the past few minutes. She stood back, her pulse throbbing. It echoed within her eardrums. One thing was clear, she would have had little success as a criminal.

George took her overnight bag into the lounge room and dropped it on the couch. The curtains were still drawn, giving the living areas a shadowy, secretive look. On the kitchen bench was a note from Kat, letting her know that she was getting some groceries and then dropping Rhyll off, but would be back by ten-thirty or so. George was a little disappointed not to see her daughter, if only to reassure herself that she hadn't spent another evening weeping over home movies. But given Kat had been present, that was unlikely. There was no evidence that Annie had been here at all this morning. Nor had she joined in the brief conversation on their group chat last night. But George wasn't worried. Even if yesterday's truce had been temporary, she was confident that today's events would provide the bridge.

She made Harry a coffee, and somewhere between the water boiling and milk being added, George had a brilliant idea. She hurried back into the study and pulled some boxes willy-nilly from the wardrobe to make it look as if she had been working in their absence. Then she removed the diary once more and brought it out to the dining room, laying it almost reverentially on the table. An hour would have been more than enough to discover it, and also read it right through. She stood back, inordinately pleased with this plan. Far better than pretending to discover it at some stage during the day. Perhaps she could have been a criminal after all.

With the scene now set, George carried Harry's blue mug care-fully down the stairs and knocked at his door before pushing it open. It was difficult to believe that this section had ever been a single-car garage. Lined with bookshelves, it had a kitchenette in the corner with a full size fridge, sink and microwave, a small lounge area and half an old table tennis table holding the larger Lego constructions. The smaller ones filled the bookshelves. Harry himself was sitting behind his desk, working on his latest kit. The television was on, with an episode of *Doctor Who*. He looked up as she entered.

'Hello,' he said, totally unsurprised that she had arrived on his doorstep carrying coffee.

George put the mug down by his elbow and examined the latest project. It was only in the early stages but judging by the box was going to be a rather impressive castle.

'It's not Windsor Castle,' said Harry, following her gaze. 'I wanted Windsor Castle because Henry VIII is buried there. But Lego Group don't do Windsor Castle.'

Clearly this would be on *his* list of pet peeves. George remembered this set being one of his Christmas presents only a month ago. She ran a finger along the top of the box.

'He exploded in his coffin on the way there,' continued Harry. 'Body gases. And fluids. Some dogs licked them up.'

'Yes,' said George, pulling her hand away. 'You told us. Apart from the dogs bit. Thanks for that though.'

Harry nodded. He took a sip of coffee and returned to staring at the instruction booklet by his elbow. On the television, the Doctor was facing down a trio of Daleks. The TARDIS suddenly appeared behind him, lights flashing, and his sidekick leaned from the doorway, urging the Doctor to run. George transferred her gaze to her brother. The discovery of his parentage cast question marks over everything that was familiar. Which of his features had he inherited from his father? Which elements of his personality? He glanced sidelong at her with a frown.

'Okay, okay. I'm leaving.'

'Good.'

Back upstairs, George busied herself with packing the Georgette Heyer books into a box for Aunt Margaret. Almost without exception, every cover bore an image of a tall, burly looking gentleman, usually clad in rippling Regency cape, and a fragile, frilly heroine. The books had been here for as long as

George remembered, yet she had never quite connected them with her mother's taste. Enid must have read them, enjoyed them, and perhaps even imagined herself in the scenes. In short, George now reflected, her mother had been a sitting duck. Or more fittingly, an apple just waiting to be plucked. She grimaced at this last analogy and then taped the box shut before checking the time. 9:55 am. She got out her mobile and using the group chat, slowly typed out the all-important text.

Omg!! I found a diary while cleaning out Mum's spare wardrobe and you're never going to believe what was in it! Too HUGE to send by message. You MUST come & read this. Un-bloody-believable!!

George re-read the message. It had to be dramatic enough to trigger Annie's FOMO, without sounding too stagey. She deleted a few of the exclamation marks, on the grounds that she wasn't fifteen, and nodded with satisfaction. She pressed send. Only then did she go into the kitchen and make herself the first coffee of the day. With it in one hand, she pulled open the lounge room curtains, flooding the room with light. Dust-motes swirled with the sudden movement. George sat down at the table to wait.

Kat was the first to arrive. She was lugging several shopping bags that she dumped on the bench before turning to George. She looked amused.

'Bit over the top, don't you think?'

'What?'

'Your message. Now she's going to be ticked off when she gets here and it's all a ruse.' Kat grinned. 'You'd better get busy and write an actual diary before she arrives.'

Rather than answer, George picked up the real diary. She held it aloft for a moment before passing it to her sister. Kat's new eyebrows shot up into her fringe.

'What the hell?'

'Read it,' said George. 'There are twenty-five entries. And let me know when you get to the one about her watching Harry sleep.'

'What the hell?' said Kat again. She began reading at the bench and then, without taking her eyes off the diary, came over to the table to sit down. She nearly missed the chair. Her face had gone soft with surprise.

George rose at the same time. She put the groceries away, glancing at her sister every so often to gauge her reaction. After about ten minutes she was rewarded. Kat frowned, and then her eyes widened. She looked over at George, her jaw slack.

'I know,' said George.

'Oh my god. She says *his* father. Do you think …?' Kat shook her head. 'No. It can't be.'

There was the sound of a key in the front door and then the familiar creak as it opened. Annie came through to the lounge room and stopped, gazing narrowly at them both before settling her gaze on George. Her left wrist was still bandaged tightly.

'Very childish,' she said curtly. 'I *was* coming to help anyway. I wouldn't *not* help.'

George pointed to the diary. She was beginning to feel quite aggrieved that her two sisters thought her capable of such subterfuge. If she *had* been dissembling, she would have been a little more subtle about it. 'You need to read that,' she said. 'When Kat's finished.'

'Oh,' said Annie. She came over to the table, gazing at the diary suspiciously.

'How's the wrist?' asked Kat, glancing up.

'Getting better,' replied Annie. She flashed a glance at George. 'Slowly.'

George didn't respond. It was rather unfair to be held even partially responsible for what was essentially her sister's inability to put her shoes on. She finished putting the groceries away and put the kettle on as Kat read through the rest of the book. Annie had settled herself at the table now, rather ostentatiously massaging her wrist. If it was that bad, thought George, then she wouldn't be touching it at all.

Kat passed the diary wordlessly to Annie when she finished. Then she sat back, staring through the sliding doors into the backyard. George made the coffees and opened a packet of ginger cookies. She brought everything over to the table and then went to the bathroom. She heard Annie exclaim as she left, and knew that she had just reached the part about Harry. She paused, listening to the low murmurs of their voices, and then they fell silent once more. In the bathroom, George stared at herself in the mirror. It was done. The diary had been shared.

She had expected to feel a greater sense of relief, but instead she just felt sad. Their mother would have hated this. It would have been top of her pet peeves. She probably would have preferred George to burn it as soon as it was found. It was amazing that she hadn't done so herself. But maybe the diary itself was a memento, like the musical ticket. The only reminders she had, apart from Harry himself. This thought made George feel sad also.

When she came back into the dining room, the diary was lying closed on the table in front of Annie. Her good hand rested on the faded cover. George pulled up a chair and wrapped both her own hands around her coffee mug. The sisters sat silently for a few minutes. George willed herself to patience. After all, she had been able to absorb the diary over several days. They had been given just minutes.

'Bloody hell,' said Kat finally.

Annie glanced at George. 'I thought you were making it up.'

'I know,' said George, feeling a flash of her earlier umbrage. 'As if!'

'O-kay.' Kat slapped the table decisively. 'We need to go through this methodically. I looked up *The Rocky Horror Picture Show* while Annie was reading. It was 1975.'

'But the diary's 1977,' said George. She felt a flush of self-satisfaction. 'Elvis Presley died in August 1977 and later on she mentions a transport strike. Three in one month, she says. That was in September 1977. I think she just kept the ticket as a keep-sake of ... you know. But the diary itself was written in the second half of 1977.'

'That fits,' said Kat slowly. 'Harry was born in July 1976.'

Annie looked from one of them to the other. 'Are we saying then, that Harry is ...?' She didn't finish the sentence. Nor did either of her sisters reply. After a moment, she tapped a finger on the diary cover. 'She had an affair. Our mother had an affair. She cheated on Dad.'

'Seems that way,' said Kat.

'But we shouldn't judge,' said George eagerly. 'After all, we don't know what was happening at the time. What their marriage was like ...' She faltered under their regard but then got her second wind. 'I'm not making excuses except, well, she wasn't just his wife. Or our mother. She was a person too.'

'Thank you for that anthropological observation,' said Annie. She was looking at George narrowly. 'She still cheated. What other interpretation is there? C'mon, you're the expert.'

'Huh?' asked Kat. 'What do you mean by that?' She looked from one sister to the other. 'George is the expert on what? Am I missing something?'

'Unlikely,' said Annie smartly. She began massaging her wrist again. 'No, I just meant that George read the diary first so she's had more time to absorb it. That's all.'

'O-kay. Sure.'

'Nice to be considered an expert anyway,' said George lightly. Her tone hid the irritation she felt inside. She hoped Annie's wrist was giving her considerable pain. From the corner of her eye she could see that her older sister was continuing to look at her with interest. Annie had reopened the diary and now bent the cover back to flick through it. George flinched. She wanted to grab it back, put it in her bag for safekeeping.

'I also resent this whole grow a backbone thing!' said Annie now, slapping the diary closed once more. 'How dare she! And that stuff about the Derwents! Calling me a sook!'

Kat leaned over and slid the diary away from her sister. 'In all fairness, she doesn't say that you didn't have a *reason* to sook. At one stage she even has a go at Dad for not holding George and me to account. She just says that you need to deal with it better.'

'She also called me a settler,' said George. 'In fact she makes me out as a bit of a pushover.'

'Yeah well, you are. A bit,' said Kat. She grinned. 'Come on, let's be honest. I'm bossy, George is overly amenable, and Annie, you *have* grown more of a backbone. You'd never have been able to dump Brad without it. Or get past all the crap he put you through.'

Annie was looking slightly mollified. 'Well, she didn't have to write it all down.'

'It was her diary!' Kat gave a sudden laugh. 'She probably thought it'd never be read!'

'Then she should have got rid of it,' said Annie. 'Or at least taken better care of her health.' Her lip quirked. 'If it was you,' she said to Kat, 'you'd have written a to-do list while lying on the floor and then organised the paramedics to carry it out before leaving.'

'Too right,' said Kat, returning the smile. She opened the diary and then sighed, her smile vanishing. 'So what we seem to have is a woman who had an affair in 1975. Then her partner in crime went away, maybe to Mount Isa. They corresponded for a while. Perhaps he stopped when he found out she was pregnant. And then she struggles to come to terms with her life. The whole diary is a midlife crisis. From start to finish. It's all rather depressing, really.'

George took a sip of her coffee. It had gone cold. 'Do you think he looks like him?' she asked suddenly. 'Harry? And his father?'

Annie shrugged. She followed it up with one of her own sighs. 'I wonder if Dad knew.'

'I don't think so,' said Kat slowly. 'I really don't.'

'God, I hope not,' said George with feeling.

'Oh what a tangled mess we weave,' said Annie. She grinned ruefully at both her sisters, her gaze lingering on George. 'When first we practise to deceive.'

George flushed, but was saved from responding by the sound of the stairs creaking. She got up quickly to put the kettle on as Harry came into the room. He put his blue mug on the bench and then sat down in George's vacated chair. He pushed her mug aside.

'Windsor Castle is the oldest castle in the world,' he said. 'It also has the largest dollhouse in the world. Queen Mary's. It has a lift and cars with engines and guns that really work. And a library with handwritten stories by authors like Rudyard Kipling and A. A. Milne. He wrote *Winnie the Pooh*. It also has plumbing and toilets that flush.'

'The castle or the dollhouse?' asked Kat. 'Because if it's the castle, I would *expect* the toilets to flush. Otherwise the Queen's in all sorts of trouble.'

'The dollhouse,' said Harry. He looked a bit confused.

'I'm liking the sound of the library though,' said George lightly. 'Can I move there?'

'No. It's a dollhouse. You wouldn't fit.'

George laughed. She collected the other mugs from the table, feeling Kat's eyes on her again. Hers wasn't the only coffee that had been allowed to go cold. She busied herself making a new lot, regretting ever having shared her private life with Annie. But if Kat raised it, she would give her short shrift. She wouldn't find her so bloody amenable now. When she looked over though, Kat had transferred her attention back to Harry. As had Annie. She guessed that they were examining his features for clues. Been there, done that.

'It was built by William the Conqueror after he won the battle of Hastings,' added Harry, more confidently.

'The dollhouse?' asked Annie. She smiled. 'That seems an odd hobby for a medieval megalomaniac. Even apart from the attention to the flushing toilets.'

'No, the castle,' replied Harry as George put his filled mug down in front of him. He adjusted it so that the handle was to his right. 'The dollhouse was built in 1924. It also has real fountain pens and packets of notepaper for writing letters.'

'Letters?' repeated Kat. She sat back, staring at him. 'Letters,' she said once more. Then she jumped to her feet, knocking the table. Coffee sloshed from the mugs. She was staring at her sisters. 'Letters!' she exclaimed yet again before hurrying from the room.

'She spilled my coffee,' said Harry mildly. 'Again. All over the table.'

George was staring at Annie, whose face echoed her puzzlement. Then her younger sister rose also and hurried after Kat. George herself paused only to rescue the diary from the

encroaching coffee. She dabbed it against her t-shirt as she followed them. They were in the study, Kat staring into the open
wardrobe. As George entered, she turned to frown at her.

'I thought you'd almost finished in here! This is still
chock-a-block!'

'Priorities,' said George, trying to keep defensiveness out of her
voice. She hugged the diary to her chest. 'I think we've got more
important things right now, don't you?'

'You think she kept the letters,' said Annie now, gazing over
her sister's shoulder.

'I'm *sure* she did.' Kat returned her attention to the contents of
the wardrobe. She began removing boxes. 'If she kept the ticket
and the diary all these years, then surely she'll have kept them
too.' She glanced at George. 'Where exactly did you find it?'

'Oh, just on a shelf.' George waved vaguely towards a stack of
books. 'There wasn't anything else with it.'

'O-kay, then we need to go through *everything*,' declared Kat.
She pulled out the plastic bag of knitting. 'They'll be here somewhere. I'm certain.'

George put the diary on the desk, out of harm's way. They spent
the next hour working methodically on the wardrobe contents,
Kat having also declared that they might as well do it properly
and box up anything that was going to landfill or charity. This
turned out to be much of it. The winter coats and dated clothing,
the wicker basket of scarves, the pile of old catalogues, the plastic
tub of broken crockery that no doubt their mother once intended
to repair. But this being something of a treasure hunt, which they
were doing together, injected a taste of fun very much absent thus
far that week. George also noticed that Annie did not seem overly
hampered by her allegedly sprained wrist. She did favour the other
one, but then she was right-handed so it was only to be expected.

Kat was the one who found the shoebox, pushed right up the back of the top shelf. *Paragon Shoes Pty Ltd*, the label boasted, a sobriquet which brought a derisive snort from Annie. Inside they expected to find the paragon shoes themselves, or perhaps ancient receipts. But instead it was instantly recognisable as a memorabilia box.

Within was an envelope of what looked like baby hair, a wedding garter, a menu from a restaurant called The Swagman, an old autograph book dated 1953 full of schoolgirl witticisms such as *By hook or by crook, I'll be first in this book* and *Let me be but a brick in the chimney of your affection.* There was also a single ruby earring and a certificate for *The Herald Learn to Swim Award 1950.* At the bottom of the box was a little dollhouse armchair, which mostly definitely wasn't up to the standard of Queen Mary's. And there was a letter, just one, postmarked 18th November 1975. It was addressed to Mrs R. Tapscott, of 7 Wisteria Avenue Ferntree Gully. There was no return address. Both Annie and George knelt by her as Kat slid the letter from the envelope and unfolded it. Her hand trembled. They leaned closer, all scanning the neat cursive script.

Dearest Enid,

I hope you are well. And Ronald and the girls. I miss their laughter. And playing euchre. I also miss the lovely weather down there. Up here it is as hot as hell. My thoughts return again and again to the very pleasant time I enjoyed with you. Best apples I've ever had in my life. Ruined me for the ones up here. But I ask again, and for the last time I swear, whether you would not consider coming up here. I've got a room at the Dalpura Motel at the moment but there is plenty of more suitable accommodation. For a family. The sunsets from Lake Moondarra would take your breath away. Please say hello to everyone from me. Also Margaret and Ken.

Fond regards, H.

'What's with all the apples?' asked Annie, leaning back. She was frowning. One of her knees creaked at almost the same time as the floor.

'It's sex,' said Kat slowly. 'The apples are code for sex.'

As one, they all turned to look at the still life that had hung on the wall by the door for as long as this room had been a study. Before that it had been in their parents' room. Glossy red apples tumbled from a wicker basket, their ripe flesh glinting against a tousled white cloth. George blinked.

'Do you think … he gave it to her?'

Kat shrugged. 'I don't know. I just remember it always being here.'

'Maybe that's where they got the idea,' said Annie. 'From the painting. You must admit, they do all look quite lush. You know, sort of … sensuous.' She suddenly blanched. 'My god! That used to hang over Mum and Dad's bed! You don't think they … did it there?'

'Well, we'll never know,' said George a little tartly.

Kat was still gazing at the still life. 'He must have kept the letter all family-friendly, in case Dad read it. But he overplays his hand a bit with the apples.'

'I think they both did,' said George with feeling. 'And in the diaries where she says she could have been eating apples in Mount Isa, she must have meant bonking. With him.'

'Bonking?' Annie glanced at her with a grin. 'God, I haven't heard that term for years!'

George returned the grin and then waggled her eyebrows suggestively.

Kat had got her mobile out and was now scrolling. 'Ah, here we are. The Dalpura Motel. In Mount Isa. Along with Lake Moond-arra.' She looked up at them. 'So we have the apple aficionado down in Melbourne for part of 1975, certainly up to when they went to *Rocky Horror* together. Then for whatever reason, maybe work, he's headed up north. He asked her to go with him and she said no. So then he writes.' She held up the letter.

'He must have sent more too,' added George. 'Because she talks about this being the *last* letter. Most likely the others were more impersonal, meant for the family with maybe just some oblique references. In this one, he gets down to the nitty-gritty. The core, if you like.' She paused, pleased with the witticism. 'He swears he won't ask again, and probably doesn't. But she kept it.'

The sound of Harry's footsteps came from the direction of the lounge room. The sisters fell silent as he made his way up the passage. But he walked straight past the study, not even glancing in their direction. A crinkling noise suggested that he had taken the packet of ginger cookies with him. He could be heard descending the stairs and then his door opened and closed. They looked at each other.

'I'm never going to be able to eat apples again,' said Annie.

Kat grimaced. 'Or watch *Rocky Horror*. Or visit Mount Isa. Not that I wanted to, but still.' She smoothed out the letter. 'What we don't know is whether she replied to any of them. Or whether he knew that she was pregnant.'

'He did,' said Annie suddenly. She took the letter from Kat with her good hand and pointed at a section. 'Here, where he underlines "for a family". He wasn't talking about her bringing Dad, or probably even us. He meant the baby.'

Kat nodded, thinking this over. 'Possibly. But she'd made her decision and she stuck to it.'

'She did hate the heat,' said George. 'Her English skin couldn't cope. Maybe she knew the taste for H's apples wouldn't last as long as the weather.'

'You're such a romantic,' said Kat. She rearranged her legs, knocking a foot against the shoebox. She started to move it aside but then paused, her grin fading as she picked it up instead. She tilted it to one side and then licked a finger and dipped it into a corner, lifting it again to display a film of grey-green crumbly fragments.

'Looks like dried herbs,' said Annie. She leaned closer. 'Maybe she had some potpourri in there once.'

Kat lifted her finger and took a sniff. Her eyebrows lifted. 'Or just ... pot.'

'Pot!' George gaped at her. 'No way.'

'Could be,' said Kat slowly. She wiped her finger on her jeans. 'But no, probably not.'

'Definitely not,' said Annie decisively. 'I'm having enough trouble getting my head around her having an affair. Let's not make her stoned at the same time. Next we'll be discovering that we were all birthed free range on a commune in Nimbin. For god's sake, this was a suburban housewife.'

Kat nodded, although George thought that she didn't look convinced. She took the shoebox from her sister and tilted it herself, watching the few grams of herb-like residue tumble together. It *did* look a little like pot. Old pot, with very little scent left. But it could just as likely be what Annie had said. She tried to imagine her mother sitting in her armchair, puffing away on a joint. It didn't compute.

'Potpourri,' said Annie again, as if reading her mind. 'It'll have been one of those little sachets Mum liked. It's just burst at some stage. Come on, our mother did *not* smoke pot.'

'No,' said George, shaking her head. She put the shoebox down.

'Yeah, you're right,' agreed Kat. 'Well, there's *one* thing I know for sure. The H is for Harold. It has to be. The rest of us are all named after someone. Me for Dad's mother, Anna for Mum's aunt, and George for Georgette Heyer. Harry was the only one who wasn't. Or at least we didn't think he was. But maybe Harry is short for Harold. She just couldn't give him the full name because it was too obvious.'

'Could be Henry,' said George. 'Or Harvey. Or Harrison.'

Annie had transferred her gaze to the bookshelves. She was frowning. 'Hey, where are all the Georgette Heyer books?'

'I packed them.' George pointed to the box by the door. 'Aunt Margaret wants them.'

'What?' Annie's v instantly deepened. 'Without even discussing it? You can't do that!' She turned to Kat. 'This is *exactly* what I feared.'

Kat looked at her evenly. 'Did *you* want them?'

'No, but that's not the point.'

'Then what *is* the point? Really, tell us. Please.'

George got hurriedly to her feet, her bruised knee objecting strenuously. She reached out a hand to steady herself against the desk. 'My god! Can we not do this again! I can't take it! Annie, I'm *sorry* if I didn't discuss it first. I was just trying to make everyone happy!'

Annie opened her mouth to reply but then must have thought twice. Instead she nodded stiffly. She got up and went over to the desk to lay the letter down, running a finger along the creases. Kat had risen also, still holding the envelope.

'This is huge,' she said. 'But what do we do with it?'

'Well, we can't tell Harry.' George looked from one sister to the other. 'Can we?'

'Of course we can!' said Annie just as Kat shook her head vigorously. They stared at each other. Kat was the first to speak.

'What would the objective be? What on earth would we gain?'

'It's not about *us* gaining anything,' replied Annie tersely. 'Or objectives. It's about his right to know. And *you* don't get to make that decision for him.'

Kat shook her head again, but more slowly this time. 'You're just saying that because you're trying to make a point with this now. C'mon, Annie, we don't even know for certain. What are we going to tell him? That Dad maybe wasn't his real father? But we don't really know who that is, except that he had a weakness for apple-fuelled adultery and his name started with H? Mum would *hate* this.'

'But it's not her decision now, is it?' Annie pushed the letter aside as if to emphasise this. She looked back at her sister. 'And for your information, I'm *not* trying to make a point. I happen to think Harry deserves to be treated as an adult, not a child. You underestimate him. Just like Mum did.'

Kat threw up her hands in exasperation. 'It'd just confuse him! He won't understand!'

'Then it's up to us to explain it better,' said Annie stubbornly. 'It's *his* information.'

George had been watching this exchange with growing confusion. She had begun with some certainty that Harry shouldn't be told but now she thought that Annie, in fact, might be right. They *did* tend to underestimate him at times, often because it was easier that way.

'And you don't get to appoint yourself gatekeeper of who should know what,' added Annie. Her mouth hooked briefly into a sneer. 'Along with everything else.'

'Stop.' George held up a hand before Kat could respond. '*Please* let's not argue. For what it's worth, I think you both have a point. But can't we just park this until we know more? Do some digging around?'

'Where?' asked Annie. Her v was still in place. 'How?'

George grimaced. She already knew the answer. 'Well, there's only one person who might be able to fill in some gaps.' She paused, the grimace deepening. 'But god, it's going to be hard work.'

'Worth it though,' said Kat. She looked down at the envelope. 'Even apart from the whole Harry thing, for my own peace of mind, I'd like to know if she was happy. Afterwards. That she didn't have any regrets.'

'Same,' said Annie after a moment. She nodded. 'Okay, let's park telling Harry for now. The question, then, is who gets to play detective?'

George blinked. 'Hang on, why can't we all go?'

'Because there's too much work to be done here,' said Kat. 'So let me see …' She bent to pluck a book of matches from a restaurant called The Swagman and then straightened, stroking her chin with her spare hand. 'How *can* we decide?'

'No,' said George.

'Sorry, no choice,' said Kat. 'It's tradition.' She flipped open the book and removed three matches before snapping one in half. She was grinning. So was Annie, albeit a little more tightly.

'No!' said George. 'I always lose! You *know* I always lose!'

'Tough,' said Kat firmly. 'Unless you'd prefer not to even go through the motions?' She waited until eventually George shook her head, and then she turned to Annie. 'Were you staying tonight?'

'I wasn't going to,' said Annie slowly. The grin had gone.

'I think you should,' said Kat. 'Now. There's lots to talk about.'

Annie hesitated and then nodded. Kat dropped her eyes, jiggling the matches and then folding her thumb over their ends so that only the heads showed, giving the deceptive impression of uniformity. She looked up at her sisters. The smile was back. 'You know the drill, team. We've done it often enough. Short straw gets the prize.'

Chapter Fourteen

Friday afternoon

The one o'clock news came on as George turned onto the main highway that wound up the mountain towards Belgrave. She increased the volume. There had only been a few wins across the fire fronts, with indeed far more losses. A woman was interviewed who had spent two nights on a Gippsland beach, her town ablaze behind her. 'We thought we were going to die,' she said, her voice oddly flat. George supposed that it was the shock, and that soon enough her voice would shake as much as her hands were probably doing right now.

The sun beat through the driver's window. George flicked the visor across and then turned the radio down and the air-conditioner up. The traffic slowed as they entered the single lane that wound through the picturesque township of Belgrave. The street was relatively empty, the weather too hot even for tourists. Puffing Billy tooted in the distance, a cloud of grey-white smoke curling up into the clear sky. George took a left at the roundabout, and then another left just past the library carpark. She coasted to a stop outside a neat weatherboard house with white sash windows.

215

Instead of getting out, George sat for a while, considering the logistics of the coming evening. She got out her mobile and sent a text to Leo. *Are you planning on going out tonight? If so, could you ask Rhyll along? I'm staying at the house so she's home alone — but I think she's finding things tough atm. Needs company.*

His answer came almost immediately. *Not a problem.*

Thanks, typed George. Then she followed it up quickly with: *Please don't tell her I asked you!* The reply was an emoji with zipped lips. She smiled as she slipped her mobile back into her bag and got out of the car. The smile vanished as the afternoon sun enveloped her. It was like a sauna. She hurried down the gravelled pathway and knocked on the door. It was answered almost immediately.

'Georgette!' said Aunt Margaret, beaming. She was wearing a cotton frock covered with roses the size of cabbages. 'I was so pleased to get your call! You hardly *ever* visit. I was just saying to Lesley the other day that the only time I get to see you girls nowadays are at the big events. Christmas, Easter, birthdays … come in, come in!'

George greeted her aunt and then stepped over the threshold, closing the door behind her. It was both cooler and darker inside, the curtains drawn and the air-conditioner humming. Aunt Margaret was already heading through the lounge room towards the kitchen.

'Christenings, anniversaries, funerals of course.'

The walls were hung with photos of Lesley at every stage of her life. Most of which Aunt Margaret was still listing.

'Graduations, engagements, weddings.'

She raised her voice with this last, just as they came into the more brightly lit country-style kitchen. To George's surprise, Great-Aunt Astrid was sitting at the pine table, leaning forward on her cane. She had jerked to attention at Aunt Margaret's raised voice. She was a triangular-shaped woman who Kat had once suggested would make an excellent Christmas tree. This impression had only increased with age, except that she now looked like she was also melting. Her bottom flowed over the chair like lava, enveloping it entirely. Great-Aunt Astrid wasn't actually a blood relative; she was Margaret's aunt by marriage. But she had been part of the extended family for so long that it made no difference. George went forward to give her a kiss.

'Astrid always spends Thursdays with me,' explained Aunt Margaret. She beamed at the elderly woman, who was already nodding off again. 'Although we nearly cancelled today because of the weather. Wee bit warm, isn't it?'

George nodded, suppressing a grimace. Her aunt was quite fond of the word wee, despite the family not having a drop of Scottish blood. But there was something particularly dissonant about using the word wee and warm in the same sentence.

'Coffee? Tea? Bonox?'

'A cup of tea thanks,' said George. She didn't think she could face any more coffee. She took a seat at the table just as a blue roan cocker spaniel came bounding into the room and straight across to the back door, where it disappeared through a dog-flap. It was the latest in a long line of blue roan cocker spaniels that her aunt had owned, all being given names that began, for some reason, with the letter F. Fiona, Flight, Frith. George thought this latest one might be called Fabian.

'Ah, how have you been?' she asked her aunt.

'Good, good,' said Aunt Margaret. She took a dimpled stainless steel teapot from the drainer. 'Sad, of course. Devastated in fact. I never thought Enid would be the first of us to go.' She cast a fleeting glance towards the elderly woman beside George and then returned her attention to the teapot. 'Although she did put an awful lot of salt on her meals. I lost count of the times I told her. There'd be a ring of it around her plate!'

'That's true,' said George, who had herself remonstrated with her mother.

'And she also still cooked in lard. 'We're not living in the Depression, Enid,' I used to say. Not that she'd listen. Last time she came up here for dinner, we had roast pork and you wouldn't believe it, Georgette, but she drained off the pork fat and took it home with her! For sandwiches, she said! And potatoes!'

George nodded again. She looked around the kitchen. As far as she could see, it hadn't changed at all since last time she had been here. A surfeit of yellowing pine furniture and matching cabinetry. It was like living in *The Little House on the Prairie*, but only if Laura Ingalls Wilder also collected Wedgwood. The familiarity of this entire house was both comforting and discordant. There was something gapingly absent. And George suddenly realised that her mother's death was going to affect her relationship with these women also. They were a threesome. The matriarchs. They had always attended functions together, Margaret collecting both Enid and Astrid, neither of whom drove. They travelled together, sat together, and shared a history that was unique to them alone. It was just too hard seeing the trio become a duo, especially when the one missing was her mother.

Aunt Margaret was still talking. 'And anybody who cooks sausages in pork fat is asking for it! Really!'

'Nothing wrong with pork fat,' mumbled Great-Aunt Astrid, without opening her eyes.

'Nothing wrong with pork fat!' repeated Aunt Margaret with disbelief. She had paused halfway to the table, teapot in hand. 'Nothing wrong with it, you say! Well, tell that to Enid!'

George flinched. She massaged her temples lightly.

'Headache, dear?' asked Aunt Margaret. She put the kettle down on a placemat and looked at George with concern. 'I've got just the thing for you.'

'Thanks, but I'm okay. Listen, Aunt Margaret, I did have an ulterior motive for this visit.'

'Here we go.' Aunt Margaret returned with a rather shabby box of Bex. 'You take that.' She patted George on the hand. 'Works a treat. I have a stash of it. Much better than that ipo rubbish they dish out now. Never trust anything that includes "proven" in the name. Little too insistent, if you ask me.'

George blinked as she disentangled this. As far as she knew Bex had been taken off the market back in the seventies, which meant that Aunt Margaret's 'stash' had to be around fifty years past its best-before date. George was quite happy to stretch things a little in that department, but half a century seemed a little risky. She concentrated on the latter part of her aunt's statement. 'It's profen though,' she said, on firm ground there at least. 'Ibu*profen*. Not proven.'

'Same difference,' said Aunt Margaret confidently. 'It's probably French.' She put the Bex down by George and then brought over the sugar bowl and a small jug of milk, along with a sliced Boston bun. 'Now, what are we missing? Cups of course! God darn it, where's my head?'

George watched as her aunt bustled back to collect teacups and saucers from a bottom cupboard. She took a deep breath. 'Aunt Margaret, we found a letter!'

'A letter?' Aunt Margaret paused, half-bent, her chin wattle almost turkey-like, and then straightened to look across at Great-Aunt Astrid. 'That reminds me, young lady. *Wheel of Fortune* this afternoon! You won't be winning so easily this time. I *shall* have my revenge!'

George glanced at the elderly woman, who was now emitting soft little snoring sounds. Each crackled across the ascent, which suggested that she needed to blow her nose. It was difficult to imagine anybody losing to her in anything. Except the race to the finish. Yet her own mother had won there.

George gave herself a slight shake and returned to the subject in hand. 'This letter we found. It was dated 1977, from a man who was working in Mount Isa, but had been in Melbourne before-hand. He sounded like a friend? Name beginning with an H?'

'H?' Aunt Margaret brought the teacups over, all the while repeating the letter h under her breath. By the time she stopped, the actual h had disappeared off haitch altogether.

'We think he might have been a friend of the family,' con-tinued George, a little disappointed that Aunt Margaret hadn't immediately identified him. 'He talks about us girls, and also says to say hello to you and Uncle Ken.'

'Oh! It'll be that Harvey from up the road,' said Aunt Mar-garet suddenly. She began pouring tea. 'Plump fellow. Lived on the corner. Obsessed with his lawn, always out there mowing and whatever. Had a harelip. And just the one leg.' She raised her voice. 'Astrid! You remember Harvey from up the road?'

Great-Aunt Astrid shifted in her chair, which emitted a spongy farting noise. 'Nup.'

'Don't know why he'd be writing to your mother though,' said Aunt Margaret to George. 'That's odd. They only lived up the road. Not sure his wife would've approved.'

'He was married then?' asked George. Plump with a harelip and one leg. And married. Harvey was not shaping up to be quite the romantic figure she had imagined. She couldn't quite picture him featuring on a Georgette Heyer cover.

'Oh yes. She was in a wheelchair. Had a stroke when she was about seventy.'

'Um ... exactly how old was Harvey up the road then?'

Aunt Margaret put a brimming teacup before George and gave this some thought. 'In 1977? He'd have been in his late seventies. Maybe eighties. They had full-time care of their grandson, you know. The daughter was a bit flighty. Oh!' She paused suddenly, gazing at George. 'Did your sister tell you I texted her?'

George blinked. 'Um. Sure?'

'About ...' Aunt Margaret flashed a glance at her older companion and then leaned towards George and lowered her voice. 'Tegan. I'm just a little concerned. I mean, I don't want to push myself in where I'm not wanted. And I didn't mean to eavesdrop yesterday. But Georgette, are you *sure* about all this?'

George stared at her as she tried to disentangle the speech without having to actually ask for an explanation. It didn't help that her aunt's right breast was currently pillowing itself across her shoulder. She recalled the discussion she'd had with Kat, in the kitchen, about Tegan receiving some of her father's inheritance. Aunt Margaret had been sitting nearby, and had clearly overheard. That must be it. George frowned. 'Yes. We're certain. Tegan *is* very responsible, you know. And we think Mum would have approved.'

'Really?' asked Aunt Margaret doubtfully. 'Enid? Are you sure?'

'Yes,' said George again, more firmly. She was a little surprised by her aunt's attitude, and also a little disappointed. 'So let's get back to Harvey up the road. I don't think it's him. For starters, the bloke who sent the letter went up to Mount Isa to work. He sounded pretty fit.'

'Roger,' said Great-Aunt Astrid suddenly. George glanced at her, unsure whether she was adding to the conversation, or simply agreeing.

Aunt Margaret looked at her, frowning. 'You're right! The bloke on the corner was *Roger*, not Harvey.' She lowered herself into a chair. 'Harvey was that older fellow who was in Korea with Ron. Harvey Eastbourne. And it wouldn't be him; he died in the sixties. Fell off a ladder. Let me think.' She sucked on her bottom lip pensively. 'There was another digger mate of theirs though, from then. But I think his name was … Jack. That's right. Jack Russell.'

George looked at her with disbelief. 'Jack Russell?' she repeated. 'Are you seriously saying my father went to the Korean War with a digger named Jack Russell?'

Great-Aunt Astrid snorted without even opening her eyes.

'Well, it was Jack something or other,' said Aunt Margaret, waving a hand dismissively. She took a sip of her tea. 'Maybe Simpson. Or Thompson. No, that was Ernest. He was friends with Billy Naughton.'

George sighed inwardly. 'Back to the H's though. Anyone with a name starting with H?'

'Let me think,' said Aunt Margaret again. She put her head back and squinted at the ceiling for a few moments, then straightened as she clicked her fingers. 'I know! Maybe it was that good-looking bloke used to work with your father. *Very* easy on the eye. They called him Hank the Yank.'

George grimaced. '*Please* tell me he was called Hank the Yank because he was American? Or just because it rhymed?'

'American,' said Aunt Margaret. 'Although probably because it rhymed as well.'

'Okay.' George thought back to the letter, trying to recall if it contained any American idiom. 'Tell me more about Hank the Yank. How old was he? Did he have all his body parts?'

'I couldn't comment on that, dear. Good-looking fellow though, as I said. Quite popular with the ladies. So I'm going to assume so.'

George glanced at her, trying to work out if she was making a joke. Aunt Margaret was leaning back, eating a slice of bun, gazing at the wall with a slight smile on her face. George suddenly had the horrible feeling that Hank the Yank had been sharing his apples with more than one member of her family.

'Not sure why he'd be writing to your mother though,' said Aunt Margaret now, with a slight frown.

'Henry,' said Great-Aunt Astrid now. Her eyes were still closed. 'That Henry what lived with Fred from tennis for a while.'

Aunt Margaret looked at her blankly. A crumb of icing clung to her bottom lip.

'They played tennis with our Ronnie,' continued Great-Aunt Astrid. 'All went off to Cohuna together one Easter. Played in a tournament there.'

'Oh, Henry!' said Aunt Margaret. 'Of course!' She turned to George. 'Nice young bloke. Bit of a hippy though. His wife died. Cancer, I think. So he moved in with Fred from tennis for a bit, maybe six months, until he got back on his feet. And yes, I *do* think he headed up to Mount Isa! Fresh start and all that. Never heard what happened to him after.'

'Dirty bird,' said Great-Aunt Astrid. She had opened her eyes and was glaring at George so fiercely that for a moment she thought the comment was directed at her. 'Always had his eye on our Enid.'

'Oh, I don't think that's true,' said Aunt Margaret airily. 'Something wrong with your tea, Georgette? You're not drinking.'

George hurriedly lifted the teacup and took a decent swig. Bingo, she thought. Henry, it was. 'Can you tell me any more about him?'

'Well, let's see.' Aunt Margaret gave this some thought. 'Average sort of fellow I suppose. Hair was a bit long. Hippy type, as I said. Nice manners though. Such a shame about his wife. Knocked him for six.' She looked at George curiously. 'Why the interest? What on earth did this letter say?'

'Dirty bird,' said Great-Aunt Astrid again.

'It was just a letter.' George shrugged. 'Asking how everybody was, that's all. It was only that Mum kept it, so we wondered if he was um, a relative or something.'

'No relative, dear. Just a young bloke down on his luck. I think your mother was quite fond of him. They had similar interests. Poetry and all that.'

Aunt Margaret made poetry sound like something exotic. Like mysticism, or perhaps conjuring up the dead. George took another sip of tea, wondering if there was a way of getting more information without sounding too keen. Great-Aunt Astrid seemed to have fallen asleep again. Somehow, in the brief period that her eyes had been open, she had managed to drain her own teacup.

'Photo!' said Aunt Margaret suddenly. 'I think I have a photo of him. Remember, Astrid? When we all went on that picnic up to Healesville Sanctuary.' She hefted herself out of her chair and went over to the dresser, opening the cupboard beneath the Wedgwood. There appeared to be a row of photo albums there. Aunt Margaret ran her fingers along the spines and then grunted with satisfaction when she located the right one. She brought it over to the table and sat down again as she flicked through.

'A photo would be lovely,' said George, trying to mask her enthusiasm. 'You know, just to put a face to the name.'

'Here we go.' Aunt Margaret slid the album across. She jabbed a finger at a black and white group photo. 'There he is. Henry Harrison.'

George looked at her with surprise. Henry Harrison. So Harry's name could have come from either first or last name. It almost seemed a little *too* obvious. She lowered her gaze to the black and white group photo. It showed about ten adults lined up in two rows, on what must have been a warm day, as those who weren't wearing hats were squinting into the sunshine. Her eyes were drawn straight to her mother, seated in the front centre. She stared at it, waiting almost masochistically for the jab of loss. Enid liked to tell a story where once, just after putting Kat and George down for a nap, she had answered the door to a travelling salesman who had taken one look at her and asked to speak to her mother. In this photo though, taken about a decade later, she had clearly matured into her role, but still not enough to be the woman who died last week. This younger version had been lost long ago. There was the same sense of nostalgia that accompanied any glance into the past, but it felt disassociated from grief.

George moved on with relief. Beside her mother sat a bouffant-haired Aunt Margaret, one hand shading her face, and then a couple of women who George didn't recognise. There was another woman standing at the side, her face mostly hidden but whose figure bore the unmistakable shape of Great-Aunt Astrid. Children sat cross-legged on the grass. George could see herself and both her sisters, all of them, even the pubescent Kat, clad in cutting-edge terry-towelling shorts, skinny legs on full display. Beside them, a teenaged Lesley wore a crop top and flares.

The men were all in the second row. Uncle Ken, two strangers, and then the figure that Aunt Margaret was still pointing at. Henry Harrison. Harry's father. George narrowed her eyes as she examined him. He was about the same height as her own father, who was standing on his other side, but much slimmer. Darkish hair that was only slightly longer than the other men's. Squinty eyes, but that may have been the sun. Rather nondescript features. George, who had been unconsciously expecting an Errol Flynn type, was a little disappointed.

'There's your mother, and your father.' Aunt Margaret moved her finger across to each as she identified them. 'And Astrid over there. And me, and Lesley of course and you girls in your wee shorts. And back there is Glenys Rawlings and Annabel Murchison. She was a shocking driver. Ran over one of her own children. And that's her husband here. Archie. He was a terrible flirt.' She paused for a moment with her finger on Archie the flirt, and then continued. 'Next to him is Fred from tennis. And of course here's your man. Henry Harrison. Nice young bloke.'

'Dirty bird,' muttered Great-Aunt Astrid.

'No, he was not. True, he fancied Enid but it was more in a *maternal* way. That's all.'

George chewed her lip. Young Henry either had a very loose understanding of the word maternal, or had experienced a very odd relationship with his own mother. She got out her mobile and took a few snaps of the photo, explaining that it was just to show her sisters. A thought occurred to her.

'Annabel Murchison. I don't suppose her nickname was Bel?'

Aunt Margaret shook her head. 'No. But if it's a friend of your mother's you're after there, you'll be thinking of Mabel Jenkins. She worked with us. Your mother used to call her Bel. Very fast typist. Seventy words per minute.'

'Floozy,' said Great-Aunt Astrid.

George blinked with surprise, mainly because her great-aunt had been looking straight at her when she said this. She slid her own gaze away, feeling guilty even though it was almost certain that Mabel Jenkins had been the target there, and not her. Aunt Margaret was shaking her head again.

'Mabel was *not* a floozy. Well, not overly anyway.' She returned her attention to George. 'They were going overseas together, you know. Enid and Mabel. They were fast friends. It was to be a grand adventure. But then they had some sort of falling out. Not sure what went down there.'

George thought she knew. According to her mother, it had been Mabel's knickers.

'I think she moved up to the country. Mabel did. Such a waste. Seventy words per minute! Anyways, last I heard she'd married a dairy farmer and had a whole herd of kids.'

Great-Aunt Astrid made a snorting noise, which either showed appreciation for the use of a cattle-orientated collective noun, or summed up her feelings for Mabel Jenkins. Nobody asked which. George drained her teacup. She wondered if the dairy farmer had been the co-conspirator in the pivotal lowering of the knickers, or whether their relationship had occurred later. She hoped that it had been happy, and that Mabel didn't look back at her sliding-doors moment with too much regret. She glanced back down at the photo.

'Aunt Margaret, do you think Mum was happy? Did she have a happy life?'

Her aunt was frowning at her. 'Happy?' she repeated, as if George had introduced a foreign concept.

'Yes, happy. Like, did she regret not going over to England with Mabel? Was she happy with Dad? And us? You know.'

'Yes,' said Great-Aunt Astrid shortly. She had opened her eyes briefly to give the word emphasis but now settled again, her head dropping forward.

'Oh yes. Most definitely,' added Aunt Margaret. 'And besides, you lot put far too much store on that sort of thing. My generation, we just made the most of whatever came our way. Happy is as happy does.'

Great-Aunt Astrid gave a snort at this last, but it wasn't evident whether this was in support or derision. George repeated the mantra to herself. *Happy is as happy does.* Her aunt had even managed to get the words in the right order and maybe she had a point. It was all about attitude. A little like rock, paper, scissors. Happy covered attitude and attitude crushed regret. If there was one thing her mother had had in spades, it was attitude. Ergo, there was every chance that apart from the brief lull evidenced by the diary, she had *made* herself happy. George thought she'd take that, for now. The cocker spaniel clambered back through the dog-flap and came barrelling across the floor. He stopped before George, his tongue lolling, and then rested his head on her knee.

'Hello, Fabian,' she said, ruffling the fur around his neck.

'Oh, *that's* not Fabian,' said her aunt with a laugh. 'This is Felicia. She's a girl. Fabian had to be put down last year. Obstruction in the bowel.'

'Sorry to hear that,' said George. She wasn't a fan of this new name; it sounded vaguely pornographic. She gave the dog another pat. 'Hello, Felicia.'

'Well, I think it's time for another cup of tea!' said Aunt Margaret, moving towards the kitchen. 'And then, oh! I have the best idea! I'll get out the other photo albums and we'll go through those also. I don't have any more of your Henry but I might have Mabel Jenkins. And plenty of family, of course! What fun!'

George blinked, and then opened her mouth to politely demur. She could think of nothing worse. Except perhaps Fabian's bowel obstruction, or even headbutting a tram like Louisa Lawson. But before she could formulate an excuse, her aunt continued.

'Oh, Georgette, you *are* a lifesaver! Here we were, feeling utterly miserable, and then you arrived to save the day. Just what the doctor ordered. It's serendipity!'

George closed her mouth. Serendipity indeed. Her aunt was now humming happily as she rinsed out the teapot. From George's right came a muffled snort. She glanced over to see Great-Aunt Astrid wide awake. As their eyes met, the elderly woman gave George a slow smile. If it had been anyone else, George would have thought they were enjoying her discomfiture. That the smile was actually a smirk. Great-Aunt Astrid leaned back, closing her eyes again as she readjusted her behind. The spongy farting sound came again, but now George wasn't so sure it was the chair.

'This is going to be such fun!' said Aunt Margaret. 'It's *so* lovely looking at old photos, isn't it? I can fill the gaps for you, tell you who everyone is. I'll get you a pad and pen so you can write it all down. And you can take photos of them with that clever phone of yours. Photos of photos! God darn it, whatever will they think of next?'

George tuned out while her aunt began listing all the possible, related things that they could think of next. The beginnings of a headache throbbed at her temples. She glanced down at the box of Bex, momentarily tempted. But then knowing her luck, she would have a reaction and be stuck here until she recovered. She resigned herself to the inevitable, the silver lining being that her mother would have been pleased she was proving a comfort to her two aunts. It occurred to her that she was seeking approval from somebody who was no longer capable of giving it. The realisation was a wrench. The cocker spaniel, Felicia, butted her head against George's leg, looking for another pat. When it didn't eventuate, the dog lay down and, in a remarkable show of dexterity, slipped her tongue beneath George's sandal strap and right between two of her toes. George jumped.

'As for those emails! Just like that!' Aunt Margaret paused in her tea-making to click her fingers. 'Every time Lesley sends me one, I think what on earth has the world come to? In my day we had blue airmail letters. And woe betide you if you didn't use the wee flap on the back! The person you were writing to would *know* you'd run out of things to say!'

George doubted this was ever much of an issue for her aunt. She pushed the dog away before it made inroads on any more toes, and looked over at the dresser. Through the open doors, she could see that there seemed to be at least a dozen photo albums inside. And they were just the ones that were visible. George took a deep breath. On top of the dresser, interspersed with the Wedgwood, were even more photos of Lesley. It seemed rather unfair that her cousin was on the other side of the world while George was stuck here, being a lifesaver to her family. Apart from anything else, Lesley was the only one who was an actual blood relative to Great-Aunt Astrid. This thought was followed by another one, which was even more unfair, and which lumped in her throat. Lesley still had two generations ahead of her. Sentient branches on the family tree. Buffers against mortality. While she, George, had had just the one. And now with her mother's death, even that was gone, leaving her totally exposed. The top of the tree, the next in line.

Chapter Fifteen

Friday evening

These thoughts stayed with George through the long afternoon, reinforced with each page-turn of every album. Sepia photos of relatives she had never met, all with complete lives spent outside the circle of hers. Women with cameos clasped at their necks, men in uniform, formal family groups clustered around their patriarch. Each of these people had once had a turn on the stage, beneath the spotlight, while she waited in the wings.

It got worse when Aunt Margaret brought out the more recent albums. Those people were not just names on a family tree. Her father's brother, dead from complications after surgery when she had been four. His mother, her grandmother, with the feather-pillow lap and feather-light scones, dying five years later from smoking-induced lung cancer. That second cousin who was killed, along with his wife, by a drunk driver in the late seventies. Her grandfather, stroke. Her own father, pneumonia. Uncle Ken, renal failure. All of these people's lives had overlapped with hers; she had *seen* them on the stage. In terms of the family tree, these were the people who had been directly above her. These were the ones who had protected her from the top. And now they too were gone, and the view was clear.

It felt almost impossible to put these thoughts into words and so she didn't. Instead she shared the news about Henry Harrison with her sisters when she got back, showed them the photo, and described the tedium of the afternoon without the excess emotion. They'd tried to place him in their memories, as clearly they had all met him at some stage, but with limited success. Fred from tennis was more memorable, owing to an impressive handlebar moustache, but young itinerant Henry simply hadn't made a big enough impression. On them, at least. Of course they had googled the name Henry Harrison almost immediately, but unfortunately it appeared that the ninth president of the United States had been called William Henry Harrison, and so he tended to dominate the search results. This version had died in 1841 though, so there was little chance he had done any international fruit-picking. The decision to park whether or not to tell Harry had been extended, by mutual agreement, when it became obvious that any other agreement would be in short supply. At five o'clock, Kat had produced a bottle of pinot grigio from the fridge and, declaring that she was heartily sick of the dining room, ushered them all out onto the veranda. She had fetched an old picnic table and some fold-out chairs from the shed earlier, but herself took the egg-chair. The rest of them were left to position themselves along the narrow space, with Annie ostentatiously finding a spot as far from the railing as she could.

George, under normal circumstances a parsimonious drinker, had finished her first glass in record time. That had been two hours, or three glasses ago, and she was now feeling decidedly tipsy, the effects of the alcohol only slightly offset by Thai takeaway. The setting sun had lost little heat and it promised to be a warm, sticky type of night. Inside the house, the old evaporative cooling unit was working overtime. The siblings picked at the food, spread across the picnic table, and indulged in spurts of conversation. Annie though was mostly quiet, making it obvious that she was still feeling slighted. Her grievances didn't seem to have impacted her appetite though, George noticed. Or her consumption of the wine.

Now Kat half-rose from her chair, refilling their glasses. Even Harry held a glass of wine, although his was barely touched. 'We should make a toast,' she said, sitting back and raising her glass. 'To Mum. We loved you dearly, and we'll miss you. Always.'

They each echoed the toast. George stared down at her glass. The word *always* had an echo. It was a death sentence in itself. She thought suddenly that when she herself was drawing her final breath, clinging to the top of the tree, she would most likely call for her mother. It didn't matter how far into the future it might be. She also thought that it would be best if she stopped drinking, before she started calling for her right now. She took another gulp.

'D'you know,' said Kat abruptly. 'For me, this last weekend was the worst. I was coping when we were planning the funeral, and I'm coping again now with this.' She waved a hand towards the house. 'It's when I don't have anything. After all this is over, I think I'd better throw myself into work. Or get a new hobby.' Her eyes slid across to George. 'Maybe have an affair.'

George flushed. She glared at her glass.

'So you told her?' asked Annie, looking from one of them to the other.

'No,' snapped George. 'But now you just have. Thanks for that, pal. And I don't want to talk about it. So both of you, shut up. Not another word.'

'Okay, okay.' Kat held up her hands. 'You can have a temporary reprieve. But I demand details at some stage.'

'Prince Charles had an affair with Camilla Parker Bowles,' said Harry. He put his glass down on the table. 'In 1989 he wanted to be her tampon.'

George choked on her wine. She began coughing. Kat reached over to whack her on the back but her attention was still on her brother.

'Do you even know what a tampon is, Harry?'

'Of course.' He gave her a puzzled look. 'It's a menstrual product designed to absorb secretions. It's held in place by the female vagina. They've been used for thousands of years. Egyptian women used papyrus. Roman women used wool. Hawaiian women used the furry part of the native fern.'

'Good lord,' said Annie.

'Well, at least they used the furry part,' said Kat. 'I believe the fronds are a killer.'

George, still spluttering, got up and went inside to get a drink of water. She was glad that they had moved on from affairs but wasn't sure menstrual products had longevity as a conversation topic. She gazed at them from the kitchen window, wishing she had brought her wine with her. Then she could have planted herself here. Sometimes there was safety in distance. Both of her sisters were now regarding Harry pensively. She knew exactly what they were thinking. Did any of his features gel with the man in the photo? Was that man still alive? She came back over to the sliding door and leaned against the jamb.

'Hey, Harry,' said Annie suddenly. 'Have you ever heard of a man called Henry Harrison?'

'Annie!' exclaimed Kat. 'No! We agreed!'

'What? How can it hurt? He might know something we don't! Stop underestimating him!'

'Yes,' said Harry, looking pleased to be asked. 'He liked peppermints. Also, William Henry Harrison was the ninth president of the United States of America. He died in office. He was also the shortest-serving president. Thirty-one days. His doctors were accused of impotence.'

Kat, who had been frowning at Annie, now transferred her gaze to her brother. Her mouth quirked. 'Impotence?' she queried. 'Really? Like, all of them?'

'Incompetence,' corrected Harry. 'I meant incompetence.'

'Admittedly, the two *can* go together,' said Annie. George flashed her a quick, questioning look. Annie had been short on humour thus far this evening.

'He left behind a wife and ten children and several grandchildren,' added Harry.

'So definitely some periods of potency,' commented Kat. She turned to her sisters. 'Do you know, I think I do remember him now. I think he used to drop in while we were at school. I have this recollection of coming home a few times and this friend of theirs was sitting at the kitchen table, talking to Mum. That *must* have been him.'

'Lucky that's all they were doing,' said Annie darkly.

'Peppermints,' said Harry. 'He liked peppermints.'

George had largely tuned out. She was picturing William Henry Harrison's bedside as his life ebbed away. His wife and all those children, plus grandchildren. The shock, the grief, the disbelief. It would have been much like her mother's. Although she doubted that anybody had been sitting in the corner playing Tetris on their mobile phone, as Harry had been. She came forward to grab her wine. 'Lesley still has two generations in front of her,' she blurted. 'We have none.'

Kat gazed at her as she absorbed the shift in subject matter, and then nodded. 'I know.'

'I was thinking that too,' said Annie, with more animation than she had shown for a while. 'A few days ago. It's like we were the sandwich generation. Kids one side and parents the other. And now suddenly, we're not.'

'We're an open sandwich,' said Kat. She gave a wry smile.

'It's not funny,' said Annie curtly.

'The sandwich is named after John Montagu,' said Harry. 'He was the Earl of Sandwich. He liked them because that way he could eat while playing cards without using a fork.'

Kat's face had sobered. 'Have you thought that humour might be my way of coping, Annie? I *know* it's not funny. And I *know* it's hard. Losing the last parent was *always* going to be hard. It's like they take the keys to your childhood along with them.'

The keys to your childhood. George ran the phrase over her tongue. She took a step backwards, leaning against the door again, staring into the darkening backyard.

'Do you know what helped me, a bit?' continued Kat. The rafter above creaked as she leaned back in the egg-chair, holding her glass against her chest. 'And this is going to sound awful, but I don't mean it that way. See, I was watching the news last night, with the fires. All those people whose lives have just been decimated. There was a father and son killed together up in New South Wales. They interviewed this woman who'd lost her daughter. And I thought that despite everything we're going through right now, we're actually lucky. *Our* people left in order. Grandparents, then parents. We might have wanted them to be here for longer, but there's nothing well, *unnatural* about it.'

George frowned as she thought this through. She took a gulp of her wine. Kat was right, it did help. But only a little. Tragedy porn.

'It's also why we have to stick together.' Kat was looking at Annie again. 'Nobody else understands the same as us. Do you remember when we were at the hospital just after she died, and we were all still in shock and I said we were now orphans? And Tom said that he didn't think it counted when you were older?'

'Oh god,' said George with feeling. 'It always counts.'

'Also it meant he didn't get his fingers all greasy,' said Harry. He was staring at his phone. 'From eating the meat without bread. Which made the cards slippery.'

Annie's v had deepened as she met her eldest sister's gaze. 'Are you trying to say something about Tom?'

'Of course not,' said Kat with obvious irritation. 'I'm just saying that he didn't understand properly. *Nobody* understands properly. Except us. For god's sake, George, stop hovering! Sit down!'

'In 2006 a court ruled that burritos and tacos were *not* sandwiches,' continued Harry. He used his finger to scroll the screen. 'A sandwich had to include at least two slices of bread. Boston. United States of America. In Australia though, the term is more narrowly defined.'

'Enough, Harry!' snapped Annie. 'Please!'

Harry looked up at her, puzzled. George reached out to lay her spare hand on his arm, but he shook her off as his face cleared. He rose to his feet stiffly and gathered up two of the leftover Thai containers, stacking them atop each other and balancing his mobile on top. Then he pushed past her through the sliding door. She turned to watch him leave.

'Well done,' said Kat. She sat back and gave Annie a slow clap.

Annie rubbed at her brow with her good hand. She got up, pushing her chair back roughly. The sun glinted across her plum-coloured hair, giving it a rather undeserved halo. 'I'll go say sorry.'

George stepped aside to allow her sister space to leave. She went over to her chair and lowered herself with a sigh. 'I'd just like one night,' she said. 'One night where we all get along. Is that too much to ask?'

'You sound like Mum,' commented Kat.

George shrugged. The backyard was now bathed in a crimson-laced golden glow. It was perfectly still, without even a breath of wind. The rumble of evaporative cooling from the house was the only sound. There was something almost lyrical about the scene, George thought, the setting of the sun a metaphor for the entire week. The notion came with a shaft of pain, its edges damp with wine. She wanted to share, but no doubt Kat would laugh at her. Humour might be her sister's way of coping, but George didn't want to provide the fodder. She felt tears prick at her eyes.

'I have to tell you something,' said Kat now. She leaned towards George and whispered, rather loudly, 'While you were gone, Tom dropped in with her bag of overnight things. Hardly spoke to me at all, the rude little bugger.'

'Oh well,' said George. She wasn't sure what else was required.

'But at least they finished their stickers. Complaining all the while, mind you. He put one on the TV, although how he's going to get it back up to the Gold Coast, I don't know.'

George took another sip of wine and then put the glass down. She'd had more than enough. 'You've got it in for him a bit, don't you?'

'What? No, I don't!'

George had regretted saying anything the moment the words had left her mouth. She really didn't want another discussion about Tom, or the dispute over stickers, or really anything divisive. Instead she wanted to talk about nostalgia, and memories, and what drew them together. In her peripheral vision she could see her sister staring at her, but George kept her own gaze on the setting sun. 'Forget I said anything.'

'Well, *that's* a bit hard!' said Kat crossly, leaning back once more. 'What a daft thing to say! I certainly *don't* have it in for him.'

George nodded, as if she was agreeing. She searched for a change in topic. 'And Annie? What did she put her priority stickers on then?'

'The dinner set and that diary.'

'What!' George turned to gape at her. The setting sun was forgotten. The diary was hers; she'd found it first. '*I* want the diary!'

Kat shrugged. She swung herself lightly in the chair. 'So put your sticker on it too.'

'But now it'll look like I just did it so she couldn't have it!'

Kat shrugged again. She leaned over to fish a carrot from one of the containers. She ate it, then licked her fingers. 'What? You worried it'll look like *you* had it in for *her*?' She gave a snort of laughter. 'So discuss it with her then. She's the one who's all up for that.'

George stared at her, trying to find the words for how unappealing that idea was. Her mobile pinged with an incoming message. For once, the distraction was welcome. She fished it out of her bag and then slipped her glasses on. It was from Leo.

All good. We're staying in tonight, playing board games and talking about Granma.

George smiled. For a moment she wished fervently that she was there, with them. He was such a good son. She recalled him offering to cancel his own plans for her on Wednesday evening, and her smile softened fondly. If she had known that his father had made other plans, she might just have taken Leo up on the offer. But probably not. She put the phone down as something skittered along the edges of her consciousness, jarring briefly before it darted away. George's smile faded as she tried to grasp it. The wine didn't help.

She glanced at her sister, who was examining her own phone as she swung the egg-chair in small, tight circles. The rafters above

creaked companionably. Annie still hadn't returned. It was something to do with Wednesday night. George backtracked, setting
the scene to nudge the thought into view. She'd been preparing a
nice meal for Simon, because of bloody Guy.

'I think Aunt Margaret is losing it,' said Kat from the egg-
chair. 'Listen to this. "I'll just say one more thing and then no
more. Georgette said Enid would agree. I doubt that." What the
hell is she on about?'

'I don't know,' said George. She didn't need the distraction.

'God, I don't need to get her sectioned along with everything
else,' said Kat. 'I'm going to text Lesley. It's her mother, after all.
She can deal with it.'

'Good idea.' George picked up her wine again and took a sip.
Leo had offered to stay, but she had told him it was fine, she was
having dinner with his father. And so he left. But of course Simon
had already made other plans. Why hadn't Leo mentioned this? If
Rhyll knew their father had gone up to Callum's, then why hadn't
he? George stilled, holding her glass out as if making a toast. *That*
was what had jarred, but the clarification brought an oilier suspicion in its wake. George put the wine down and picked up her
mobile again. She typed quickly, her fingers fat.

When did your dad tell you he was staying at Unvle Callum's?

Staring fixedly at the phone, George willed her daughter to
reply. Before long the dots appeared, hovering tantalisingly, and
then came a response.

Are you drinking? Lol. Unvle Callum. He told me that day. Why?

George blinked. It hadn't been planned then, only coming into
being after he met Guy. The correlation formed a fist in her gut.
She got up quickly, her chair skittering back.

'Are you okay?' asked Kat.

'Fine. Fine. I just need to … um, do something.' George took
the phone inside the house, going through to the lounge where

she stood with it heavy in her hand while she tried to order her thoughts. The glasses of pinot grigio were not helping. How had she not put two and two together sooner? Simon had made an *unplanned* visit to his brother just after the man she was having an affair with had dropped around. Leo had been there for some of the conversation, but not all. She raised the mobile, pulling up Guy's last message and then adding another. Even typing the words made her feel ill.

Does my husband know?

The reply was slow in coming, although she knew for a fact that Guy always kept his phone nearby. But when it came, she almost wished it hadn't.

Yes

George stared at it. The confirmation pulsed at her temples. Another message arrived before she could even think through the ramifications.

You probably won't believe me but I didn't mean that. I only went around there because I was worried about you. I sincerely regret that now.

She blinked. The pomposity of this succeeded in overlaying her anguish with anger. It throbbed along the periphery of a burgeoning headache, pinching behind the bridge of her nose. She marshalled her fury, jabbing at the keypad as she typed.

Bullshit. You went round because your ego was hurting. You're an arsehole. George had barely pressed send before she was typing again. *My mother died and all I needed was time to sort through everything. But you couldn't allow me even that. Instead you've destroyed my marriage because you felt ignored. You are the lowest of the low. I only hope that there is such a thing as karma. Rot in hell.*

The row of undulating dots had appeared while she was composing this last, then vanished, and appeared again shortly after it was sent. George realised that she was holding the phone so tightly that her knuckles were white. She took a deep breath and loosened her grip as his message appeared.

Not true. I admit I should have restrained myself, not gone to your house. But my intentions were good. I regret any part I played in your current difficulties but it was actually your text that did it. Not me.

George frowned. She scrolled back through the conversation thread until she reached the one he had sent her on Wednesday. It suddenly dawned on her that he sent that *while* he was there, not afterwards. It would be just like Simon to invite him inside, give him a drink. They had probably been sitting on the couch, watching the tennis *together* when she had texted him, telling him he was an arse and that it was over. Her face paled. Kat came inside from the veranda and gave her a curious look.

'Are you sure you're okay? What's up?'

'Nothing,' replied George curtly. 'Just sorting something out.'

'O-kay.' Kat shrugged. She got the bottle of wine from the fridge and took it back outside.

In the meantime, another message had popped in from Guy. *And tbh, I think it wise if we keep our distance for a while. Don't you agree? Give you time to sort things out. I really do wish you all the best for the future.*

George shook her head numbly. She knew the suggestion of distance had nothing to do with her, or the position he had placed her in, but with his fear of what might happen if her marriage actually broke up. In the cold light of the past few days, no doubt he had realised that she might turn up on his doorstep with a suitcase. She began typing another response but stopped halfway through. After a moment she deleted it. There would be time for that later. Right now she needed to acknowledge that not just had her husband known about her affair since Wednesday, but no doubt he thought that she knew that he knew – and was ignoring it. Two whole days. She flicked across to their last conversation and stared at it for a while before typing, this time far slower.

You will never know how sorry I am. I never wanted to hurt you. Ever.

She pressed send and then waited, her eyes on the text. No dots appeared and nor did his icon, indicating that he had even read it. Minutes slid by. Nausea swirled within, fizzing with wine. Her marriage was over, finished. Kaput. The moving finger having writ, had moved on. Without her even having realised.

Chapter Sixteen

Friday (late) evening

'So we're doing the division at lunchtime tomorrow?' asked Annie, massaging her wrist.

'You asked that question before,' commented Kat. 'And the answer's still yes. Can't put it off past that. We need to get everything cleared over the weekend.'

George barely heard them. She was leaning back in her chair, her chin concertinaed. The sun had set some time ago, the golden glow having given way to graduating shades of grey. Annie's bandage looked grey. The moths that fluttered against the outside light were grey too, just a softer feathery grey. Even her mood was grey. The conversation had ebbed and flowed for the past hour or so, with her contributing very little. Her nausea had long since evolved into self-pity, and a generous dollop of resentment. It bubbled just below her sternum, like gas. Resentment at Guy, at Simon, at her mother, at everything.

'My daughter writes a blog,' she said now, staring at her wineglass. 'It's very good.'

Annie made a soft, snorting sound. 'Yeah we know. What, have we moved to that stage of the evening where we start listing our offspring's accomplishments? Bags not.'

'That's not what I meant!' George glared at her sister, her bubble instantly enlarging to include Annie.

'Besides, that's not a game I can win,' said Kat lightly. 'And I prefer ones I can win.'

Annie made her snorting sound again, but this time muffled it by taking a gulp of wine.

George watched her narrowly. She took her glasses off and folded them, then unfolded again. '*I* want the diary,' she burst out suddenly. '*I'm* putting a sticker on it too.'

Annie's v appeared. 'I'd expect nothing less.'

'Good!'

'Fine!'

'Oh, for god's sake,' said Kat crossly. 'So put your sticker on it then. Or discuss it. I don't care. Just don't bloody argue about it. Hell, it wasn't even that good a read. Self-indulgent waffle. No dialogue. No plot. No real resolution. Ends left untied. I'd give it two out of five stars on Goodreads.'

George stared at her. From the corner of her eye she could see Annie doing the same. After a moment, her mouth quirked. It was either that or bursting into tears.

Kat took a sip of wine. 'And I'm only being generous because I knew the author.'

'Oh, I don't know.' Annie leaned forward. Her v had vanished. 'Perhaps we *should* publish it. Perhaps the emerald-eyed Martin Pratt would like to read about missed opportunities. He might even reach out. He could even be your new hobby.'

'Oh god,' groaned Kat. 'What was wrong with me? Bloody hell. Kat Pratt.'

Annie was now grinning. 'How did you know that his hair was like cornsilk? Did you run your hands through it during recess?'

Kat threw her head back, gazing at the ceiling. She straightened again. 'I remember him too. I thought he looked like that guy from *The Waltons*. He even had a mole on his cheek. Thankfully my taste has improved a little since then!'

'Do you know cornsilk is actually a greenish-yellow?' said George. She heard herself slur slightly over the word greenish so continued quickly. 'It looks like a nest. Not all that attractive really. And it can be used as a diuretic. Like, to produce more urine.'

Kat was staring at her now. 'You sound like Harry!'

'Well, I definitely don't need any of that then.' Annie rose, a little unsteadily. 'Off to the loo again!'

While she was gone, Kat got up to collect the empty Thai containers. George tried to calculate how much she'd drunk, but it was too hard. There was a little left in this bottle, and two empties on the drainer by the sink. But she was glad of the alcohol; as much as it dulled her thought processes, it also numbed them. At least as far as her husband was concerned. Sitting here, the veranda a pool of light in the darkness, she could pretend *that* wasn't happening. Tomorrow was another day. Annie came back outside. She picked up her phone as she sat down.

'I was thinking I might go home,' she said, already typing. 'I'll get Tom to pick me up. He's got the car.'

'Oh don't,' said Kat. 'Don't go home. Stay.'

'Nah. Maybe another time.'

'Fine. Suit yourself.'

'I will.'

Kat turned away. She stacked the containers on Harry's abandoned chair and then gave the table a perfunctory wipe with one of the serviettes. George reached across for the bottle and drained it into their three glasses. A moth fluttered across the back of her hand, its wings like eyelashes against her skin.

'Oh. Tom's out. He can't pick me up,' said Annie. She gave a heavy sign as she put the phone down. 'But look, I had another thought. I'm prepared, *reluctantly* ...' she paused here to give them both a look, underscoring this reluctance, 'to shelve telling Harry in case we find out more. But we should tell Tegan. In fact, she should be involved in the decision whether or not to tell *him*.'

'Yes,' said Kat without hesitation. She flopped back into the egg-chair. 'Definitely. It's her parentage too. And you know what else? We need to start involving her in all the decisions being made about Harry. We should've already been doing that. I was thinking about it last night. What we seem to have forgotten thus far is that *she's* his next of kin. Not us. Her.'

'Sure, but he's also an adult,' said Annie flatly. '*He* needs to be involved in the decisions too. Mum treated him like a child, but there's no reason we should.'

Kat didn't reply, instead lifting two fingers to pinch the bridge of her nose. George leaned forward to check her phone. There was still no reply from Simon. She sent through another, in the same vein as before. That made five unanswered messages. Then she sat back, trying to focus on what had just been said. Tegan was Harry's next of kin. It felt discordant, as if the order that Kat had been referring to earlier had just been knocked asunder once more.

'Hang on though,' said Annie now, her brow furrowing again. 'But are you saying that Tegan should get control of his money? When things get settled? I don't know about that.'

'Well, maybe *Harry* should have control,' said Kat smartly. 'After all, he's an adult. We need to start treating him as one.'

'Now you're being ridiculous,' snapped Annie.

'Probably,' said Kat. 'But it's all about where you draw the line, isn't it?' She kept her eyes on her youngest sister for a few moments and then sighed. 'Look, anyway, I don't think we have a choice. Tegan is his next of kin now. We can get some legal advice, but do we really want to fight about this anyway? She *should* be on board. She's his daughter. And let's face it, out of all of them, she's the best anyway. Hands down.'

George glanced automatically at Annie, who was gaping at Kat. She looked like she was about to have an apoplectic fit. George felt a sudden chuckle rise and swallowed it quickly.

'I mean because she's a social worker,' added Kat hurriedly. 'That's all.'

Annie didn't look convinced, but nor did she appear willing to pursue the matter. George thought it just as well. If she was to be honest, even if Tegan hadn't been a social worker, she would still probably be the best for such a responsibility. Tom was too self-involved, Leo too well, quirky, and Rhyll … George tried to imagine what would happen if her daughter was suddenly responsible for another human, with a healthy bank balance. She grimaced.

'And also,' continued Kat, 'George and I were talking earlier and we thought Tegan should take a portion of Harry's inheritance earlier. Help set herself up.'

Annie was still staring at her. Her v had reappeared. 'So you two decided this?'

'No, we didn't *decide* that,' said Kat, a little curtly. 'We *discussed* it. You weren't here at the time. So we're asking your opinion now. So, thoughts?'

After a moment, Annie dipped her head to stare at her wine. She shrugged.

'I'll take that as agreeance then,' said Kat. 'And we're also agreed about telling her about the other stuff? About Henry Harrison? If so, I'll send her a message. Suggest she come by tomorrow a little earlier. Before everyone else gets here. And then she can chip in on the decision about whether to tell him or not. Everyone happy with that?'

Both George and Annie nodded. George didn't want to think about tomorrow though.

'You know what still annoys me?' asked Annie suddenly. She ran a finger around the rim of her wineglass. 'You know where Mum was talking about the Derwent pencils and she called me a sook? That's *so* unfair. It really is.'

George took another sip of wine so that she wouldn't have to answer. With all the things currently on her plate, there was no room for Annie's annoyance. Which straddled the edges of sooki-ness anyway. For herself, she was more perturbed about being called a settler. She thought about this for a while. Perhaps it was true. She did seem to have settled for things rather than seek them out. Reaction rather than proaction. She considered her life as it now was. Treading water. Now, drowning. And then she recalled her dreams of London. Earl's Court. Windsor Castle. The Tower. Anne Boleyn, who had also cheated on her husband. Allegedly.

'Yes, I suppose it is,' said Kat eventually, into the silence.

'It's better than settling,' said George abruptly. She frowned at her glass. 'At least you complained about stuff. *I* just put up with it.'

'So you're saying I *am* a sook then?'

This time George was saved from answering by her phone. It pinged against the table and she jerked herself forward, snatching it up. It was Simon.

Stop texting me. I don't know what hurts fucking more. That your having an affair, or that it's with a slug like that.

You're, she thought numbly, with the only part of her brain that seemed to be working. He must be pretty upset to have misspelt that word. He knew how much it irritated her. But then maybe that's why he'd done it. Perhaps now they were even. She blinked. The pinot grigio swilled nauseously in her stomach, along with guilt. The two did not mix well. She hit reply and then paused, her finger hovering over the keypad. In the end, she kept it simple. *I'm sorry.*

This time the answer came straight back. *Fuck off.*

George put her phone down and then took her glasses off. She really was sorry; she never wanted him to be hurt. Regret clamped her bowels. Tomorrow had arrived too soon. She rubbed at her eyes, smudging mascara across her hand. When she lowered her hands, it was to find both her sisters staring at her.

'Don't ask,' said George simply. 'Please, I mean it. Just don't ask.'

'O-kay,' said Kat. She exchanged a rapid glance with Annie. 'Sure. Well, to go back to what you were both saying before George took a message that obviously upset her but she refuses to discuss, then I'd add this. If you don't like being called a sook, don't sook about it. And if *you*' – she turned to George – 'don't want to be called a settler, then don't settle. Do something different. Spread your wings. Take the leap.'

'I will,' said George.

'What?'

'I will,' she repeated. It all suddenly seemed crystal clear. 'I'm going to London. I'll stay with Lesley. I'm going to write my book.'

Annie was staring at her. She snorted. 'You so won't.'

'Oh, yes I will,' said George with certainty. 'I'll show *her* I'm not a settler.'

'Hmm. If you're talking about our mother, you do realise that she's not around to notice?' said Kat. She was regarding George quizzically. 'Too late to go looking for her approval now.'

'I don't need her approval,' replied George. This didn't ring true, even to her. But her sister's expression was more than a little annoying. She put her glasses back on, swiped away Simon's last text before she was forced to read it again, and then quickly typed a message to her cousin. She held it up to show her sisters.

'Lol,' said Kat. 'You'll just take it back in the morning. When you're sober. And you don't have mascara spread across your face.'

'Really?' asked George, raising her eyebrows. She brought back the phone and scrolled through her contacts for the travel agent they used two years ago, for their trip to Bali. There she was, Kate Thatcher, just beneath Enid Tapscott. George blinked, dragging herself back to the matter in hand. She thought for a few moments, trying to ascertain the most suitable timing for the trip. Rhyll's birthday was at the end of the month. It was also high season at the moment, so it would be more economical to wait a while. Plus a replacement teacher would have to be organised, for her TAFE classes. Then there was Easter. George glanced up at her sisters with a tight smile. They were both watching her, looking bemused. Her smile widened. She was impressed by how sharp her thought processes were now. Perhaps she should have turned to drink years ago. She typed quickly, requesting that they book her a ticket for May. One way. She hit send and then held her phone up once more.

'O-kay,' said Kat. 'I'm impressed.'

'I'm going to do what Mum didn't,' said George firmly, this thought only just occurring to her. 'You know, in the diary. Go to London. I'll stay for a year and see what happens. Maybe I'll even take some of her ashes and sprinkle them there.'

'I think that's illegal,' said Annie. Her v had reappeared between her eyes.

'Ha! I laugh at the law,' said George airily. She proceeded to do just that.

'Um ...' Kat's batwing brows had risen. 'Are you *sure* you're okay?'

George nodded, beaming at them both. 'I've never been better. In fact, for the first time in *years* I'm seeing things clearly,' she said just as, behind them, all the lights went off.

They were instantly plunged into near-darkness. The only illumination came from the moon, and the iridescent green of a distant garden ornament. From George's left came a yelp, presumably from her younger sister. Then all was quiet once more. She realised that the steady hum of the evaporative cooler had ceased as well. It all seemed oddly comforting, almost reflective. George thought she could just stay like this until May, and then go straight to the airport.

'Electricity blackout,' said Annie, rather unnecessarily. 'Too many people using their bloody air-conditioning, no doubt.'

'Like us?' said Kat. A rustling noise followed and George guessed that her sister had just risen from the egg-chair. A single beam of light appeared as Kat flicked her mobile phone torch on. 'I'll go check on Harry. Do you two want to see if you can find some candles?'

Annie had used the illumination to locate her own torch. As Kat left, she stood and went inside to the kitchen, tucking the phone against her chest with her bandaged hand. George could hear her opening and closing cupboards and drawers, muttering the whole time.

'Your battery'll run out soon,' called George helpfully. 'Those things eat the charge up.'

'Great,' said Annie. She slammed the pantry closed. 'I don't suppose you know where she keeps the candles?'

'No idea. But she does have a proper torch on top of the fridge.'

'Really? Thanks for letting me know.'

'You're welcome.' George checked her own phone to see if she'd had a reply from either Lesley or the travel agent. The former would be more likely, she supposed, given the time.

'Damn,' said Annie. She came back to the sliding door, shaking the torch. 'It's got no batteries. We need four double As. Do you know where she keeps those then?'

'Maybe with her candles?'

There was silence for a moment. 'You're a great help.'

Another beam of light sliced through the lounge room and then Kat reappeared. 'He's already gone to bed. Oh good, you found a torch! My phone charge is almost gone.'

'No batteries,' said Annie. 'We need four double As.'

'Bloody hell.' Kat pushed past to come outside. She flicked her torch off and took a sip of her wine. 'Maybe the electricity company stuffed up the transfer? That girl *was* an idiot.'

Annie had followed her. She put her mobile down on the picnic table, where it shone a beam straight up into the night sky. Behind it, her face looked elongated, her eyes dark pools. 'If that's so, we probably won't get it back on until tomorrow.'

'True,' said Kat. She sat down in the egg-chair once more, folding her arms crossly.

'I know where there might be double A batteries,' said George helpfully. 'But they're in the bin. And I'm not getting them.'

'What? Why would they be in the bin?'

'Because we threw them out,' explained George. 'On Tuesday. Or was it Wednesday?'

'Don't,' said Kat. 'Because now you sound like Aunt Margaret. It's like drawing blood from a stone. Why the hell would we throw them out?'

'Oh!' Annie's head came around to the side of the light. She was staring at George. She gave a snort of what might have been dismay, or laughter. 'No. No way.'

'What?' Kat looked from one of them to the other. Then realisation dawned. 'Oh.'

'And we're not doing the draw-straws thing either,' said George firmly. 'If you want them, you get them. No more amenability from this girl. I'm perfectly happy in the dark.'

Kat sighed. She looked across at Annie. 'So the question is, how badly do we want to save our phone charge? Badly enough to find our mother's vibrator where it's buried under rubbish, open it up and get the batteries out?'

Annie shook her head. 'That's not a question I ever thought I'd have to answer.'

'To be fair,' said George equably, 'I don't think you're alone there.'

'Nor do I particularly want to know if the batteries in there are well-used.'

Kat got up again. 'Bugger it. *I'll* get them.'

George moved her chair so that her sister could squeeze past to get to the steps. Her mobile light came on as she descended, and then it disappeared. Annie sat down.

'Switch yours on, George. So I can give my battery a rest.'

George felt around for her glasses and then realised that she still had them on. She squinted at her phone, trying to locate the torch icon. She was quite proud of herself for not giving in. Normally she would have either gone with the short straw option, which she always lost, or just volunteered beforehand. A people pleaser, that's what she was. She flicked on the torch and slid her mobile towards the centre of the picnic table where it wasn't so blinding. As she did so, Annie turned hers off and almost instantly a message flashed up on her sister's screen. George glanced over automatically.

Soz Mum. Hope its not to awful. Dont let them push u round!

George blinked. She glanced up and met Annie's rather horrified gaze.

'Ignore that!' said Annie. 'It's from, um, before!'

'Before what?' queried George. She was rather pleased that her voice was so even. 'Before things became *unawful*? When we were pushing you around?'

'Not quite.'

'Or back when you both realised that relatives were just people who shared your blood?'

'Oh. You saw that?'

'*Everybody* saw that, Annie,' said George. 'It was on Facebook. Before your charming son defriended us.' She took her glasses off and polished them. The effect was ruined somewhat by her dropping them mid-polish. She fumbled on her lap for them and then looked back at her sister. 'Do you know something? You're your own worst enemy.'

'Really?' Annie stared at her, then sat back and folded her arms. 'How so?'

'Well, for starters you're so bloody sensitive.' George slipped her glasses back on. Her sister's face swam into focus, weirdly lit by the mobile. She didn't look happy. George continued regardless. 'You're always on the lookout for being slighted. You're like a … an offensive *bloodhound*.'

Annie's lips thinned. 'Did you just call me offensive?'

'Huh? No. I said you're an offensive bloodhound. Like you search out *offence*.'

'You're drunk,' snapped Annie. 'And you're the one who's offensive. You're *always* offensive. Both of you. Ganging up on me and—'

'Fuuuck!' said George, her voice rising through the stretched syllable. 'Not this again! Oh my god! Have you ever thought that it's all in your imagination?' She leaned forward, tapping a finger to the side of her head. 'And that if you didn't *sook* so much, we wouldn't gang up on you?'

'Well, if you didn't bloody … never mind. You wouldn't understand. Not in a million years.'

'Really? Well, by all means explain it. Come on, you're the one who's into discussion.'

'Oh, just shut up. Do us all a favour and put a sticker over your bloody mouth.'

'And you know what else? I *am* having that diary. I found it!'

'Over my dead body!'

'Fine! Suits me!'

The side gate banged, severing the heated exchange. Moments later the light from Kat's mobile torch came into view as she mounted the steps. She tossed four double A batteries onto the table. One hit George's glass with a dull clang.

'Success!' exclaimed Kat. 'I deserve a medal for that! Now we just …' She petered off as she took in her sisters' faces. 'What now? I was only gone five minutes!'

Annie pushed her chair back. 'I'm going to bed.'

'But hang on, what happened?'

'Let *her* explain.' Annie lifted a shaking finger to point at George. 'As for me, I can't bear to look at either of you anymore.

And don't worry, I'll still help out the next few days. Along with my *charming* son. But then I'm out of here. Forever!'

Kat's eyes had widened. She watched her sister leave and then turned to George. 'Well, that was a little dramatic. What the hell did I miss?'

'A message from Tom,' said George. She could feel the adrenalin leaving her body. It left just weariness, and a little nausea, in its wake. 'Apparently we're both awful. Also he needs some remedial English.'

'Oh, hell.'

'She's an idiot,' said George. 'So I told her a few home truths.'

'Oh, hell,' said Kat again. She took a deep breath. 'I'll go talk to her.'

'Whatever,' said George, channelling her daughter. She waited until Kat left, still using her mobile torch, and then turned her own off. The darkness settled again, like a weighted blanket. She took a sip of wine, but it had become a little warm. Also, she thought that perhaps she'd had enough. From inside, she could hear voices slowly rising. She thought that if she got up and moved into the lounge room she could probably have heard everything. She stayed where she was.

After a few minutes, George pressed at her phone screen and checked whether any messages had been received. Nothing. She wondered what Simon was doing, right this moment, but then quickly shut that line of thought down. It was too much to bear. Instead she scrolled through to the message sent to the travel agent and re-read it before texting a follow-up. She needed that ticket booked earlier. Hang the expense.

Chapter Seventeen

Saturday morning

In the dream, George was with her family in the goldfields country town of Majic, not far from Bendigo. This was where her father had grown up, before moving to Melbourne in his late teens. It was also where they had spent their summer holidays until she was about twelve. In her memory these were perpetually sunny days, where rules were as optional as shoes, laced with the smell of gum trees and zinc cream. Jovial uncles who seemed permanently tipsy, soft-bosomed aunts with feted culinary skills, and so many cousins that it didn't seem to matter what you wanted to do, there was always someone to do it with.

Over the years, the duration of their stays had gradually lessened as her father's roots loosened. The older generation had died off, while the younger ones moved away or simply drifted apart. Life got in the way. Then one year they holidayed with friends in Rosebud instead and that was that. But in this dream they were all there again, even her grandparents, and her father's cousin Sid, who had a fatal altercation with a chainsaw when she was seven, and Uncle Martin's manic Yorkshire terrier with his paralysed back legs fixed within their rickety, makeshift wheeled contraption.

They were picnicking along the bluff overlooking the town. Seersucker tablecloths lay across the ground, loaded with Loy's lemonade and sandwiches and Aunt Tilly's prize-winning scones. Her mother sat with her legs to one side, slicing bananas onto buttered bread and then sprinkling them with sugar. George watched with fascination as this youthful Enid deftly worked the paring knife, stopping just short of her thumb. She willed her mother's concentration to slip, just for the briefest moment. Not because she particularly wanted her to be hurt, but because each successful slice carried a sliver of disappointment.

In the dream she was neither child nor adult, but something nebulous. She was acutely conscious of this, although nobody else seemed to be. She could see her sisters sitting cross-legged with the other girls, their swap cards spread across the grass. Annie's wrist was bandaged. A nearby pram held the curled form of a baby. One of the aunts was spraying Aerogard. Her father sat with the men around a radio, listening to a VFL match. *To the wing position on the members' stand side and oh! Alex Jesaulenko! You **beauty**!* The men roared and Uncle Martin picked up his dog, wheels and all, and kissed it roundly on the snout.

They all belonged, fitting together perfectly like jigsaw pieces. Except her. There was no place for the child–woman that she was and, even more upsettingly, there didn't seem to be a gap where the girl was missing. She was a watcher, not a player. She lifted both her hands, staring at them, willing definition. And now there was a wall between her and everyone else. She explored it with her fingertips, itsy-bitsy-spider style, and then opened her eyes into darkness. The ambiguity travelled with her, adding to her confusion. Perhaps she didn't belong here either.

It took a while for George to ground herself. She was in her father's single bed, in her mother's room, in her childhood home. The wall formed part of the latter. She could hear her sister's feather-light snores from the other bed. And now, with time and place sorted, she realised that she also felt ill. *Really* ill. Her head throbbed and her stomach churned and her mouth felt as dry and scratchy as cat litter. It was also sauna-hot in this room. George sat up gingerly and, slightly buoyed by the success of this venture, pushed the tangled sheet from her legs and swung them over. A strip of light beneath the door suggested that, thankfully, the passage light was on. Which meant the electricity was back. She made her way slowly across the room and eased the door open just enough to slip through.

The study door was closed, and she now recalled Annie having claimed it for the night. Not verbally of course, as by then they were no longer on speaking terms. Recollection came with a vice-like grip to her temples. George flinched. She went into the bathroom and sat on the toilet, lowering her head into her hands and trying to decide whether she wanted to vomit. It was an appealing thought. After barely eating for over a week, a surfeit of Thai spices probably hadn't been the best choice. After a while her stomach settled, so she stood up to gaze into the mirror. That was a mistake. She was accustomed to the mohawked bed-head hair, but not the pallid skin, the pouchy jowls or the sunken eyes. She looked a little like her mother had, just before she died.

George took a few deep breaths and then used the toilet before taking the bath towel and making her way slowly back to the bedroom. She laid the towel by her bed, just in case, and then lowered herself onto the mattress, pulling the crumpled sheet over her. She felt hot and ill and miserable. The minutes ticked by with excruciating slowness, sliding into hours. Along with the recollection of the fight with Annie came the text messages from Guy, and from Simon. They rolled within, agitating, like washing. With each turn she recalled something else, or realised a fresh ramification. Occasionally she fell asleep, but only briefly, her body maliciously dragging her back from any respite. Nor were there any more dreams, or family reunions, just a ground-hog night of wretchedness and cloying heat.

She woke the final time into full light. The blinds were no match for the sunshine that now glowed along the edges. Her mother's bed on the other side of the room was empty, the covers pulled back. George lay still, staring at the ceiling. She tried to calculate how much sleep she'd had altogether, but gave up when this threatened to reawaken her headache. Instead she let herself slip into a fantasy where her mother was right now out in the kitchen, boiling eggs and cutting toast into soldiers. She would look up as George came in, with her particular smile. It quirked up one side of her mouth, and lifted the corner of her eye. Enid hadn't been the most tactile person, but she didn't need to be. Not with that smile. It was both a welcome and an embrace. And it slotted George into place.

A car revved up the road and then took off with the sound of spitting gravel. It was enough to fracture the daydream. George rolled over and pressed her fingertips against her eyes. Compart-mentalisation was the only way she was going to get through this day. She felt marginally better, physically, but the sure knowledge of what lay ahead was nauseating in itself. It lay atop the wine and Thai food like an oil slick. She rolled over again and slipped her glasses on to check her mobile. No messages. She sighed and then lay still, postponing the inevitable until the waiting became tedious in itself. When she eventually got up, George didn't bother to dress. She just visited the bathroom briefly before padding out to the living area wearing her oversized t-shirt.

The sliding door was open, but the northerly breeze already felt clotted with warmth. Her mother was not in the kitchen. Instead Kat was leaning against the island bench, typing on her iPad. Annoyingly, she looked none the worse for wear. She had on a sleeveless, dusky-pink sundress that matched the roses in her tattoo. She glanced up as George came in.

'Sweet Jesus.'

'Yes,' said George. She put her phone and glasses down on the table and then pulled out a chair and sat down facing her sister. 'Exactly.'

'At least do something about your hair.'

'I did. This is the improved version.'

Kat continued examining her for a minute or so, then grimaced. She turned away to put the kettle on. 'You need Eno, but I think Annie got rid of all that when she did the pantry.'

'Where is she?'

'Still in the study.' Kat lowered her voice. 'Door closed. She had a shower before and I caught a rather disturbing glimpse of her, stark naked, rummaging through the linen closet for a towel.' Kat paused to grimace again. 'I'm going to store *that* away with things I never want to see again.'

George opened her mouth to ask why Annie hadn't just used the towel already in there, at least to cover herself, but then remembered that it was currently lying beside her bed. She closed her mouth.

'Anyway,' continued Kat, 'I asked if she wanted coffee, but she said no. She's leaving soon. Coming back later.'

George shrugged. She slipped on her glasses and then picked up her mobile. The screen felt sticky. It was nearly eight o'clock.

If it was already this warm, this early, the day itself was going to
be another stinker. Her temples pulsed. She didn't know how she
was going to get through it. Even her aunt's half-century old Bex
would have been welcome right now.

Kat was still talking. 'So we've got Tegan coming by around
one. And I've let your two know that they need to pick up their
stuff from two onwards.'

George nodded to show that she was listening. There were still
no new messages on her phone. She took a deep breath and then
pulled up the brief exchange that she'd had with her husband last
night. She re-read it, her stomach turning.

'Which means the afternoon's going to be quite busy,' continued Kat. 'Then that's it.' She brushed her hands together in a
finale gesture. 'My removal's coming first thing Monday.'

George nodded again. She tried to imagine how shocked Simon
must have been, how wounded. He very rarely swore for starters.
*I don't know what hurts fucking more. That your having an affair, or that
it's with a slug like that.* And he was right, Guy Weston *was* a slug.
A traitorous, malicious slug. She felt flushed with embarrassment
and remorse.

Kat brought over a cup of coffee along with a glass of water and
two paracetamol. George took the latter and then a grateful gulp
of the former. It burnt her tongue. She wondered if it would be
possible to negotiate the day like one of those nodding dolls that
sat on dashboards. She rubbed her eyes behind her glasses. She
simply couldn't do it.

'So I thought for the morning we could concentrate on the
wardrobe and—'

'No,' interrupted George. 'Sorry, but if you don't mind I might
go home for a bit too. I think there was something wrong with
my pad thai. And I didn't sleep very well.'

'Yeah, that's it,' said Kat with a smirk. 'Salmonella and a bad night's sleep. Nothing to do with the bottles of wine I put out in the rubbish this morning.'

George closed her eyes briefly. She didn't even want to hear the word wine. 'I'll grab a quick nap and be back by noon. I promise.'

'Fine. And from the look of you, that's probably a good idea. But don't forget your stickers. You're the only one who hasn't done your priorities yet and it'll be too late by the time we do the division.' She lowered her voice. 'We don't want to give Annie another reason to complain.'

'Sure. I'll do them quickly before I head off.' George's phone pinged so she glanced down with an equal mix of hope and trepidation. But the incoming message was from her cousin Lesley. Her eyes widened as she read it.

OF COURSE you can stay! Yippee! And if you come over in April, that's perfect! It gives me a month or so to show you round and then you'll have the flat all to yourself while I'm in Aus. Don't rush looking for your own place either, stay as long as you like. The whole year if that suits! I'M SO EXCITED! I'm going to start redecorating my spare room RIGHT NOW! This is going to be so MUCH FUN!!! Woo hoo!

George was still gaping at the message as recollection returned. She blinked as she absorbed it. From the bench, Kat let out a snort of laughter. She had leaned across to stare at George's mobile.

'You'd probably need to make time in your busy schedule to break the news to your husband,' she said, looking up at George with a grin. 'Woo hoo!'

'Oh god,' said George. She lowered the phone.

'Probably best to do it before the travel agent gets back to you.'

'Oh god,' said George again. Her stomach churned. She could feel the two paracetamol tablets within, riding the waves. She removed her glasses and cleaned them on her t-shirt. One thing at

a time. That was the only way she was going to get through this
day. And the first thing on the list was putting her sticker on the
diary. Second was going back home to crawl into bed. She would
pull the sheet over her head and pretend the last twenty-four
hours had never happened. Or even better, the last year. Then she
would swear off both alcohol and adultery. And as a silver lining,
her mother would still be alive.

***

George drove home slowly and carefully, mainly because she suspected that she shouldn't be driving at all. The dreadful thought
occurred to her, as she neared her house, that Simon might be
home already. If that was the case, she was going to drive straight
past and book in at a hotel. But his car wasn't there, and neither
was Leo's. To add to her relief, as she came up the path, she could
also hear the hum of the air-conditioner. She let herself inside,
revelling in the instant drop in the temperature, and left her overnight bag by the door. She hung up her handbag, first removing
her glasses and mobile, then slipped off her sandals and padded
down the passage into the lounge room. To her surprise, Rhyll
was sitting at the table, her laptop open before her. She seemed
equally shocked.

'What are you doing here?' asked Rhyll with a distinct lack of
welcome. She closed the laptop.

'I live here. Remember?'

'Well duh. I meant, I thought you were at Granma's house all
day?'

'Sorry to disappoint you.' George went past into the kitchen.
She poured a glass of water from the tap and took another two
paracetamol tablets. One lodged in her throat and she coughed
helplessly until it spat into the sink. She watched it dissolve, her

head thumping. When she turned around, Rhyll was still frowning at her.

'You look like shit.'

'Thanks.'

'Had a big night then, huh?'

'Something like that.' George went into the laundry to check
on Puddles. The labrador looked up with rheumy eyes. Sebastian
the bear was nestled by his side. The dog stretched his head towards
her, his tail twitching with happiness. George squatted to fondle
him between the ears. At least somebody was glad to see her.

'Well, we had a good night here too,' called Rhyll from the
family room. 'Leo filled me in on some stuff.'

George stood, her bruised knee emitting an audible crack.
Once upon a time, Puddles would have jumped up also. He would
have wound his way between her legs, his whole body undulating with unrestrained joy. Now even his tail barely moved. They
were going to have to do something about him soon. But this
knowledge was definitely more than she could deal with today.
She went back into the kitchen and regarded Rhyll warily.

'What sort of stuff?'

'Oh, this and that. And about that friend of yours dropping
around.' Rhyll put her head to one side and for a moment she
looked like her cousin Tegan. 'He said he was an odd sort of
bloke. Bit full of himself.'

'Ah.' George reached up and got down her favourite mug.
Please do not annoy the writer, the slogan read. *Or she may put you in
a book and kill you.* George turned it round to face her daughter.
'And what else did Leo say?' she asked.

Rhyll put her elbows on the table and rested her chin in her
hands as she gazed at her mother. 'Did you sleep with him?'

'*What?*'

Rhyll shrugged. 'Just a theory. We're wondering why Dad took off so soon afterwards. And then you texted last night about how long I'd known he was going up to Uncle Callum's. Which suggests you didn't know he was shooting through either.'

'I see.'

'So if you *didn't* sleep with him, then what'd he say that upset Dad so much?'

George felt her chest tighten painfully. 'Leo said your father was upset?'

'Yeah.'

It occurred to George that if she and Rhyll had one of those Facebook mother–daughter relationships, then she could have collapsed into the chair opposite her and spilled the beans. She probably would have cried a little. Rhyll would be shocked but sympathetic. She would pat her mother's shoulder and give her ... if not advice, then at least support. George felt a sudden sense of loss. The kettle boiled. It gave her an excuse to turn away.

'Well?'

'I don't know what it's all about.' George wrapped her hands around her mug as she faced her daughter again. Guy's flowers sat on the table beside Rhyll, along with a bowl of apples. George stared at them and then grimaced at the juxtaposition, before realising that might have made her look guilty. She wiped her expression as she continued hurriedly, 'And I'm not sure why you'd jump to the conclusion that I was sleeping with him. I'll just have to ask your father tonight. But I'm sure it's all fine.'

'Yeah. Sure.'

Silence fell between them. 'What are you working on anyway?' she asked, nodding towards the laptop. She was fairly sure it was most probably the blog, but didn't think this was the right time to raise it. She needed more sleep before that.

'Nothing.'

'Ah. Okay. And you know we're doing the division today? Everything'll have to be collected?'

'Yes, Mother. I know. You don't need to like, remind me of everything.'

George resisted the urge to roll her eyes. 'Fine.'

Rhyll picked up her mobile from the table and examined it, scrolling. Then she put it down and glanced back over at her mother. 'Hey, I asked Tom about why he defriended you two. He said it was because he didn't want to be censored.'

'Censored?' George stared at her, befuddled.

'Yeah. Apparently Aunt Annie had a go at him for that thing he posted. About relatives just being those that share your blood.'

George tried to reason this through. It seemed to make little sense. She shook her head, dismissing it. 'Well, I had a really bad night's sleep so I'm going to have a nap. Okay?'

Rhyll shrugged. 'Whatever. You do you.'

George kept her gaze on her daughter for a few minutes, but Rhyll had now opened the laptop slightly and was peering into the gap. George sighed, but under her breath, and then collected up her glasses, mobile and coffee and retreated down the hallway into her bedroom. To her relief, everything there looked exactly as usual. Simon had clearly not been back. The bed was made, cushions were scattered across the cover. There was no suitcase on the bed, or *Fornicator!* scrawled across the wall in scarlet lettering. She put everything down on her bedside table and went to the wardrobe. All his clothes were still there, and so were hers. There had clearly been no sudden packing, and the guilty person's belongings hadn't been thrown outside or donated to the local charity store.

George took a quick shower and then, with her hair still wet, threw the cushions into a corner and stripped back the bed-covers.

She climbed in, revelling in the crisp coolness of the sheets, the familiarity of her pillow. As soon as she closed her eyes, it felt like a weight had been removed, but her mind still raced. She methodically slackened her jaw, loosened her shoulders and then took seven deep breaths. When that didn't work, she called up the image from this morning's dream. The seersucker tablecloths, the grassy bluff, the scones, the family, her mother slicing bananas. She pressed play and they all sprung to life. Children laughed gleefully and the men roared as Alex Jesaulenko took his mark. The Yorkshire terrier hurtled past, wheels spinning. And her mother paused, mid-slice, paring knife pressed against her thumb, and turned to George with that smile. 'This too will pass,' she said, putting everything down so that she could rest one hand gently on George's shoulder. 'But isn't it funny? We're more alike than we thought.'

Chapter Eighteen

Saturday (early) afternoon

By quarter past twelve, George was parking in her usual spot outside the house. She was feeling significantly better than when she had left that morning. Not back to normal by any means, but certainly more human than she had. This was largely due to a deep, dreamless two-hour sleep followed by another blissfully indulgent half-hour spent dozing on and off. It was during this final part that she also did some good thinking. Running through the events of the previous evening. The situation with Simon, the argument with Annie, the impulsive and rather ridiculous notion to move across the world for a year. She was even able to give a wry chuckle at this last, especially when she rolled over to check her mobile and found an enthusiastic message from her travel agent. Along with one from Kat, asking her to bring milk, another from Aunt Margaret, about villages and children, and a long screed from Lesley, together with photos of her spare room, and the street-view from her lounge room window, and a squirrel.

Simon still hadn't arrived back from his brother's, or the tennis, or wherever he was now. He had rarely stayed away even one night before, let alone two, not in all the long years of their marriage. But then she had never cheated before either. She had repeated the word several times into her pillow. Even muffled, it had a sinuous, slimy feel, which seemed fitting. She had brought this all on herself. But George eventually arrived at a feeling of fatalism. When all was said and done, she had simply forced a situation that had been a long time coming. In a way, she'd done them both a favour.

To make things even more palatable, the heat of the past few days had finally broken some time while she slept. A cool change had rolled in, bringing grey, gravid clouds and a threat of rain to come. George collected up her handbag and the shopping bag with milk and pastries and then for no particular reason, even though she was already late, sat for several minutes with them on her lap. She felt a little like a child dragging its feet on the way to school. Finally she took a deep breath and got out, skirting Kat's car on her way to the front door and then pushing it open. This afternoon there was no sound of voices coming from the living areas, just a silence that felt even stranger for knowing that both her sisters were there.

She found them at the dining table, as usual. It felt like she had spent much of the last week sitting at this table. And, for that matter, the fifty-five years before that. But in all those previous years, her mother would have been there and she would have given the current disagreement short shrift. George felt a shaft of the now-familiar loss. It was almost comforting. Both of her sisters looked up from their phones as she rounded the corner.

'Good afternoon!' said George, a little louder than intended. She continued with determined cheerfulness. 'Sorry I'm late! Loving this change in weather, hey? And look what I brought!' She slid the pastries from the bag and then realised that there was an almost identical box on the bench. 'Oh! Snap!'

'I brought those,' said Annie, rather grimly. She nursed her bandaged hand, avoiding eye contact.

'Lovely! The more the merrier, I say!'

Kat lifted one of her still-shiny eyebrows. 'Did you overdose on Berocca?'

'Of course not!' George dialled herself back a notch. 'I'm just trying to set the mood.'

'Well, all my mood needs is coffee. Please tell me you brought milk? Annie forgot.'

'I didn't know!' said Annie with a defensiveness that was almost accusatory. 'I don't *always* check my messages.'

'I wasn't blaming—'

'Never mind!' interrupted George. 'I've got some!' She pulled out the milk with a flourish and then crossed to the kettle to switch it on. There was a red sticker on the kettle, and also on the cooktop. Silence fell again behind her as she got down the mugs. She began to wonder if there had been yet another exchange of words before her arrival, or whether this was just the residue from last night. The kettle boiled and she made coffees, bringing the mugs over to the table. She took a seat on the other side of the table, facing the kitchen. A messy pile of papers spilled across the end of the table, alongside the bowl holding the rolls of coloured tape. A few drops of rain had begun to splatter across the glass sliding door.

'Speaking of messages,' said Kat. 'Did anyone else get some weird ones from Aunt Margaret this morning?'

'Yes!' said George.

'No,' said Annie. She stared dourly at her coffee.

George exchanged glances with Kat. She searched for a change of topic. 'So, um, how's your wrist?' she asked Annie after a few minutes.

'Fine.'

'Okay. Good.' She turned back to Kat. 'And how was your morning? Get much done?'

'Yeah, the wardrobe's finished now. No more surprises there.'

'Pity,' said George, not really meaning it. She took a sip of coffee and then, just for something to do, fished her mobile from her bag and sent a message to Rhyll. *You weren't there when I got up? You'll be here this afternoon though? To get your stuff?*

A response wasn't long in coming. *Ediquet dictates only 1 question per text. Your skating on the edge of anarchy.*

George gritted her teeth. *You're,* she typed. *Not your. Plus that would only be amusing if you knew how to spell etiquette.*

Your 2 easy 2 annoy, replied Rhyll quickly. *If u must know, Leo took me around 2 the house 2 so I could finish my stickers & yes, we'll both bbl. Funny thing tho, Tom dropped Aunt Annie off while we were there and I think they redid theirs altogether!*

George blinked. Looking up, she locked eyes with her younger sister, who immediately glanced away. George felt a surge of irritation. Redoing your choices at the last minute mightn't be against the rules, so to speak, but it certainly wasn't in the spirit of things. Especially from the person who had spent the week making a big deal about manipulation. She just hoped that meant Annie had changed her mind about the diary.

'Well, we better get going,' announced Kat. She pushed her phone aside and leaned over to gather together the pile of papers. 'I've made a head start. I used one of these for each person.' She paused to hold up a sheet of paper. It had Tegan's name written on top. 'And listed everything they wanted, starting with their two priorities.'

Annie reached across with her good hand to snag a few sheets. 'You've been busy then.'

'Yes,' said Kat. She sounded a little tired.

'But I'm sure you don't need to worry,' interjected George. She wrapped her hands around her mug as she smiled at Annie. 'Late changes would all be included.'

Annie flushed. Her lips thinned. 'No doubt that comes as a relief to you also then, with *your* late additions this morning.'

'That was hours ago,' retorted George. 'It was hardly last minute.'

'Really?' Annie drew back in her chair. Her v was on full display. 'So, not like your daughter who arrived here at eleven to do hers?'

George stared at her sister, tingly with indignation. She knew, in a small corner of her mind, that much of this was actually frustration in disguise, and due to things totally unconnected to Annie, but there was joy also, in having a target. 'Rhyll hadn't *finished* hers! And *she's* been busy all week helping out here, so there hasn't been *time* to—'

Kat slapped a hand down in the table. 'SHUT UP!'

George drew back, breathing heavily. In truth, she was a little surprised at herself. She had been determined to wear a cheerful face and instead, at the first opportunity, *she* had been the one to send things off the rails again. She, who usually avoided confrontation like the plague. She was also surprised at the depth of her irritation towards her younger sister. It simmered just below the surface, refusing to be compartmentalised.

'My god!' Kat glared at each of them in turn. She seemed genuinely angry. 'We haven't even started! Do you think you could keep it together just long enough to get through this? *Then* you can have at each other, if that's what you want.'

George stole a glance at Annie. Her lips were almost non-existent, her v still in place.

'Tegan will be here in under an hour,' continued Kat. 'So we need to get this done.'

George nodded. 'Okay. Sorry. Got a lot going on.'

'Who hasn't?' said Kat shortly.

George took a deep breath. She doubted that Kat's busy morning measured up against adultery, a failing marriage, a secretive daughter, and the total inability to work out what to do next, or how, or where. But the other burden, which superseded all else anyway, *was* something they shared. It was their mother who had died. So instead she just nodded again.

'Let's start with the easy ones,' said Kat now. She plucked the sheet of paper from Annie's hand and picked up another from the table. 'Tegan has prioritised the grandfather clock and the secretaire. Nobody else has, so they're hers.' She reached over and got a highlighter from the bowl with the coloured rolls of tape and then used it to emphasis those items on Tegan's page. 'And then Leo has gone for the pewter knight bookends and the hanging egg-chair. Nobody else has prioritised those either, so he gets them both.'

'Really?' asked George. 'I thought Rhyll was going for the chair too?'

'She must have changed her mind,' said Annie. She gave her sister a flat smile. 'Maybe last minute.'

George was saved from answering by the sound of Harry's footsteps. He came into the room carrying his mug and deposited it on the bench. A strip of red tape traversed the blue ceramic. They all greeted him and Annie rose quickly to put the kettle on. While it was heating, she brought over a box of pastries and placed it on the table.

'Sorry,' she said, without making eye contact.

'Good,' said Kat. 'Keep that attitude, because you're going to need it. Harry, sit down. We're just sorting out who gets what.'

'I want this table,' said Harry. He pointed to a red sticker on the edge as he took the seat beside George. 'It's for my Lego.'

George smiled at him. 'Excellent idea. You can get rid of that old table tennis table then.'

'No.'

'Fine,' said Kat quickly, shooting George a warning, pick-your-battles look. 'It's all yours, Harry. And now ...' she paused as she ran a hand through her hair. 'We get to the harder ones. First, me. I put the Eames chair as number one, and the war medals as two. Dad's Korean ones and his father's, from World War II. I get the chair, but not the medals.'

'Why not?' asked George. She leaned over in an attempt to read the other papers on the table. She could see hers, with the diary listed first and the Eames chair second. This had seemed an inspired move this morning, because if Kat had the chair as her first choice, then she, George, wouldn't get it and therefore her claim to her own number one, the diary, despite Annie also list-ing it, would be stronger. Surely she would have to get *one* of her priority picks. She had been quite proud of herself.

'Because Tom put them as his top choice,' replied Kat. Her voice was tight, her face expressionless.

George's jaw had slackened. She looked across at Annie but she had her back turned to them as she prepared Harry's coffee. She tried then to make eye contact with Kat instead but she was now busy highlighting. George felt a surge of her earlier indignation. Tom had done that deliberately, she was certain, to get back at his aunt. He had checked out the lay of the land this morning and changed his choices accordingly. And her sister had the gall to accuse others of manipulation.

'The Korean War killed 2.5 million people,' said Harry. 'And it never actually ended.'

'So Dad's AWOL then?' asked Kat lightly. She busied herself stacking the highlighted sheets. 'Good luck charging him.'

Annie brought Harry's coffee over and then sat down heavily. She stared at her own mug. George gazed at her, seething, willing her sister to look up.

'So we might as well do Tom next then,' said Kat into the silence. 'He gets the medals as his first pick but doesn't get his second, mainly because Rhyll put that as her first. The *John and Betty* book.'

Because George had still been looking in Annie's direction, she was able to see the shock that mirrored her own. She whipped her head around to face Kat. 'Rhyll did? The *John and Betty* book? Really?'

'Yes. And she also gets her second choice, which is the leadlight lamp.'

There was a choking sound from her younger sister's end of the table, but George was too busy with her own thoughts to pay any attention. So it seemed that Tom had gone for both of his aunts. Kat with the medals and her with the book. Even though she hadn't prioritised that, her sticker had been plain to see. It had been a smart move, if scoring points was the objective. George smiled. Because it had all been foiled by Rhyll who, it appeared, had simply waited until they'd finished to make her own choices. George wondered what *her* objective had been. Did she really want the book, or had she too been scoring points?

'Leadlight has been around for a thousand years,' said Harry. 'Not Mum's lamp though.'

'Doubtful,' said Kat. She shuffled some papers. 'Given electricity would have been rudimentary back then.'

'Electricity wasn't around at all,' corrected Harry. 'Except with electric fish. People with gout or headaches were made to touch electric fish to cure them.'

'I don't have gout,' said Kat. 'But I *do* have a headache. Are they better than Panadol?'

'No,' said Harry.

'So Rhyll put down the *John and Betty* book as her first choice,' said Annie slowly. She was staring at George. 'How ... interesting.'

George opened her mouth to retort but was stopped by Kat slapping a hand down on the table yet again. Harry jumped, dropping the profiterole he had just selected. Icing sugar spattered across the table.

'Sorry,' said Kat to him. He ignored her as he picked up the pastry. Annie reached over and brushed the icing sugar off, leaving a smudged white trail. Kat shrugged, returning her attention to her sisters. 'Okay, let's cut to the chase before we go on,' she said firmly. 'I'm not going to use the word manipulative ...' She paused to flash a glance at Annie. 'But there's no doubt quite a few people have been rather ... um, *strategic*. Tactical, if you like. And I take some of the responsibility. The whole sticker thing was my idea, but I didn't realise it could be used like that. And before you say I told you so ...' she settled her gaze on Annie again. 'It also demonstrates that discussing everything wouldn't have worked either.'

'I'm not sure about that,' muttered Annie.

'Well, we'll never know,' continued Kat briskly. 'For good or bad, we went with this. And it's clear that more than one person has been man ... *strategic*, so there's absolutely no benefit in pointing fingers.'

George took a sip of her coffee. It had gone cold. She knew that Kat was right, but she also felt that Annie was being let off the hook. It was clear that she and her son had started the move towards tactics, and that others had simply followed their lead. Sure, she herself had put her second choice on the Eames chair earlier yesterday to bolster her claim towards the diary, but then

Tom had altered his choices altogether. If that wasn't manipulation, she didn't know what was.

Nevertheless her irritation was also offset by a smug awareness that Annie had been hoist by her own petard. She couldn't very well complain about Rhyll having abruptly chosen the *John and Betty* book, thereby robbing Tom of it, when he himself had left things to the last minute. She took another sip of the cold coffee, this time hiding her grin.

'Which brings us to the last of them.' Kat took a deep breath and then tapped on the sheet of paper before her. 'You two. And you've both put the exact same thing.'

George's grin vanished. She turned to stare at Annie, who kept her attention on Kat.

'The diary first,' said Kat. 'And the Eames chair second.'

'Charles Eames married Bernice Kaiser in 1941,' said Harry. Icing sugar was dotted across his upper lip. 'She was called Ray. For their honeymoon they took a road trip to Los Angeles and collected tumbleweeds which they then hung from their ceiling.'

Nobody paid him the least attention. The rain outside had picked up in intensity, pattering against the veranda. George had dragged her gaze away from Annie and now stared fixedly at her eldest sister, waiting for her to continue.

'So obviously I get the Eames chair,' said Kat now. 'Because I was the only one with it as a first choice. But the big question is the diary.' She stopped to massage the back of her neck. 'I didn't foresee this happening.'

'Not sure why not,' said Annie tightly.

Kat looked at her. 'And I very much doubt that leaving you two to *discuss* things would help here.'

'No,' said George, curling her lip.

'So … I've been thinking this over for the past few hours and rather than toss a coin or anything stupid like that, I've come up with a solution.' Kat sat back. She looked from one of them to the other. 'Neither of you get it.'

George blinked. 'What?'

'Well, better both of you hate me than one feels like they've been hard done by. It's the only answer. You've both got it as your number one, and neither of you get your second choice because it was my first.' Kat levelled her gaze at George. 'And don't even get me started on why you both did that.'

George narrowed her eyes. She wanted to mount an argument but there really wasn't any. Rain now formed a silvery curtain beyond the sliding doors. The sound was a steady backdrop to their conversation. She could feel the diary slipping away, and it hurt.

'So who gets it then?' asked Annie stiffly.

'One other person had a sticker on it,' said Kat. 'And although he put stickers on almost everything in the house, he didn't actually include any priorities. He also happens to be the one most affected by the contents. I vote he gets it.'

George shook her head. 'But … no! It's not just about him! It's about all of us!'

'True,' said Kat. 'But mostly, indirectly, him.'

'Anne Frank had a diary,' said Harry. 'And so did the Wimpy Kid.'

'Besides, it'll get trashed down there!' continued George. 'You know he doesn't care about books!'

'Not true,' said Harry. He frowned at her. 'I *do* care about books.'

'She didn't mean it, mate,' said Kat. She turned back to George. 'Anyway, if you'd let me finish, that's not my suggestion. I think it should be given to Tegan for safekeeping. Let her have it. She's almost as much affected.'

George opened her mouth and then closed it again. She sat back, folding her arms.

'I second the vote,' said Annie suddenly. 'Well done. A great compromise.'

George transferred her gaze to her younger sister. She blinked, struck with the realisation that Annie didn't seem terribly upset. And this was followed by certainty that part of its appeal had been in George herself wanting it so much. And that her surge of acquiescence now owed more to the fact that even if Annie didn't get it, then at least George didn't either. A lump of anger and frustration rose to lodge in her throat. She swallowed painfully.

'But what now?' asked Annie. 'Because that means neither of us get a priority at all.'

Kat was nodding. 'I know. Which is why I think you should do them again. Obviously some stuff has gone but there's plenty left. Most of the furniture for starters. And the Spode dinner set. Nobody ended up choosing that.'

'I have all my Lego Group instruction books,' said Harry crossly. 'I have a shelf just for them.'

'I know,' said George shortly. 'Sorry. I shouldn't have said that before.'

Harry slid his gaze towards his mobile phone. The frown was still in place, indicating that forgiveness was not yet in the offing. George sighed, and then stared down at her folded arms. She suspected that they were being punished and that Kat had thought this all through before they'd even arrived. She could have started with this dilemma, and allowed them both to choose from the range of alternatives before allocating most of them to others. But no, this was their punishment for being manipulative, and also a way of preventing any further tactical manoeuvres.

'So I suggest you both go do that now,' continued Kat. 'Take your time. Tegan should be here soon though, so if it's okay with you two, I'll take her outside and start filling her in on everything else.'

George nodded stiffly. She couldn't trust herself to speak. She rose, plucking her roll of tape from the bowl before going straight to the study. The diary had been put back in the desk drawer but when she pulled it out, it did indeed have one of Harry's stickers alongside Annie's and hers. Both the latter bearing the number one. To make matters worse, Annie had stuck her tape right across the fragile front cover. That was going to leave a mark. She flicked the diary open, gazing at her mother's tight cursive script. Curlicues above and below. *Today I went to Ethel Ferguson's Tupperware party. I have no idea why.*

'I really did want it,' said Annie from behind her. 'I didn't do it just to spite you.'

George didn't reply. The diary felt warm between her hands. Familiar.

'It's like hearing her again, you know. Even when she calls me a sook.'

Annie's voice had lightened with this last and George knew that she was trying to inject humour. But that just made it all worse. This wasn't funny. She slid the diary back into place. Her eyes burned with unshed tears.

'Fine then, don't answer me. Be childish. See if I care. *I'm* trying to take the high road.'

It wasn't so much that George was choosing not to reply, as incapable of it. The lump in her throat prevented any sort of coherence, which was probably just as well. There would be no going back from what she really wanted to say to her sister.

'This is probably going to come as a shock to you,' snapped Annie now. 'But you don't always have to get everything you want. Maybe learning that will be the silver lining here.'

George whipped around but Annie had already made her exit. Fury frothed within, caught painfully behind her ribcage. And now that it was too late, words jostled for egress. Pot, kettle, black. How dare *Annie*, of all people, accuse her of always getting what she wanted. Annie, with her passive aggressive prickliness. Her excess of feelings, her sensitivity, her hyper-vigilance for anything that could be considered a slight. *Look at me, I'm Annie and you have to make allowances because I've had the rockiest road through adulthood.*

Rain thrummed against the roof, providing a soundtrack for the resentment that throbbed at George's temples. She stared at the doorway, a little taken aback by the depth of her emotions. It wasn't just about the diary. Nor was it anything to do with Tom's antics. Unlike Kat, she didn't much care about those. No, with her it was all about Annie. It had been simmering for days. Maybe, if she was to be honest, even for years. And it was shadowed by her mother's voice, urging her to be nice. Every time Annie took offence, got prickly, stomped off in a huff. *Be nice.* But at the moment George herself wasn't having the easiest time either. The big difference was that she wasn't asking for special treatment. Nor was their mother now around to support *her*. It was all incredibly, horribly unfair.

From down the hallway came the sound of the front door opening, followed by Tegan's voice as she called a greeting. George could hear Kat answer, and then their voices fading as they rounded the corner towards the dining room. She looked at the still life print on the wall. The luscious red-gold apples tumbled from their wicker basket. It had three stickers on the frame. Lime-green, purple and salmon-pink. George's lips thinned as she took a biro from the desk and scrawled the number one across her sticker. If she couldn't have the diary, at least this was related.

With that done, George went to the doorway but could no longer hear Kat or Tegan at all. Her sister had probably taken their niece out to the veranda, away from Harry, to explain everything. She was glad that Kat had volunteered to take on the task. Tegan's shock, her questions, were more than she could have handled right now. Their mother would have hated this, the uncovering of her past and the division of her possessions. But she had also loved Tegan. She had been more than a grand-daughter. And if someone had to have the diary, then Enid probably wouldn't have been too devastated that it had fallen to her.

This realisation settled slowly, like a mantle, easing the tension across her shoulders. She played with it, examining the edges until the worst of her anger fragmented like lace, leaving just a curling residue behind. This she tucked aside, because it was all about Annie anyway. She would deal with that later. After this weekend, she wouldn't even have to see her sister again for quite some time. Compartmentalisation. But when it came to the diary, if George herself couldn't have it, then at least she could console herself with the idea that it was going somewhere worthy. Not to Annie, or her son, but to Tegan. It was Tegan's heritage also. And of all the cousins, she was the most responsible, the most grounded.

She took a step back, returning her attention to the still life. It really was a very calming picture. Placid and invariable. She took a few deep breaths, letting it wash over her. The apples were caught mid-tumble, the wicker basket a perfect counterfoil for their glossiness. She would hang it somewhere that she could see it every day. Perhaps she could even photocopy the diary, secure the pages to the back of the frame. They belonged together. Losing the diary still hurt, but it was no longer clotted pain. The knot in her stomach loosened slightly. Maybe the unexpected result was the one with the best fit. Maybe things had turned out how they should. And maybe, just maybe, everything else in her life would too.

Chapter Nineteen

Saturday (mid) afternoon

By two o'clock, the house looked like it was hosting a giant garage sale. While George and Annie redid their priority picks, Kat had cut up a roll of black electrical tape and adhered pieces to all the bigger items that hadn't been allocated, letting everyone know that these were up for grabs as well. She'd also dragged some boxes into the lounge room, labelled *Free stuff! Take what you like!* They were each filled to the brim. Normally, this might have called for some humour. Because while not a hoarder, their mother's philosophy appeared to have been why buy one when you could get a pack of fifty? This went for everything from textas to soap, light globes to unicorn-shaped erasers with diamanté eyes. She had even found the spare batteries, around thirty of them, in a box at the back of the linen cupboard.

After much consideration, largely contained to the study, George had chosen the desk as her number two pick. Of course she had one at home, but *this* desk was where her mother had sat throughout much of George's childhood, writing letters, paying bills, tallying up budgets. And, no doubt, writing the diary.

This desk had history. On her part, Annie had avoided the study altogether while deciding her replacements, eventually settling on the Spode dinner set along with the filigree brooch that they had given their mother for her previous birthday.

All that had remained was to work through the rest of the division. This was made a little easier by Tegan's enthusiasm to be involved, and her continually expressed shock regarding her heritage. While they worked, she devoured the diary and the letter, studied the photograph with a magnifying glass, re-examined her grandmother's study in case anything else was hidden there, signed up for ancestry.com, and ordered a DNA test for both herself and Harry. She had also googled all Harrisons with an online presence in Mount Isa, which turned out to be a surprising amount of middle management there, and also a cockatiel with its own YouTube channel. This latter featured an impressive breadth of obscene vocabulary. The former, not so much.

Much to Annie's barely hidden delight, Tegan had also come down firmly and without hesitation on the side of telling her father. She had in fact been rather shocked that they might have considered *not* telling him. According to her, this was nothing more than infantilisation, and she came quite close to criticising her grandmother for having used this approach at times. The only concession Kat managed to pull was a delay until at least the following week. She had argued that 1) this week was already hard enough, and 2) this gave Tegan a chance to do some investigating of her own. Far better to give Harry a complete story, if possible, rather than bite-sized chunks that may yet prove to be wrong.

George suspected that the others agreed only because they had won the main argument. And besides, they simply didn't have time to continue the debate. There was too much to get done. Surprisingly, the final division went relatively smoothly. Having recovered quickly from losing the argument over Harry, Kat took charge. There were many items that more than one person had stickered, but given they weren't priorities, it was fairly easy to ensure that everybody got a fair swag. The highlighted sheets of paper were now spread neatly across the dining room table, waiting for their owners to use them as a guide.

Tegan left shortly after two, with a carful of boxes, bags and the diary. The rain had eased up, leaving the garden damp and the driveway slippery. A bird, perhaps celebrating this brief respite, flew straight into the lounge room window with a shuddering thump, leaving several feathers and a fissured crack. It was a measure of the current tension that even the response to this was muted. George concentrated on getting the furniture ready for collection. This meant stripping the beds, clearing the bookshelves, taping down loose drawers, while intermittently checking her phone and rehearsing the conversation she would eventually have with her husband. If he ever came home.

Meanwhile Tom had arrived in his mother's car, his manner studiously polite. Whenever George crossed his path, he seemed to be striking a pose that had him staring off into the middle distance with folded arms. Oddly, it was the staginess of this performance that first began to sand down the sharpness of her resentment. After a while it was actually difficult to suppress a giggle. It was just too ridiculous; especially given it was *him* who had created this distance, not them. *Him* who had defriended them, for whatever ridiculous reason, not the other way around.

At around two-thirty, George came into the lounge room to find Kat standing by the window, gazing outside. A box sat by her feet, half-full of what looked like linen. George went over to join her sister. The clouds hung heavily, promising more rain to come. The crack in the glass glimmered like a vein of diamonds. Tom was now striking a version of his pose on the nature strip, beside their car, as his mother rearranged the back seat.

'Good lord,' said George.

'I know.' Kat rolled her eyes. 'He looks like he's auditioning for the role of Maligned Hero in a 1930s silent movie.' She mimicked the pose, turning side on and jutting her chin out.

George grinned. 'Yeah … no. Your eyebrows work against you there. They glisten too cheerfully. You look like a cartoon.'

'Hmm.' Kat straightened, raising one of the eyebrows in question. 'Not sure cheerful was what I was going for. That'll clash with my resting bitch face.'

'Might be useful for work,' said George. 'You can be a woman of contradictions.'

'True. Lure them in with my eyebrows, destroy them with my face.'

George laughed. The easy exchange of nonsense was soothing. It was unique, difficult to replicate with even good friends. It needed a lifetime of familiarity. It needed sisters. She glanced outside, where one of the aforementioned stood by the car, her expression in direct contrast to their banter. George felt a surge of her earlier anger. It shouldn't be like this.

'You did that deliberately before,' she said to Kat without turning. 'Punishing us both for trying to be clever. I think you let Annie off too easily though.'

After a moment, Kat shrugged. 'It wasn't punishment. It was compromise. Not sure what else we could have done. I wish I'd never suggested the stupid stickers now.'

'No, it wasn't them,' said George with certainty. 'It was Annie. She's been a total pain in the arse.' She lowered her voice, even though there was no chance of the pain in the arse overhearing.

'This was always going to be hard, but *she's* made it almost unbearable.'

Kat turned to face her. 'You accused me of having it in for Tom last night, but I could say the same to you. About her. I mean I'm a little annoyed with her about the whole let's-tell-Harry thing, but you … you seem to be annoyed with her about everything.'

'Not at all!' objected George, taken aback by the accusation. 'I'm just sick of having to watch everything I say around her. And she didn't really want that diary; she just didn't want *me* to have it!'

'I don't think that's strictly true,' said Kat. Exasperation bled through her tone. 'She mightn't have wanted it as *much* as you, but even that's subjective. You can't blame her for choosing it. That was the deal. To be honest, I'm sick to death of hearing about it.'

'Fine,' said George stiffly. Her stomach churned unhappily. The last thing she needed was to fall out with her other sister as well. 'Let's change the subject then.'

Nothing was said for a few minutes. Down by the car, Annie and Tom appeared to be having a conversation of their own. As she watched, he put one hand on his mother's shoulder and leaned in, quite suddenly gathering her into a hug. George blinked. They broke apart, Tom dropping a kiss atop Annie's head and then bending to collect the box containing the Spode dinner set. As he slid it into the back seat, his mother glanced up towards the house. They locked eyes for a moment, each expressionless, and then Annie broke away.

'Awkward,' said Kat with a grimace. 'She probably thinks we were talking about her.'

George's lip twitched. She rather hoped that was exactly what their sister thought. It was no more than she deserved. But nevertheless she took a step backwards, so that if Annie happened to glance up again, she wouldn't see the two of them standing so close.

'It all went well with Tegan before, don't you think?' asked Kat now.

'Definitely.'

'I'm not sure why Aunt Margaret has a bee in her bonnet about it,' continued Kat with a frown. 'That's what I think she's on about with all these messages. It's really odd. But I *know* we're doing the right thing. And I think Mum would have approved too. About that at least.'

George nodded. She couldn't quite trust herself to speak. She had a sudden, eerie feeling that their mother was in the room with them. And she was nodding too. The thought sent an involuntary shiver up her spine at the same time as it warmed her, from the inside out. She returned her attention to the roadside, where Annie was trying to lever a box up from the nature strip. Her bandaged hand didn't seem to be much of an impediment now.

'Do you think I should say something to him?' asked Kat suddenly. She had followed her gaze. 'Like, get it all out in the open?'

'No,' said George. She was sure about that, at least. Tom was due to leave the following day. Any discussion while it was so raw would only end badly, and the fallout would affect Annie most of all. Maybe he simply wouldn't come down here again. As annoyed as she was at her sister, she didn't want that.

Kat sighed. Down at the car, their nephew was fitting another box into the boot. 'Do you think he's becoming more like his father?' she asked, still watching. 'Like this move to Queensland hasn't done him any favours?'

George thought about this. 'Maybe. A little.'

'I just get the feeling he's behind a lot of the issues we've had this week. With Annie.'

'Maybe,' said George again. 'Probably. Learned behaviour. But I also think with her, some of that's ancient stuff. And we can't really blame him for that.'

'I suppose,' said Kat with clear reluctance. 'But I swear he's been stirring the pot.'

George shrugged. 'Whatever.'

Kat turned to look at her quizzically. 'What's going on with you anyway? This isn't just about Annie, is it? Is it that message you got last night? When you got upset?'

'Of course not,' said George defensively. 'I just think how much Mum would have hated this. Us fighting like this. She would've banged our heads together and said—'

'Be nice,' Kat finished for her. She sighed. 'Maybe it's all just grief. Bringing out the worst in people. They do say that there's three things that put families under the most pressure. Weddings, deaths, and I can't remember the third one.' She paused to run a finger along the fissure in the glass. 'I was thinking about that last night actually. Maybe Annie, and to a lesser extent Tom, *needed* a target. It gave them something to focus on other than grief.'

George looked at her sister with surprise. This was very similar to what she had been thinking a few days before. She was just about to respond when she was distracted by the sound of a car reversing into the driveway. It was Leo's SUV, manoeuvring the trailer down the slight dip and into the narrow gap beside Kat's car. It was rather expertly done, requiring a miniscule adjustment that tucked the trailer at an angle with only inches to spare. George was particularly pleased that her son had performed the difficult operation in front of his aunt and cousin. They themselves had paused to watch. She returned her attention to Leo's car as the driver's side door opened. To her shock, Simon emerged.

'Ah!' said Kat beside her. 'I thought that was a bit too cleverly done for Leo!'

George was temporarily robbed of the ability to speak. Nerves soared into her chest, fluttering like moths against her ribcage. She felt like a teenager, catching sight of a crush. It was not a sensation she had ever missed. She took another step backwards and became aware of her sister watching her with a puzzled frown.

'There *is* something going on,' said Kat. Both shiny eyebrows had drawn together. 'Come on, spill! Is this anything to do with what you were upset about last night?'

'No!' exclaimed George, a little more shrilly than intended. She swallowed, to help modulate her tone. 'For god's sake, let's not create drama where there's none!'

'Hmm, sure. O-kay.'

Kat didn't look convinced, but George didn't have time for that at the moment. She flashed a glance outside. Her view was now limited to the top of the driveway and the verge where Annie's car was parked. Both Leo and Rhyll had joined their aunt and cousin, all four laughing at something. George felt a wash of envy at the easy amity. Leo was wearing pinkish-red coloured pants and a brown t-shirt. He looked like a strawberry that had been dipped in chocolate, then sprinkled with icing sugar. But Simon wasn't with them, meaning that he was most likely heading towards the front door. George was filled with a sense of flight or fight, except with very little of the latter. She mumbled something about needing to finish getting things ready, and fled to the study. The room was rapidly becoming her safe haven.

Once there though, she felt a little ridiculous. This was her husband of twenty-seven years. She knew him intimately. She knew that he had cried at the births of both their children. She knew that he threw out the receipts for Puddles' expensive organic dog food lest she query the cost. She knew that he didn't particularly like red meat, but sometimes pretended to at very blokey barbecues. She knew that he had researched hair regrowth last month for his emerging bald spot. She knew that he farted before waking most mornings. And she also knew that the *before* part of the equation wasn't really accurate, even though he always claimed that it was.

She could now hear greetings being exchanged in the hallway and then they faded as the speakers moved towards the living area. George stared at the wall, arms folded, and then after a while realised that she was striking a very similar pose to that which her nephew had earlier. She gave a short bark of laughter and then loosened her arms, giving them a shake and rotating her neck to release some of the tension.

'Um, is that some new dance?' asked Rhyll from behind her.

The tension came flooding back. George turned slowly. Her daughter was leaning in the doorway, gazing at her contemplatively.

'Doubt it'll catch on,' continued Rhyll. 'It's a little too, like, jerky.'

'Very funny.'

Rhyll nodded agreeably. 'Yeah, that's me. A laugh a minute. Listen, what are you doing in here anyway? Hiding?'

'Don't be ridiculous.'

'Thanks, but giving me life advice doesn't answer my question.' Rhyll pushed herself away from the doorframe. 'Anyway, Aunt Kat sent me to see if you wanted coffee.' She gestured with her head towards the other side of the house and then suddenly grinned. 'Just say the word and I'll save you a seat beside Dad.'

George looked back evenly. Her daughter appeared to be in a particularly push-button mood. She actually didn't feel like coffee, having already drunk more than enough today, but it seemed like a good opportunity to casually join the rest of the family.

She nodded. 'Thanks. I'll be out in a minute. Listen, first though …' She lowered her voice. 'Why did you pick the *John and Betty* book?'

'Lol, that? Just to piss Tom off.'

'Oh.'

'And also, like, I thought it might save me getting you a Mother's Day present.'

'Oh. Really?'

'Anyway,' said Rhyll hurriedly, as if concerned her mother might become sentimental. 'Get a move on, would you? We're missing your scintillating conversation.'

After her daughter left, George took a deep breath and then rotated her neck once more before following. She could hear their voices as she left the study, getting louder as she entered the lounge room and then stopping altogether when she came into view of the table. Harry, sitting closest to her, was staring at his mobile, but all other eyes were on her. Kat on his other side and Rhyll at the head. Tom, leaning against the wall by the sliding door, as if planning a quick escape. Leo, sitting atop the island bench, swinging his legs. Annie, lining up mugs one-handed behind her nephew's butt. And Simon, opposite Harry, his gaze now flicking away as he examined his fingernails. He looked tired, but disturbingly normal.

'There she is!' exclaimed Kat brightly. 'The hard worker!'

George, who was still gazing towards Simon, caught sight of Annie rolling her eyes behind him. This served to reignite her annoyance and oddly, also break through the awkwardness she felt. She smiled at everyone in turn, even those no longer making eye contact.

'You look like you're channelling the queen,' commented Rhyll. She lifted one hand, cupping it slightly as she gave the royal wave. 'Greetings, peasants. Hark, I have arrived.'

'Remind me not to get you to do my PR,' said George lightly. The only spare chair was between Simon and Rhyll so she manoeuvred herself behind her husband and pushed past Leo's legs. She pulled the chair out a little further so that it was wedged in the corner by the island bench, and then sat down.

Annie began bringing coffees over to the table, along with a plate of the leftover pastries. It had started raining again, lightly, the sound like white noise. Harry reached over for a muffin, examining it carefully before eating. The sound of his chewing did nothing to relieve things. She surreptitiously watched her husband as he continued to examine his fingernails. It was certainly more attention than George had ever seen him pay them in all the years they had been married. But did him being here, in her family home, helping out, mean that he had taken the first step towards reconciliation? Did she even want that?

Leo cleared his throat. He had repositioned himself so that he was now cross-legged on the bench. One jutting knee was dangerously close to George's head. 'So, Tom, when're you heading back to the sunshine?'

'And the Dick breaks the silence!' announced Tom, with a rather flat grin. 'Well, since you ask, I'm off early tomorrow morning. Why? Missing me already?'

'Always,' said Leo blithely. He glanced outside, at the rain. 'Although if this keeps up, I might follow you.'

'Ha. Good move.' Tom had folded his arms once more. He flicked a glance at his mother. 'Trying to talk Mum into that as well. Do her the world of good. Fresh start and all that. It's not called the Gold Coast for nothing. Beautiful one day, perfect the next.'

George couldn't see her younger sister as she was still in the kitchen, largely hidden behind Leo. She looked over at Kat instead. She sensed Tom watching the exchange. He must have sensed her, sensing him, because he turned to gaze out onto the veranda.

'There's no gold there though,' said Harry, still focussed on his mobile. 'It used to be called the South Coast, but got changed because everything was so expensive there. Houses too.'

Leo laughed. 'Maybe they should change the name to Palladium Coast then, given that's the most expensive metal.'

'What the hell's palladium?' asked his sister.

'It's sort of like silver. But rarer.'

Simon looked up. 'Haven't you ever heard of Long John Palladium? He was Long John Silver's brother. Just wasn't seen around as much.'

Groans greeted this weak attempt at a joke. George glanced back across at her husband. It had been the first he had spoken since she had come in, and the band around her chest loosened slightly. If he was able to speak so lightly, then surely that was a promising sign?

'This is so weird,' said Rhyll suddenly. 'Us all being like this. Without … Granma.'

Kat, sitting beside her, squeezed her niece's shoulder. 'I know.'

'Yeah. I keep expecting her to come in,' said Leo. 'No doubt with some scathing comment.' He plucked at his strawberry-coloured pants and then put on a high-pitched voice. 'Nice pants, young man. You trying to match the broken capillaries in my cheeks?'

George shook her head even as she laughed along with everyone else. 'She didn't sound like that!' she protested. 'More …' She tried speaking from the base of her throat. 'Good job on the eyebrows, Kat. Auditioning for the Thunderbirds, are we?'

'Hey!' Kat poked at George's arm. She continued, mimicking the husky version of their mother's voice. 'What on earth possessed you to write about Margaret Thatcher in that column, George?' She turned her head slightly, making a spitting gesture. 'Scraping the bottom of the bitch barrel there, aren't we?'

Simon let out a bark of laughter and then continued in the same vein. 'I'm going to give you lot to the count of three to clean up this mess! One!'

'Thomas!' exclaimed Tom from the sliding door. He rubbed a hand across his light stubble. 'Shaver broken, is it, young man?'

'Two!' said Simon.

'My dear Rhyll,' said Rhyll, drawing out the words. 'Don't you think you're getting a little too old to carry off all that angst?'

'Three!' said Simon. He slapped a hand down on the table and then gave an exaggerated glare towards each of them in turn. Except George.

Laughter greeted this end to the banter. George exchanged a rueful grin with her older sister. If she didn't count the fact that her husband was so clearly ignoring her, these last few minutes had been the most enjoyable of the day.

'Huh,' said Annie suddenly, in her own voice, from behind Leo. She coughed and then cleared her throat. 'The Sorter, the Settler and the Sook.'

'What?' asked Simon after a moment.

None of those that knew offered an explanation. George felt another flash of annoyance at her younger sister, this time for sabotaging the convivial exchange. For a few minutes, they had actually felt like a family again.

'I miss her,' said Rhyll. 'Granma,' she added, as if there might be some confusion.

'We all do,' said Kat. 'She was special. Unique.'

'She's dead,' said Harry.

George blinked. She gazed at her brother, at first concerned for him, but then realising that he had simply added this as a piece of information. Much like commenting on her eye colour, or new haircut. She was, but is no longer.

'Breaking news,' muttered Tom by the sliding door. He looked across at his cousin. 'Anyway, Rhyll, congratulations on securing that *John and Betty* book. Bit of a coup, hey?'

'*I* like books,' said Harry, sending a hooded glance in George's direction.

Simon was still looking at Tom. He gave a grunt of laughter. 'You make it sound like she's a reporter. You know ...' He lowered both his brow and his voice. 'Well done, Lois Lane. Great scoop there.'

Tom's mouth quirked but he didn't reply.

'She *could* be though,' blurted George, surprising even herself. With everybody now looking at her, she felt obliged to continue. 'She's a good writer. A really good writer.'

'Gee, thanks, Mum,' said Rhyll.

George frowned at her. 'Well, you are. That blog is, well, great.'

'What blog?' asked Simon.

'Are you kidding?' asked Leo incredulously. 'Dad, have you seriously not read Rhyll's blog?'

'I didn't even know she *had* a blog!'

George felt a wave of camaraderie with her husband, alongside validation for herself. Nevertheless she wasn't about to let on that she hadn't known either. Not in front of the others, anyway. '*Beyond the Peripherals,*' she explained. She waited a moment, willing him to look at her without avail. She continued quickly. 'It's all about women who are one or two steps away from well-known history. Sisters, wives, servants, of those more famous.'

'Sort of a copy of yours, hey?' said Tom. 'Like fan fiction. How cute.'

George dragged her gaze away from Simon and towards her nephew. She opened her mouth but Rhyll got in first.

'Cute?' she repeated, staring at him. '*Cute?*'

Leo cut across her. 'Goes to show you haven't read it much either,' he said to his cousin with a laugh. 'Totally different. Both really good, but in their own way. And far from cute. We'd better pull our socks up hey, Dad?' He transferred his grin to his father. 'We're being eclipsed by the women in our family.'

'Yeah,' said Simon. Finally he glanced over at George. He was not smiling. 'They're way ahead of us.'

George flushed. Aware that everybody except Harry was looking at them curiously, she picked up her mug and drank slowly. Almost immediately she realised that this was a mistake. The coffee was sickly sweet. She schooled her expression, even as she felt another burst of fury towards her sister. Annie knew full well that she didn't take sugar.

'Hindus believe that eclipses are caused by a demon called Rahu,' said Harry, breaking the silence. 'He was beheaded for going to a banquet, and his decapitated head flies across the sky chasing the sun. Sometimes it catches it.'

Rhyll gave her uncle a nod of approval. 'Cool.'

'Not sure Hindus *still* believe it, Uncle Harry,' said Leo. 'I think you'll find it's mythology.'

'Yep,' said Harry. 'Can I have more coffee?'

Annie put the kettle on and then came over to the table and gathered up all the mugs, except George's. She disappeared behind Leo once more as she began making fresh coffee. George caught Kat's eye and grimaced.

'So, what's on the agenda then?' asked Simon. 'What am I moving?'

'Mum's desk,' replied George, assuming he was talking to her. 'And the hanging chair on the veranda. I think that's it for the big stuff.'

Kat leaned back in her chair and sighed. '*Sure* you don't want anything else? Like the washing machine and dryer? They're not that old. Or the lounge suite? Or any of the bedroom furniture?'

'No,' said both George and Simon at the same time. She flashed an appreciative glance at him, but it wasn't returned. In fact she thought he even inclined his head further away. The childishness of this brought a bubble of unexpected laughter to her throat. She swallowed it quickly. No doubt laughing at him would not improve things.

'I want the table,' said Harry. He laid his spare hand on it, grasping at the edge, as if somebody might decide to remove it then and there.

'Nobody's taking your table,' said Kat. She moved her body sideways, peering past Leo. 'What about you, Annie? Do you want any of the other furniture? Washing machine? Dryer?'

Annie came into view, bringing Harry's blue mug over to the table. She didn't reply until she had returned to the kitchen. 'Actually, I wouldn't mind those. Even the lounge suite. If nobody else wants them.'

'Excellent!' exclaimed Kat. She clapped her hands together. 'They're all yours!'

'Yeah, okay. But they have to stay here for a while. I'll need to organise a truck.' She lifted her bandaged hand. 'And it might have to wait till this is better.'

'I've been meaning to ask you what happened,' said Simon. 'Kat working you too hard?'

Tom gave a snort of laughter. 'Nah, that was from George trying to kill her the other day.'

'What!' George gaped at him, then transferred her gaze to her sister. 'I did *not* try to kill you! I tried to help you!'

Annie nodded slowly. 'Yes, you did. But you also moved the planter in the first place so that the rotten railings were exposed. Not that you were trying to kill me, of course. Tom's just joking there. But it *was* a little dangerous.'

'So was hopping around the veranda with one shoe on!' protested George hotly. 'And can I also add that you *knew* about the rotten railings beforehand. I didn't!'

'Hey!' Tom put a hand up. He was grinning. 'Calm down, George! Mum's right, I was just joking. Ha, ha. You know, just a joke?'

George was incapable of replying. Her anger caught in her throat like phlegm. She was conscious of the fact that several of those watching, who had been grinning, were doing so no longer.

Simon abruptly rose to his feet. 'Well then, how about I make up for my wife's murderous intentions by dropping the stuff off for you today. I'm sure Kat'd like them out of the way and we've got the trailer here anyway. Might as well get it done with.'

'Really?' asked Annie, clearly taken aback. 'You'd do that?'

He gave her a puzzled look. 'Sure. Tom and Leo can give us a hand.'

Rhyll snorted. 'Oh great. I'll just hang around in the background being *cute*, shall I, Dad? Or will I get in your way?'

'Thanks, Simon,' said Tom, a little gruffly, ignoring her. 'That's good of you. Oh, and George?' He turned to his aunt. 'Sorry. I really was just joking.'

George glared at him, but gave the slightest of nods. Her mobile pinged. She had forgotten that she'd left it on the table earlier. All thoughts of Tom vanished as she grabbed for the phone, covering the screen with her hand as she dragged it over. Even while doing this, she automatically looked across at Simon, knowing that guiltiness was writ large across her face. He met her eyes expressionlessly and she cursed inwardly. It was extremely unlikely that Guy would be texting anyway, but any high ground that she could have claimed later, on the basis that the affair was over, had just been undermined by overreaction.

Simon pushed his chair back towards the table. 'No rest for the wicked,' he said curtly. 'Let's get this trailer loaded. Lounge suite first, I reckon.'

Leo slipped off the island bench, his right knee striking George on the side of the head. He said sorry with a chuckle that rather negated the apology itself. Tom left also, along with Rhyll, still protesting about her earlier lack of inclusion, and finally Annie. George listened as Simon began instructing who was to take the couch, and who the armchairs, while Rhyll lectured him about gendered expectations. It took quite a few minutes for them to get themselves organised. Then their subsequent progress from the lounge room, and down the passage to the front door, was punctuated by curses, along with thumps as the furniture bumped against the walls. As soon as the coast was clear, Kat leaned towards George, speaking in a low voice.

'What the hell is going on between you two?'

'Nothing,' said George unconvincingly. She pulled her glasses over and slipped them on as she looked down at her phone. There was a message from the travel agent.

Hi again George! I'm holding that ticket for you but will need payment by 9:00 am tomorrow. Can only hold for 48 hours.

'Bullshit,' said Kat now. 'But fine, be like that. Don't tell me then. At least you can agree that Tom *is* fuelling the fires now though, can't you? Just a joke, my arse.'

'Definitely,' said George. She closed off the message and sighed. Why hadn't she already told the travel agent to cancel it? Why didn't she do that right now?

'I mean, if you'd really tried to kill Annie, you'd have been a little more imaginative, wouldn't you? Poisoned pastries perhaps?'

'Yep,' said George. She wasn't really listening. Nor did she have the energy to unpack Tom's idiosyncrasies. He was leaving the following day, Simon wasn't. Well, not that she knew of anyway.

'The 1858 Bradford sweets poisoning killed twenty-one people,' said Harry, looking up from his phone. 'Two hundred people were poisoned. Somebody accidentally used arsenic instead of sugar.'

'Yeah, "accidentally",' said Kat darkly. She used her fingers to insert inverted commas. When George still didn't react, she rose, stretching. 'You're no fun. I'm going to go supervise. And try to talk Annie into taking even more.'

George glanced up as her sister left the room. She put the phone down and then turned to Harry. 'Just us two, yet again. And you know what's good about that?'

'What?' asked Harry with obvious lack of interest.

'Well, *you* won't judge me.'

Harry nodded. 'Judge Buller was known as Judge Thumb.' He straightened his coffee mug. 'He was a judge in 1782. He said that a husband could hit his wife with a stick, so long as it was no wider than the man's thumb.'

'Sounds like a charmer,' said George. She looked at her brother thoughtfully. 'You know something, Harry? You're special. Unique. I'm sorry about what I said before, about books.'

Harry nodded again. He held his hand up and then made a fist, sticking out his thumb and staring attentively as he flexed it. He frowned, as if not altogether happy with the result. George took her glasses off and then massaged her temples. It was especially tender on the side where Leo had kneed her. She could hear faint voices from the driveway as the couch and armchairs were manoeuvred into the trailer. From the sounds of it, there was more direction than anything else, except perhaps chaos. Sitting where she was, wedged against the island bench, she couldn't really see the gaps left in the lounge room. No doubt they were marked by differing shades of the carpet, and dust bunnies. She didn't want to see them either. It occurred to her that this was like a metaphor for life. It was impossible to go backwards, and so very difficult to go forwards. Much easier, when all was said and done, to just remain exactly in place.

Chapter Twenty

Saturday (late) afternoon

George was still mulling this over as she drove home a few hours later. She had made her escape after Simon left for the second run to Annie's house, and Kat had been busily ordering pizza via Uber to be ready for their return. Her back seat was loaded with boxes, along with the apples print and Rhyll's leadlight lamp wrapped in old sheets. As she turned the corner onto the main road, she wondered whether this was her problem. Had *always* been her problem. She simply stayed in place. The status quo was not just the safest option, it was also the one that required the least of her. There were no decisions to be made, no changes to be made, no mountains to be climbed. Yet even so, the status quo came with its own set of risks.

She pulled up at the traffic lights and glanced into the car beside her. An elderly woman sat ramrod straight in the driver's seat, both hands grasping the steering wheel. They were like claws, with far more papery skin than flesh. She looked to be in her late eighties. George was struck by a deep sense of injustice. Why did this woman get more time than others? No doubt she was off to visit her family right now; perhaps it was a grandchild's birthday. They would all sit around a laden table, taking each other for granted, totally unaware of how lucky they were. Then later this evening the elderly woman would drive home and potter around her house before putting herself to bed, and then waking up again the next morning. It simply wasn't fair.

Enid had never driven. This was something George had always just accepted but now she wondered why. For such an independent woman, this suddenly seemed odd. She wanted to ask her now. Not just about that, but about everything. Did she ever feel gut-wrenching guilt over her affair? Did she regret not having gone to Mount Isa? Had staying with the status quo, in her case, brought happiness? The lights turned green and George took off, leaving the elderly woman behind.

The big issue was the balance of risk with reward. Less of the first also meant less of the second. It was a trade-off. George shook her head even as the thought formulated. That was wrong. Because even if Enid, or someone like her, had taken the gamble, it could have ended badly. The theory was often much better than the practice. Rewards weren't guaranteed. She chewed her lip as she flicked her blinker on, turning off the main road. Perhaps it wasn't about risk and reward at all, but regrets. Minimising those wherever possible. Maybe that was the point, so that when you arrived at the end of everything, the final sign was one where satisfaction outweighed sorrow. Maybe life was like a zucchini; it worked best when every last drop was wrung out of it.

George slowed as she approached the roundabout that led towards her own house. There was another car to her right, revving noisily as it negotiated a bend in the road, and she debated putting her foot down to beat it across but then decided to play it safe. Instead she returned to her thoughts. Had her mother's final sign been one of disappointment? Of regret? The notion made George feel ill.

The noisy car had fishtailed slightly as it came out of the curve. She could now see a P plate prominently displayed on the windshield. George rolled her eyes. Within moments though, her irritation turned to consternation. The car was clearly approaching too fast to negotiate the roundabout safely. The driver must have registered this at around the same time as the brakes were suddenly applied, too hard. They screeched, smoke billowing from the tyres as they tried to grip the tarmac. And then gave up. What happened next seemed to unfold in slow motion, and yet was over in a blink.

The car began to spin halfway into the roundabout, emitting a squealing roar that brought with it the suffocating smell of burning rubber. George could see the passenger, a young blond guy, reach out to grab the dashboard as he whipped past her. Then the front end of the car mounted the central island, the lowered bumper-bar scraping furiously against the concrete. But this also worked in their favour because as the car continued its turn, grating the bumper back onto the road, it had slowed considerably. Within seconds it came to a halt, straddling the island, facing George. Smoke billowed around it as if part of a dystopian movie set.

She stared at the occupants and they stared right back. Both young men, barely more than teenagers. The passenger was still clinging to the dashboard. The driver had a pimple on his cheekbone. Life hung, seemingly reluctant to recommence. After a few seconds, George blinked, and it was as if this broke the spell. The driver let out a cheer and then mouthed the word 'sorry' as he restarted his ignition. He reversed, angling the car away, and then took off down the road to George's left, driving a little more sedately. She gazed after them, her heart still thumping.

Logic told her that the risk had never extended to her. Apart from the young guys, and their car, the only thing in any real danger had been the nearby foliage. But still. Maybe it was a sign. If she *had* been at risk of joining her mother, then one thing was for certain, she would have been too laden with regrets to have even been capable of sliding into her grave sideways. That in itself was telling her something. Ergo, even if it hadn't been a sign, she was going to take it as one.

George dragged her gaze from the black tyre marks that now swirled across the tarmac, and checked both ways, once, twice, before moving. But as she drove slowly towards home only one thought throbbed against her temples, repeating itself over and over until any misgivings were washed away by a burgeoning excitement. Her decision had been made for her. There would be no regrets here. She was going to London.

Chapter Twenty-one

Saturday evening

The decision brought a sense of purposeful serenity that was as welcome as it was unexpected. It was aided considerably by the stiff Scotch that George consumed as soon as she got home, and then the second one that she was now enjoying on the deck outside her house. Along with cheese and crackers. She could have been killed. She had actually, nearly, almost, had a near-death experience. With the second glass of Scotch, she began imagining how her funeral would have played out. With their mother's debacle fresh in mind, she was sure that her family would have put together a much better showing. And as heart-wrenching as the death of an eighty-three-year-old was, there was something particularly tragic about mourning the death of one cut down in their prime. Or just past it.

Perhaps they would play 'Wind Beneath My Wings' by Bette Midler, or even the rather more maudlin 'Seasons in the Sun' by Terry Jacks. The latter was the one that, as a young teen, she had imagined being her funeral song. There would be plenty of tears, she was sure, especially from those who had cause to regret their last interactions. Simon would always be sorry he had shot through to Daylesford. Tom would feel guilty for baiting her. As for Annie ... George smiled grimly. Maybe, in recompense, her sister would suggest that the most fitting place for the diary now was inside the coffin, with George herself.

From his bed by the rattan table, Puddles gave a short, sharp bark without even opening his eyes. George shuffled across on her chair and leaned over to fondle his velvety-soft ears. No doubt he was having a lovely dream. One where he gambolled joyfully across the backyard, instead of having to be coaxed outside with leftover lasagne and ceaseless encouragement. She hauled herself out of the wicker chair and went to stand by the balustrade. A light drizzle had set in for the evening, with a fish-grey, overcast sky that had triggered all the solar lights early. The garden glistened, fern fronds dripping into the rockery, the pockets of gloom offset by splashes of light. The effect was almost magical.

Earlier, she had thrown out Guy's flowers. She had also contemplated sending him another text, this one with something suitably emasculating. Like rating his prowess in bed, or a scathing comment on his bent penis, but the serenity had helped here too. She simply didn't care enough. And if his life was so shallow that he couldn't handle being ignored for a week or two, then surely that was punishment enough. She had already moved on.

Puddles barked again, but this time he opened his eyes and popped his head up, tail wagging. George knew what that meant. The others had just arrived home. She hurried back over to her chair and arranged herself with knees tucked beneath her caftan, cushion on her lap and book in her hand. Despite the serenity, she could feel her heartbeat echoing in her eardrums. Now she could hear them in the kitchen behind her. The murmur of their voices went on for a while before one of the French doors to her left swung open. The echo of her pulse seemed to stop altogether, and then Leo lowered himself into one of the wicker chairs by her side.

'Nice,' he said, staring out into the backyard.

George nodded as she lowered her book. 'It's moments like these that make all that gardening worthwhile.'

'Yeah.' He stretched out his long, strawberry-encased legs and then yawned.

'Did you get everything done?' asked George.

'Yeah,' he said again. 'Aunt Annie's house now looks like an op shop. Mission accomplished. So anyway, Rhyll and I are heading out in a minute. Drinks with friends.'

'Rhyll's going with you?'

Leo twisted to face her. 'We thought we'd give you two a chance to talk. Sort out whatever's going on.'

'Nothing's going on!'

'Sure.' He yawned again. 'Well, maybe you'll take advantage of our absence then to discuss whatever's *not* going on.'

Rather than respond, George picked up her glass and took a sip. She silently cursed Simon for having made it so obvious that they were having issues. But then she recalled the source of those issues, and cursed herself instead. Leo had leaned over to pat Puddles and now he rose, helping himself to a handful of crackers.

'See ya,' he said, popping a cracker into his mouth.

George gave him a wave, then returned her focus to the book. The words swam across the page. Puddles got up and stretched a little drunkenly, and then lay back down as if rethinking the need for movement. George sympathised. The French doors opened again and this time, by straining her peripheral vision, she could see that it was Simon. He was holding a stubbie of beer. Her pulse caught in her throat.

After a few moments, he walked across the veranda and then leaned against the balustrade, staring out into the garden. Only then did George glance up. He had gotten changed since arriving home, and was now wearing the black seersucker shirt that she had given him for Christmas. She wondered if that was a good sign, or perhaps he intended going out again tonight. Maybe he had met someone already. She swallowed at the thought. Simon remained still, gazing away. George knew that as the guilty party, she was the one who should start this conversation. An apology for starters, a mea culpa. But the words had caught in her throat also. It was like a logjam in there.

Simon turned, quite suddenly, and George whipped her eyes down to the book. The only sound was the overfull guttering dripping steadily onto the crazy paving below. She could feel his gaze on her. The seconds stretched, each punctuated by the sound of the drips and the pounding of her pulse. It was beyond uncomfortable; almost a battle of wills. She felt a borderline hysterical giggle rise and trap itself behind her ribcage. She swallowed, keeping it in place. Giggling was unlikely to help the situation. Finally Simon spoke.

'Good book?'

'Huh?' George looked up with surprise. 'Um, yeah. Sure. Really good. Very interesting.'

He nodded agreeably. 'It must be, given it appears to have restored your sight.'

'Huh?' asked George again. She frowned as she tried to work out what he meant, even as she followed his gaze to her glasses. They sat on the table beside her. She flushed.

'It's a miracle,' said Simon.

George didn't reply. She laid the book down and reached for the glasses, polishing them slowly on the sleeve of her kaftan. It bought her time to accept that the only way forward was to dive off the edge. 'I'm sorry,' she said. 'I can't even explain how sorry.'

'Try harder then,' said Simon. He was leaning back against the balustrade now, regarding her expressionlessly. 'C'mon, George, words are your stock in trade, aren't they?' His lip curled. 'This should be the easy bit.'

George put her glasses on and almost immediately regretted it. Simon was more defined now, more stiff. More present. 'I *am* sorry,' she said in a low voice. 'I don't know why I did it. I didn't know why I was doing it, even *while* I was doing it.' She regretted that choice of words immediately, so continued with a hurry. 'I think I was looking for something to make me feel, I don't know, more *me*. Younger maybe. More alive.'

'Christ!' he said, displaying anger for the first time. 'Shut the fuck up!'

George flinched. Simon never spoke like that. 'You're scaring the dog,' she said stiffly. This wasn't the best response because both of them could see that, apart from sighing in his sleep, Puddles hadn't even stirred.

'Younger? More alive?' repeated Simon now. 'Could you *be* more of a fucking cliché?'

George felt tears spring to her eyes because he was right. She *had* been a cliché. A walking, talking, adulterous cliché. She blinked, and then aware that he was still glaring at her, followed it up with a shrug. There really wasn't anything to add.

'So what was he like then?' asked Simon. His tone was once again measured, even conversational. He took a swig of beer. 'Come on, spill. Tell me the goss. What was the sex like? Good? Bad? Did the earth move for you?'

George blinked again. She was fairly certain that responding with details wasn't going to improve things. Nor did she think

Simon would be buoyed by the things she *hadn't* liked. Like the kink in Guy's penis, or his annoying habit of crying out *Mama mia!* whenever he climaxed. No, not the best angle to take. If she was going to score them both out of ten, then Simon would win by far, but she suspected that he wouldn't be terribly impressed by that either, right now.

'Come on. What, *now* you're holding back? Give me some details.'

'No.'

'Then at least satisfy my curiosity about *one* thing.' Simon folded his arms across his chest, tucking the beer into the crook of an elbow. 'Why him? Why that smug little git? What was it about *him* that made you drop your knickers? Huh?'

George stared down into her lap. Each word was a missile, because they were true. Guy *was* a smug little git. It suddenly seemed important to let Simon know that. 'You're right,' she said, looking up. 'He *is* a git. It was a huge mistake. I despise him. It's over.'

Simon scoffed. 'Of course it is. Never as much fun when you're found out, hey? Loses the sparkle?'

'It was already over,' insisted George. 'That's why he came here. He was annoyed because I wasn't answering his texts.'

'Oh, *so* sorry it didn't work out,' said Simon sarcastically. 'Whatever could have gone wrong with such a match made in heaven?'

'He wasn't you,' said George. The words slipped out before she had even realised they were there. She locked eyes with Simon, both looking equally surprised. He broke it off by shaking his head, then he took a swig of his beer.

'I would've thought that was the whole point.'

'No. It wasn't.'

'Then what was? What the fuck was worth throwing our marriage away for?'

George took a deep breath. She knew she owed him at least this much, but it was hard to explain when she barely understood it herself. She took off her glasses and turned them over in her hands, staring at them. 'It was like a different me. The person I might have been if I'd published earlier, or better. If I'd lived that life. The affair was never the point. That was like the least of it. It was a glimpse of, I don't know, sliding doors I suppose.' Through her glasses, the batik pattern of her kaftan was magnified. It swam across her lap. 'Separation was the only way I could do it. Like *that* had nothing to do with *this*.'

George finally looked up, first at him and then at the backyard beyond. The solar lights twinkled. 'Then Mum died and I started seeing it for what it was. And when I found out he came here, the other day, it was devastating. Not just because you now knew, but because everything was suddenly merged. And I couldn't pretend that they ever weren't.'

Simon was silent for so long that George brought her gaze back to him. She felt a shaft of lateral pain. He had deserved more than this.

'I am so very sorry. I never meant to hurt you. I … I did something stupid. It's my fault.'

'How long?'

'What?'

Simon met her eyes. 'How long? You say you did something stupid, like it was a one-off. Exactly how long did you continue doing something stupid? How many times?'

'I didn't keep count,' snapped George before she could stop herself. She took a deep breath. 'Almost a year.'

'Yeah, thought as much.' Simon's lip had curled once more. 'It was that conference you went to last February, wasn't it? I've been thinking about it. That's the one where you came back with presents for everyone. When you said we just had to celebrate being us. A family.' He snorted. 'Unbelievable.'

George didn't reply. She was a little surprised that he had even put this together. She reached across for her Scotch and took a gulp. 'I had a near-death experience this afternoon,' she blurted, putting the glass down.

Simon lifted an eyebrow. 'Well, fortunately for us you seem to have survived.'

'Only just.'

'Another sliding-door moment then?'

'Something like that.' George put her glasses back on and then shuffled forward forward until she was sitting on the edge of the chair. She stared at her husband, at the familiarity of him. His ever-so-slight paunch, his receding hairline, his eyes. Usually so warm, but now like agate marbles. 'I *am* sorry,' she said. 'More sorry than I can even put into words. I'm also embarrassed, and humiliated by the whole thing. You were right before. I *am* a cliché, and it's nothing more than pathetic. I'm also devastated that I hurt you. I never meant that.'

Simon gave another of his snorts. He pushed himself away from the balustrade and went over to one of the chairs on the other side of the table. He sat down, leaning forward to fondle Puddles before settling himself with his stubbie nestled between his thighs. After a few moments, he sighed. 'What a fucking mess.'

George nodded. 'Sorry,' she said again.

'Yeah, you said. So what now?'

This was where she felt herself on surer ground. She was taking responsibility. 'You stay in the house. It's only fair. I'm the one who stuffed up. I'll leave.'

Simon glanced across at her. 'Hang on. So my reward for *not* having an affair is that I get to stay here, with our kids? And ...' he glanced down at Puddles, 'an incontinent dog? *That's* my reward? Is that what you're saying?'

'Um, yes.'

'Hmm. Not sure that's much of a reward.'

George looked at him, trying to work out if he was injecting humour. His eyes didn't seem *quite* as marble-like. They stayed like that for a few moments, gazing at each other. George felt an almost insurmountable urge to apologise again, but she swallowed instead. It slid down her gullet painfully and settled somewhere around her heart. She felt tears spring to her eyes once more.

'We should have talked back then,' said Simon now. He sounded more sad than angry. 'Things weren't great. Haven't been great for a while.'

'No,' said George. 'Where did it go wrong?'

'Well, the easy answer is when you fucked another bloke,' replied Simon with a little of the earlier antagonism. Then he shook his head. 'But it was way before that. When the kids left home? When we stopped talking?'

George nodded slowly. She took another sip of Scotch, just to have something to do. 'I'm going to London,' she said, without looking in his direction. 'I'm going to stay there for a year. Sort myself out. Decide what I want to do next.'

'Are you kidding?'

She turned back to him, grimacing inwardly at the expression on his face. 'I'm staying with Lesley. I'm going to try and write a book.'

'Fuck!' exclaimed Simon. The anger was definitely back. 'This is all about you, isn't it? What about Leo? What about Rhyll? What about *me*? You just giving up then, are you?'

George shook her head. It wasn't like that at all. It was so hard to explain how adrift she felt. Disorientated. She looked back at Simon. 'I need to orientate myself.'

'Huh?'

'I need to do this.'

He stared at her for a few moments and then suddenly his face cleared. 'Ah, I see! You're running away. This isn't just about the mess you've made, it's about your mother as well.'

'Leave my mother out of this!'

'You did the same thing when your father died,' continued Simon. 'But that time you just wanted to shift out to the back of beyond. Remember? You even lined up a job at a TAFE near Poowong. Bloody Poowong, for god's sake.'

'There's nothing wrong with Poowong,' retorted George hotly. 'Wilfred Burchett came from Poowong! He was a famous war correspondent.'

Simon snorted. 'It has a population of about twelve.'

'Actually, nearly four hundred. *And* a vibrant dairy industry.'

'What, were you going to milk cows in your spare time?' asked Simon sarcastically. 'Udder in one hand, quill in the other? Come on, George, you just wanted to run away from your grief. And that's exactly what you're doing now too. Except this time you're also running away from having to face the fucking mess you've caused.'

George sat back again, folding her arms across her chest. 'For your information, it's not like that at all. I'm not running away from anything. I'm running *towards*. I'm trying to—'

'If you say "find yourself", I swear to god I'm going to throttle you with my bare hands.'

George thinned her lips. That was exactly what she'd been about to say. She considered trying to use her zucchini analogy, but suspected that wouldn't come out quite right either. 'It's all booked,' she said instead. 'I'm leaving on the 3rd of April. It's a Friday. At ten-fifty pm.'

Simon stood abruptly, his chair skittling backwards. He looked down at his stubbie for a moment and then suddenly hefted it back and flung it out into the backyard. It disappeared into the darkness, followed by a thud as it hit the back fence. Puddles jerked his head up, looking around. Simon strode over to the French doors and yanked one open.

'I'm sorry that you don't understand,' said George stiffly.

'Oh, I understand all right,' snapped Simon, turning back with one hand on the door. 'Things are too hard here so you're dumping them on everyone else and shooting through to *find yourself.* Well, good luck with that, darling. Good. Fucking. Luck.'

The door slammed behind him with such force that the glass rattled. George felt her eyes well again, so she took her glasses off to wipe at them angrily. She hated confrontation, and it was even worse when she herself was the cause. Puddles stretched both front legs out stiffly as if intending to rise, but then curled them back onto his bed. George transferred her gaze to the darkening garden, trying to recapture the serenity of earlier. It was now overladen with guilt. Beneath this, though, was also a vein of relief. She didn't know what she would have done if Simon had begged her to stay. But his angry, accusatory response had simply hardened her resolve. She'd show him. And if she lost him in the process, then that was the price she had to pay. In fact, it would be a fitting punishment. George took a deep breath. The serenity might have vanished, but the certainty had not. She *had* to do this. Not just for herself, but for her mother also. It was all she had left.

Chapter Twenty-two

Sunday morning

George spent a fairly restless night on the living room couch. This, she could justifiably blame her husband for. He had a favourite television-watching end of the couch and over time his butt had made a particular indentation there. This meant that whichever way George positioned herself, either her head or her feet were in a dip. At about two in the morning, she decided that there was some ironic humour to be found in the fact that even as he was curled up in their queen-size bed, he had managed to leave behind an instrument of torture. She was definitely the butt of this joke. It was no less than she deserved.

As such though, George slept in, only waking when she heard the sound of movement in the kitchen. The remnants of a dream clung, where she had been running late for a bus and Simon had been waiting. However, she had forgotten to pack her sleeping tablets. She couldn't possibly leave without them, but if she went back, she would miss the bus altogether. The dream faded and she opened one gummy eye to see Simon at the island bench, fully dressed, drinking coffee. George snapped her eyes closed. Far easier to pretend to be asleep. She hadn't seen him again after their exchange on the deck the previous evening. Simon had taken himself off to their bedroom while George herself had waited until after the kids got home to make up her bed on the couch. She didn't need their questions, mainly because she didn't have the answers.

Footsteps sounded, coming across the room. George made a deliberate effort to relax her eyelids. The footsteps paused, leaving the ensuing silence to stretch interminably. It tingled. She opened a slither of eye, and could see Simon's Volley runners through her lashes. By a process of elimination, she tried to work out what his plans were. They weren't the runners he wore for jogging, or gardening. Or golf. He didn't play tennis on a Sunday. He wasn't a fan of meeting friends for breakfast. Brunch, maybe?

'I know you're awake,' he said, his voice even.

George didn't move. At what point did continuing to pretend become childish? Or was she already past that?

'Okay, have it your way. I'm off to the tennis. We need to talk tonight though, sort out the details of your desertion.'

'It's *not* a desertion,' replied George. She frowned as she peered up at him. 'It's a ... a—'

'A journey of discovery,' said Simon. He lifted his mug of coffee as a sort of salute. 'Yeah, you've already told me. Potato, potahto.'

George hoisted herself into a sitting position. Her back protested painfully. 'Well, it's not going to be much of a discussion if you keep that attitude.'

'Oh, *I'm* sorry,' said Simon caustically. 'Please do write me a list of dot-points for the socially acceptable way to behave when your wife's just admitted to an affair, and now plans on shirking all responsibilities to jet off to the other side of the world for a year. I'll make sure I study them up.'

George gave him a deprecating look, but she knew it lacked her usual sense of justification. He sipped his coffee, watching her, as if waiting for a verbal response.

'So tell me,' Simon asked finally. 'Where exactly do you plan on living up till ten-fifty pm on Friday the 3rd of April?'

'I thought, well, that I could make up a bed in my study,' said George. She examined his expression or rather, lack of one. 'But I could always stay with Kat if you prefer.'

'Whatever,' said Simon as if he was not interested in her answer, despite having asked the question himself. He glanced down at his watch. 'Anyway, I'm off.'

George tried to decipher this brief exchange as she watched him leave. After a while she gave up. She packed up her bedding and then went down to the bedroom to shower and change. Simon had made their bed neatly, even replacing the scatter cushions on top. Barefoot, George padded back out to the kitchen and checked on Puddles before making herself a mug of coffee. It was an insipid-looking day, the remnants of yesterday's clouds like old men's beards in the sky.

'Where's Dad?' asked Rhyll, sliding herself onto one of the stools at the island bench and putting her mobile down in front of her.

'At the Australian Open,' replied George. She flicked the kettle back on. 'With Uncle Callum, I'm guessing.'

'Pfft,' said Rhyll. 'Boring.' She regarded her mother with a thoughtful expression. 'Sleep well? Was the couch comfy?'

George sighed inwardly. 'Yes, thanks. Perfectly nice.'

'So you two didn't sort things out then?'

'Never mind that,' said George. She got down a mug for her daughter. The thought occurred to her that she was actually better off telling both her children about her plans while Simon was gone, otherwise they would be sure to hear it from him that evening. She turned back to face her daughter. 'Actually, there's something I need to talk to you and Leo about, but seeing as you're here … well, here's the thing.' She paused, taking a deep breath. 'I'm going to London in April. I'm going to spend a year there.'

Rhyll had picked up her phone. She glanced at her mother. 'Cool.'

'See, I've always wanted to go there. From when I was even younger than you.'

'Yeah, I know. You've said.'

'I'll be staying with Lesley at the start. But it's not like I'm deserting you or anything. It's just something I need to do, for me.'

Rhyll put the phone down and propped her head in her hands. 'Yeah, sure. Good for you.'

George blinked. 'Do you mean that?'

'Of course.' Rhyll frowned. 'Shit, Mum. Why wouldn't I mean that?'

The kettle began to whistle, which saved George from answering. She made Rhyll a mug of coffee and slid it across, leaving her hand wrapped around it just long enough for their fingers to touch. 'Thanks,' she said.

'London, baby!' yelled Leo, sliding into the room from around the corner. He was dressed in nothing but a pair of yellow boxer shorts patterned with dancing avocados. His hair swept up from the sides into a frosted peak.

George gaped at him, and then back at her daughter. Rhyll grinned as she tapped on her phone by way of explanation.

'Smuggle me into your suitcase!' said Leo. He levered himself onto the stool beside his sister. 'I've always wanted to take London by storm!'

Rhyll glanced up at his head. 'Well, you do look like you've *been* in a storm.'

'Yet my natural good looks remain undimmed.' Leo was still looking at George. 'Seriously though, Mum, I didn't think you had it in you! Can I come visit? Promise I won't cramp your style.'

'Um, sure.'

'Excellent! Let's see, if you head over in April, maybe I could follow around September?' Leo frowned as he thought this through. 'Nah, maybe October. That's the off-season, so flights are pretty cheap.'

Rhyll gathered up her mobile and mug, then slid off the stool. 'After six months putting up with you by himself, Dad'll probably shout you the fare.'

'Good plan!' Leo nodded enthusiastically. 'I shall commence my campaign of obnoxiousity on April the first! Very fitting, as initially he'll think it's an April Fool's joke but then ...' Leo lifted both hands into a praying gesture and then let his fingers dance against each other. 'Mwa ha ha, he shall henceforth realise his mistake.'

'I think you've already commenced,' said his sister. 'And also, obnoxiousity isn't a word.'

'Minor details,' said Leo.

George turned away to fill the kettle. She got down another mug for Leo and then drank some of her own coffee, buoyed by the upbeat attitude of her two children. Talking over the details with Simon tonight was going to be a lot easier with them on board. She felt a flash of sympathy for him. When she turned back, Rhyll had disappeared, but Leo remained at the bench, grinning at her.

'Going on an adventure then, hey? Good for you, Mum.'

'It's something I've always wanted to do,' she said. 'But are you sure you're okay with it? I mean, I don't want you to think I'm, you know, *dumping* you or something.'

'Hey.' Leo beckoned her over and then grasped her hand between his. He looked deep into her eyes. 'Let's call it a trial separation. After all, if you love something, set it free.'

George snatched her hand back. 'Very funny. You know what I mean.'

'Sure I do. But you do pick funny words. Dumping me!' He laughed. 'Besides, I'm twenty-five. So's Rhyll. We're both adults. You do what makes you happy.'

George wasn't quite sure that Simon would agree with this latter sentiment. The kettle whistled again so she made Leo a hot chocolate. He didn't drink coffee first thing in the morning. Puddles padded into the kitchen, yawning. She ruffled his fur and then got down some of his soft dog food and spooned it into a bowl.

'So how does Dad feel about this plan then?'

George remained where she was. 'Not overly keen.'

'I bet,' said Leo. 'Hey, maybe he could come over at some point too? He could come with me. We'll drag Rhyll along too. Maybe Tom too, if you guys manage to sort out your differences. Oh, and Tegan! That is, if she goes through with the ... you know.'

George glanced up. 'The you know?'

'The *you know*,' repeated Leo, enunciating each word as if that might help. He looked at her enquiringly, and then frowned. 'You don't know? I thought you knew!'

'Clearly not.' George straightened. 'So perhaps you could just tell me.'

Leo grimaced, rubbing at his chin. 'I wouldn't have said anything if I'd known that you didn't. I was under the impression that you knew *before* I knew. And that—'

'For god's sake!' interrupted George irritably. 'Just tell me!'

'Maybe it's just as well,' continued Leo, still rubbing his chin. 'You *should* know. She might need support. Tegan's pregnant.'

George gaped at him as the words registered. She had not been expecting that. She closed her mouth as she ran through the last few times that she'd seen her niece. She hadn't *looked* pregnant, but then that meant very little.

'She's going to have a termination,' added Leo when his mother still hadn't spoken. 'Not sure who the father was, but if it's early days, I'm guessing it's that guy she broke up with so spectacularly at my birthday party. You know, the one she caught cheating that night. Bit of a wanker. She's well rid of him.'

All of this was news to George. She hadn't known that Tegan had been going out with anyone, let alone that he was a wanker, or that there had been a scene at Leo's party on New Year's Eve. For a moment she wondered what else had been happening right in front of her that she'd missed, but then she cast that aside. Priorities. Tegan was pregnant.

'How far gone?' she asked now. 'Is she sure about termination? Has she spoken to anyone?'

Leo shrugged. 'Dunno to any of it. And can you not let on that I'm the one who told you? I was sworn to secrecy. It's just I thought that you knew before I knew.'

'Yes, we've been through that,' said George distractedly. She would have to talk to Tegan. Not about her choices as much as to just let her know she was there, if needed. They were all the family that the girl had. Her mobile pinged from the bench so she slid it across. There was a message from Kat.

Picking you up in ten. Now that Tom's gone, let's go to Annie's to resolve things. Please say yes. We need to draw a line here so we can move on. No answer means you're on board.

George blinked as she re-read the message. She felt like she was entering information overload. Her fingers hovered over the keypad but then instead she put the phone down. Maybe it was for the best. Loose ends were flying around her like tentacles on a sea-creature. She needed to get rid of some of them. Too much had happened this week with her younger sister to hope for miracles, but at the very least perhaps some bandaids could be put on the more painful parts. Maybe a year apart would help mend the remainder. Or offer Annie an attitude adjustment.

Leo drained his mug and pushed it aside so that he could fold himself forward within his arms. George didn't know if he was checking his phone or he'd fallen asleep. She returned to her thought processes. Going for a drive with Kat would also provide the opportunity to share her plans, and apologise for leaving her with everything for a year. Kat wouldn't have grounds to complain about the latter, given she had spent more than that time overseas on her last secondment. Then this afternoon, with all that accomplished, George could ring her niece and offer support in that quarter. It was the least she could do. Her mother would most definitely approve. That would just leave the conversation with Simon this evening. George smiled grimly. She already had the kids onside for that.

She took a deep breath. This was all doable. One tentacle at a time. Onwards and upwards.

★★★

Despite her best intentions though, George did not get a word in edgewise through the entire trip to Annie's home in nearby Ringwood. Kat kept up a running monologue which danced, butterfly-like, from topic to topic. Just some of those covered in the twenty-minute trip were how much had been accomplished the previous day, how she had arranged for both balustrade and gutter repair *and* a hard rubbish collection the following week, her concerns about Aunt Margaret's possible senility, her plans to revamp the kitchen, Tom's immaturity, and how many idiots were on the road nowadays. This last was in response to being stuck behind a car that was not quite doing the speed limit. It wasn't often that George was in the passenger seat while her sister drove, and she was quickly reminded of why she avoided it. The driving was just as single-minded as the conversation.

By the time they pulled to the kerb outside Annie's block of units, George's fingernails had left moon-shaped indents across the fleshy part of her palm. Her sister had purchased her unit, the front right, shortly after her divorce. It was tumbled brick, with a curving concrete pathway and trellis-edged porch. Holland blinds were pulled half-down in every window, giving the unit a som-nolent, heavy-lidded appearance. Annie's red Mazda was in the adjoining carport, so she was definitely home.

But when Kat opened her car door, George reached across and laid a hand on her arm. She suddenly had second thoughts. 'Are you sure this is a good idea?' she asked.

'What? Why not?'

'I just wonder if we should give her more time.' George peered over at the unit. Now it seemed more watchful than sleepy. A bit like Annie had been all week. 'I mean, *I'm* still furious at her, so I'm guessing she feels the same way. And whenever we've tried to talk things through lately, it's ended badly.'

Kat shook herself free. 'You're just trying to avoid things.'

'No, I'm not!'

'And besides, given I just saw her peek through the side of the blinds, if we drive off now it'll do more harm than good. She might think we're casing the joint.'

George sighed, and then followed her sister from the car. They trudged over the nature strip, still soggy from the previous day, and then made their way to the front door. Kat rang the bell, the chimes echoing inside the house. Moments later Annie opened the door. She had an Aztec-patterned turban wrapped around her plum-coloured hair. Holding her bandaged hand against her chest, she regarded them silently. They regarded her silently back. Kat broke the impasse.

'Hi there!' she said brightly. 'Can we come in?'

'What for? Have you come to take back the stuff I got yesterday?'

'Don't be ridiculous,' said Kat. Her buoyant tone had slipped a few notches. 'Now are you going to invite us in or not?'

Annie shrugged. 'Sure. But take your shoes off.'

Kat pulled a face at George as their sister turned away. They slipped their sandals off, George having a little trouble with the buckle of one. She leaned against the doorway and bent over, eventually wrenching it free, almost smacking herself in the face with the momentum. It reminded her of Annie a few days earlier, staggering through the railing. She flinched at the memory, then bent to position the sandals neatly by the door.

'Look what you did,' said Kat.

George straightened as she followed her sister's pointing finger to the wall directly opposite them. About halfway down, a small clump of mud clung to the white surface. Even as they watched, it began the long slide to the floor, leaving a thin trail of earthy-brown in its wake.

'Whoops,' said George. 'I'll get a cloth.'

Kat grabbed her arm. 'Leave it. Let her think we didn't realise it was there.'

'Certainly not,' retorted George primly. She removed a tissue from one pocket and moistened it on her tongue as she went over to the wall. She began to mop from the original blotch down but this just turned the relatively unobtrusive trail into swirls of brown. Slightly panicky, George spat on the tissue and tried again. She took a step back. The wall now looked like a child's faecal finger-painting.

'Told you so,' said Kat.

'What the hell!' exclaimed Annie from the doorway.

'Sorry,' said George with feeling. 'A bit of mud flew off my sandal so I tried to clean it up.'

'Sterling effort. Leave it. I'll do it.'

'But I can—'

'No!' exclaimed Annie. 'Go, sit down. I insist.'

George grimaced at her younger sister, hoping that would convey yet another apology. This wasn't a good start. She followed Kat out of the small hall and into the lounge room. Boxes were stacked everywhere here, some half unpacked, along with bags of what looked like they might be soft furnishings. Sheets and pillows and cushions. Underneath it all was their mother's nubbly lounge suite. Leo was right, the place did look like an op shop. They went through into the dining room where Kat took a seat at the round table while George continued into the kitchen to wash the mud off her fingers. Then she joined her sister. Annie came past to fetch a cloth and a bowl of soapy water. She avoided eye contact.

The unit was a very similar layout to their mother's house, albeit on a smaller scale. Annie had also removed the island bench shortly after moving in, replacing it with her wooden butcher block on wheels. George thought it looked ridiculous. It also always reminded her of a brief rift around twenty years ago, at Annie's old house, which still rankled. While the adults had been sitting in the lounge talking, five-year-old Tom, along with his two cousins, had used the butcher block to reach the biscuit cupboard. According to both Leo and Rhyll, Tom had then left them atop while he clambered down and gave it a good push. Leo had taken a tumble, grazing one knee, while Rhyll had been found half-on the counter, hanging onto the overhead cupboard. Fortunately, apart from shock, no great damage had been done to either child, although it could easily have been much worse.

The real problem began *after* the event. Neither Leo nor Rhyll had actually seen Tom push the butcher block, and he steadfastly denied it. This gave his father the opportunity to accuse her two of making it up. He had lectured them on circumstantial evidence, and then threw a parting comment on false accusations at them as they left. She and Simon had been furious. All the while Annie had stood by silently, her arms around her son's shoulders. They hadn't spoken for a month after that, and it might have been even longer but that was about the time Anne and Brad had separated for good. The butcher block incident was swept under the rug.

'God, is she washing the whole wall?' muttered Kat now.

'Probably,' said George. She idly pleated the snowy-white tablecloth between her fingers as she tried to recover her earlier optimism.

Kat was watching her. She frowned. 'Who on earth even *has* tablecloths anymore?'

'Me,' said Annie, coming back through the room with a sponge in her hand. She glanced at George on her way to the kitchen. 'And can you not do that please.'

George dropped the cloth. There was now a fan of small pleats in the folds. 'Sorry.'

'And for your information,' continued Annie as she washed her hands at the sink, 'the tablecloth hides the scratches on the table itself. Makes it look far more presentable. Not *every*one can afford to just rush off and replace furniture at the drop of a hat.'

George blinked. She didn't think she had ever in her life just rushed off to replace furniture. In fact she knew that she drove Simon crazy with her deliberations before any large purchase. While it was unlikely that Kat had purchased any furniture at all since before she left for her overseas jaunt.

'Yeah, o-kay,' said Kat, the two words injected with disdain.

Annie didn't reply. She began filling a glossy chrome coffee machine on the counter. George recalled her having said that Tom had given it to her for Christmas. It looked expensive. He had certainly been generous. She wondered whose money he had used.

'Tom get off okay?' she asked her sister, with the idea that bringing him into the conversation might perhaps ease the tension.

'Yes,' said Annie. She plucked three mugs off a little pine stand.

'Um, good,' said George. She persevered. 'How's your hand then?'

'Getting there.'

George exchanged glances with Kat who gave an imperceptible shrug. This was hard work. She felt fresh annoyance at her younger sister, given she was largely responsible and didn't seem to even recognise this. The machine hissed on the bench, sending a thin stream of steam curling towards the ceiling. Annie made the coffees and brought them over to the table. She sat down opposite George.

'So then, to what do I owe this pleasure?'

'Well it's like this,' began Kat, leaning forward. 'We thought we should have a chat about what went down during the week. Mend some fences. And clearly there's some underlying issues here, otherwise it wouldn't have gone off the rails like that. We need to unpack them so we can move forward.'

'No,' said Annie. She wrapped her hands around her mug, the bandage white against the earthen pottery.

Kat frowned. 'What?'

Annie took a sip of coffee and put the mug down. She adjusted her turban slightly and then looked from one of them to the other, her eyes settling on Kat. 'I said no. This may come as a surprise, but you don't get to dictate when someone is ready to talk about stuff. And I'm not. Frankly the way you both treated me is still far too raw.'

'The way we ...' George petered off. She blinked, having no idea what to do with the rest of this statement.

'Come on,' protested Kat. 'That's a bit rich. You weren't exactly a shining light.'

Annie shrugged. 'Whatever helps you sleep at night.'

'I sleep just fine, thanks!'

'Why doesn't that surprise me?'

'Stop!' said George. Both her sisters turned to look at her. She held up a hand like she was directing traffic. 'This isn't getting us anywhere! Can't we at least be adults here?'

Annie snorted. '*I* certainly can. But I don't want to.' She paused, most likely realising the self-sabotage. 'That is, I think the past week has proven that no, *some* people can't.'

'Oh my god,' said George. She took a deep breath and tried again. 'Don't you see, Annie, this is *exactly* why we need to talk it through. You're, I mean *we're* all being so subjective!'

'No,' said Annie. Her v had appeared on the bridge of her nose. 'And you can't bully me into it either. I don't need to *unpack* anything. Not now and not ever. I've been giving this a *lot* of thought and I know exactly what happened and I know why.' She let out another snort. 'Do you really think I'd give you two *another* chance to turn on me? How stupid do you think I am?'

George opened her mouth to respond, but then closed it once more. Supplying an answer to this last question probably wasn't helpful. She felt the irritation that had bubbled in the pit of her stomach for the past few days threaten to surge once more.

'Nobody's trying to turn on you,' said Kat stiffly. 'Look, I get what you're doing here. Probably without even really realising it. All this crap is really about you being flattened by grief. If you turn us into the enemy, it gives you something else to concentrate on. But we're *not* the enemy. We're on your side.'

Annie was staring at her. 'What the hell? What sort of psycho-bullshit is that? *I* didn't make you into the enemy, you did that all by yourself! Don't put this on me!'

'But hang on,' said George, leaning forward. '*Nobody's* the enemy!'

'And what's more,' continued Annie, ignoring her, 'if anybody here needs to be psychoanalysed, it's you. Maybe they could work on your need for power and control. It's borderline abusive.'

'What?' Kat reeled back, her eyes on her youngest sister. 'Are you calling me abusive?'

'That's not what I said,' retorted Annie immediately. 'And this is half the problem! You don't listen!'

'Well, try talking bloody sense! Then I might listen more!'

'Okay, fine.' Annie sat back and folded her arms over her stomach. 'Listen to this then. I've decided that Tom's right. There's clearly nothing for me here now that Mum's ... moved on. That's been made abundantly clear. So I'm shifting to the Gold Coast. I've got an agent coming tomorrow for an appraisal. I plan to have this place on the market by the end of the month and make the move in April.'

George stared at her. The speech had been equal parts offensive and astonishing. She couldn't remember a time in her entire life that Annie hadn't been more than a stone's throw away. And even apart from that, she knew that Tom was quite wrong. His mother would be leaving all her supports behind to move to a place where she knew nobody except him, and his father.

Kat was staring at her also. 'What about your job?'

'I'll get another one,' said Annie. 'That's the good thing about being a nurse.'

George looked away. In the lounge room, Annie's tortoiseshell cat emerged from behind some boxes and preened as it rubbed itself against the couch. She wanted to mount an argument against Annie's plans, but the words jumbled against the weight of her resentment. And, also, the fact she herself was planning to leave in April.

'Are you sure about this?' asked Kat. 'Have you thought through all the ramifications?'

'Yes,' said Annie. 'And yes. My mind is made up.'

'I see.'

They sat in silence. The cat came over to wind itself between George's legs and then disappear in the direction of its owner. Outside, somebody started up a whipper-snipper, the sound swelling as it was put to use. George stared grimly at her coffee and then took a sip, just to have something to do, but it slid down her throat without flavour.

'O-kay then,' said Kat finally. 'I think I speak for George as well when I say that naturally we'd rather you not go. We'll miss you. But if you're determined, then it's even more important that we resolve … this. Somehow.'

Annie's v deepened. 'I told you, I'm not unpacking anything. I'm not your therapist.'

Kat's eyes widened at this last comment but then she shook her head as if trying to clear it. 'Sure. Well, I'm just going to park that over there for now.' She made a pushing gesture with her hand, as if doing exactly that. 'And I wasn't suggesting that now anyway. It's like this. I think we've all been under horrid pressure this week, and then when you throw grief into the mix, well, it's a toxic combination. We've all had moments where we could have done things differently. So how about instead of unpacking it, we just draw a line between then and now, and move on?'

'Draw a line?' repeated George. She shook her head. That was something that she already knew she couldn't do. Not a chance in hell. Drawing a line didn't erase other people's behaviour, it just swept it under the rug. The same rug that they had already stumbled over throughout the week. 'That's not—'

Annie interrupted with yet another snort. 'Oh you'd both like that, wouldn't you?'

'Huh?' asked George, turning to her.

'Yes, actually I would,' said Kat crisply. 'For starters, I was counting on a bit of support over the next twelve months, not acrimony. And also, to be honest, I rather enjoy a peaceful life.'

Annie shook her head, even as she kept her eyes on Kat. 'No, what *you* enjoy is a lack of accountability. They're two different things.'

Kat's eyes widened. 'What?'

'You heard me. You don't want to be held accountable for anything. The stickers were your idea and—'

'Who gives a fuck about the stickers!'

'Oh, *now* you say that.' Annie leaned back even further, as if wanting to create extra distance. 'But you were certainly hell-bent on them before. *Despite* me saying that it'd be manipulated.' She paused to flash a glance towards George. 'And then when it *was*, somehow it's my fault.'

'Oh no,' replied Kat, almost sweetly. 'We don't blame you. We mostly blame Tom.'

'Stop!' said George. She too was furious with Annie but she knew absolutely, without a doubt, that if Kat continued down this path, there was no going back. 'Annie! We came here with good intentions! Can't we just—'

'How *dare* you.' Annie was still staring at Kat. Her eyes were as flat as marbles. 'That's just bloody typical. You've *always* had it in for him. *Always.*'

'That's bullshit. Utter bullshit.'

'Really?' Annie's lip curled. She glanced across at George and then back. 'You've both made your feelings perfectly clear this week. You've hardly spoken to him. Like, did *either* of you ring him this morning? Or text him? To wish him a good trip back?'

'Well, I *would* have sent a Facebook message,' Kat shot back. 'But he defriended me, remember?' The sweetness had gone. Her words were like gravel. 'And you want to talk about account-ability? How about you giving him some? Or even taking some yourself? After all ...' She paused to push her mug aside so that she could point at her sister. Her finger jerked to emphasis each word. '*You* started this!'

'*I* started this?' Annie gaped at her. 'Me?' She shook her head and then honed back in on her sister, eyes narrow. 'When *you're* the one who swept in bossing everyone around and insisting on having your own way, no matter what? My god, you must have been pissed when Tegan sided with me about telling Harry. *One* thing you didn't get your own way on!'

'*What?* I couldn't give a flying fuck whether we tell him or not! I just think it'll confuse him! And you *know* Mum wouldn't want that. She'd prefer—'

'For him to be treated like a baby! Yeah, we get it. And it suits you as well, doesn't it?' Annie's lip curled. 'You can boss him around then like you do everyone else. Let's face it, the main reason you're annoyed with Tom is because you *can't* do that with him.'

'What the *hell*?'

'Yeah, that's right! You're just annoyed because he tried to stand up to you!'

'No, I'm annoyed because he's an entitled little shit!'

Annie's lips thinned. She shook her head once more, her arms still folded, and then suddenly jerked to face George. 'As for *you*. I thought we were *friends*. I thought you at least would have my back.'

George blinked. She felt a rush of defensiveness alongside her frothy fury, even though she wasn't sure what she had to be defensive about. To add to her consternation, she realised that Annie's eyes had filled. They stared at each other.

'And you have the damn gall to accuse *me* of having a lack of accountability?' continued Kat, as if unaware of the brief exchange. She was still pointing but now her finger was steady. 'When you're so busy drowning under victimhood to have any insight into yourself? Talk about pot kettle black! Tell us, please, what *is* it you want? Because it seems to me that you don't want to talk about it, except to point the finger at others.' She paused for a moment, as if suddenly aware of the irony that the only person actually pointing was her. She curled her finger over and hurried on. 'And you *certainly* don't want to take any responsibility, but you don't want to draw a line either. So please tell us, Annie, what the hell do you actually want?'

Annie sat up a little straighter, arms still folded. 'Do you know, that's the first time all week you've asked me what I want. Well, I'll tell you. I want you to get out. Go on, leave. You know where the door is.'

'Fine,' spat Kat. She pushed her chair back. The cat let out a yowl and shot across the room, disappearing back behind the boxes.

George had risen also. She frowned, trying to make sense of it all. The anger was still there, but higher up, pressing against her ribcage, was hurt. Annie wasn't even willing to make the effort.

They were being asked to leave. 'We were trying to do the right thing,' she said now to her sister. 'Which is a sight more than you.'

'Too little, too late,' said Annie flatly.

'God, I can't believe you.'

'Right back at you.' Annie stared at her and then jerked her head towards the doorway. The turban slipped sideways. Her eyes shone like jewels. 'But you'd better get a move on. Your mate's already left. You don't want to be left behind now, do you?'

'Annie …'

'Just go. Now. Fuck off.'

George kept her eyes on her sister for a few more moments and then picked up her bag and made her way with dignity through the untidy lounge room. By the front door, the bowl of soapy water sat on the hall table. The wall was still shiny from being cleaned. They hadn't even been there long enough for it to dry.

Kat had left the door wide open so George closed it quietly, withstanding the temptation to slam it. She felt tears prick at her eyes but wasn't sure if they were from anger or frustration or dismay. Perhaps all three. She paused to slip on her sunglasses and then walked down the pathway to join her older sister by the nature strip. They looked at each other and then Kat drew a deep breath, letting it out with a rush.

'Well, that went well,' she said.

George nodded but didn't reply. She simply didn't have the words.

Chapter Twenty-three

Sunday afternoon

The nature strip outside their mother's house was piled with discarded furniture and boxes of household goods. Several had clearly been rifled through, leaving their contents vomiting across the grass. Stained saucepans and mismatched crockery, towels and pillows, rusty gardening tools. Annie's old couch sat in centre-stage, like a pit stop for pedestrians. George supposed that Simon must have brought it back for her on one of his trips. She felt a flush of pride in him, alongside additional resentment at her sister.

In fact she was so full of emotion, much of it conflicting, that George had fully intended on going straight back home. Kat however had insisted on a debrief session and given she was driving, there wasn't much that could be done. Except perhaps have her charged with kidnapping, which seemed a little extreme. Accordingly they had debriefed all the way, or rather in her usual style while driving, Kat had kept up a continuous monologue. The only time George had been able to add anything was when they stopped off at the supermarket, and then while waiting in line at the local Subway for lunch. None of this debriefing seemed to have got them very far though; they were both still exactly as angry, and hurt, and befuddled as they had been when they left.

'Do you know what it is?' asked Kat now, as she locked the car. 'She *likes* being a victim. It's her safe space. Where she's most comfortable.'

George juggled her bag, sandwich and container of soft drink. 'Maybe.'

'It's her default. So when she's under stress, she heads straight for it. Do you think I'm bossy?'

'Yes.'

'Fair enough. But I meant what I said before, that I don't really care about the outcome – I just like order. Son of a *bitch*!'

'What?' George whipped around, nearly losing her drink in the process. Her sister was pointing at the nature strip.

'Some arsehole has dumped his washing machine there! And there's paint cans too!'

'Ah well,' George shrugged. There was only so much resentment she could hold. 'It'll still all get picked up together next week.'

'It better be,' said Kat darkly. She strode over to examine the scene of the crime.

George made her way up to the front door, but it was too hard to extract her keys from her bag so she stood there, gazing at the thready lacework of the clouds. For the first time she was facing the realisation that her relationship with Annie had changed irrevocably. She would never be able to move forward without some sort of analysis, and Annie would never want to give one. Not if it also meant self-examination – and examination of her son's behaviour as well. Her sister had been one of her best friends, for years. George thought that at some stage she was going to have to grieve this too.

Kat came past, muttering about vandalism, and fumbled with her keys to unlock the door. Inside the house, the hallway yawned and the lounge room was as empty as Annie's had been over-crowded. George hesitated in the doorway. The carpets had been freshly vacuumed, with lines imprinted in the pile. Some darker shapes on the walls and floors were the only sign that once this room had been furnished. Even the free-for-all boxes were gone.

'Amazing, hey?' said Kat proudly. Her voice echoed.

George blinked. She felt as hollowed as the room. She slipped off her sunglasses but that just made things worse.

'Hang on,' said Kat. She went into the kitchen and returned having swapped the groceries for two tea towels. She gave one to George and then laid the other on the carpet, right beneath the light fitting, before deftly lowering herself into a cross-legged position. She began arranging her lunch like a picnic.

'Your drink's going to spill,' said George. She still hadn't moved.

'I beg to differ.' Kat tucked the container of soft drink neatly between her thighs. 'Voila.'

George sighed. Over the past decade, her fondness for non-table picnics had diminished on par with her flexibility. She came over to her sister and squatted, one of her knees creaking, to lay down her load. Then she dropped down, her bottom hitting the floor with a thud. She grabbed at her drink before it could spill and wedged it against her crutch. Her eyes widened.

'Do you think she even realises what a hypocrite she's being?' asked Kat now.

'No,' said George. With one hand on the drink, she shuffled herself backwards until her back was against the wall for support. Then she rearranged the container a little further from her nether regions and unwrapped her sandwich.

'I suppose at least we're not arguing about money,' said Kat. 'That's the usual thing that breaks up families at times like this.'

'Give it time,' said George. She felt a flash of disloyalty, as she didn't really think that Annie would do that. But then she hadn't thought she'd do half the things she'd done that week.

Kat had opened up her own sandwich and was now picking out the excess of onion rings. 'I'm not letting her off the hook, but I blame Tom mostly. I think he did it deliberately. He wanted his mother up there so he pushed and prodded.' She jammed her sandwich back together angrily. 'Little shit.'

George gave this some thought. 'I don't think so. At least not in the beginning. But then later, yeah, no doubt he took advantage of it. He probably misses her.'

'Well, sure. But that's about *him*. I doubt he's really considered *her* in all this. For god's sake, she'll be back within a stone's throw of bloody Brad!'

'I know.' George began eating, even though she wasn't really hungry. It was difficult to know which was worse, the earlier anger or this oddly queasy numbness.

Kat sighed. 'Well, I have to say that I didn't anticipate this with my SWOT analysis.'

'A weakness in itself,' said George.

'Definitely.'

They ate in silence. For a while George thought about her sister, but it was a little like poking her tongue into a tooth abscess. She pushed it all away, only then registering that something integral was missing. With a jolt she realised that it was the sound of the grandfather clock ticking in the hallway. It had always been there, punctuating the entire fifty-five years of her life. This brought her thoughts back to her mother, and what she would say if she saw her house gutted like this. It was another abscess, but this one wasn't compartmentalised so easily.

'Do you think Mum was like the glue?' she asked now. 'Holding us all together?'

Kat frowned, considering this. Then she shook her head. 'No. I can't think of it like that. Because then it's all inevitable.'

George sighed softly. Inevitable or not, that was exactly what seemed to have happened. And so quickly. Their mother would have been devastated.

'Did you bring me some?' asked Harry from the doorway.

'Oh!' Kat gazed at him. 'No, sorry. But there's rolls and cheese and stuff on the bench.'

'Okay.' Harry didn't seem too perturbed. He disappeared around the corner into the kitchen.

Kat turned back to George, lowering her voice to a whisper. 'Do you think he's going to expect me to supply food all the time?'

'You'll have to establish ground rules,' replied George. 'Mum used to get his groceries and then he'd take them downstairs. Just keep a tally and take it out of his pension.'

Kat chewed her lip and then nodded. 'And we still have to work out all that financial administration stuff. I don't want to be landed with the whole thing just because I'm here.'

'Um, yes.' George laid down the remains of her sandwich. 'There's something I need to tell you.' She paused, took a deep breath. 'I'm not sure how to say this, but—'

'You're off to London for a year,' said Kat equably. 'I was wondering when you were going to share that gem.'

George looked at her, surprised. 'How did you know?'

'Rhyll texted a few hours ago. She wants to move in here after you leave.' Kat picked up a piece of her discarded onion and popped it into her mouth. 'She figured it was about time she was a little more independent, but at least here it'd be affordable. She could manage that at least, alongside uni.'

George was now gaping at her. She didn't know which part of this to fix on first.

'I said yes,' continued Kat. 'I hope you don't mind. But it does make sense, doesn't it? And to be honest, it'll be nice to share ...' She gestured with her head towards the kitchen. 'Everything.'

'Uni?' asked George, finally having settled on one part. 'You mean ... university?'

Kat looked at her questioningly. 'You do know she's applied for uni, don't you? A Bachelor of Arts, majoring in creative writing I think it is. At RMIT.'

'Oh my god,' said George. She knew that she should be offended that Kat had known while she hadn't, but her joy overshadowed this. It was all the more welcome because she herself had just been feeling so miserable. Rhyll was going back to university. She had direction. And creative writing no less. Harry came in from the kitchen with a plate holding a cheese roll. He contemplated the seating arrangements for a few moments and then disappeared once more. They heard the sliding door open.

'I hope it wasn't a secret,' said Kat now, frowning. 'Maybe she meant to surprise you. Pretend you don't know!'

George nodded. She had no intention of pretending any such thing. She couldn't wipe the smile from her face. This was something good, amongst everything else. There would be a celebration that evening. Maybe she'd get Indian food, which was Rhyll's favourite takeaway.

'And you don't mind? About her shifting in here?'

'Not at all,' said George warmly. Even if Rhyll only moved out for the year that Kat was here, it would still be good for her. And it wouldn't have happened if George herself hadn't decided to move to London. Her smile broadened. 'I think it's a marvellous idea!'

A clattering noise came from the dining room, followed by the sound of the sliding door closing. Harry reappeared, this time carrying a folding chair along with his plate. He deftly flipped the chair out just inside the lounge room and seated himself, his lunch on his lap.

'The World Health Organisation has issued a comprehensive package of technical guidance,' he said. 'For the road ahead.'

'Fascinating,' replied Kat. She turned back to George. 'Let's get back to you flitting off, though. Firstly, I've got no grounds for complaint, given I haven't been back all that long myself. But what I really want to know is why? And what's the go with your marriage?'

George shrugged. She wanted to hold onto her happiness.

'Tell me one thing then,' continued Kat. 'Are you really having an …' she paused, glancing at Harry before lowering her voice to a whisper, 'affair?'

'*What?*' George stared at her. Her smile vanished. 'Why on earth would you ask that?'

'Oh come on. You and Annie made it perfectly obvious the other day. Plus the way you and Simon were acting yesterday. And you haven't answered.' She lowered her voice to a barely-there whisper. 'Are you?'

'I can't hear you,' said George, knowing that she was both stalling for time and hoping that Kat abruptly forgot what she was talking about. The former never worked and the latter never happened.

'Bullshit.'

George closed her eyes for a moment. When she opened them, Kat was still staring at her. 'Okay, yes. I was. But it's over now. I don't want to talk about it. It was a mistake. And it's got nothing to do with my decision.'

'Well, well, well.' Kat was grinning. 'You dirty dog. I wouldn't have thought you had it in you. And absolute rubbish it has nothing to do with your decision. You're running away.'

'Prince Charles had an affair,' said Harry. 'With Camilla Parker Bowles. He wanted to be her tampon.'

'Yeah, you told us.' Kat hadn't taken her eyes off George. 'So I gather Simon knows?'

'Yes,' replied George stiffly. This was the second time she'd been accused of running away. 'He found out on Wednesday.'

Kat folded the sandwich paper over the rest of the onion and screwed it up before shoving it into her empty drink container. Then she stretched out her legs with a groan. 'Do you want to know what I think?'

'No.'

'I think your marriage has been in trouble for a few years, but neither of you have done anything about it. So you've had this affair – and by the way, I'm going to be wanting details later.' She bent her knees and wrapped her arms around them, gazing intently at George. 'And now you're also devastated about Mum. Probably the situation with Annie too. So rather than dig in and deal with everything, you're running away.'

George had begun shaking her head halfway through her sister's speech. 'You're wrong. This is something I've always wanted to do. You *know* that. And didn't you read Mum's diary? She wanted to as well! So in a way, I'm doing it for both of us.'

'Bullshit,' said Kat. She gave a short laugh. 'Next you'll be telling me that this is a pilgrimage. And you *do* want to take her ashes and scatter them over there.'

'And besides,' went on George, ignoring this last, 'even if a small part *is* running away, so what? Sometimes that's the best thing to do. It's not called fight or flight for nothing.'

Kat snorted. 'That's for if you meet a bear in the woods, not for avoidance. And in your case you need *less* distance, not more. If I had my way, I'd lock you and Simon in your house for a few months, and not let you out until you've sorted things. One way or the other.'

George was saved from responding to this bizarre proposal by the sound of a knock at the front door. Harry glanced towards it but didn't move. Kat grinned at her.

'We haven't finished here,' she said as she rose to her feet.

George leaned over to peer through the front window. Tegan's blue hatchback was parked in the driveway. The fractured section of glass gave it a jewel-like appearance. She straightened just as her niece appeared in the doorway. She stopped there, beaming, and then tilted her head to one side as she fingered the blonde plait that lay across a shoulder.

'I have had the *best* idea! Guess what I want to do?'

'Go to London?' asked Kat from just behind her.

'No!'

'The Gold Coast?'

'No!'

'Then I give up.' Kat came past and lowered herself back to the floor. She waved a hand expansively. 'Come, pull up a pew and tell us.'

Tegan bounced across the room and dropped a kiss on her father's forehead before flopping down beside his chair. She folded her legs, heels touching, then despite wearing rather tight jeans, managed to pull up both feet to sit atop her knees in a yoga-like pose. She grinned at them. 'I want to buy this house!'

George was too busy admiring her niece's elasticity for this to immediately register. When it did, she frowned but Kat was the first to respond.

'That's a lovely thought, Tegan,' she said gently. 'But even with the portion you're getting from your father's share, it'd still be beyond your means. Even if we gave you the best possible price. As a single earner, I doubt you'd even get the mortgage.'

'No, hear me out.' Tegan leaned forward eagerly. 'I've thought it all through. I want to buy it outright, and then move in here and let Dad stay in his apartment downstairs. I won't be able to do it until the end of the year though, because I'm under lease where I am. But I've done my research so I know the equivalent market value. I don't want to pay any less.'

'Tegan …' began George doubtfully. She also knew the worth of this house.

Tegan put up a hand. 'I know what you're going to say. But I know exactly what I'm letting myself in for. And he's my father.' She paused to give Harry a big smile. 'I *want* to do this. And rest assured I'll be putting support services in place also. That's the beauty of me being a social worker. I know the system.'

'That's actually not what I was going to say,' said George. 'It's more, well, even if you got the home loan, and your father paid a generous board, the mortgage would be crushing.'

'Maybe …' Kat frowned. 'Maybe he could invest some of his share.' She shook her head. 'No, it'd still be too much. And then we run into problems if it doesn't work out.'

'Stop!' Tegan's grin was still in place. 'You don't understand. I want to *buy* it. Outright.'

Kat raised an eyebrow. 'Did you win TattsLotto?'

'Not quite.' Tegan looked from one aunt to the other. 'I suppose Granma never told you. See, I got a substantial inheritance from my grandparents a few years ago. My other grandparents, that is. My mother's parents. I've got it in a term deposit.'

'Oh,' said George. So much for them trying to ensure that Tegan was financially secure. But the inheritance did make sense. Vanessa had been her parents' only child, and Tegan their only grandchild. Now that George considered it, she assumed that it was indeed a significant amount. She felt a rush of fondness for her niece that she would even consider using it all to buy this house. And she was even gladder now that Tegan had been given the diary. 'But are you sure?' she asked now. 'It's a big investment. Huge.'

'Absolutely, definitely,' said Tegan. 'I *love* this house.' She paused to glance around the empty lounge room. 'I loved my other grandparents' house also, but that got sold by the executors because I was under twenty-one. This time though, it's my choice. This house is part of my childhood. It's like, like, *family*.'

Kat sat up, wrapping her arms around her knees again. Her tattoo peeked from beneath a sleeve. She gazed at her niece pensively. 'It does sound like you've thought this all through.'

'Oh, I *have*! Except for asking Dad how he feels about the idea. Which I probably should have done first.' Tegan leaned to the side, tilting her head up. 'Sorry, Dad.'

Harry looked a little surprised to be included. He nodded.

'Can I ask you to park it then,' said Kat now, 'just until say, September, October? I mean obviously it'd be marvellous if you wanted to go ahead, but we need you to be absolutely sure. If you still feel the same then, we can start going through details. And in the meantime, I'll consult with you about any renovations. Just in case you hate them.'

'I'm sure I won't,' said Tegan confidently. 'You've got great taste and I'm not *ridiculously* sentimental. I know stuff has to be done.' Her smile broadened. 'But thanks. Appreciated.'

Harry leaned over to put his empty plate down on the floor. 'In 2017, people doing renovations in Montreal, Canada, found skeletal human remains in the basement ceiling,' he said. 'It was a seventy-year-old baby.'

Kat and Tegan immediately began questioning Harry further, particularly around whether this was some type of geriatric infant mutant, or if he meant the remains had been there for seventy years. George wasn't really listening. She had stilled, suddenly remembering that Tegan herself was pregnant. With everything else that had happened that day, this had completely skipped her mind. She gazed at her niece now, searching for confirmation. Certainly she was remarkably limber for somebody who was expecting, but then it was most likely early days. Particularly if she planned on a termination.

'Tegan,' she said now, a little hesitantly. 'Um, I know about the … you know.'

'Huh?' asked her niece.

George flashed a glance at her brother but he had taken his mobile from a pocket and was staring at the screen. She turned back to Tegan. 'The you know,' she said again, this time lowering her eyes meaningfully.

Tegan's grin had finally faded. 'No, I really don't. The you know what?'

'What the hell are you talking about?' asked Kat, looking from one of them to the other.

'You don't have to say anything,' said George, ignoring her sister. 'I just wanted you to know that I know. And if you need any support … you know.'

'I really don't,' replied Tegan. She frowned, fingering her plait. 'Is there something I should know that you know, and I don't?'

'Oh my god!' exclaimed Kat. 'George! Just say it!'

George flashed her sister an irritated glance before settling her gaze back on Tegan, with more sympathy. 'The baby,' she said quietly.

'What baby?'

Now it was George's turn to frown. '*Your* baby.'

'I have a baby?'

George's frown deepened. Tegan was not that good an actor. She cast her mind rapidly over the conversation with Leo that morning. He had definitely said Tegan. He wouldn't have made that up. She lowered her voice. 'Um, aren't you pregnant?'

'Fuck, no!' exclaimed Tegan. She immediately flushed. 'Sorry, didn't mean to swear. You just gave me a shock.'

Kat snorted. 'I bet!' She turned to George. 'What made you think she was pregnant?'

'Leo told me!' protested George. She felt like a fool. 'Tegan, are you *sure* you're not pregnant?'

'Absolutely, definitely positive. What the hell?' She let out a snort of laughter and then jumped to her feet. 'I'm going to give him a ring. Find out what's going on.'

Kat had also begun laughing as Tegan left the room, mobile phone in hand. 'Look at you, starting rumours to divert attention from your own shenanigans. Sure you're not projecting? Perhaps *you're* pregnant!' She raised both hands in the air. 'It's a miracle!'

George rolled her eyes even as she kept one ear out for the conversation happening in the hallway. Leo did enjoy a bit of gossip, but it was not like him to create something from nothing. She could hear Tegan start to giggle and then a moment later, she popped her head around the corner. Her phone was still at her ear.

'He got it from Rhyll. I'm ringing her now.'

'Interestinger and interestinger,' said Kat as their niece disappeared once more. 'But let's take advantage of her temporary absence. What do you think of her plan?'

George shrugged, a little distracted. 'It sounds like it might work. She *is* a social worker.'

'Well, we've got a good few months in hand anyway. Which will give her a chance to be sure this is what she wants. It's a hell of a responsibility.'

George nodded. 'At least that'd mean he wouldn't have to move to a you-know-what.'

'Although, then again, maybe we should just ask him.' Kat had lowered her voice. 'So we don't need to say things like you-know-what. Maybe Annie had a point there. Maybe we do treat him like a child.'

George nodded slowly. It was the habit of a lifetime, inherited from their mother. It would be difficult to break. 'Yeah, maybe. Probably.'

'Anyway.' Kat shot her a grin. 'Don't think I've let you off the hook. Temporary reprieve only. You and your pilgrimage.'

'It's not a pilgrimage,' said George, although she was growing to like the sound of that. 'And anyway, it's only a year. I'll be back before you know it.'

Tegan ducked her head around the corner once more. 'Rhyll got it from Lesley. In London. Apparently she sent her an email last night saying she thought I should have someone my own age to support me. What a hoot!'

'Lesley?' asked George, frowning again. '*Cousin* Lesley?'

'Yeah, apparently. I'm going to ring her now.'

'Hang on!' called Kat, twisting to face the doorway. 'It'll be the middle of the night there. Beside, you don't have to. We all know the only place that Lesley could have got it from.'

'Aunt Margaret,' said George and Tegan at the same time.

Harry's head popped up at this last. He looked around as if expecting his aunt to leap from somewhere. When this didn't happen he relaxed, focussing back on his phone.

'*I'll* ring her,' said George determinedly. She scrabbled through her bag for her mobile. 'I want to know how this all started.'

'Put it on speakerphone,' said Kat. 'This is going to be gold.'

George keyed in her aunt's contact and then pressed the speaker icon. Tegan came back and bobbed down beside Kat. The phone rang and rang, and George was about to hang up when they finally heard Aunt Margaret's rather tinny voice.

'Hello? Who is this? Who's there?'

'It's me, Aunt Margaret. George!'

'Turn the volume up,' hissed Kat. She reached over and George jerked the phone away.

'Georgette! How lovely! How are you, dear, how are you coping?'

'I'm good, thanks. I'm here with Kat and Tegan. And Harry. You're on speakerphone.'

'What sort of phone?'

'Speakerphone!' repeated George, raising her voice. 'So everyone can hear you!'

'All right then!' yelled Aunt Margaret. 'Is this better?'

George briefly considered trying to explain but then dismissed the idea. She turned the volume back down instead. 'That's perfect! Listen, we wanted to ask you something.'

'Certainly! Is it about your mother?'

'No,' called Kat, leaning over. 'It's about Tegan. Aunt Margaret, did you tell Lesley that Tegan was pregnant?'

'Oh dear!' Aunt Margaret fell silent for a few moments. They could hear her breathing. 'God darn it, I am *so* sorry. You'll think I broke your confidence, I know. It's just I was up all night wrestling with my conscience. It takes a village you know, and I consider myself part of that village. So I thought if Enid was alive, what would she do? What *would* she do?'

George looked at her sister, thoroughly perplexed. Kat didn't look any the wiser.

'Aunt Margaret!' said Tegan, coming closer. 'It's Tegan here. What we want to know is—'

'Oh, you'll think I'm such a fuddy duddy,' interrupted Aunt Margaret. 'But it's not like that at all. I'm a feminist! Women's liberation! Rosie the Riveter! I even waved placards about this back in the sixties! Your uterus all the way!'

'Huh?' said Tegan. She sat back on her haunches. 'She waved placards about my uterus?'

Kat was shaking her head. 'Aunt Margaret, what the hell are you talking about?'

'I'd like a cup of coffee,' said Harry from the doorway. 'I have my blue mug.'

George put up a hand. 'Hang on! Everyone shush!' She lifted the phone closer. 'Aunt Margaret, TEGAN IS NOT PREGNANT.'

'She's not?'

'No! But what we want to know is where on earth you got the idea that she was?'

'But you said so!' exclaimed Aunt Margaret. 'I distinctly recall you saying so. Or was it Kathryn? It was one of you two certainly! In the kitchen!'

George looked over at her sister questioningly but Kat was shaking her head again.

'Not me,' she hissed. 'Why would I say that?'

'Aunt Margaret,' said Tegan, leaning in again. 'Could you tell us exactly what was said?'

'I'd really like a cup of coffee,' said Harry plaintively. 'I got my blue mug.'

'In a minute,' said George impatiently. 'Aunt Margaret, Tegan's right. If you could tell us precisely what you heard, we could perhaps sort this out.'

'Well, certainly,' came the reply. 'I was sitting there, at the table reading the paper. About the tennis. An article about that Djokovic fellow. And you and Kathryn were talking in the kitchen but I accidentally overheard. And you said that Tegan was pregnant. That she was going to get a termination.' Aunt Margaret lowered her voice. 'You know, an *abortion*.'

Kat suddenly rocked backwards. She stared at George, her eyes wide, and then suddenly began laughing. George frowned at her but her sister was now laughing so hard that she was in no condition to explain. It was clear though that she had come to a realisation that the rest of them hadn't yet.

'Aunt Margaret,' said George, still frowning at Kat. 'I'll ring you back soon. But please don't tell anyone else that Tegan's pregnant, because she's not.' She hung up even though she could still hear her aunt's voice, and then put the phone down on the carpet. 'Okay, Kat, what's the go? Care to explain?'

'Oh my god,' spluttered Kat. She groaned, putting a hand on her stomach. 'This is why she's been acting so weird! She *was* sitting at the table and we *were* talking about Tegan, but not about pregnancy! We were talking about giving her a portion of Harry's inheritance! Get it? A *portion*. And she heard—'

'Abortion,' finished Tegan for her. 'Oh lordy. And then she's stewed on this until she told Lesley, who told Rhyll, who told Leo.' She looked at George. 'Who told you.'

Kat began laughing again. 'The moral being that if you ever *do* get pregnant, Tegan, keep it to yourself until you're ready to share!'

'Unbelievable,' said George. She was grinning also.

'Coffee?' asked Harry. He had made it over to the dining room where he stood, blue mug still in hand.

'I'll get it, Dad,' said Tegan, rising gracefully. She went past her father into the kitchen. He followed her, holding out his mug like some sort of offering.

George shook her head, still grinning. 'Someone needs to break the news to Aunt Margaret before she takes out a full page ad.'

'Dibs not,' said Kat.

George rolled her eyes. She got up stiffly, her joints protesting all the way. She could hear Tegan talking with her father in the kitchen. He seemed to be telling her some facts about pangolins, and markets. It occurred to her that for the past hour or so, she had forgotten how empty the house was. Events had filled it instead. She looked down at Kat, who had stretched her legs out on the carpet. 'Mum would have loved this bit. Even the ridiculousness of it. All of us laughing. Looking after Harry.'

'Yes, she would've.' Kat's smile faded. She took in a deep breath, then let it out with a rush and followed up with a smaller, softer sigh. 'It'll get better, you know.'

'Will it?'

'Yes. Have you ever heard of the old guy with the house on the hill?'

George looked perplexed. The conversation had taken an unexpected turn. 'What?'

'I can't remember where I heard it,' said Kat. 'But it's sort of helped me this week. It goes like this. This old guy who lost his wife explained his life after her death. He said that for fifty years or so he lived in a house on top of a hill and the view was just wonderful. Then after she died, he plummeted to the bottom and lived there for a while. He couldn't see anything. His view was obscured by the shadows of the hill itself. And how big it was. Overwhelming.' She paused, and then cleared her throat before continuing. 'But over time, his house moved back upwards. It'll never be right at the top again, but even halfway the view wasn't too bad. It was different, but he could live with that.' She rose from the floor with a groan, and then looked back at George. 'It's a metaphor. For life.'

'I get that,' said George tightly. Her throat hurt. 'I'm going to the bathroom.'

She made her way across the empty room and up the hallway, past the Encyclopaedia Britannica set. She knew why Kat had stickered that, even though everything it contained could now be accessed on a mobile phone. Their mother had purchased it off a travelling salesman about fifty years earlier, paying it off in instalments that she saved out of her housekeeping money. She had received as much enjoyment from each of the volumes as her children. They had thrown open the windows of their suburban home to the world. Past, present and future. Jason and the Argonauts, the Colosseum, Tutankhamen, the Bermuda Triangle, the gold rush, the space race. Many a time, George had come into the house to find her mother sitting at the table, book in hand.

'Look, Georgie,' she might say. 'This was William the Conqueror! He invaded Britain in 1066 and changed the course of history.'

All these years later, George felt tears prick at her eyes. The course of her own history had been irrevocably changed. Not just hers but also Kat's, and Annie's. Recollection of the earlier scene with her younger sister threatened to crowd its way in, but George pushed it resolutely aside. She cast one more glance at the encyclopaedias, which held so much more than a phone ever could, and then made her way into the bathroom. She stared at herself in the mirror. The view wasn't great, but sooner or later it had to improve. She was moving up the hill if it killed her.

Chapter Twenty-four

Sunday evening

That evening found George in a very similar position as the previous night. She was even wearing the same kaftan. Once again, a glass sat on the rattan table by her chair on the deck, and once again a small platter of cheese and crackers was nearby. There were significant differences though. She was drinking wine, not Scotch and it wasn't raining tonight. The garden was still, caught in the glow of the setting sun like an oil painting. The initial and most difficult discussion with her husband was in the past, and if awkwardness still lay ahead, at least the worst was over. Her daughter was no longer directionless, Harry might not have to move into care, and her ticket was now fully booked and paid.

Earlier that day, after finally being dropped back at home, George had run herself a bath and well and truly poked the abscess. She had autopsied the altercation with Annie and tried, as much as possible, to probe where it went wrong. Where it had gone wrong all week. This endeavour brought her no closer to any particular insight, but by the time the bath grew cold, it did have the effect of grinding down the sharpness of injury. What remained was a congealed sadness. She had never realised that their relationship was so fragile. There was a grim irony also, in that Annie had created her worst fear. Her sisters had *not* been ganging up on her at the beginning, but they most certainly were by the end.

George also had an idea. She resolved to write it all down before the details became murky, and then share it with Lesley when they met. What they needed was a facilitator of sorts, one who was objective. Lesley was perfect. She was bossy, and family-orientated, and she had known them their entire lives. She was also visiting in June and no doubt, once she knew what had happened, would also fit in a trip to the Gold Coast. George held no illusions that their relationship would ever be the same, but if they could find a place where they could communicate, or Annie was reminded that she had a safe place if it all went awry up on the coast, then that at least would be something.

This plan did not offset the sadness altogether, but it did give her an excellent excuse to compartmentalise the cause. Just as victimisation was Annie's default, procrastination was her own. So she now cast another admiring glance at the garden, and returned to reading Rhyll's latest blog post. It was about the two wives of Samuel Morse, who had both died young. Apparently it was the death of the first one, Lucretia, and the deafness of the second one, Sarah Elizabeth, that had inspired him to come up with the Morse code. The post had already gathered 234 likes, seventy-eight comments, and three laughing emojis, which seemed a little inappropriate. George slipped her glasses off and laid them in her lap with the phone. She wondered how many more of Harry's anecdotes would be turned into entire posts, after Rhyll shifted over there. Maybe she herself should have used him as a source after all.

With unusually impeccable timing, Rhyll pushed open one of the French doors and slid through. Her laptop was under one arm. She eyed her mother warily.

'Why'd you send Leo for Indian food?'

'To celebrate,' said George happily.

'What? You leaving?'

'No. Well, maybe that too.' George leaned back, resting her hands on her stomach as she smiled at her daughter. 'But mainly you. Going back to university.'

'Oh.' Rhyll chewed her lip for a moment and then crossed the deck to flop down in a chair on the other side of the table. 'Aunt Kat told you then.'

'Yes. But I don't know why *you* didn't! I couldn't be more pleased.'

Rhyll helped herself to some cheese from the platter. 'That's exactly why. I haven't even been accepted yet.'

'You will,' said George confidently. She held up her phone. 'All they have to do is have a look at your writing. You're a natural.'

Rhyll popped the cheese in her mouth. She looked sidelong at her mother. 'Really?'

'Absolutely. You're very good. Have you told your father?'

'Not yet.' Rhyll grabbed another bit of cheese but this time just tossed it from hand to hand. 'Did she also tell you that I asked if I could move in there for a while?'

George nodded. 'And I think that's a great idea too. It'll give you some independence. Away from … us.'

'Well, I thought with you gone I didn't want to be the only female around. You know what happens then? They end up doing all the housework.'

George looked askance at her daughter and then realised that Rhyll was joking. How little she did around the house had long been a bone of contention. It was highly unlikely that would have changed whether George was there or not. She grinned back, enjoying the moment. It certainly wasn't the right time to tell Rhyll that there was a chance that her cousin Tegan might be buying her grandmother's house by the end of the year.

'But Dad doesn't know that either,' said Rhyll now. 'Not yet. So please don't say anything. I'll tell him in my own time.'

'Sure,' said George warmly. It was a nice feeling, to share secrets with her daughter. Maybe with some independence, and the return to university, Rhyll would gain some confidence. Maybe she would start sitting up straighter too. Make some friends. 'Hey,' she said now. 'Did you mend fences with your cousin before he left?'

'Close enough,' said Rhyll. 'We'll get there.'

'Don't bank on it,' replied George with feeling. 'And don't let it fester. I hate to think all this affected you guys too. You've always gotten on so well. Address it head on, before it becomes something more.'

Rhyll looked at her, one eyebrow raised. 'I gather you're leading by example. Mended fences with Aunt Annie then?'

'Not quite.' George stared out into the backyard. The setting sun bled across the horizon beyond the tree line, painting the landscape with a coral-tinted sepia. It occurred to her that in a few short months, she and her sisters would be gazing out at vastly different sunsets. Kat would have their childhood one, Annie the straight line of sun above ocean, and she would have the English twilight. A suspended hiatus in itself.

'He gave us a medal each,' said Rhyll now. 'Tom did. Me and Leo. Tegan too. One of Grandpa's old war medals.'

'Really?' George stared at her. Those were the medals that Kat had wanted. She wondered if Tom had always intended to share them, or if that gesture had been a sudden, conciliatory one. Either way, she felt a rush of warmth towards her nephew, and renewed sadness that they themselves had ended things on such a prickly note. Maybe, despite everything, she *should* have sent him a text the previous night, wishing him farewell. Maybe Annie had a point, there at least. She was genuinely fond of him, and had always thought he felt the same way, and it hurt that their relationship had been treated almost as if it was disposable. Like mother, like son.

'Besides, *I've* still got him on Facebook,' said Rhyll with a sidelong grin.

George nodded. She pushed the thought of Tom away. Perhaps space might work wonders there also. 'Speaking of Facebook,' she said. 'When I do go to London, shall *we* be Facebook friends?'

'Not a chance,' said Rhyll firmly. 'I don't need you all up in my business. No offence.'

'Oh, no offence taken.' George waved a hand to emphasise the airiness of her tone. 'In that case I'll just start commenting frequently on your blog, so we keep in touch.'

Rhyll looked at her narrowly. 'Are you serious?'

'Well, it's either that or Facebook,' said George. 'Your choice.'

'That's blackmail,' said Rhyll grumpily. 'How about we settle for regular FaceTiming? Or maybe Zoom? I mean, it's not like I have Dad on Facebook either, you know.' She paused, waiting for her mother to respond. George just smiled at her serenely. 'Whatever,' said Rhyll, opening her laptop. 'Anyway, I found your bloke for you.'

'My what?' For a moment George thought she meant Guy, and her stomach clenched accordingly. But then Rhyll swivelled the laptop and she could see that the screen was filled with the picture of a far older man. He had white hair and a rather plump nose, with smiling eyes surrounded by pleated wrinkles. George had never seen him before. She looked back up at her daughter, puzzled. 'Um ...'

'It's your bloke,' said Rhyll impatiently. 'You know, Henry Harrison.'

'*What?*'

'I know what you're going to say,' continued Rhyll defensively. 'That I shouldn't have taken that diary. But in my defence, you'd never have told me otherwise, would you?' She paused, and then nodded at her mother's expression. 'No, of course not. I know she was your mother, but she was my granma too. *You* act like you're the only one who misses her.'

George stared at her, gobsmacked. She had barely registered that yes, the diary *had* been taken, when defence had become offence. Somehow she was the one at fault. She glanced down at Henry Harrison, who smiled cheerfully back. 'But how did you even know—'

'I saw you reading it. So I just took it for the night, so I could too. Then Aunt Margaret rang on the landline yesterday, because apparently nobody was answering her texts. She said you'd visited. And I thought well, *that's* odd.' Rhyll paused to give her mother a smirk. 'So I did a little prodding and she mentioned a letter, from this guy called Henry Harrison. It wasn't that hard to do the maths.'

'Oh my god,' said George. She shook her head to try to clear it.

'Did you know he moved back down to Melbourne? In the mid-eighties.'

George dropped her eyes to Henry once more. She knew that she should be more annoyed that Rhyll had rifled through her bag, stolen the diary, but it was overshadowed by the tumbling information. 'So ... he lives here then?'

Rhyll shook her head. 'No. Sorry, he died a couple of years ago.'

'Oh.'

'But there's more.' Rhyll straightened the laptop and hit a few keys before turning it back to face her mother. A newspaper death notice had appeared on the screen.

Henry James Harrison (1942 – 2018).
Much loved husband of Valeria
Loving father of Harry, Aurora and Ariel
Adored grandfather of Jackson, Charlie, Brandon and Evie
Forever missed

George scanned the notice and then re-read the third line, her mouth falling open. After a few moments, she raised her gaze to Rhyll. 'Loving father of Harry. But how? Is it …?'

'Yup, it's our Harry,' said Rhyll cheerfully. She straightened the laptop. 'He married late, just had the two daughters. Twins. Not sure I can forgive him and his wife for naming them after Disney princesses though.'

'But … then he knew? About Harry?'

Rhyll looked over at her mother quizzically. 'Did it ever occur to you guys to actually ask Uncle Harry? I did. Showed him the photo yesterday. Turns out he's met him a few times. Then he started telling me about where the word funeral came from. So I'm guessing Granma took him to that too.'

'Oh my god,' said George again. She shook her head, trying to absorb the implications. 'Mum must have taken him there. She must have met them all. His wife too.'

'Look here,' said Rhyll. She turned the laptop to face her mother once more. 'Aurora is pretty chatty on Facebook. She has the three boys and Ariel has the girl. She's gay. Ariel that is, not the little girl.'

George stared at the family now filling the screen. They were crowded around a large table holding a train-shaped birthday cake. One of the children was holding a knife. Henry wasn't in this photo though, so George assumed it was more recent. There was an older woman sitting towards the side and two younger ones, perhaps in their late twenties, clearly related. A cluster of children leaned forward across the table, their eyes on the cake. None of them looked like Harry though.

'She posts lots about her father too,' continued Rhyll. 'Especially on his birthday. Apparently he liked going on cruises, and playing bowls, and eating peppermints.'

'This is amazing,' said George slowly, still examining the photo. She stilled, her finger on his face. Peppermints. Harry had *said* he liked eating peppermints. He hadn't been talking about the ninth president of the United States at all, he'd been talking about his father. They should have listened then. Instead they'd underestimated him, just as Annie said. She pushed her sister aside deftly. 'How on earth did you track all this down?'

'It's called research,' said Rhyll a little pompously. 'It's what I do.'

George started to answer but then her eye was drawn to a picture that hung on the wall behind the partygoers. She leaned in. It was a still life of apples, in a gilt frame, very similar to the one that was now leaning against a wall in her lounge room. George's breath caught.

'So Uncle Harry has two sisters,' continued Rhyll. 'And Tegan has four new cousins.'

'Unbelievable,' said George slowly. But she wasn't talking about Harry's extended family, or even her daughter's sleuth work. She dragged her eyes away from the apples. There would be time for that later. 'Listen, can you keep all this to yourself? At least until I've spoken to Kat. Tegan needs to be told also.'

Rhyll snapped the laptop closed. 'Sure. But it wouldn't hurt you to say well done.'

'Well done,' said George. Then she caught sight of her daughter's expression. 'No, I mean it. Not well done on stealing the diary, but certainly well done on the rest. You've done an amazing job. I'm very impressed.'

'Oh good,' said Rhyll sarcastically. 'That's my ultimate aim in life. Impressing you.'

George didn't bother responding to this. She was still trying to unpack Harry's new family. Ariel and Aurora. She grimaced. Kat was going to be astonished. There was no question now, Harry would have to be told. It didn't matter how confusing this might be, or how much their mother would have hated it. He had a right to know. Tegan also. These people were their direct relatives. Whether they then reached out or not was their choice.

Rhyll leaned across to grab another piece of cheese and George noticed a little silver ring on her finger. The tiny diamond chips matched the stud in her nose. It was the one from her mother's house. She felt a lump form in her throat. Had Enid ever intended them to discover this? Or had she just taken Harry there so that his real father could meet him? *Loving father of Harry* ... It must have been more than once, and it seemed that they had even attended the funeral. The family probably didn't even know that her mother had died.

The French doors opened and Leo came through bearing plastic bags of takeaway food. The smell of Indian spices and jasmine rice encircled him like an aura. Puddles followed unsteadily, and then promptly curled up on the decking by George's chair. Rhyll leaned across and fed him the cheese that she had been holding.

'We having a party?' asked Leo, depositing the bags on the table. 'If so I'll grab a beer.'

'And plates! And cutlery!' called George after him as he disappeared back inside. She turned to make space on the table. 'Does *he* know?' she asked.

'About Harry?' asked Rhyll.

'Yes. And about you – with university.'

'No to the first and yes to the second,' said Rhyll. She frowned. 'And about that, please, Mum, let's not make it a big deal.'

'It *is* a big deal,' began George. She caught sight of her daughter's face. 'Okay. Sure.'

'Good.'

George's phone pinged so she slipped her glasses back on. There was a new message from Kat. *Annie just left our group chat.* George shrugged, and then found the matching emoji to send back. Another text followed. *Same.* A few seconds later came yet another. *Maybe you were right and we should have left it a while.* George's fingers hovered over the keypad for a few seconds, but then she put the phone down instead. As gratifying as it was to have her opinion acknowledged, Annie had already taken up too much time today. And she didn't want to get into another conversation with Kat just yet anyway, not when she had so much to tell her.

Leo came back out with plates and cutlery so they busied themselves sorting out whose meal belonged to who. George had also ordered Simon's favourite, palak paneer, which she put to one side. She topped up her wine and settled down to eat. The food was delicious. Her mother had taken Harry around to Henry's house. The affair hadn't been the end. Perhaps they had even become friends. The notion was oddly comforting.

'Remember that time Granma was round here, and we had Indian?' asked Rhyll suddenly. 'And she said she didn't eat that type of food, but then demolished the leftovers?'

Leo laughed. 'They weren't just leftovers! She got Mum to make her a toasted sandwich and then ate half her food while she was waiting!'

'I remember it well,' said George grimly. But she was putting it on. In reality she had been thrilled to have introduced her mother to a new type of cuisine. It had been like getting approval, by proxy. She felt the now familiar throb behind her eyes and ducked her head, wondering if it would ever ease up. There were seven stages of grief apparently; however, she seemed to have opted for a fusion. Disbelief, along with pain and anger and sadness. Perhaps that meant she was progressing more rapidly than most, and the upward turn was just around the corner. Or perhaps this synthesis meant that they were here to stay.

'You okay, Mum?' asked Leo now, around a mouthful of butter chicken.

She nodded. 'Let's change the subject.'

'Sure. So did Rhyll tell you then that she's deserting me and Dad as soon as you skip the country? It's gonna be a bachelor pad around here.'

'Shh!' hissed Rhyll. She jerked her head towards the house.

George barely had time to turn before the French doors opened once more and Simon emerged with a stubbie of beer in one hand. He ran his eyes over the tableau expressionlessly and George felt a flush of guilt even though, on this occasion at least, there was no reason to feel guilty.

'Hey, Dad,' said Leo brightly. 'We've got Indian for dinner. Mum got you your favourite.'

'Generous of you,' he said, flashing the same flat look in her direction. 'But then you're known for your generosity, aren't you?'

George looked away, catching her two children exchanging a glance of their own. In an instant she knew that they knew a lot more than they had let on. She flushed. Simon came over and picked up a fork along with his container of palak paneer. He took it over to the balustrade and balanced it on top as he began eating. George didn't know if this was a good sign or not, but at least he hadn't taken it back inside.

'Something really funny happened today, Dad,' said Rhyll, heaping more rice onto her plate. 'Aunt Margaret misheard something that Mum and Aunt Kat said, so she told Lesley that Tegan was pregnant. Then Lesley told me, and I told Leo, and he told Mum. Tegan just put it on Facebook. How funny is that? You can't keep secrets in this family!'

'Oh, I don't know. Some people can.'

Leo rolled his eyes. 'God, Dad. Did you like get attacked by rabid tennis fans today or something? What's got you in such a mood?'

Simon shrugged, turning his attention back to his food. After a few moments, he looked across once more. 'Has your mother told you about her plans? London?'

'Sure she has,' replied Leo as his sister nodded. 'We think it's fantastic. Good on her.'

Simon frowned at him and then slid his gaze to George, still frowning. She took her glasses off and polished them on the sleeve of her kaftan, just to have something to do.

'I'm going to visit her later in the year,' continued Leo. 'I'm trying to talk Rhyll into it as well. You should come too!'

His father snorted. He took a swig of his beer and stared down at his food. George put her plate down and tore a piece off the spare roti. She chewed slowly, sure that the sound was extra loud in the silence.

'Look here,' said Leo suddenly. 'We know you two are having problems, but do you really have to make things so awkward for us too? *We* didn't do anything.'

'Nothing at all,' adjoined his sister, a little sanctimoniously.

'So maybe you could at least pretend for our sake?' continued Leo. He appeared to have been appointed as spokesperson. 'They say that an acrimonious atmosphere has a detrimental effect on children. Impacts on their cerebral cortex. We might need therapy if this keeps up.'

'You're both twenty-five!' protested George. 'Your cerebral cortexes are finished!'

'Besides, neither of you can afford therapy,' added Simon. 'And we're not paying for it.'

'Harsh,' said Leo. 'But fair.'

Rhyll grinned. She put down her food and plucked a few grains of rice off her top. 'Maybe you two are the ones who need therapy anyway. It'd be nice if, no matter what happens, you could at least be friends.'

George blinked. She stared at her daughter but Rhyll was now brushing her top off. Even though there didn't seem to be any rice left there. She looked across at Simon instead and they caught each other's gaze. Behind him, the setting sun leaked orange across the horizon. She gave him what she thought might be a rueful smile. It wasn't returned but at least, she thought, they were having eye contact.

'You'd better be careful, Dad,' continued Rhyll. 'Leaning against the balustrade like that. You know what happened to Aunt Annie. Mum might have sabotaged that one too.'

George whipped back around. 'There was *no* sabotage! She fell through by herself!'

'Sure thing,' said Leo. 'We believe you.'

'And that would require carpentry skills,' said Simon. 'Of which your mother has none. No, if she was going to kill me, she'd be more likely to poison this food.' He held up his palak paneer. 'Or maybe bore me to death with a game of Monopoly.'

George turned back to him. She frowned. Was it possible that was … humour?

'What a great idea!' said Leo. 'Who's for Monopoly?'

'We actually played Monopoly the other day,' said George. 'Your father and I.'

Leo raised his eyebrows questioningly. He glanced across at his father as if needing confirmation for this unlikely claim. After a moment, Simon gave a slight nod.

'Well, shame on you both for not including us,' said Leo. 'Now we definitely need to play. You owe nothing less. So which one will it be? *Simpsons*, *Doctor Who*, or *Game of Thrones*?'

'*Game of Thrones*!' exclaimed Rhyll, jumping to her feet. 'Bags me the direwolf!'

Leo had now risen also. 'We'll set it up,' he said to his parents. 'Give us ten minutes.'

They both pushed at each other as they went through the French doors, arguing over the tokens. Puddles lifted his head to watch them go, and then laid it back down. His tongue snaked out to collect some rice that had fallen nearby. George took a sip of wine and gazed across at her husband.

'Looks like we're playing Monopoly.'

'Looks like it.'

'I *am* sorry, you know.'

'It's not your fault. If memory serves, we both bought them the board games.'

George kept her gaze steady. 'That's not what I meant.'

'I know.'

'Do you think they're right?' she asked. If it was good enough for her mother and Henry Harrison, then surely it was good enough for her. 'Could we be friends again? Eventually?'

Simon shrugged. 'Ask me again in a year.' He broke eye contact, looking over at the table instead. Dirty plates had been abandoned along with empty takeaway containers. 'Nice of them to leave us their mess.'

George smiled. 'They must have been raised by wolves.' She paused for a moment, and then forged ahead. 'When was the last time we've done this?'

'What? Cleaned up their mess?'

'No. Talked out here, you and me. Or spent the evening together, with them, playing a game.' She willed him to look back over, and finally he did. 'It feels like years. When did we stop? *Why* did we stop?'

Simon shrugged again. 'I don't know. Maybe we wouldn't be in this mess though, if we hadn't. Anyway, if we're going to have a game of bloody Monopoly, then I'd better have a shower first. It's been a long day.'

'Go ahead,' said George. 'I'll clean up out here.'

Simon looked at her. 'I should think so. After all, you had an affair.'

'Exactly,' said George smartly. 'So that'll make us even.'

One of his eyebrows rose just slightly, but otherwise he remained expressionless. He pushed away from the balustrade and then collected up his leftover food and beer and headed inside. At the doorway though, he paused, and looked back at George. She still couldn't read him. After a moment, he broke away and disappeared, pulling the French doors closed behind him.

George gazed after him for a little while, trying to work out what that last exchange meant. Then she shook her head. No doubt she would know more by the time the game of Monopoly was over. It was amazing to think that it had been years since she had last played that board game, and yet she would have now endured it twice in one week. It was not her favourite game by any means, but this was certainly her favourite family.

It also occurred to her that she had been sitting in this exact same spot one week ago, but then her family had been giving her space because she had demanded it. She had been crying, with violent, all-consuming sobs that had racked her body. Eventually she joined in the group chat with her sisters, using them both as her strength and comfort. One week later her mother was still gone, and the knowledge was like a permanent ache that lined her ribcage with lead. But she was no longer bowed by its weight. She wondered if this was due in no small part to the events of the week, crowding for space. Perhaps the grief still crouched there waiting its chance. Which was all the more reason that she had to keep moving, planning, packing. It wasn't running away, it was self-preservation.

George stretched, grabbing at her glasses before they could slide off her lap. She put them on, bringing the garden into focus just as the solar lights came on. It really did look lovely. She wondered if Lesley's apartment building had a garden, or whether she would need to wander to nearby Hyde Park for a dose of nature. She smiled. It didn't seem too onerous. She could sit there with a book, and just watch the world go by. The kitchen window slid open behind her and turning, she saw Rhyll's face behind the flyscreen.

'C'mon, we're starting as soon as Dad's ready.'

'I'll be there in a minute.'

'And Dad said you should be House Lannister.' Rhyll chortled, as if this was amusing, and then slid the window closed. It rattled lightly in its frame.

Having never watched *Game of Thrones*, George wasn't entirely sure what message Simon was trying to send with his comment. Although she thought she could guess, and she supposed she deserved it. The thing was, she realised with a burst of insight, that she didn't want to be wholly forgiven by Simon. If she was wholly forgiven, then it would make it harder to leave in April. And she most definitely wanted to go. This was the chance of a lifetime, something that she would regret forever if she abandoned now. She didn't want to share her mother's regrets. Instead she wanted to do this for both of them. It *was* a pilgrimage of sorts, whether or not she took some of the ashes. She fancied that her mother would have approved of the gesture at least, and her approval was still as important as ever. She thought it always would be.

After a few moments, George wiped at her eyes impatiently. In just over two months she would be winging her way across to the other side of the world. She was going to accomplish what the universe, and Mabel's wayward knickers, had prevented her mother from doing. Living Enid's dream would be a final gift, and a final collaboration. She would prove that she wasn't a settler, not anymore. The year 2020 might have begun in the most dreadful way possible, but she was going to wrest it back. Conquer it and bend it to her will. Despite the tears still pricking at her eyes, a smile spread across George's face and it felt good. It felt marvellous. Because nothing was going to stop her now.

Epilogue

Beyond the Peripherals

Plague Lockdown #3![1]
Saturday, 13th February 2021

So this column is going to be a little different. For Lockdown #1 (can you believe that's almost a year ago?), I wrote a series about women widowed by the bubonic plague (including the two Mrs Wards, whose simultaneously shared spouse was the inspiration for Captain Jack Sparrow!). For Lockdown #2, I delivered with poor Mary Mallon (aka Typhoid Mary), the Spanish flu (aka the Spanish Lady), and the various tentacles of the coronavirus family (aka the bastards that threw a grenade into 2020)[2]. Now, of course, we've just been tipped into Lockdown #3. I should write a book called *Assorted Plagues & How They Never Bloody End*.

But yesterday, as I joined the pre-lockdown lines at the supermarket (toilet paper? Wtf Melbournites?), it occurred to me that

---

[1] AKA, here we go again.
[2] If you haven't yet read any of those columns, you can find them here in the Archives.

this blog is all about the margins of history and **we are literally living those right now**. In a hundred years, school children will be learning about COVID-19 on their surround-sound, immersive whiteboards. Virtual reality will mean they'll be able to *smell* the baking sourdough, *feel* the weight of PPE, and *see* the pinpricks of burst blood vessels across the cheeks of angry anti-vaxxers. Maybe my book *Assorted Plagues* will be on the high school syllabus.

So I thought I would do something that I haven't done since starting this blog three years ago – write about my own family. And I'd like you to do the same – tell me about yours in the comments. Take a photo, a snapshot, with words. It doesn't have to be earth-shaking, because mine's not, and it doesn't even have to be particularly interesting, because mine's probably not that either. It just has to be yours. That's what makes it unique.

My family has treated the pandemic like a giant game of the grass-is-greener-over-there musical chairs. Example #1: my brother spent the first lockdown at home with our parents, before shooting through literally as restrictions lifted to move in with a friend[3]. That must have worn thin also because after Lockdown #2 he shifted into our cousin's spare room when *her* flatmate moved back to the country. Me, I began in a spare room at my granma's house, with my aunt and uncle, and then spent Lockdown #2 at my friend Casey's (thanks Case!) before heading over to my cousin's place to share with my brother (said cousin having now moved across town into Granma's house to help out there). My other aunt? Well, she shot up to the Gold Coast just after Lockdown #1 and vanished for nearly four months before suddenly

---

[3] And I mean literally quite literally. He moved out at midnight on 13th May 2020.

resurfacing back in Victoria. Apparently she's now spending Lockdown #3 with my Great-Aunt Margaret and Great-Great-Aunt Astrid. And trust me, that should test her commitment!

So you see, if my family had been on the *Titanic* then yes, we would have been those rearranging the deckchairs. But oddly, the biggest shift may well have been with the two who didn't move at all. My parents[4]. See, pre-COVID my mother was on the *point* of moving, with plans to desert the marital home in favour of rediscovering herself in England or some such douchebaggery. Tbh though, good on her. Life's short. But the flight was booked for the 3rd of April and lockdown hit on the first. Fucking irony, right? The upshot was that she spent Lockdown #1 with a face like a basset hound (I took a screenshot each time we FaceTimed and then put them together into an Andy Warhol-type collage for her[5]). My father, on the other hand, initially wore this smirk that was equally irritating, but the basset hound proximity must have proved infectious because seriously, FaceTiming those two in the latter half of Lockdown #1 made me want to yeet myself off a cliff. Which is possibly why my brother left the moment he could.

Anyway, then for Lockdown #2 – all 111 days of it – they were on their own. And while I wouldn't like to say that it turned into a second honeymoon or anything like that[6], there's no doubt that gradually they became less basset hound and more Cheshire cat. So either they resolved some stuff, or got his and hers facelifts[7]. They even – unbelievably – bought a COVID puppy. How cliché

---

[4] I'm grinning right now because I know my mother reads this blog and at this point she's staring at the screen gobsmacked and going, 'No, Rhyll! No! Don't go there!' Too late, Mumsy, too fuck-a-doodling late. Lol.

[5] She didn't appreciate the gesture.

[6] Mainly because even the thought made me throw up a little in my mouth.

[7] And given elective surgery was off the table it's most likely the former.

is *that*? They said it was to keep our old dog company, but that makes no sense because much as I hate to say it, our Puddles is on his last legs. Also he's partly blind, mostly deaf, and fully arthritic. Not exactly puppy play-date material. Although since they called this new dog **Mabel** (yep, seriously), perhaps they were trying to speed up the ageing process there too. I don't think anybody – animal or human – has been called Mabel since the 1940s. There you have it. That's my family, warts and all. I wrote about them for a creative piece at uni and the lecturer sent me the contact details for student support. I kid you not. But we, like you, are about to slither down the margins of history into Lockdown #3. Footnotes for the future. So let's look beyond the peripherals – beyond all the celebrities and influencers and attention-seekers – and amuse ourselves by documenting our own. *Real* life. My granma, who died pre-COVID, kept a diary that we only found when we were clearing out her stuff. It wasn't much – just a kaleidoscope of short vignettes. But it was so special that people fought over it after she died. Words can do that. So let's call this a gift exchange. Pop your lockdown stories into the comments below and maybe I'll turn *those* into a book! *Beyond the Plague: the good, the bad, and the goddamn ugly.* I like it.

In the meantime of course, stay safe, stay well and, as always, be prudent with the toilet paper.

Acknowledgements

At times, this was a difficult novel to write. There were sections that took me back to the death of my own mother nearly eight years ago – a period that I have no real wish to revisit, even temporarily. It reminded me that the tide is never truly out on grief. Those first tumultuous, swollen, swamping waves might recede, but you can still feel the dampness between your toes. Even apart from the ever-present possibility of a rogue wave, always, the bruises remain forever. It's a bugger of a thing, grief. A high price to pay for love.

But overall, those moments were far outweighed by the enjoyment I take from writing. Let me assure you, I am far too self-indulgent to spend time on something I don't enjoy! And those brief forays into the past might have been unpleasant but they were also a little cathartic. Because of that though, I did have to be conscious of keeping a distance. This is a work of fiction, and the characters are entirely fictional. So I would like to start this section by thanking my daughter Caitlin Evans, for reading through three separate drafts and telling me, in no uncertain terms, when that distance was being even slightly breached. I would also like to thank my niece Sara Woodroffe, for offering advice on the same thing, and my sister Robyn Evans, for unintentionally providing some inspiration.

Thanks also to my mother, always, for all that she did and continues to do. Nowadays without effort. And I also know that she would want a line here assuring everybody that she is **not** the mother in this book. For starters, she never had an affair and nor did she own a vibrator. And yes, I'm certain. Nor did she ever have a friend called Mabel, with or without knickers, and although she did read Georgette Heyer, it was mostly for light relief. She preferred non-fiction. But in other ways, she *is* the mother. If we are lucky, we all have one of those. Much-loved, sorely missed, and leaving behind a chasm that yawns at the periphery of our lives.

Huge thanks, as always, to my agent Sarah McKenzie, of Hindsight Literary Agency. And thanks also to all those at Harlequin and HarperCollins. Rachael Donovan, Suzanne O'Sullivan, Rochelle Fernandez, Natika Palka, Virginia Grant and anybody else that I have forgotten – please don't be offended. When I get to the end of a book, I have a mind like a sieve. But one person that I can't forget is Nicola Robinson, who took me on as a mid-career author with *The Unusual Abduction of Avery Conifer*, and who followed it up with unwavering support for this book. I wish you all the best with your new position as publishing manager at the Indigenous Literacy Foundation. I'm sure you'll be freaking amazing.

And lastly thanks as always to my own little family. Michael and Kate, Jaime and Jack, Caitlin and Rachael. Elijah, the most adorable three-year-old in the world (a totally objective opinion). I couldn't do what I do without you all, and nor would I want to.

Book Club Questions

1. Do you think the book's title of *Family Baggage* reflects the story within? You may be interested to know that the working title was *The Story of Her Life*. If you had been able to title it, what would you have gone with?

2. The Johari window is a psychological model that details the 'blind spot': those aspects of ourselves that are seen by others but not ourselves. An example might be Annie declaring that George was a follower when George herself saw herself more as a mediator, despite not really doing a lot of mediation. What other examples can you think of throughout the book?

3. In a similar fashion, their mother had nicknamed the three sisters 'the Sorter, the Settler and the Sook', but George and Annie were quite confronted by this. Did their mother have a point, or could her labelling have helped create the very aspects that they described?

4. Does George also label her own children? Could this be why she is so blindsided by Rhyll's blog?

5. Should Enid Tapscott have burnt her diary, or did she owe her children the truth? Do *you* have anything that you should consider burning?

6. Does *Harry* deserve the truth? Would you tell him?

7. In your opinion, was there a pivotal moment in the book where things went awry, or was it more of a compilation of small moments that built up? Or, perhaps, had the build-up begun long before Enid's death – and if so, was the breakdown of relationships inevitable?

8. At one point in the book, George realises that her cousin Lesley 'still had two generations ahead of her. Sentient branches on the family tree. Buffers against mortality. While she, George, had had just the one. And now with her mother's death, even that was gone; leaving her totally exposed. The top of the tree, the next in line.' Yet Lesley is older than George, so really this shouldn't make any difference. Statistically Lesley will pass away before George regardless. So why does this realisation hit George so hard?

9. There are no villains in this story (except perhaps Guy!) – rather a collection of people who all have lapses in judgement that they expect to be overlooked while refusing to overlook the lapses of others. How true is this statement?

10. Which part, or paragraph, resonated with you the most? And why do you think that was?

11. Family is one of the themes of the book, along with grief and motherhood. What are some of the other themes?

12. Towards the end of the book, George thinks 'There was a grim irony also, in that Annie had created her worst fear. Her sisters had *not* been ganging up on her at the beginning, but they most certainly were by the end.' How correct is she here?

13. The three sisters disagree over whether Harry should be told of his parentage. Is one point of view correct, or are their varying opinions simply reflective of their personalities?

14. In Rhyll's blog entry at the end of the book, she mentions that her parents called their new dog Mabel. What do you think was their motivation here?

talk about it

Let's talk about books.

Join the conversation:

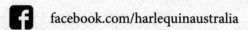 facebook.com/harlequinaustralia

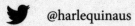 @harlequinaus

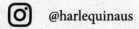 @harlequinaus

harpercollins.com.au/hq

If you love reading and want to know about our
authors and titles, then let's talk about it.